THE LEGEND OF THE LAST KNIGHT

The Saga of Terminus Mundus

Michael Mazzaro

The Legend of the Last Knight: The Saga of Terminus Mundus
by Michael Mazzaro

Signalman Publishing
www.signalmanpublishing.com
email: info@signalmanpublishing.com
Kissimmee, Florida

Cover design by: Kate Danailov

ISBN: 978-1-940145-09-9 (paperback)
978-1-940145-10-5 (ebook)

Library of Congress Control Number: 2013950146

Signalman
Publishing

To God, Family, and Country

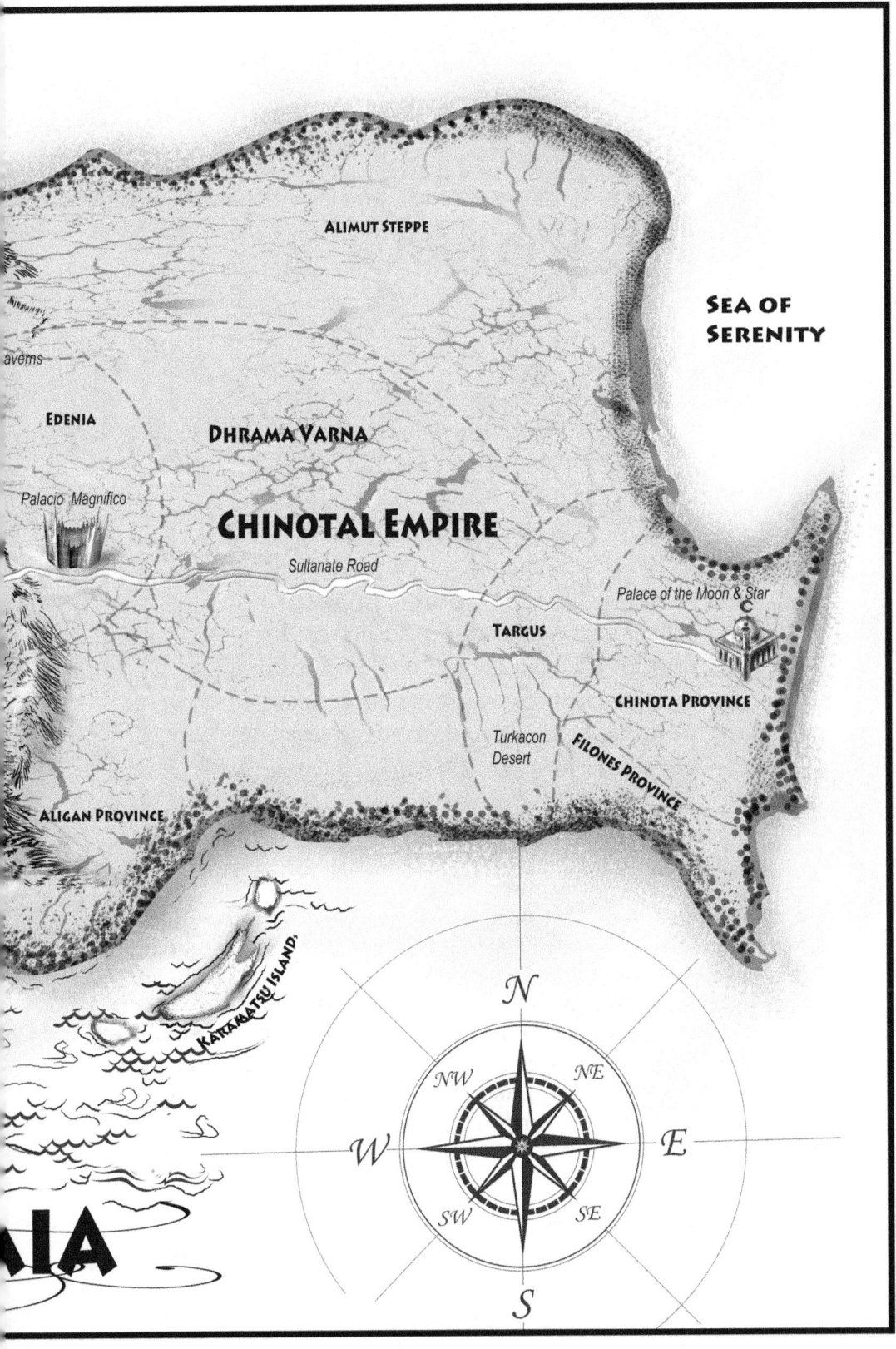

PROLOGUE

In the beginning was the Word
And the Word was with God
And the Word was God
He was in the beginning with God
All things came to be through him
And without him nothing came to be
What came to be through him was life
And this life was the light of the Universe
The light shines in the darkness,
And the darkness has yet to overcome it
—*The Scriptures of the Christ, the Titan Evangelist*
(Chapter 1:1–5)

In the beginning was the Father who reigns eternally in the Celestial Realm beyond human comprehension of time and space. At the heart of His realm was the "City of God," the eternal Jerusalem. Bathing his city in light, the power of the Father reflected off of the ivory towers like that of a thousand suns. Lush gardens and rivers flow throughout the realm, an eternal sustenance to its inhabitants. There was no temple; rather, at the center of the city is the "Throne of God." Countless numbers of unblemished buildings extend in circular rings from the Throne. The Eternal Father, our Lord God, reigns over his perfect eternal watchmen, the angels.

The angels were beings created by God, possessing all possible physical, mental, and spiritual perfections. Beyond the weakness or blemish of time and space, these beings were not subject to the frailties of humanity. The angels were ordered into a strict caste system based in three Triads and nine Choirs. In spite of this caste system, seven angels were designated by the Lord God to be Sefiroth, captains of the heavenly host: Michael, Gabriel, Raphael, Uriel, Jophiel, Zadkiel, and Camael. Possessing tremendous powers, the captains reported to a single commander, Lucifer. Lucifer, "the light-bearer," was the most beautiful and was believed to be the most powerful of all the angels.

In the strictest confidence, the Lord God would reveal to Lucifer his ultimate plan. God would create the Temporal Realm bound by the laws of time and space. He would fill this realm with an abundance of life and create a race of beings called "humans" in His own likeness and image. Bestowed upon these children would be the gift of free will. The humans would not be forced to live a life directed by God but rather would have the freedom to come or refuse God as they chose.

Driven insanely jealous by the gift to be bestowed upon a race of inferiors, Lucifer plotted an insurrection. The angel could not understand why his kind was bound to the "will of God" but the humans could still maintain grace in total defiance of God. Journeying deep into the caverns of Tartarus beyond the "the gates of Heaven;" Lucifer used his blood and magic to create an army.

Chanting endlessly and invoking his spells, Lucifer's piercing blue eyes focused on a bloody pentagram traced on the ground below him. The illumination once brought about by his celestial robes darkened and dulled with each word. Rising from the pentagram was a web of red light and Lucifer's tone sounded foul and sinister. The angel vomited blood and a wretched genesis began.

"Arise, my children!"

The first of the creatures birthed from the pentagram. Covered in a primordial slime, they tore at the sheath with their fangs. As the creatures emerged, Lucifer could feel changes transmuting his own body. Golden hair blackened to the color of night and the tint of his skin turned to copper. Horrified by these changes, Lucifer used his powers to maintain his original form. Eating the cocoons that covered them, hideous spawn presented themselves to their creator.

Varying greatly in size, it was not uncommon for the children to have extra limbs or heads. Lucifer disdained at the sight of his demon offspring. Overconfidence and pride blinded the light-bearer to the fact that his powers were derived from God and thus, using a corrupted form of that magic created an inferior race. Stupid and festering demons stood no chance against the full might of the angels of God. Asserting his authority, Lucifer subjugated his spawn under his new title the "Prince of Darkness." The light-bearer had one dangerous tool left at his disposal; his silver tongue would find the perfect commanders for his army.

Lusting for power and swollen with jealousy at God's plan, angels were quickly turned by the serpent's tongue. Soldier, scholar, steward, or singer, it made no difference. When he was finished, Lucifer had convinced one-third of the angels in heaven to swear allegiance to their new prince. Unsatisfied with this number, he attempted one last temptation. Seeking out the angel Camael, Lucifer used every manipulation possible to turn the noble leader of the sixth choir. Camael would resist and for that the prince invoked a powerful curse on him. Within the Sefiroth's very soul, an inner darkness spawned to corrupt him, but Camael would not yield. Defiantly, the insurrectionists toiled endlessly within the Caverns of Tartarus, training, arming, and perfecting his demonic army. When they were ready, the prince and his "fallen angels" lay siege to the gates of Heaven.

The Asphodel fields were a vast plain that consisted of terra firma but also endless mist. Shining on one end of the fields was a large, gilded gate floating upon two white clouds. Perched on top of this gate was a white dove, tail consumed in flames. Staring across the vast plains, the dove witnessed Lucifer emerging ahead of his army. His seemingly infinite army of demons stood with venom and saliva dripping from their mouths. Restless, hungry, and wroth with unquenchable cruelty; the spawn were ready to devour whatever was placed in front of them.

Anxiety filled his red eyes as the principality angel Abaddon stood behind Lucifer. Wearing his silver plate legion armor, his long brown hair was cloaked in a silver helmet with ram's horns on each side. Towering over his fellow angels and carrying two large, long, curved swords, the young principality was eager to slaughter his former comrades. At his command, were angelic soldiers that had sworn loyalty to the Prince of Darkness, the overwhelming majority carrying burning swords.

"Abaddon," barked Lucifer.

The young angel eagerly responded.

"I am at your command, my prince."

"The honor of the attack on the gates of heaven shall belong to the principality choir. My commando unit is yours to command. Your orders are to hold back while our pawns engage their forces. Then flank the angels and strike at their rear."

"I shall not fail you! The time for you to take your rightful place on the throne is at hand, my prince."

Clanking and creaking of the great gate drew the attention of the rebels. The dove perched on top of the gate flew upward and outward. It flapped its wings and began to hover over the military force leaving the gate in perfect unison. Appearing as trained legionnaires ready for battle with spear, shields, and swords, the angels marched behind the dove. They wore shining tunics over their armor which had been washed clean in lamb's blood, and their wings wrapped around their necks to give the appearance of a cloak. Bringing up the rear, a small archery contingent carried long ivory bows with draw strings made completely out of light. In front of the angels was the archangel Michael, who had been elected general by the seven Sefiroth to lead them in battle against Lucifer. Jophiel and Zadkiel volunteered to act as his shield bearers, while Raphael stayed in the rear to command the archers.

"Form the phalanx!" commanded Michael.

Snapping into formation, the angels organized the defenses. Sheathing their swords, the defenders of Heaven pushed forward with shield and spear. Michael turned his attention to the rear and found a second division of angels advancing into position. These angels were of the powers choir, and they were commanded by the Sefiroth Camael. Unlike the angels in the phalanx, these angels appeared as knights armed in silver plate from head-to-toe, and each held a sword in front of them that was consumed in white fire. These angels did not have the traditional white wings but rather dark green wings that appeared black.

Cloaked in four large black wings, Camael wore black plate armor. A long-brimmed hat covered his face; a claymore remained attached to the back of his armor. In his left hand was a diamond shaped shield with a metal whip projectile at its bottom. Krystos, Camael's shield bearer, stood at his right with brown eyes and short brown hair. His physique was impressive, and the appearance of a spear, sword, and bow distinguished him as a weapons master. On his left was his second-in-command, Cassiel who carried his own fiery sword. Though he had sworn to follow Michael in this battle, Camael answered directly to God. Fearing the power of

Lucifer and his armies, the angels wanted the battle-hardened powers choir commander to lead them. However, Gabriel counseled that Lucifer's poisoning of Camael's soul made him a liability. Embracing the light and darkness, Camael was truly two halves to one self, and the angel was caught in a constant struggle against the corruption of his eternal soul. Only the love of God kept Camael from falling into darkness. In spite of this, Michael would entrust no angel with the orders he had given to Camael. Anticipating a trap, the powers choir was ordered to stay behind the main force and destroy any force who dared to assault the gate. Michael knew that Camael would defend it to the last angel. Foolishly, Lucifer smiled at the sight of Michael's army and took the bait.

"The archangel leads them and not the warrior," observed Lucifer. "Father why don't you just hand me the throne!"

Lucifer held a trident high in the air and shouted, "Charge!" Eagerly the first waves of demons broke towards the lines of the defenders of heaven. The dove stopped its hovering and suddenly flew at the attackers. Blazing a fiery trail, a barrier was formed between the demons and defenders. The first demons that came in contact with the holy fire were incinerated to dust. Dancing flames soon took the form of an impenetrable pillar; teeming with fear at the dove's power, the demons ended the charge. As the dove returned to the gate, Michael took the opportunity to draw his sword.

"HOLD THE LINE!"

Blinded and disorganized, the demons limped past the pillar of fire. Forced into a bottleneck, the spears of the angelic phalanx impaled the first waves. Angelic bowmen opened their wings to take to the sky. They drew their bows, creating arrows of fire and light. Raining down on the enemy, the arrows instantly incinerated the attackers. A second wave of demons headed for the Powers choir. Camael ripped the large sword from behind his back. Invoking the powers of the Lord God, the sword was engulfed in white fire. A single swing from his sword created a wave of fire that consumed the charging demons.

Resolute as ever, the rebels would continue to send wave after wave at the angels of God. Splintered spears gave way to drawn swords in close-quarter combat. Purple and yellow blood splattered over the defender's armor and wings but the blithering monsters were forced to retreat. Spears, spells, and supporting range struck the hulking giants. They were hurled to the ground and squashed many of their demon comrades in the disorganized retreat. Undeterred by his earlier defeats, Lucifer simply smiled and organized his final assault.

"While they are distracted," ordered Lucifer as he raised his arm in the air, "Abaddon, lead our commando unit against their rear. I'll deal with Michael myself."

Abaddon uncrossed his swords, letting them taste the soil of the Asphodel fields. The rebels spread their wings and flew around the frontline troops. Michael turned back to warn Camael of the coming danger. Looking into his subordinate's eyes, the general knew his Sefiroth comrade would not fail him. The archangel general turned his focus back to Lucifer, who was now rallying his demon children to his banner. At the beck and call of the insurrectionist was a personal honor guard, he had named devils. These demons had smooth, flawless, and red, skin. Black horns spiraled out of their heads and their wings were devoid of feathers. Rapidly they crossed the fields on their cloven feet and sharp talons. Fearlessly diving into the phalanx, they forced the defenders to break ranks. Scattered across the plains, Michael fought tirelessly to reorganize his command. Attacked by a devil, he drove his sword deep into the creature's chest. Realizing his sword was trapped, Michael unleashed a spin attack with his spear. Two devils dropped dead as Lucifer's trident pierced the general's left shoulder. An inevitable battle began between the two former friends as Abaddon's command made for the gate.

Abruptly stopping his charge, Abaddon's anxiety turned to outright fear. Camael and his choir had lured the principality right into a trap. The deafening voice of Camael issued a final warning

"The Lord God is merciful . . . lay down your arms and be welcomed back into the embrace of the Father. If you continue to oppose us, you will risk eternal separation from the Father!"

"Lord Camael, I stand before you with half of your own forces joining our brethren," stammered Abaddon. "The prince has long waited for you and your choir to join arms with us. Lucifer wishes to make you his second in command if you swear him fealty and help us destroy Michael."

Camael said nothing, but a great force of darkness crept steadily across the whole of his body. Carefully examining the Sefiroth's body for changes, Abaddon witnessed the front incisors of Camael transform into snake fangs. Krystos stepped forward and placed his right hand on the shoulder of Camael. Bursting white light seemed to come directly from Camael's soul, dispelling the darkness. The Sefiroth brought the hilt of his sword to the level of his eyes. Abaddon realized that any further conversation was futile. The principality prepared for the inevitable confrontation.

"Then it is... To the death!"

The angels loyal to Lucifer charged the powers choir. Chanting, Camael spread his wings. He rose six feet above the ground as his wings glimmered.

"Winged Angel of Death!"

Heated pieces of silver formed on the feathers of the Sefiroth. Recognizing the attack, Abaddon barked out commands.

"Shields!"

Raising their silver shields, the rebels hoped the devastating attack would be halted but to no avail. The projectiles melted through their armor and lodged themselves in the attacker's bodies. Noxious scents of melting skin and wings filled the field as the rebels covered their wounds. Krystos and Cassiel led the screaming powers choir against the insurrectionists. Swords started to sing as the foes met one another. Fire leapt across the scorched fields igniting a grand conflagration. Screaming in agony, the rebels limped away from the coming barrage, but the powers choir would show them no mercy. Camael struck the finishing blow on many of his former subordinates. Even when surrounded by foes, the Sefiroth could move his sword like falling rain. He left only a trail of bloodied wings and fallen bodies behind. Sensing the battle lost, Abaddon wagered that only one solution could net him a victory.

"I have to kill Camael... to win the war... "

Abaddon shoved a powers choir angel away from him and struck at the Sefiroth from behind. Anticipating the attack, Camael retaliated with the projectile whip on his shield. Abaddon staggered back as his left gauntlet splintered into a million pieces. Gritting his teeth, the principality screamed, and lunged at the commander repeatedly. With two swords, Abaddon could continually change the level of his attacks. Challenged by the style, the sword master was forced to drop his shield. The second hand on the hilt allowed the claymore to respond rapidly to the principality's style. The strategy of dodge, evade, and parry frustrated Abaddon. Pressing their blades into one another, both angels prepared to strike a final blow.

The strength of the two foes was so intense that both weapons soon became red hot, and it was only a matter of time before a sword shattered.

Dread overtook Abaddon as he felt his muscles weakening from overwhelming exertion. Camael preserved his cool and confident expression. Determined to the end the battle, Camael thrust forward. Abaddon's swords were shattered but the rebel would not be denied his victory. A flap of wings forward caused the shattered pieces of his swords to lodge themselves into the neck, chest, and arms of Camael. The Sefiroth began to gasp in agony from his wounds but would not yield. Spinning one-hundred-eighty degrees caused his hat to fall off and a blinding halo to emerge. As he shielded his eyes from the light, Abaddon found Camael's blade lodged into his heart. Without God's blessing, his silver armor disintegrated. As he fell off the claymore, the young angel staggered back two steps. He clutched his chest and bowed his head.

"God... is the superior... "

Though engaged with Michael, the sight of his retreating forces caught the eyes of the Prince. His commando unit cut to pieces, Lucifer realized that his insurrection was hopeless. Michael took the opportunity to lodge his spear under Lucifer's trident. The attack threw the two weapons away. Dripping with purple, demonic blood, Michael ripped his sword out of a fallen devil. Raising his blade high in the air, it was struck by a blue bolt. The impact of the bolt knocked Lucifer back.

"Who is like God... I smite thee in HIS NAME!"

Michael drove his sword deep in Lucifer's chest. Radiating blue light from the sword began to distort the body of Lucifer. Every angel bore witness to Lucifer's true form. The ground swelled underneath him and massive holes sprouted in the fields. The smell of sulfur and brimstone contaminated the fields as the angelic defenders covered their noses. The growing distortion swept in the angels sworn to the prince, his demon spawn and the traitor himself. Running or flying made no difference; the strength of the singularity was too great. Screaming and cursing God not one of the traitorous angels sought forgiveness. As punishment for his rebellion, the Lord God decreed Lucifer and those sworn to him would be cast into the great furnace known as hell. Separated absolutely from God for all eternity, the realm would become a place of torment and despair. Yet, Lucifer saw great opportunity in this final condemnation. He would finally command a realm of his own and boasted a chilling warning to the general.

"It is better to rule in hell than serve in heaven. Enjoy your short-lived victory, Michael, for I will do everything in my power to bend the will of creation away from God. When they fall to temptation, I shall return and tear down the gates of heaven once and for all."

Filled with pity, Michael stared helplessly as his former comrades were drawn into hell with the wretched demons Lucifer spawned. His moment of regret was interrupted as a guardian angel named Teman flew to the powers choir position. In his right hand was an ivory staff with blue orb on top of it. A katana blade flapped against a golden chord tied around his waist. Though many guardians had chosen to abstain from the battle, his blood stains showed that Teman did not share their philosophy. Michael hurried to the same position to find Teman's brown eyes diagnosing the multiple wounds on Camael's body. The guardian rubbed the sweat from his short brown hair as he shook his head.

"Teman!" asked Michael. "How bad is he?"

"The wounds are great, Lord General. He cannot survive as he is now. Lord Camael . . . I must act quickly if I'm going to save your life."

Camael studied Teman's face but his attention was soon drawn to his right ring finger. The seal of God, a dove covered in flames was engraved on the ring. The Sefiroth was at peace knowing a friend was taking care of him.

"You are the liaison between my choir and the Lord Father."

"I am Teman of the dominions choir. We are known as the guardians. Sefiroth, I can save you, but in order to do so I must banish that darkness that tears at your soul. Lucifer needs you to die here so he can corrupt your soul and join him in hell."

"What's the catch?"

"If I do this, you will no longer have the power to serve as a Sefiroth."

"Then if God wills it... tear this serpent from me. 'Tis better to be in the kingdom of heaven with half my strength than to be in Gehenna with all of it."

Raising his staff in the air, Teman covered Camael's body with blue light. The Sefiroth closed his eyes and was reborn.

The Lord God continued with his plans, and he created the universe. Over eons and epochs, the human race rose from the ground. Humans were conceived with both a physical form and the eternal soul consisting of reason and free will. Armed with his knowledge of free will from God, Lucifer would tirelessly tempt these humans. When corruption did not take root, he sent his angels, the Acolytes, into creation. Breeding with each other they gave birth to a race of Nephilim. These beings possessed the innate qualities of human and angel but were sworn to Lucifer. Acting on the front lines, they sought out weak-willed humans to turn into Demonkin; thoroughly corrupting these beings until their eternal souls were bound to fell spirits.

The omniscient Lord God would preserve creation by sending Sentinels to combat the Acolytes. Though they would surrender some of their divine powers to fall from grace, these angels were more than a match for their demonic foes. Time eventually wore them down and they gave into carnal temptation siring Divikin. For countless eons Acolytes and Nephilim had battled the Sentinels and Divikin in an endless holy war, with all of creation lying in the balance.

In the bounty of life that was the universe, one planet was different from all others. In the farthest reaches of the Milky Way Galaxy rests the planet Terminus Mundus, borderline between the celestial realms and the temporal universe. In spite of the constant war between heaven and hell, Terminus Mundus remained the most developed planet in creation. In an era where many had come to question the existence of a God, a new fear was prophesized: Lucifer had forged a new body for his trusted Lieutenant Abaddon and bound him to fulfill a special mission. A power had been discovered on Terminus Mundus the universe had never seen before. If Lucifer possessed this power, he would have the ability to fulfill his final promise to Michael, and the gates of heaven would be open to the armies of hell. Terminus Mundus was not without its defenses, for an ancient prophecy told of a time filled with war and despair when a knight would make a stand when all others failed, and this knight would destroy evil. He is called *Permaneo Eques Ordinares*, or in the unified tongue, "The Last Knight."

The Kaiser Mountains, the 25th Revolution of the Reign of King Stephen Acadia

In Our Hour of Darkness
When Evil Infests Our World
When Courage is No Longer a Shield
When the Hearts of the Bravest Lie Broken
The Last Knight Shall Take up his Sword and the Prayers
of the World
And Inherit the Power to Destroy Evil.
—*The Legend of the Last Knight,*
translated by the elf scholar Demetrius

Alpha, Beta, and Gamma were in their new phases, creating the rare astronomical event known to the inhabitants of Terminus Mundus as the darkest night. Shadowing the sea of grass were the rocky points of the Kaiser Mountains. The night wind blew over the eastern Acadian Plains reflective of the first rotation of the one-hundred rotation growing cycle. Standing alone was the Nephilim Basarabas covered in bearskins to keep his copper skin from freezing. Long black hair flapping in the evening breeze, Basarabas stomped his feet. Focusing his golden eyes on the area directly in front of him, the tall and muscular warrior was clearly waiting for something or someone.

This night is certainly different than every other night, thought Basarabas as he pulled the bearskins tighter over his black wizard robe.

The Nephilim were descendants of the Acolytes of Lucifer. Though they did not possess the angelic powers of their forefathers, their cunning and strength made them a force to be reckoned. Enslaving primitive man with their powers and conjures proved to be child's play. Towering monuments to their leaders and greatness were erected in the shadows of the Kaiser Mountains. Their empire stretched east and west of the mountain chain and their leaders foolishly believed no one could challenge their powers. Forcibly enslaving a high elf race during a famine would be their downfall. A great prophet would arrive to deliver the high elves after revolutions in bondage. The Lord God had ravaged the Nephilim Empire with ten terrible plagues. The high elves were set free, and over the revolutions won devastating battles against their former masters. However, it was the kingdom of Titanus that struck the final deathblow, and all that remained of the vast empire were the ruins east of the mountains.

Basarabas stood there with secret information. Visions showed him that the Prince of Darkness had not abandoned his own and an Acolyte was sent to Terminus Mundus. His Nephilim subordinates secretly hoped that this warrior was coming to restore their empire but as a leader he was realistic. Rationalizing that the Prince's designs for Terminus Mundus did not coincide with his own, Basarabas accepted the honor with reservations.

His thoughts were interrupted by the sudden distortion of space in front of him. Noxious smells of sulfur caught the nostrils of his black tattooed nose. Casting aside the bearskins, Basarabas felt extremes of hot and cold. Apprehension took hold of the Nephilim as time stopped. In that moment, a burst of energy shot up from the grass in front of him, and everything in the area was burned to a cinder. Hot wind threw Basarabas back a few steps as a figure began to take form. Prostrating himself on the ground, the Nephilim immediately recognized the face of Abaddon. Stamping the fire out with his steel-toed boots, the acolyte took a moment to breathe the air of creation.

Basarabas could only wonder what Abaddon had promised the Prince to gain his favor after his failure at the gate of Heaven. Lucifer had made Abaddon one of the lords of hell, giving him a castle in the sixth plane and the title of the "Locust King." Slighted, the former principality sealed himself in his castle, secretly creating an army and waiting for his opportunity. The fallen angel had crafted a new armor consisting of a chainmail underneath black tempered plate mail. Basarabas stared at the symbol of a locust head on the breastplate. Abaddon's large, white wings were slowly being retracted from their extended position. His gauntlets were an unnatural size because bucklers had been melded onto both of the forearm plates. The fallen angel had forged new swords and kept them crossed behind his back. Removing his closed helmet by its rams horns, Abaddon let his long red hair fall loosely behind him.

"Lord Abaddon, I did not expect someone of your stature to come," stammered Basarabas. "Forgive me for not preparing a better welcome."

"You need not concern yourself. The imperative was for secrecy. I don't want anyone to know of my arrival just now. You can rise and tell me your name."

Basarabas did so immediately.

"My name is Basarabas. I am currently the commander of the 666 Nephilim that remain on Terminus Mundus."

"I guess that's a starting point. What of the Demonkin? What are their numbers?"

"We stand apart from the Demonkin, my lord. They were originally our slaves, but our defeats caused them to break from us. They sell themselves as mercenaries now; however, they could number in the millions."

"The wretched scum of a god-forsaken race. Mark my words, Nephilim, they will soon learn their place. I care more for their numbers than their feelings, and I need strong lieutenants to lead them. Are you willing to serve me, Basarabas?"

"I am humbly at your command, my lord. Though I do not know the purpose of your arrival, I am willing to follow you to whatever end."

"And do the other Nephilim feel as you?"

"There are many who had hoped that you would come and restore our empire."

"Do not waste my time with the vanities of a lost world! The Nephilim are here to serve my purposes; it is the order of our Prince."

Basarabas nodded in agreement, but Abaddon put up his hand to stop him from speaking. Removing the sword from his back, the fallen angel turned behind him. He stared deeply into the night as if he was looking for something but wasn't able to detect anything. Abaddon returned his sword to its place and calmed himself.

"Is anything wrong, my lord?"

"Someone is out there. At first I thought it was one of yours, but he was able to mask his signal as quickly as I picked it up."

Abaddon focused his gaze on a wall of fire rising north of his position. Shaking his head, he was curious of its origin.

"Is that some wildfire?"

"No, it is the campfires and artificial lights from two encampments. The kingdoms of the west and the empire of the east are warring again."

"Perhaps my job will be easier than I thought. Warring parties could provide the chaos necessary to cover our actions."

"What is your mission, my lord?"

"I'm on a recovery mission. The Prince has discovered something that he was missing for a long time. Are you familiar with the "daughters"?

"Yes. They are his six direct blood offspring and seductive temptresses, if I heard correctly."

"Indeed. You see, many of your revolutions ago, an angel fought his way into hell and brought one of these daughters out. The concept of time has no meaning to the celestial realm, but the Prince believes that an angel and this daughter conceived a girl. Now, rightfully, that child belongs to Lucifer, but since she carries angelic properties, she has the ability to enter the gates."

"This girl would penetrate the gates and leave them open for our horde to enter."

"What can you tell me about Cassandra Acadia?"

"She's the daughter of King Stephen Acadia. He's kept her a virtual prisoner in Castle Acadia in the city of Verian. She makes very few public appearances."

"We believe Cassandra to be the girl we are seeking."

"I'm afraid that might be a problem," informed a now-concerned Basarabas.

"What is it?"

"Her hand has been promised to Prince Cedric Rhone."

"I'm not going to worry about some fop prince standing in my way."

"He is no fop, my lord. Cedric Rhone is the greatest enemy the Nephilim and Demonkin have ever faced. They call him *La Morte Angelus*."

Abaddon grabbed his sides and started to laugh.

"Basarabas, I know the Angel of Death, and that boy is not the Angel of Death. I'll deal with this pretender and those with the vanity to call him such. Now I think we've overstayed our welcome. Do you have something I can travel in?"

"Yes, my lord. I brought some robes for you, but I hope they're long enough."

Basarabas tossed Abaddon a long purple wizard's robe. Taking his time, the fallen angel tucked his wings around his armor. He put the robe on over his body and pulled up the cowl to cover his head. As the two began to leave, a noise could be heard in the plains once more. Smoothed out grass a hundred meters from the meeting place betrayed the fact that someone else had witnessed the meeting. It concealed a being of considerable muscle mass that was about six feet two inches. Black and white angel feathers were on the ground.

ACADIAN HEARTLANDS, EASTERN ACADIAN PLAINS

"The Western Alliance of Kingdoms is made up of four nations: the kingdom of Evengard, the Napolitan Imperium, the kingdom of Titanus, and the seat of the alliance stewardship, the kingdom of Central Acadia. The alliance was formed specifically to challenge us, their rivals to the east, the Chinotal Empire, and the enemies within their own borders, the Tribal Confederation. The key to their military dominance is highly trained, class-specific warriors."

–Writings of Saladin, Chief Advisor to Sultan Assad Khan of the Chinotal Empire

The Red Highway cut the Acadian Heartlands like a grid between the capital of Verian and the Kaiser Mountain Pass. The surface had been designed with a combination of paved gravel and stone so horses could travel the road with enough give so they wouldn't be injured. The highway was so named because of the blood spilled over the revolutions between the west and east. The heartlands was an area of rich, fertile soil, and as such Central Acadia had divided the lands into both large and small farms to feed the nation. Proximity to the imperial encampment at Lake Cancer, kept the local famers on high alert. Five kilometers was all that separated them from the empire. There was still a job to do, and Renior's farm had to plant with the growing season.

The rays of sun were just beginning to peek over the Kaiser Mountains, and those outside were bundled up. A boy was hanging on the wooden fence that extended from the stone wall surrounding the small family farm. Renior's farm was directly adjacent to the road, which was good for transport but carried the risk of being the first farm burned in the event of invasion. However, the farmer was lucky to get a plot, given the long waiting lists delved over by the morass that was the Acadian bureaucracy. The boy watched intently as a large grasshopper leapt from the plains and onto the fence. Renior shook his head at the young boy as he tilled away at the rows of soil behind him. The boy followed the grasshopper as it moved along the fence until the slightest vibration began to spark movement of gravel on the road. Sensing danger, the grasshopper leapt from the fence and flew away. The son's attention was now focused west along the highway as something approached in the distance. Vibrations from the road began to affect the soil in the area and Renior was no longer able to ignore the situation. Concerned with the safety of his family, the farmer pulled his son away from the road. The frightened farmer stared down the road and could make out three figures on horseback tearing down the highway. The approach of the riders suggested they were allies, but Renior wasn't going to take a chance. He searched hastily through his toolbox but in the end the only weapon he had to defend his family was a wheat sickle. Renior doubted the blunt sword he kept over his fireplace would do him any good.

The riders on horseback closed on the farm and the first thing Renior spotted was the two standards carried by the horsemen behind the lead rider. The left standard bore the sigil of a golden eagle on a red and black banner, the coat-of-arms of House Rhone. The right standard bore the flag of Titanus: red, gold, and black horizontal stripes with a golden eagle surrounded by fifteen stars at its center. Satisfied they were allies; Renior turned his attention to the lead rider, now clearly visible. The rider wore a black samurai-style helmet bearing three golden crescent moons as an ornament at the forehead.

"Saints protect us!" shouted Renior. "It's the Rising Moon helmet of Prince Cedric Rhone!"

Cedric's breastplate was made of black tempered steel worn over a chain mail shirt. The armor could barely contain the massive pectorals, biceps, and triceps of the barely six-foot-tall knight. The sigil on his breastplate was a red cross. Two golden pauldrons held a long black and scarlet riding cloak in place, which flapped in the wind as he rode. A black-and-gold pleated kilt covered his waist and thighs. His black boots were protected with steel shin guards, and a similar type of armor covered the thighs underneath his kilt as well. His black gauntlets decorated with silver swords tightly held the reigns of his massive white horse, Jericho.

Titan horses had been bred over the decades for size, speed, and endurance, but Jericho was still considered a freak of nature. Its red eyes, white legs, and silver horse boots were the only parts visible underneath interlocking steel plate armor. The riders behind him wore full silver plate mail from neck to toe and silver sallet helmets in the closed position. Their horses were covered in steel plate as well.

Upon reaching the farm, Renior spotted the legendary two-handed war sword Ragnarok, hidden carefully behind Cedric's cloak. The cross-shaped golden hilt was fixed with an enchanted diamond on each side and four enchanted rubies. Ragnarok, considered the finest work of the dwarves, was hooked with a gold chain to the back of his breastplate. The blade itself was four feet long and made of silver, giving it a light-blue tint when drawn, and it was grooved in its center to allow Cedric to swing it faster in battle.

The heavy gaze of the Titan prince fell upon the terrified farmer and son. Renior dropped his sickle in a sign of total submission. No longer detecting a threat from the farmer, Cedric concentrated on the road and his mission. The riders would disappear as quickly as they came into the farmer's life. The boy was in awe, but his face began to fill with fear as he saw his father cry for the first time. His mother and sister had come running to the front porch in tears of relief. Renior knelt before his son and hugged him tightly.

"My son, you must never forget this. You'll be telling stories to your grandchild of the time the Angel of Death passed you by."

Undeterred by the brief distraction, Cedric quickened his pace along the highway. He had gotten used to the timidity that often appeared in men's faces at his presence. The Titan prince had seen a mere thirty-five revolutions, but more than half of them had been on the battlefield. His Divikin blood gave him the appearance of a young man, and his handsome facial features made him the object of many young maidens' desires.

Born in test tube, rather than conceived in love, Cedric and his twin sister Cecilia had been trained in the arts of war since they were young children. Graduating at the top of the military academy, the prince needed a campaign to solidify his position in his kingdom. Eradicating the Wildmen of the Griffin Mountains earned him the knight title, La Morte Angelus.

During the fighting, his soldiers described the prince as an avenging angel dealing fire and death. War after war, Cedric's victories piled up against the tribes and empire. Considered the most formidable warrior on the planet, the knight was both feared and revered.

The Titan Battle Manual, his book on strategy and personal ethics, was required reading in every nation's military academy. Bearing the unique warrior class of Sword Master, the knight had mastered every potential use of his blade, including saber magic, the ability to enchant a sword with one of the eight elements of Terminus Mundus.

Cedric and his bodyguards slowed their horses to a trot as they left the highway for the grassy terrain. Breeze off of Lake Cancer filled his nasal cavity as the knight closed in on his destination. When the horses got within one hundred meters of a grassy ravine, Cedric raised his hand and gave the signal to stop. The bodyguards staked the banners in the ground as the prince dismounted. Reaching into a saddle bag, he pulled out a red apple. Jericho stomped his front hooves into the grounds, grunted, and shook his head. Cedric rubbed Jericho's neck, and the horse inhaled the presented apple in one bite.

"Easy, Jericho," assured Cedric. "You'll need your strength for the battle."

Jericho nodded and chewed on the apple. Removing his helmet, the sword master wiped the excess sweat from his short auburn hair. The sides of his hair were shaved to make his helmet fit more comfortably. Scanning the area, he found his friend Christian DeVries lying in the grass overlooking the ravine. The Titan spymaster was about six feet tall with a body built for speed and agility. In any light, he maintained perfect eyesight, by wearing a thin pair of gold-rimmed glasses with one lens tinted red and the other green. His chestnut brown hair was combed back to cover the top portions of his ears. Christian held the class of Nightblade and wore a light armor breastplate made of silver and the elven ore vanadium. He was wearing black pants, black boots, and brown leather gauntlets on his hands. Christian was wearing a gold coat over his armor that had a hood that could be pulled over his head. The black belt on his waist and two sheaths held his golden-hilted daggers made out of the rare ore orichalcum, making them impervious to magic.

The spymaster wasn't alone, as the hulking, young Colin Wilkins was sleeping soundly on the ground next to him. The massive, six-foot, two-handed sword Deathbringer was staked in the ground behind him.

Colin had already built up quite a reputation for himself as an assassin, even though he hadn't even seen eighteen revolutions yet. His armor was built to strike fear in his enemies, as the steel plate mail that he wore had ornamentations of bone sticking out of it. Resting on top of his head was a protective mask carved in the shape of a skull dripping with blood.

If great men stand on the shoulders of other great men, Cedric Rhone could attribute his successes to the work of his two closest confidants, his spymaster Christian DeVries and his assassin Colin Wilkins. Christian was brought to Titanus as a young boy from Evengard, seeking asylum with an Edenian ranger, Anton DeVries. The refugee was taken in by Wilhelm von Angelhardt, who had also taken Cedric as his ward. Facing the trials of training and education together, Christian vowed to serve Cedric. After graduation, DeVries was granted authority by Queen Civilia to start an intelligence agency in Titanus called the Eagle's Eye and commanded a special forces infantry unit known as the Eagle's Talon. Colin Wilkins was an Acadian slave rescued by Cedric Rhone during his campaign against the Wildmen. Cedric noticed his innate abilities from their first encounter and took the golden brown–haired boy as his apprentice. The Titan war master Horace Irvine had wanted the boy for the army originally but gave him to Cedric to serve as his assassin. Blessed with inhuman speed, strength, and stealth in his kills earned him the dubious reputation of the Lunar Falcon. Christian turned his brown eyes to Cedric and simply laughed at his irritated friend.

"I don't find it funny, elf," chided Cedric. "Do you realize that my mother brought in fresh eggs and sausage this morning? Now you call me out here, and all I can do is shove two scalding cups of coffee down my throat."

"Well, I'm sorry you won't be able to break your fast this morning, your excellency," teased Christian. "I just thought that the potential end to this war would be more important than your meal."

Gritting his teeth at his friend's taunt, Cedric reached into a specially designed pocket in his battle cloak. He pulled out a silver flask marked with a flaming skull and two angel wings behind it. Spotting the well-maintained graduation gift from twenty revolutions prior, Christian surmised that it was filled with the prince's libation of choice. The spymaster didn't approve of his friend's drinking habits but knew full well that his Divikin blood could metabolize it without any ill effects.

"It's a little early in the morning for brandy, Cedric."

"I told you a thousand times that brandy helps get a man's heart started in the morning. Now tell me what my wood elf vassals found so important."

"If you take a look down into the ravine at a seventy-two degree angle, I think you'll find the trip was well worth it."

Cedric strapped his helmet back on. The prince pushed a button on the side of it and scopes came down over his eyes. He zoomed in at the position Christian told him and spotted fifteen soldiers sitting around a fire drinking coffee. The soldiers were wearing bronze scale mail covered by white cloaks. They carried tulwar swords on their black belts and composite bows on their backs. Their heads were covered with white turbans that had sandstone-colored cockades on the side. The Titan prince took a deep breath when he noticed a brown satchel marked with the imperial seal of a phoenix in flight.

"Sandstone cockades!" analyzed Cedric. "If the cockades were topaz, then Sultan Khan would have committed the Imperial Army. It's bad enough that we're outnumbered by conscripts, but the Regional Army is coming as well."

Christian went into a compartment on his belt and brought out a PDA. He pressed three buttons and took pictures of the janissaries in the ravine.

"I'll prepare the log," announced Christian as he pushed a recorder in front of his mouth.

"The twenty-fifth revolution of the reign of King Stephen, second rotation of the growing cycle, Prince Marshal Commandant Cedric Rhone and Colonel Christian DeVries, Eagle's Eye reporting. In the waning rotations of the winter cycle, negotiations had been taking place for the end of the third Tribal-Acadian Trade War when imperial conscripts were observed crossing the Kaiser Mountain Pass in direct violation of the First Alliance–Imperial Armistice. The conscripts constructed a fort in the Acadian Heartlands, twenty kilometers east of Lake Cancer. Marshal Rhone assaulted the fort five rotations prior and forced the conscripts into retreat. Imperial conscripts are now camped at Lake Cancer. Under the cover of the darkest night, wood elves in the Arudin Forest observed fifteen janissaries crossing the Kaiser Mountain Pass and settling in a ravine in the Acadian Heartlands. The observers making this report can now assure visual confirmation of this unit. It was the unbiased belief of both the marshal and the spymaster that this unit was of the Regional

Army due to certain identifiers on their uniforms. It was their opinion that the Regional Army would cross the pass this rotation and join forces with the imperial conscripts.

"Thank you Christian for establishing the legality of our actions."

Standing up, Cedric walked a path leading to the ravine.

"Cedric, I'd like to know where you're going?"

"Despite my haste, I was still able to open my Bible this morning. I was drawn to the ancient scriptures, and the passages I read assured me that the Spiritus Sanctus was inspiring me."

"God, why did you stick me with the one commander who treats the scriptures as a military history text?"

"Grab your crossbows and take cover positions on the ridge," Cedric ordered his bodyguards. "If they charge us, we're getting out of here, but if they ask us to come to them, begin the assault."

Nodding their cloudy blue eyes, the riders took firing positions along the ravine without questioning the prince's orders.

"I should have known," joked Christian. "I wish I brought my commandos with me this morning, but at least I had the good sense to have Colin tag along."

Christian stood and kicked Colin in the boot. Opening his brown eyes, the assassin brushed back his short, golden-brown hair back before adjusting his mask.

"Time to earn your keep, Colin!"

"It's about time I had some fun," exclaimed Colin as he pulled his sword out of the ground.

Disturbed by the last statement, Christian dutifully followed his commander into the ravine. Cedric walked over to the edge and slid down the hill. Christian and Colin followed suit behind him. Taking a few seconds to regain their strength, the three walked very slowly and deliberately toward the campfire of the janissaries. The sergeant in charge of the unit dumped some water on his face and blinked a few times. Squinting at the three men approaching him down the ravine, the janissary attempted to identify the encroachers. The sergeant was no fool and quickly spotted the glint from the hilt of Ragnarok.

"To arms!" screamed the sergeant.

The janissaries stopped whatever they were doing and went into formation. The sergeant and nine others took position in the first line and drew their swords. The remaining five drew their bows and took position behind them. Cedric stopped walking and shifted his front foot into a fighting stance when he spotted this. Christian and Colin followed suit.

"I'd know you anywhere, La Morte Angelus!" screamed the sergeant. "These men are regional janissaries, and we do not fear your reputation! If you don't believe me, why don't you charge right in, and we'll prove that we won't run like cowardly conscripts!"

"Wrong choice," murmured Christian softly.

"God has once again delivered my enemy to me this day," said Cedric with a smile. "Colin you take the ones of the left."

Pulling Ragnarok from behind his back, Cedric charged toward the janissaries. Colin sprinted left, with the tip of Deathbringer dragging across the ground. Christian dashed right and didn't bother to draw his weapons. The simultaneous attack patterns caught the janissaries by surprise, and the archers kept their arrows drawn in their bows. Jumping in the air, Cedric twisted his sword in a down-thrust position. He drove the sword through the scale mail of the sergeant in the middle of the formation. Instantaneously, the sword master withdrew the blade and performed a spin attack. Ragnarok sliced deeply into the archer directly behind the dying sergeant and the two swordsmen surrounding him. Leaping off the side of the ravine, Christian drew his daggers midair. He landed behind the archer on the right flank and slashed him across his throat. Christian thrust his other dagger forward and gutted the midsection the swordsman off the far-right flank.

Colin bull-rushed the three swordsmen on the left and knocked them off balance. The ravine didn't allow them to spread out, so when they attacked, Colin managed to block all three sword attacks at once. The assassin pushed them back and slashed Deathbringer sideways with all of his strength behind it. The power attack managed to kill all three janissaries at once. With their sergeant dead and half their company destroyed in a matter of moments, the regional forces broke formation.

Raining down from above were bolts from the crossbow of the bodyguards. The two archers on Colin's side of the ravine futilely attempted to rip the bolts from their necks. Cranking their weapons quickly, a second wave of bolts put them down permanently. The janissary archer on Christian's side tried to climb the ravine to get away, but Christian pulled him down. After slashing his throat, the spymaster noticed the satchel he was searching for was on this archer's waist. Cedric pulled a dagger from his right boot and tossed it into the neck of one of the swordsmen. Fearlessly, a janissary charged him but Cedric swung at his legs, sending him flying into the air. A second strike across the chest ended his life before he hit the ground. Fleeing for his life, a swordsman was cut down by Colin.

The last surviving janissary managed to sprint down the ravine while the Titans were distracted. Cedric was furious, but his rage calmed when he noticed the hair on his arms begin to stand up as if the entire area was filled with static electricity. In the middle of a clear sky, a bolt of lightning came down from the heavens and struck the retreating foe. The crackling sound of burnt skin echoed in the ravine as he fell dead on his knees. Cedric focused his gaze upwards and tipped the hilt of his sword to his helmet in salute.

Princess Marshal Amuro Jenitzen was sitting atop her mount Maiden with a playful smile on pink lips. Promptly pulling down the lower left eyelid around her royal blue eyes, the elf princess teasingly stuck her tongue out at Cedric. She swept her long, golden blonde hair—kept off her forehead by a gold tiara decorated with leaves and a sapphire at its center—behind her pointed elf ears. Hugging her chest was a light armor made of the same vanadium as Christian's armor, cut to accommodate her modest breasts and athletic figure. Underneath, Amuro dressed in a crimson wizard's robe made of velvet cut like a long skirt below her waist. She held her falchion Enhancer in her white-gloved hands. While the blade was made of vanadium, the dwarves had oxidized it during the tempering process to give it a red color. Amuro's gloves were marked with red magic circles to represent her class of Red Wizard. A red wizard was a spellcaster with the discipline to use high-level spells in the arts of restoration and destruction. Enchanted swords and necklaces increased her internal magic pool.

Maiden had been Amuro's faithful companion ever since she found the injured, winged unicorn in the Forest of the Eternal spring. Despite her youth, Amuro was able to use her magic to heal the creature. Maiden's golden tail and hooves glistened in the rays of Primus. Though the injuries in her youth had permanently grounded the mare, Maiden had formidable battlefield skills. Sensing no battle, her wings were folded against her side.

Amuro Jenitzen had always been a jack-of-all-trades tomboy who preferred the lure of adventure to her duties at court. Her high intelligence and intellect allowed her to master a variety of spells in her youth. Such mastery led the elven leaders to believe, she was destined to be a powerful sorceress in the mold of the last Queen Gwendolyn Marisol. Yet, it wasn't her destiny. Tempted by the art of swordplay, Amuro could easily slay with either sword or spell. Disappointing her father, her unique abilities made her perfect for command. In time, she would come to command the army of Evengard and eventually took her rightful place as a Marshal of the alliance army. When it came to battle, Amuro was dead serious, but possessed the innate ability to keep things light around a campsite by teasing her comrades. The princess marshal had the best claim of all the potential successors for the vacant throne of Evengard.

Amuro was flanked by two elf lancers in golden vanadium scale armor and gold helmets with blue plumes carrying the banner of House Jenitzen—a white magic circle on a blue and gold background. After Cedric and his men had made it back up to the ravine, Amuro held her hand out to him. Never missing an opportunity to take advantage of Cedric's chivalric nature, she reveled in the moment. While he groaned at having to do it, the sword master indulged his friend. When Amuro's brown-heeled boots touched the ground, she playfully hugged him and kissed him on the cheek.

"Marshal Amuro Jenitzen," pronounced Cedric, "what do I owe the pleasure of your company?"

"It was so boring at the camp," teased the honey-voiced elf maiden. "I heard about this exclusive party taking place in the heartlands and just had to attend. I may be fashionably late, but like a true gentlemen you were kind enough to leave me a treat."

"I appreciate you coming to back my play, Marshal."

"After your mother sent me a personal note, I couldn't refuse. You can't bury your head in the sand when janissaries show up on our side of the mountains."

"I thought Julius was supposed to be the responsible one. You were just wondering whether I cut you out of any of the spoils."

"It's expensive trying to keep a body like this in tip-top shape. What's this all about anyway?"

Having already broken the seal on the parchment and studying its contents, Christian prepared his assessment. Positioning herself next to Cedric, Amuro put her arm around his waist. Feeling a silk favor against his armor, her curiosity got better of her and she had to peek. The princess smiled widely as she saw the black silk favor marked with a golden roaring lion. Christian didn't appreciate the flamboyant affection Amuro was displaying but chose to focus on his report instead.

"We had credible intelligence that the Regional Army of the Chinotal Empire moved through the Kaiser Mountain Pass. Against my better judgment, his excellency thought it would be a good idea to slow them down by attacking the advance column."

"We should have anticipated that when the conscripts returned to Lake Cancer for the winter encampment," said Amuro. "Three lunar cycles without a battle, and now they're bringing in a steamroller. Did you make for contingencies?"

"Our agents in the Arudin are laying an ambush for the Regional Army before they make for the trade city of Deniva," described Christian. "If they can turn them into the old growth portion of the forests, it will take them much longer to get to the encampment. However, his excellency will not allow them to strike and waste their lives if we're going to turn tail and run."

"Cedric Rhone, you're always putting others above yourself," joked a nodding Amuro.

"Did I rub your feathers the wrong way this morning, Amuro? You've been on my back all morning."

"You can't take a little ribbing from a friend, my dear knight?"

"You know you're a much more attractive maiden when you're honest with your feelings, Amuro. Whenever a woman says 'dear' to me, it's because they want something."

Amuro blushed slightly.

"Prince Cedric, is it your intention to seduce every single eligible bachelorette on Terminus Mundus?"

Grabbing Cedric in an embrace, Amuro kissed him on the cheek, blew a little into his ear, and began to whisper.

"I know your type; you and I would be a fine match. We'll just take off right now and let things fall as they may."

"I'm tired of you testing out your flirting skills on me! Why don't you stop playing around and actually take the fight to your clueless beau?"

"I wish he was more like you, but what can I do, I always fall for the odd ones. Besides, she would never forgive me if I stole you away."

Amuro rubbed the favor around Cedric's waist, and an exchange of smiles displayed the comment was understood between friends. The she-elf returned to her marshal demeanor and stared at Cedric with all seriousness.

"I don't mind fighting imperial conscripts that flee when you kill a few of them. However, the soldiers in the Regional Army are pretty well trained. It sounds like we're up against it. What's your play, Cedric?"

"We can't let those armies join forces. The Regional Army is going to take a long time to cross the Kaiser Mountain Pass. We need to attack the conscripts swiftly and send them running."

"Chinotal won't be expecting us to attack. They're counting on Julius to keep us in the encampment after you won that victory at the fort. My first instinct would be to fall back, but my army is tired and wants to go home. About five revolutions back, I attended a knight's tournament and everyone was telling me I was crazy to bet on some Titan prince to win the joust. Yet he unhorsed his foe and won me a lot of gold. If we don't win this war soon, we're not going to win it. I'm doubling down on your gamble."

Moving gracefully, Maiden butted her head against Amuro's back. The elf princess put out her hands demanding Cedric place her on the winged unicorn. After a moment of staring at her to determine her intention, the prince grabbed her around the waist and lifted her up on Maiden's back. When it was over, Cedric and his men got back on their horses.

"We've got to get the intelligence back to the camp," stated Cedric. "After that, I need you to help me convince Julius and King Stephen to attack the conscript camp."

"Julius isn't going to like that idea."

"Once he sees the evidence, Julius will know that we don't have a choice. He knows I'm right; he just needs a kick in the butt to get going sometimes."

"May the Father save us all!"

Amuro stroked the mane of Maiden tenderly. Acknowledging her presence, the winged unicorn brushed against her glove and turned west.

"With haste!"

The riders took off for the alliance camp.

ALLIANCE ENCAMPMENT, TEN KILOMETERS WEST OF LAKE CANCER

"My answer, lords and ladies, is that I am all in! I will fight every battle! I will pay any price! I accept the recommendation of the last will and testament of Lord Marshal Hector Reed. As alliance steward, I offer the following proclamation. I name Prince Julius Imperia, Princess Amuro Jenitzen, and Prince Cedric Rhone marshals of the Alliance Army. Know that I will be dead before I ever surrender Central Acadia."

—King Stephen Acadia, on the appointment of the three marshals

The Western Alliance had arranged their encampment in a nine-grid square, the system preferred by its three commanding marshals: Prince Marshal Julius Imperia, Princess Marshal Amuro Jenitzen, and Prince Marshal Commandant Cedric Rhone. The entire perimeter of the square was a giant stockade complete with steel gates, wood stockade walls, and barbed wire. Torches and artificial light generators were positioned in every grid of the camp. Grid five in the center of the square was a large loading station where the pinnacle of Terminus Mundus transportation technology, the hover train, was in station. The train rose two feet off the ground when the fusion engine was fired, was twenty cars long, and traveled at speeds up to 600 km/hour. The cars to all of the freights were open, transferring supplies and taking the wounded back to the facilities at Fort Orion. The grids directly north, south, east, and west of the train station remained open so the train could travel through the steel gates in those grids.

Central Acadia occupied the northwest position in grid one. The flag of the seat of the stewardship was a white vertical stripe flanked on either side by dark blue vertical stripes. A lion emblem with a crown was against the white portion of the flag. In the center of camp was the king's tent, consisting of a large central tent with three small tents attached to it. The tent was colored with blue and white stripes. The banner of House Acadia, a lion's head on a background of blue and white, was staked outside the tent. Boasting the smallest number of soldiers in the entire encampment, King Stephen failed to convince the Acadian generals to commit all of their forces. Interspersed between these circular white tents were wooden corrals where armored horses waited for battle. The clanking of steel cuirass breastplates slightly startled the horses as their cuirassier masters arrived. In contrast to armored knights, Acadian cuirassiers wore blue pants, black boots, and armet helmets with blue plumes. Basket-hilted swords hung from their black belts. Halberdiers, as named from the use of the halberd poleax, made up the remaining Acadian forces. These troops were dressed in iron plate mail and combed morion helmets.

Bathed in a tradition of discipline and organization, the Napolitan Imperium occupied grid seven. Arranged into five rows, each tent was placed in a precise slot, so every legionnaire faced the two rectangular tents of the Centurion and commanding Legate. Currently the four standards the legion carried into battle were staked outside the centurion's tent. The first standard was the Napolitan flag, which was all dark green with a golden dragon breathing fire at the center of it. The second was the coat-of-arms of House Imperia, featuring a crown with a dragon at its center against a green and white background. Committing the first and second legions to the battle, the last two standards showcased the sculpted heads of a golden dragon and a wyvern. The legate's tent had a blacksmith in front of it, where the quartermaster distributed supplies. Exclusively made up of heavy infantry, the legions wore segmented steel plate mail over green tunics with green cloaks covering their backs. Soldiers buckled open face helmets made of gold-tempered steel with green plumes, and carried elongated, oval, golden, scutum shields. The legionnaires fought with spears and the gladius broad sword on their belts.

Evengard's encampment was in the northeast. Blessed with magical superiority, the Elves had no need for tents. Rather they simply erected an energy shield over their sleeping rolls and armor mannequins to protect themselves from the elements. Amuro's desire for privacy made her elf subordinates construct a blue and white-striped tent adorned with golden unicorns. Elf rangers garbed themselves in green cloth uniforms, brown boots, and camouflage green cloaks to blend into the forest. The rangers carried quivers filled with arrows, daggers on their brown belts, and longbows. Elf battle mages wore blue robes. The female version of this robe was cut similar to the one Amuro dressed in, while a male robe was cut like a pair of pants on the bottom. The battle mages wore vanadium cuirasses over their chest and had flanged maces made of orichalcum on their waists. Like their commanding marshal, battle mages loaded themselves up with enchanted shields, rings, tiaras, and helmets in order to enhance magical powers. Amuro's personal guard of Elf Lancers paraded around the encampment inspecting the other forces.

Titanus's camp in the southeast reflected their technological superiority. In lieu of tents, the Titans had three long buildings made of corrugated steel. The first building housed the barracks and showers. The second building was a stable for thousands of horses. The third building was the command and control center with quarters for the royal family. Similar to the Evengard encampment, the standards were missing. Pounding away at forges and anvils, four blacksmiths toiled away at the center of the camp. Titan Lord Knights wore silver plate mail, black boots, and silver great helmets. They wielded either silver long swords or silver flanged maces along with armorial shields when mounted. Restricted to female lancers was the Titan Valkyrie Core, wearing silver breastplates over chain shirts, black battle skirts, and black guarded boots. Inspiring fear in the hearts of primitive men many revolutions past, these lancers were identified by gold sallets which were decorated with gold angel wings on either side. Silver cavalry spears were their primary weapon, but silver sabers hung on their waists for close quarter combat. Light-armor knights wore chain mail shirts under a black tunic with a golden eagle on it and black boots. These knights were skilled in both the composite bow and saber. No matter the rank, each cavalry unit in the armada wore a special undertunic designed by Martha Heinrich, the Titan chief scientist. This black tunic fit like a shirt, prevented heavy perspiration during battle, and increased the endurance of its wearer. Females would wear an additional pair of tights, and males would wear shorts. Black capes flapped on the back of every rider in the armada, except for the Scarlet Riders, whose cloaks were red on the inside and black on the outside. Scarlet riders served as the personal house cavalry of the royal family. In addition to the cavalry, Landsknecht infantry complimented the army, carrying large, silver, two-handed war swords. These infantry were known for their puffy sleeves and ornate uniforms interlocked with their steel plate mail.

The command and control building featured a long desk in the main room. Four female technicians sat at computers and monitored developments on a viewing screen. The screen showed the position of the Alliance Camp, the Imperial Camp, Lake Cancer, the Arudin Forest, and the Kaiser Mountain Pass. The technicians wore the Titan military uniform a red military jacket, white blouse, black tie, black skirt, black tights, and black boots. They were supervised by a male officer. This officer's uniform consisted of a red military jacket, white shirt, black tie, black pants, and black boots. Seated in the right corner of the room were the eagle's talon commandos. These commandos wore black versions of elf ranger garb, hooded black cowls, and black boots. Covering this garb was a black-tempered steel breastplate. Built for stealth, the commandos were skilled in the use of the crossbow and dirk. Guarding the door opposite the viewscreen, royal guards maintained constant watch.

Anticipating trouble from the sound of the door opening, the supervising officer straightened his tie. Promptly getting his subordinates standing, all five saluted Princess Cecilia Rhone. The tall, big-breasted, muscular, and voluptuous twin sister of Cedric clicked the heels of her black boots against the steel floor. Her brown eyes divulged her foul mood as she brought her gold gauntlets to her golden winged-war crown to answer the salute. Cecilia tied her long auburn-brown hair back in braids in anticipation of battle. Her tri-pronged Göttin-Speer was attached to the back of her golden breastplate underneath her scarlet and black cloak.

Cecilia Rhone lived her entire life balancing the demands of her first love, the battlefield, and her duties as a princess. Seeking perfection, Cecilia's precision with needlepoint was equal to her skill with a spear. The Titan princess's beauty, charisma, and womanly assets should have made her as desirable as her brother; however, men were terrified of her reputation. Perpetually egged on by her mother to find a proper suitor, Cecilia shunned all manners of proper courtship. In truth, she had a secret crush on Ethan de-Milly, son of the Margrave of the independent country of Deniva. The princess held the rank of Vanadis, translated war-goddess in the unified tongue, which made her the marshal commandant of the Titan Valkyrie core. Like her brother, Cecilia was an accomplished spell-slinger.

"Is my mother still here?" asked Cecilia.

"Yes, ma'am," answered the officer.

"Carry on."

Cecilia marched by the officer with the intent of paying her mother a visit in her personal chambers. Queen Civilia was seated at the table, dressed only in undertunic and tights. Breaking her fast on sausage and eggs, a maid dutifully attended to her every need. Pouring tea from a porcelain pot, a second maid tried to maintain her composure despite the obvious distraction of Civilia's daughter. Civilia had seen eighty revolutions, but her Divikin blood blessed her with the appearance of a woman about thirty. Her daughter certainly did not inherit neither her beauty nor facial features from the Queen. Civilia was significantly shorter than her children and remained quite thin due to extensive military training. Lying unkempt for the time being was her auburn hair, while her brown eyes focused vigilantly on intelligence briefings.

Civilia Rhone had been Queen of Titanus for thirty revolutions now. Her willingness to sacrifice anything for her children and war-torn reign had earned her the title "Matriarch of Destruction." Civilia had been chosen successor by her father, Justin Rhone, much to the dismay of her brother, Ivar. Defying his dying father's wish, Ivar had led a pretender revolt against her but had failed. Civilia's greatest strength as a ruler was her ability to forge uncanny alliances. As a light-armor knight, she had the support of the military, but her appointment of Martha Heinrich as chief advisor earned her support among entrepreneurs and scientists as well. Tired of the demands of the throne, she planned on abdicating in favor of Cedric. However the last two wars had opened her eyes to the dangers remaining in the west. Behind closed doors, Civilia was well-versed with the raised voice of her daughter. In spite of the distraction, she was not going to deny herself the satisfaction of a fresh meal. Entering the room, Cecilia removed her war crown and accepted her mother's invitation to sit in the open seat. Crossing her legs, Cecilia observed proper protocol by folding her hands on her lap.

"Is this behavior befitting a Titan princess, my daughter? I will not have you stomping around this compound like a mad horse!" commented Civilia in between bites. "The armada is tense enough."

"Sorry, mother," acknowledged the annoyed voice of the haughty Vanadis. "How could you allow my brother to abandon the camp at first light?"

"You're just upset at the thought of him killing more imperials than you."

"My share of the imperial spoils is another matter. Please answer my question."

"Would you break your fast with me?" deflected her laughing mother. "We received fresh supplies this morning."

Walking over to her seat and shaking, the maid poured Cecilia a cup of tea. When they tried to serve her a plate, she put her hand up and refused.

"Since when are you watching your weight?" queried her mother.

"I hate eating rich foods before a battle; the riding makes me nauseous. I had some granola and yogurt in the barracks."

"Martha warned me that you and your brother would share a deep connection. You needn't worry about where he's gone. I sent two of our finest royal guards as his escort. Christian and Colin are with him as always."

Naming his companions calmed Cecilia's rage for the time being. The princess had built up a bad reputation of being overprotective of her beloved brother. Patiently, she was waiting for the end of the war so she could have a nice long chat with his betrothed. Relaxing for a moment, she enjoyed her tea and set it down.

"Why did you let Cedric go off instead of a full division, mother?"

"Christian DeVries spends a night out in the wilderness and you do not deem that important enough to send one of our senior officers."

"Plenty of men and women in this camp are capable of performing such a menial task that doesn't risk the life of the marshal commandant! Why didn't you make him take me along at least?"

"A woman needs her beauty sleep! Must I constantly remind you of your duties as a soldier and a woman? You are expected to handle every situation gracefully."

"I'm sorry."

"Besides, I sent Amuro after him!"

"You sent that flirtatious elf instead of me!"

Closing her mouth before she finished spitting out the sentence, gears started to turn in the princess' head. Mortified, she closed her eyes and bowed her head in respect. Finishing her breakfast, Civilia sympathetically smiled at her daughter. Cecilia took few deep breaths before regaining the guile to confront her mother again.

"I'm sorry. You sent Amuro Jenitzen because you needed an objective eye to observe the situation. The evidence and her endearing elf nature will serve as the counterweight to Julius's planned strategic retreat. I must say, Mother, you're more devious than I could ever hope to be."

"You have nothing to apologize for, my daughter. Passion can be a blessing as well as a curse, and we mustn't miss the forest for the trees."

Looking at the storm raging on her daughter's face, Civilia knew this wasn't the time for a lecture. Interrupting the awkward silence was a call on the intercom system.

"Your Majesty, Freigraf Irvine is here and says there's trouble in the camp," broadcasted the officer. "He needs to see you as soon as possible."

"Thank you, Lieutenant," replied the queen. "I'll see him as soon as I've dressed."

"Looks like our allies have gotten wind of our shenanigans," added Cecilia.

Civilia switched off the intercom and stood from the table. Walking to the armor mannequin by her bed, the queen started to don her battle gear. After clearing her table, the maids began to set the queen's hair in a golden war tiara featuring fifteen opal stones. Per Titan tradition, Cecilia assisted her mother by lacing up her chain mail and attaching her golden tunic. One maid put on the queen's boots while the other placed a scarlet rider cloak on her shoulders. Cecilia handed her mother a black war belt with her saber already attached to it. The queen buckled the golden buckle marked with a red poppy. She put on her brown gloves and turned to her daughter. Seeking reconciliation for the earlier argument, mother and daughter embraced before leaving the room.

Freigraf Horace Irvine, war master and commander of the scarlet riders, stood in the main room dressed in a Titan lord's knight armor. His breastplate was marked with the sigil of his house, a ram's head. The same sigil was on the armorial shield slung over his back. As a reward for his victory over Ivar, the queen had the dwarves craft him a giant flanged mace with a silver head and gold handle. Horace had shaved his head down to the scalp, but maintained a trimmed black van dyke across his face. Muscular from revolutions of weight training, the dark-skinned war master towered over his comrades in his armor. As he sniffed the pleasant aroma of the cigar in his left hand, Horace knew he made the right selection from his humidor this morning. Striking a stick match in his right hand, the freigraf enjoyed only a single puff of the cigar before his queen entered the room. He clicked his riding boots together and saluted with the cigar still in his right hand.

"Your majesty, I'm sorry to interrupt," apologized Horace.

"It's quite all right, freigraf," accepted the queen as she answered the salute. "I expected this."

"News passes a little too quickly in a camp this size. The Acadians are demanding answers, and King Stephen is appeasing them by calling a War Council."

"We're in for it now," assumed Cecilia.

"Walker came over to escort us to the king's tent," explained Horace. "He's trying to buy us some time with a nice slow walk."

"Bless his noble heart for that," said Civilia. "We won't keep him waiting anymore."

"Any word from Cedric yet?" asked Horace.

"No, but if everything is in order, he should be back soon," replied the queen.

Tossing his blue cape lined with white rabbit fur behind him, Jonathan Walker stood at the well in the center of the Titan camp waiting for the queen to arrive. Walker stood about six foot two and, like most knights of Terminus Mundus, had developed strong muscles in order to bear the weight of heavy armor. The lord knight's armor was a gift from his late father, Lord Commander Hector Reed, and made of the same silver-steel meld that the Titans used. Walker had sharp blue eyes and a blond fade. In his hands was an open-face silver armet helmet with a long light-blue plume hanging from the top. Slung over his right shoulder was his most prized possession, the Oath Shield. Forged by the dwarves, this large silver kite shield was lined with runic stones of blue, red, and yellow with a sigil of a castle tower in the center. Tempered seven times to prevent it from cracking in battle, the protective runes gave the Oath Shield the power to absorb magic spells as well. His father's sword, Sigmund hung at his side.

Born the bastard son of Hector Reed, Walker had no right to his father's holdings or titles. Identifying his natural abilities, Reed burned out all of his connections to make Walker a knight and got him appointed as Princess Cassandra's bodyguard. The wars against the tribes and empire had forced Acadia to employ every soldier they had in the defense of the crown. Taking advantage of the opportunity, the shield of the princess had won much glory and respect in the recent campaigns. King Stephen aided his meteoric rise by appointing him vice-marshal of the alliance army. Hearing the door to the command center open, Walker clicked his black boot heels together and bowed in the presence of Queen Civilia.

"I am honored to receive such a flattering greeting, Captain," declared the queen.

"My father always believed that respect should be given when due. I'm afraid that I've been ordered to bring you over for a War Council."

"Ordered!" screamed Cecilia as she reached her boiling point. "Perhaps King Stephen needs to be reminded of the shoulders he stands on."

"I wish I could call it a poor choice of words, but that is the words he used," said Walker as he tried to soothe his fellow vice-marshal. "I tried to take my time, but I see by the missing standard that Cedric hasn't come back yet."

"My son will be returning shortly. I'm hoping my presence will buy him some time."

Walker nodded. Horace signaled to two royal guards, who joined Civilia, Cecilia, and Horace as they walked across the grids to the Acadian camp. Stopping at two valkyries, Cecilia gave them orders. The two nodded before rushing to spread the word around the rest of the camp. Noticing a favor tied to one of her subordinates lured Cecilia's attention to her comrades throughout the camp. Favors or flowers in the arms and waists of the warriors gave the impression that every soldier had someone waiting for them except the vanadis. Consumed with jealously, Cecilia could feel the disconcerting stare of a mother eagle descending on her. The princess blushed and retorted her mother.

"I'm perfect just as I am!"

"I think it would be good at your age if we finally got you married. As a crown prince, it was necessary for your brother to wait for a political marriage, but you have no excuses!"

"There isn't anyone worthy!"

"I was thinking of that nice young man from the trade city."

Cecilia was bewildered by the mention of her crush by her mother. Wondering if her mother had been reading her diary, she was forced to sprint in order to catch up with the party pulling away from her.

Julius Imperia stood over a wooden table in the centurion tent of the Napolitan stockade. Already standing at six-foot five, his lean muscular frame made Julius appear even taller when dressed in his armor. In contrast to the legions, Julius was adorned in silver plate mail. The Napolitan crown prince held the rank of Paladin, and his breastplate sigil featured a dragon clutching a sword. Tugging at the brown hair of his ponytail, Julius's green eyes stared nervously at intelligence reports. Thirty revolutions of age, Julius still had his youth about him, but the pained countenance on his face matched the pounding of his gauntlets on the table in front of him.

"Bro, we're up!" a voice called out to him.

Julius jumped out of his skin when he saw his brother pull back the canvas of the tent.

"Cagius, don't startle me like that!" screamed Julius.

The Dragoon, Legate Cagius Imperia was slightly shorter than his brother but much more muscular. Historically, the class had been made up of dragon slayers, and Cagius was the only person in the west who held the class rank. Designed to give the appearance of dragon, Cagius's armor was metallic green, tempered steel plate. Resting on the spike of his right pauldron was an ornate helmet shaped like a dragon's head. A silver trident with a gold handle was attached to his back plate. Cagius threw his long braided blond hair behind him and looked his brother over with his blue eyes.

Julius never seemed to be able to do enough to gain the recognition he deserved. His father, Caesar Constantine, saw him as no less than perfect, and Julius had always tried to live up to that image. Forced to train as a Paladin, Julius lost the respect of the legions. Instead, praise was showered upon his brother Cagius who properly rose through ranks. While they still saluted Julius, the legionnaires regard his brother as a true leader of men.

If his problems in his own country weren't enough, the dragon prince never expected a rival the likes of Cedric Rhone. Perpetually haunted by the memory of Cedric defeating him in the finals of Cassandra's Quize Jousting Tournament; Julius hoped the wars would provide an opportunity to overcome the embarrassment. Julius's military strategy relied on defense, and his actions prevented the defeat of the alliance at the Battle of the Istle Hills. Loyal to his brother, Cagius preferred to play the role of cavalier, which had made him very popular with the most beautiful maidens on Terminus Mundus.

"Sorry, Julius, but there's a lot of activity going on."

"Did you see these reports yet?"

"No, the questor sent them right over to you."

"Well, take a look at them now."

Cagius grabbed the briefings and began to read them. It didn't take long for the dragoon to gain the same expression as his brother. Shaking his head, the legate handed the reports back.

"Three empty regional forts." observed Cagius. "That means we're going to have the second, fourth, and seventh regiments coming to the party. Fortunately, that means the Horde and Mammoths are staying home."

"Khan's pressing the attack. He wants to goad us into a fight with his conscripts while the Regional Army flanks us."

"What's our course of action, bro?"

"I think we should get out of here and fortify our position at Fort Orion."

"You're going to have a hard time explaining that decision to our allies."

"It's better than being slaughtered in an open field again."

Interrupting the brothers was the sudden appearance of Antonio Valentine, the spymaster of Napolitan. Valentine was from a fallen noble house, and determined at a young age that he could make the most money to support his family by rising quickly through the military ranks. The spymaster had green eyes, spiked brown hair, and a handsome face. Valentine wore a black garb that was heavily quilted to provide him armor protection without the heaviness of mail and a black cloak. Infiltrating every brothel on the planet, Valentine secretly trained a network of prostitutes as spies and assassins. Always ready for battle he put his hands on the hilts of a dervish Dawn and dirk Dusk.

"King Stephen wants a war council," announced Valentine.

"How can we have a war council when two of our marshals are out gallivanting in the wilderness?" asked the paladin rhetorically. "Vincenzo!"

An eager green-eyed teenager rushed into the tent, brown hair tied back in a ponytail. Serving as Julius's squire, he wore the leather armor of a legion auxiliary. Vincenzo Gravius was the son of Magistrate Matthias Gravius, one of the chief advisors of Caesar Constantine.

"What do you wish of me, milord?"

"King Stephen requires my presence, so I need to dress."

Vincenzo walked over to an armor mannequin and grabbed a green cape and hooked it onto Julius's pauldrons. He took a heater shield with the same sigil Julius wore on his breastplate and placed it over the cape. Placed on his head was a war crown forged with a sword at its center. Lastly, Vincenzo took Julius's long sword Excalibur and handed it to him. Enchanted with holy saber magic, Excalibur was a legendary weapon crafted by the dwarves. Thus the Paladin could tap into one of the powers of a sword master without the intensive magical training. Taking the blade with reverence, Julius honored his most prized possession.

"Thank you, Vincenzo. Ready my horse in case we need to ride."

"Of course, milord."

The brothers and Valentine left the tent.

"I think I could get used to having a minion waiting on my every need," teased Cagius.

"I don't know what your father was thinking," scolded Valentine. "A Gravius serving in the military is like putting a wolf in the middle of a flock of sheep."

"It's not like I had a choice in the matter," defended Julius. "Besides, I can handle a small fish like him."

The king's tent was already filled with members of the alliance war council. At the head of a long, rectangular table sat King Stephen Acadia dressed in a white shirt, with blue pants and brown shoes. Huddled under a blue robe lined with rabbit, Stephen protected himself from the bitter morning chill. The king had curly blond hair set underneath his golden crown adorned with diamonds. Retaining his good looks despite the fifty-five revolutions he'd seen, the king sustained his neatly trimmed beard.

Reigning twenty-five revolutions, the first of his name, Stephen Acadia had served twice as long as any Central Acadia King. Marred by a lunatic of a grandfather and sickly father, his ascension would have ruined a lesser man. Yet, by following a series of principles based in justice and wisdom, Stephen managed to hold the Alliance together. During his reign, the alliance had won two wars and strengthened the economic bond between the four kingdoms. Despite his political brilliance, Stephen certainly was not lucky in love. His first marriage to Sharon Fenidor was a rebound after being jilted by Civilia Rhone. Sharon's infidelity and failure to produce a male heir prompted him to take an additional wife, Penelope Orpheus. Barren after giving him another daughter, Stephen dealt with a full-blown succession crisis.

King Stephen was being protected by Sir Jonas Marimon, the commander of the Acadian Templar Army and holder of the title "Sword of the Saint." This title meant only he and the five knights under his command could protect a king. Jonas was shaved bald to the scalp with calculating blue eyes. The knight wore steel plate mail covered with a specially designed tunic marked with the six diadems of the saints. Jonas Marimon had built quite a reputation for his cruelty on the battlefield, especially when fighting the tribes. Accusations of war crimes and atrocities followed the march of the Templar Army. An investigation had begun into an incident at the Terrace River, where the armies of Jonas Marimon and Cedric Rhone clashed swords at a tribal village

Seated at table with the king were the representatives of Evengard, Malcolm Fenidor and Master-Mage Cerwin Faulkner. Malcolm stood about six foot three but always seemed taller due to his lanky frame and green ranger garb that fit him to form. His shoulder long blond hair was covered by a green beret with a long pheasant feather coming out of it. Slung on his shoulder was quiver of arrows and his longbow Apollo. The bow was two meters long and made of vanadium. Impacts from his arrows could knock a rider from his horse because Apollo required over one hundred pounds of pressure for Malcolm to draw it. Keen blue eyes made Malcolm the best shot on Terminus Mundus, and his confirmed kills were innumerable. Frustrating to Amuro was Malcolm's complete lack of social skills and his inability to pick any of the subtle hints she's dropped him. The ranger prince preferred the serenity and beauty of nature to industrialization of society. Cerwin Faulkner was the oldest living elf on Terminus Mundus and its most powerful wizard. Becoming indifferent to his appearance long ago and blind in one of his blue eyes, Cerwin was clean but unkempt. Refusing to wear anything but blue wizard robes two sizes too big for his frail body, the mage was long past due for his journey to the Forest of the Eternal Summer. The sudden death of Queen Gwendolyn Marisol and the absence of a prophet of the Father, granted Cerwin the title of "judge of the change." Toiling over claims for thirty revolutions, Cerwin concluded that a union of House Jenitzen and House Fenidor would produce the next king and queen. The old mizer constantly meddles in their affairs of Amuro and Malcolm trying to move the relationship to the next level. Resting his oak staff against the table, Cerwin's thoughts turned to his final project, the training of his niece Cassandra Acadia in the art of sorcery

"Prince Malcolm," asked Stephen. "Did not Marshal Jenitzen hear my summons?"

"The princess is currently on a mission," replied the stoic elf archer. "I have been asked to attend in her stead."

"A mission, Lord Cerwin?" inquired a doubting Stephen.

"I'm an old elf and I need my sleep. If I bothered to pay attention to every single piece of rumor and gossip, there wouldn't be enough time in the rotation. The marshal knows what she's doing."

"A fierce wind blows from the Turkacon desert!" alleged the concerned king.

Julius, Cagius, and Valentine entered the tent.

"Well, at least one marshal is still on call," taunted an arrogant Jonas Marimon.

Julius bowed his head to Stephen.

"Prince Marshal Imperia, thank you for heeding my call," said the king.

"King Stephen, have you seen Titanus's intelligence reports?" probed Julius.

"Indeed I have, Marshal Imperia. We anticipated this was going to come to pass when the empire attempted to establish that fort. The alliance owes a great debt to your colleague for stopping the incursion."

Even though he meant no insult, Julius was burned by the king's comment. In spite of the paladin's counseling to leave the fort alone, Cedric executed his own operation. Under cover of darkness, fifty Titans took the fort. Chastised by his father for an act of cowardice, Julius wondered if his next proposals would be met with greater scrutiny.

"There are many rumors flying about the camp this morning. I want to be brought up to date on the latest intelligence," continued Stephen.

"Well, then, I can only bring you bad news."

Laying down the various intelligence reports in front of the king, Julius studied Stephen's reactions. The movements of empire concerned the Acadian leader.

"The Regional Army? Sultan Khan has grown desperate indeed."

"My guess is that the Khan is trying to take advantage of our poor military position. Our armies have suffered greatly because of the recent war against the tribes. Our military capacity is currently about sixty percent."

"Quality will always defeat quantity!" boasted Civilia Rhone.

Looking up, the king watched as Walker led Civilia, Cecilia, and Horace into the room. Delighted to see the Titan queen, Stephen wasted no time in greeting her properly.

"I should have expected no less than to see the 'Matriarch of Destruction' ready for battle," admired Stephen.

"My war master believes I would serve my people better by sitting on a throne rather than recklessly charging into battle. However, not even the queen is above serving her country."

As Stephen embraced her, Jonas moved to protest. Despising the close relationship between his king and the war-mongering bitch, Marimon kept his mouth shut for now.

"I'm glad you are here with us, dear."

"I swore on my honor, Darling, and Titans keep our oaths."

Breaking their embrace, Stephen turned to Cecilia.

"While I am graced by the presence of the Vanadis, I do not see La Morte Angelus."

"My brother has taken steps to secure our victory."

"It must be a grand rotation for battle if the Titans still speak of victory," quipped Cerwin.

"Well, Grandfather, you should know better than anyone of Titan victory against overwhelming odds," boasted Cecilia.

"I assume you know of the latest intelligence reports," said Julius.

"That is why my son left in the morning. Our wood elf allies have kept us abreast of the enemy's movements."

"Then they know the Regional Army left Edenia this morning."

"Colonel DeVries was alerted before dawn and left immediately. My son followed him some time later."

"Why did you not bring this to our attention earlier?" shouted Jonas.

"Until we had visual intelligence to act upon, there was no point in panicking the entire encampment," explained Cecilia.

"This is what happens when you give a trio of young bucks too much leeway, your majesty," mocked Jonas. "They think they can do as they please without paying respect to the mood of the camp."

"Titanus was kind enough to present us with intelligence showing Sultan Khan has committed the Regional Army to the war effort," interrupted Stephen as he rubbed his temple to relieve stress. "We already have two hundred thousand conscripts camped at Lake Cancer. Marshal Imperia, you may have the floor."

"It's imperative you understand that we're outnumbered two to one against the conscripts alone. When Pasha Melmut arrives with two hundred thousand more troops, we'll be forced to dip into our national reserves to match them."

"If that's all that is holding you up, I can have one hundred thousand riders here in four hours," asserted Civilia.

"This isn't a time for boasts, Queen Civilia," stated Julius. "We have to look at our army's strength and pull back to Fort Orion."

Aggravated by the direction of the conversation, Cecilia was ready to break into a diatribe. However, she remembered her conduct from earlier in the morning and chose to take her mother's advice.

"I don't believe we have time to gather provisions for a protracted siege," interjected Malcolm.

"We also run the risk that the empire may avoid Fort Orion altogether," expounded Cecilia calmly. "If they turn north, there's a lot of tribal land they could raze before they even got to us."

"Who cares what happens to those barbarians!" yelled Jonas.

"We certainly would care if they managed to resupply themselves for a two-cycle campaign against us," retorted Cagius.

"The vice-marshals of Titanus and Napolitan make excellent points," declared Stephen. "However, I do believe in the prudent approach of Marshal Imperia."

"I fear that our best option may be to retreat to Fort Orion and fortify the defenses," requested a sighing Julius. "We do what King Frederick Rhone did in the War of the First Alliance when he forced the empire to attack Eagle's Gate."

"Fort Orion is not Eagle's Gate," criticized Cecilia. "We'd lose all of our advantages."

"Even the strong must retreat sometimes," argued Cagius, drawing the approval of the others in the room. "We'd be outnumbered four-to-one in an open field. I don't like playing those odds."

"I'll take those odds!" challenged Cedric as he entered the room with Christian and Amuro.

"Well, friend, it's nice to see you made it back in one piece," joked Julius. "My brother and I were taking odds on whether you would choose to confront the Regional Army by yourself."

"Just where have you been, Titan?" demanded Marimon.

Ignoring the comments of the Templar Knight, Cedric signaled to Christian to begin his presentation. The nightblade stepped forward and cleared his throat.

"We bring pressing intelligence from the field. Our agents were able to isolate the convoy that was bringing the conscripts stationed at Lake Cancer news of the coming of the Regional Army."

"And?" pried Stephen.

"Let's just say that they won't be getting any delivery confirmation on the package," jested Amuro.

Except for her intended target, Malcolm, the entire tent broke out in laughter.

"Why didn't you leave any for me?" whined Cecilia as she playfully slapped her brother on his back.

"And you are sure the message didn't get through?" asked Stephen.

Christian handed Stephen the scroll. Opening the scroll and reading the orders, the king's eyes brightened. A wide smile formed across his face, inspiring the warriors at the council.

"Those conscripts are blind to the fact that the Regional Army is on their way," confirmed Malcolm. "We'll never get another chance."

"How long do you think we'd have before a relief column arrives?" asked Julius.

"The marshal commandant has commanded our vassal agents in the Arudin to launch an ambush against the Regional Army," stated Christian. "We believe they might be able to give us four hours to deal with the conscripts unhindered."

"Retreat to Orion would be the prudent course of action," decided Julius. "This factor, however, may give us the advantage if we were to launch an attack."

"You said it yourself, Julius, we're down to 60 percent capacity," asserted Cecilia. "If we knock out the conscripts, then we've got four divisions of the Regional Army outnumbered."

"Most of those conscripts are nothing more than farmers and slaves picked off the fields," said Cagius. "They are armed with nothing save for some chainmail and a spear. Some of them don't even get that much."

"Imperial conscripts travel light without horse, so we have a distinct cavalry advantage," added Walker. "If we break their ranks, the Titans can run them right into the ground."

Signaling for a private conference, the three Marshals walked out of earshot of the others. Placing their arms around one another, they formed a huddle.

"We'll never get another opportunity like this," explained Cedric. "We win this battle at Lake Cancer and we can win the war."

"Don't you ever get tired of being right?" bantered Julius.

"Give me the opportunity to break them, Julius, and I will get you the victory crown. We can do this!"

"What do you say, Amuro?" queried Julius. "Do we let the 'Riverboat Gambler' try to draw another royal flush?"

"If they don't take the bait and head for Orion, we'll put ourselves in a tactical disadvantage," reasoned Amuro. "I think we've been given a gift, Julius; we can't afford to waste this gamble. Let's win this war and go home!"

"I'll save any objections and revisionist history for my personal journal. All right, marshals, let show them what we're made of!"

Breaking the huddle, the marshals returned to the meeting table. A passing look at her brother's face told Cecilia everything she needed to hear.

"King Stephen, the three marshals of the Alliance Army unanimously concur that an immediate attack on the imperial conscripts at Lake Cancer is the best course of action," announced Julius.

"My liege, permission to speak," demanded a fuming Jonas.

"Yes, Lord Captain," replied Stephen.

"I believe these three young and naïve aristocrats are making a terrible mistake," counseled Jonas. "It is far too dangerous to rely on the intelligence and military prowess of a few tree-dwellers! We should retreat and regroup!"

"The marshals have always been the first to speak about victory over our enemy," professed Stephen. "They defeated the tribes when the war seemed lost, and I will not doubt their judgment now. Prince Marshal Imperia, Princess Marshal Jenitzen, and Prince Marshal Commandant Rhone, I accept your recommendations. Make any preparations as you see fit! The blessings of the alliance go with you."

Cagius and Cecilia gave each other a high-five as Walker pumped his fist. The marshals went back to the table and pulled up a map of Lake Cancer.

"All right, Amuro and I will take our infantry and range to the western side of Lake Cancer," presented Julius. "We'll bombard their army and force them to move on our positions."

Julius pointed to the forest.

"Cedric, will you risk taking your cavalry into the Arudin Forest?"

"Our commando units can clear the path. Don't worry, nothing will prevent us from reaching the rendezvous point."

"They'll fall right into trap and we'll break them," explained Amuro.

"We can't allow for a retreat. It has to be total surrender, and this is the only way we can be certain. On our signal, Cedric, you will break through the forest and strike them from the rear. They'll be disorganized and fleeing in terror."

"What signal should I expect?"

"I'll use an explosion spell," Amuro casually stated.

Concern filled the faces of her male counterparts. On more than one occasion, Amuro's had been reckless with her spellcasting and nearly turned the tide of battle for the worst. Realizing they didn't trust her, the elf marshal sought to defuse their doubts.

"Don't worry, I'll only hit the enemy . . . this time."

"And now I'm worried . . ." teased Cerwin, shaking his head.

"How long do the camps need before we're ready to march?" requested Julius.

"Titanus is ready to march," declared Civilia.

"We'll need ten minutes," said Malcolm.

"Walker, Jonas, we'll have the Acadian cuirassiers and templars fill in behind our ranks," ordered Julius.

"Our duty is to the king," interrupted Jonas. "Marshal Imperia, the Templar Army is not yours to command. My liege, I would go so far as to remove all Acadians from this reckless battle. I would not wish to see the 'shield of the princess' die for nothing."

"I thank the templar commander for his concern, but it is unnecessary," rebuked Walker. "It will be an honor to join with the marshals for this battle."

"Thank you for your service, Captain," acknowledged Stephen. "I will address the army at the center of the encampment in ten minutes."

The deep sound of a horn was heard coming toward the camp.

"You didn't, Queen Civilia?" questioned Amuro.

"Since we were 'short' on allies, I believed it would be appropriate to call in our vassals."

Rolling his eyes in disdain, Cerwin stared outside the tent and watched three divisions of dwarf warriors entering the camp. As the aristocrats and warriors left to prepare their armies, Civilia and Julius greeted their coming allies. Brash and defiant, a dwarf with a graying red beard and black eyes stepped forward in melded plate armor. He held a horned helmet under his arm and a large axe on his back.

"King Lurac, I see that Minister Yueh delivered my message," said Civilia.

"We have come to honor our allegiance to the kingdom of Titanus," vowed Lurac.

"We're happy to have you," remarked Julius. "As you can see, our numbers are sh— I mean diminished."

"That's because, lad, you rely too much on those elves!" chided Lurac.

"I think you're within earshot of the Evengard camp!"

"LET THE ELF WITCH HEAR ME! One dwarf warrior is worth ten elves in any fight. Where do you need us?"

"Get in behind the legions. After the initial defensive, you can charge in and get to work!"

"Aye, lad! Just you wait; we'll show them some fighting!"

Prepared for battle the dwarves moved to center of the encampment. Elegantly strolling back to her camp, Civilia avoided the incredulous stare of the centurion. Throughout the encampment, workers began to disable the stockades and moved the supplies to the hover train. If the battle went poorly, the marshals were prepared to retreat. Inspecting his archers, Malcolm was interrupted by Amuro's approach on Maiden.

"Are we ready, Vice-Marshal?"

"All is accounted for, Marshal."

"Battle Mage Core prepared for battle, princess," added Cerwin.

"Want to give me a kiss for good luck, Malcolm?" teased Amuro.

Malcolm continued to look at Amuro with his same countenance. Trying to look as attractive as possible, Amuro was playfully flipping her hair.

"Why?" asked the befuddled ranger. "I doubt that fate or the Divine Father would smile upon us simply over the exchange of bodily fluids."

"I was hoping to avoid any incidences of friendly fire sweetie pie."

"Marshal, I believe that would be highly inappropriate at this time. Besides, in all of the battles in both the war against the tribes and the empire, we've never hit one of our own troops. I request that you wouldn't use such language, as others may get the wrong idea about me."

Stung by her subordinates comments, Amuro's eyes narrowed and the inflections in her tone and breathing sent the signal to stay clear.

"By the book as always, Vice-Marshal. Then make sure that we're at the front of the camp on time or else you'll have hell to pay from me!"

Amuro reared Maiden and rode off. Confused at what just happened, Malcolm tried to return to his duties. Cerwin walked over to him and put his hand on his shoulder.

"Malcolm, you are one of the finest archers I know and I think the world of you," Cerwin reassured him. "Still, you're a putz."

"A putz?"

"It would be appropriate for you to offer some friendliness and affection to the woman who will eventually be your wife."

"Cerwin, I don't think it's appropriate during the hour of battle."

"Dammit, son, it's most appropriate in the hour of battle! You have much to learn about women and that's why you're a putz."

"I see... I will try to learn as much as I can, since I don't believe this putz characteristic is a good thing."

"I'm sure you will," said Cerwin, though certainly not convinced. "Now let's not keep the lady waiting."

"Right, Captain Sirius."

Sirius emerged from the middle of the archer brigade cloaked in ranger garb. Cursed with albinism, the elf captain let nothing prevent him from serving his country. Even for an elf, his stoic expression was quite grave. Sirius wore a medallion around his neck bearing a unicorn's head. The captain had no love for any of the elven royal houses, but still served with distinction due to faith and love of country. Sirius' unit was most disciplined on the planet and these elves pledged to avenge the death of the late Queen Gwendolyn Marisol

"Yes, Vice-Marshal," responded Sirius.

Forming ranks, Sirius hustled the elven units to the front of the camp. Riding side by side was Cedric on Jericho and Cecilia on her gray mare Myst. Working on the same cigar, Horace waited for the twins at the front of the armada.

"Your excellency, the armada is armed, saddled, and awaits your orders."

Cedric nodded. Carrying the banner of House Rhone was a middle-aged man wearing the robes of a bishop covered with a scarlet rider cloak. A tonsure had been shaved into his brown hair and his brown eyes studied the approach of Civilia. Two priests carried crosses behind him. Civilia rode up to her twins and greeted the bishop.

"Archbishop Arthur, we would appreciate some divine intervention!" declared Civilia.

The bishop smiled. Arthur Langley, the shepherd of the faith, was the most powerful man in the Catholic Christian Church on Terminus Mundus. Arthur was a member of the Titan Royal Court; however, he was neither the puppet of the queen or Titanus. The archbishop even excommunicated the queen when Civilia genetically engineered her twins. The queen was forced to endure a humiliating penance before the bishop reinstated her seven long revolutions later. Staking the banner into the ground was the signal for the riders to remove their helmets and crowns. The bishop opened his hands for the blessing, which all followed:

"In nomine, Patri, Fillia, Et Spiritus Sanctus. O God, I beseech you, watch over those exposed to the horror of war, and the spiritual dangers of a soldier's life. Give them such a strong faith that no human respect may ever lead them to deny it, nor fear ever to practice it. By your grace, O God, fortify them against the contagion of bad example, that being preserved from vice, and serving You faithfully, they may be ready to meet you face to face when they are so called through Christ our Lord."

All replied, "Amen."

"Sacred Heart! Inspire them with sorrow for sin, and grant them pardon. Mother of God! Be with them on the battlefield during life and at the hour of death, and grant that they may live and die in the grace of thy Son."

All replied, "Amen."

"Consort of the Holy Mother, pray for them. May their guardian angel protect them!"

The Titan Army broke out in the Prayer of Saint Michael:

"Saint Michael the Archangel, defend us in battle, be our protection against the wickedness and snares of the devil, may God rebuke them we humbly pray, and do thou O prince of the heavenly host by the power of God cast into hell Satan and all evil spirits who prowl about the world seeking the ruin of souls. Amen."

After concluding his blessing, Christian came forward to receive his orders.

"All ready, your excellency."

"Get into the Arudin Forest and clear us a path. I don't want empire to know we're there," ordered Cedric.

"Yes, sir."

Twenty revolutions of battle gave Christian perspective. Getting the drop of enemy was more important than listening to another inspirational speech. Signaling to the commandos, Christian took his troops into the Arudin Forest. Counting on his spy master to clear the road, Cedric inspected his troops before giving the order to ride.

"Okay, Cecilia, call the birds!"

Pulling a whistle from under her chain shirt, Cecilia let loose a call. Twenty-five raptors consisting of eagles, hawks, and falcons flew out of a tent at the edge of the camp. Saving their strength for the battle, the raptors used the riders pauldrons as perches. A golden eagle landed on Cedric's shoulder, while a silver falcon landed on Cecilia's forearm.

"Eat well, Calvary!" said Cedric.

The eagle nodded as if to understand what he was saying. A small transmitter was present on the back all of the bird's heads. Cecilia kissed her falcon.

"We'll show them, Talon!"

Shrieking loudly, the raptors announced the march of the riders. Sensing something was wrong, Cedric turned his attention to his twin sister.

"Well, let's pay some lip service to what Stephen Acadia has to say," stated Cecilia with disdain.

"It's not honorable to use such disparaging tones about our allies," warned Cedric.

"Come on, Cedric, an Acadian lecturing a Titan about war . . . that's like letting a high elf construct a dwarf tunnel."

"We've had the other kind in the past, Cecilia, and it hasn't been pretty."

"You're marrying his daughter, not him!"

Cedric turned and glared at his sister, who grew nervous at seeing her brother so angry. She immediately tried to deflect the damage.

"I'm sorry Cedric."

"Don't think I've gone soft!"

"I never would... it's just... everyone knows that you should be the one leading this battle! If it weren't for you, we never would have gotten this far."

The mood of the armada reflected Cecilia's concerns. She wouldn't say a word, but Civilia's eyes confirmed the same desire.

"For everything there is a season, Cecilia. It is prudent for us to be good little girls and boys... at least until after the wedding. Sister, dear...

"Yes, dear brother."

"God help me the day that I make you my enemy."

"Well, Cedric, I can still be ruthless if you let me."

"Freigraf, we go to war," ordered Cedric.

"Yes, your excellency," exclaimed Horace.

Horace dropped his hand and screamed, "Forward." The units formed ranks and marched perfectly out of the camp with Civilia and the twins leading the way. Waiting for them were Julius and Walker on horseback, as Cagius commanded the legions from the ground. In spite of their victories, contempt and distrust ran rampant between the four kingdoms. Lurac and Amuro, with their respective forces, had to be separated.

"This is going to work out just fine," observed Cagius. "I'm just glad the only thing they hate more than each other is the empire."

Stephen approached the soldiers on foot, with Jonas flanking him. Staring with pride at the courage and honor of the alliance soldiers gathered, Stephen climbed on the caboose of one of the hover trains. Though he had prepared remarks for the moment, the king improvised.

"I want to thank the marshals for gathering you here. As you know, we face our most dangerous foe, the Chinota Turks, and the whims of Sultan Assad Khan. He has never hid his desires to subordinate our kingdoms into his empire. This Alliance of the Western Kingdoms is the only resistance against the empire's dreams of a single world order. Never can we allow ourselves to lose the freedom that we hold dear. The freedom our ancestors died for is now ours to defend. Despite the odds against us, I have faith the three marshals, who led us to victory when all hope was lost against the tribes, will bring us to victory once more!"

Stephen's oratory swayed the mood in the camp. The soldiers understood they weren't perfect but they were called to defend their homes. Cheering and beating their spears against shields, the warriors demanded victory. Julius signaled to Cedric. Raising his arms in the air, the marshal commanded his armada to enter Arudin Forest. The Titans looked almost too relieved to get away from the sappiness of Stephen's speech. Amuro trotted over to Julius.

"We're going to need to give Cedric some time to get in position," reminded Amuro.

"We'll take a nice slow march. I know we'll be cutting it close, but if they can retreat, it will be just as if the reinforcements got there first," determined Julius.

Julius raised his arm and screamed, "All out." The alliance infantry and range passed King Stephen. Reaching out to shake his hand, Stephen took the time to honor every soldier he could. The king stared helplessly as the infantry continued at a deliberate pace towards Lake Cancer. Would he be celebrating a victory or consoling four defeated kingdoms when it over?

Maintaining silence was a priority, so Julius wouldn't allow the beating of drums. Responsibility fell on Cagius' shoulders to keep the cadence so the troops would have the strength to fight when ready. Chided for studying dancing, his knowledge of rhythm served the alliance well. When they reached the ridge above Lake Cancer, Julius and Amuro dismounted. Crawling on the ground, they investigated the enemy camp. No word of the alliance attack reached them because the tents were still up and the camp fires were lit at the southern edge of Lake Cancer. Observing they were in the middle of a midday meal, Amuro and Julius winked at one another. Morale was devastated in the camp after their defeat by Cedric five rotations ago. Bribes of food and gold were offered by officers to an army ready to break.

"We've got them!" said Julius. "Order the men to form ranks. We wait on Cedric's signal!"

Julius and Amuro jumped back on their mounts. Gliding silently up and down her lines on Maiden, Amuro whispered to her soldiers to form ranks. Reacting to this, Cagius positioned the dragon legions in front of them. The dwarf infantry and battle mages were held in reserve to prevent the enemy from flanking them.

ARUDIN FOREST

Omne Verum A Quocumque Dicatur A Spiritu Sancto Est
—Inscribed on the Entrance to the Eagle's Eye, Rhinegard, Titanus

Patrolling the forest paths were seven desert spearmen, armed in scale mail and holding spears. The weather was fair—the sound of rustling branches, birds, and animals the only noises present. Trembling, the spearmen walked designated routes. Alerted by his senses, a spearman turned around quickly and pointed his spear. Not satisfied, he turns in three other direction. Seeing nothing, he shook his head and breathed a sigh of relief. But as he returned to his path, he found Colin Wilkins waiting for him.

"Surprise!" whispered Colin.

Colin swung his sword and cut the spearman nearly in half. His presence alerted three more spearman, and they started running to his position. Calmly assuming a fighting stance, Colin shifted his weight for combat. No match for his agility and strength, the assassin ended their lives before the battle began. Choosing life over valor, the remaining soldiers were in full retreat. Two more spearmen attempted to escape down the path but were cut down with bolts fired from crossbows. The last spearman fell as he staggered backward. As he went to stand, Christian stood above him. Without a word, he plunged his dagger into the spearman's throat.

"That's apparently all of them," observed Colin. "The empire's going to need some more scouts. Pathetic really, forcing amateurs into service to satisfy one man's greed."

"Yes," concurred Christian, tapping his ear to get in communication with Cedric. "All clear, Cedric!"

61

The operatives heard only the slightest treads on the forest paths muffled by heavy cloaks. Seemingly emerging from behind the trees, the twins led the riders into a forest clearing.

"I would have sent fourteen just to make sure," commented Cecilia.

"They must have been awaiting those janissaries," analyzed Cedric as he tapped his earpiece. "Hey, Julius, are you ready?"

Observing the camp from the ridge, Julius readily answered Cedric's call.

"We're in place here! You ready?"

"We'll break from the forest on Amuro's signal. Maintain radio silence until then! Good luck, and keep your head up!"

Cedric overheard Julius tell him: "Good luck! Over and out!" Cecilia awaited her brother's final orders.

"What formation? Pincer or wedge?"

After some contemplation, Cedric smiled and responded, "Wedge."

"My favorite."

"Let's show them the meaning of fear!"

Cedric pulled out his flask and took another drink. Offering his sister a nip, Cecilia happily obliged him. Toast concluded, the sword master ordered Christian over.

"What about the Regional Army?" questioned the Titan prince.

"They're taking their sweet time crossing the path," announced Christian. "I've signaled for Gerard and his army to give them our welcoming present when they enter the forest."

"Good. This war ends here!" proclaimed Cedric as he took a final drink before putting his flask away.

On the ridge, Julius readied his forces for battle. He drew his sword and rode down his lines for a final morale boost.

"Marshal Jenitzen, give them a volley!"

"Range!" screamed Amuro as she drew her glowing red blade. Malcolm drew two arrows from his quiver while Sirius and the others each drew a single arrow. Patiently waiting for the final command, they loaded their bows with perfect precision. The she-elf marshal put her sword in the air and thrust it downward.

"Fire!"

The sound of tens of thousands of arrows composed a song as they screamed toward the encampment. The conscripts looked to the sky and saw arrows raining on their camp. Futile shouts of "incoming" could be heard everywhere. Soldiers that could react to the sudden attack either ducked for cover or held their shields over themselves. Those that couldn't were pierced before the battle began. Resonating throughout the camp were cries of death and agony, in contrast to the horns sounding the call to arms. The imperial commander exited the command tent with his scale mail only half on. It was just in time for Amuro to yell for a second flight. The imperial forces once again sought cover as others attempted to duck the coming arrows. Weaving to avoid the attacks, the commander reached his officers, who were using binoculars to scout the ridge.

"What's going on?" asked the imperial commander.

"Alliance forces on the ridge. I'm scouting Marshal Imperia," observed the officer. "Marshal Jenitzen and her army must be on top of the ridge since we're under fire."

"Are our scouts reporting anything?"

"No word, sir."

"It's unlike Melmut not to send some warning forward, but we have to assume the Regional Army is on the way. Form ranks and prepare for battle! If anything else was going on, our scouts in the forest would have reported already."

The officer saluted and got the conscripts in line. The shouts of "form ranks" were passed between the officers around the camp. The conscripts rushed into position, desert spearman in front with spears forward and archers behind them. Witnessing the changing behavior with her keen eyesight, Amuro adjusted her orders.

"Fire at will!"

Despite shifting to rapid fire, the elf archers maintained their accuracy. Imperial officers found themselves in the difficult position of holding scared conscripts in ranks as arrows pummeled them. These officers became prime targets for arrow fodder.

"All forward!" shouted the imperial commander.

The conscripts ran up the ridge thinking they were about to confront the archers. However, heavy infantry awaited them. The arrows decimated the conscripts; every step they took, hundreds would fall from the arrow assault. The rest pushed and huddled themselves together to avoid the arrows. Limiting their maneuverability was part of the plan; Julius readied his troops for the coming battle.

"All right, bro, they're all yours!" ordered Julius.

"Legions! Dragon formation!" commanded Cagius.

The Legions held up shields and pointed their spears forward. Crouched down, the phalanx defended all members. Cagius took position in the center and put a whistle to his lips. Julius turned his horse to Walker.

"Hold your cavalry to the rear while the infantry engages," ordered Julius. "I'll join you for the charge."

"Yes, Marshal," Walker acknowledged.

The cuirassiers drew their swords, and formed up behind the infantry. The first conscripts reached the top of the ridge and stared in disbelief at the dragon legions waiting for them. However, officers whipped them forward. When they reached a position of one hundred meters from the Alliance Army, Amuro gestured to her troops to cease fire. The archers ended their attacks and drew daggers to defend themselves. The dwarf and battle-mage lines moved forward to reinforce the frontline dragon legions. The conscripts altered from the quick march into a full charge while the legions held their ground.

Conscripts contacted the shields of the legions, and in the initial stages of the trench battle, the legionnaires were pushed back by the superior numbers. Cagius blew his whistle three times, which ordered the legions to readjust their position and shift their weight. Fully expecting to overwhelm the legions, the conscripts were shocked to find themselves in a stalemate. When the legions moved to sure ground, Cagius smiled and blew his whistle twice. The legions, in one motion, shoved their shields forward and threw the frontlines of the conscripts back. Thrusting their spears forward, the front line of attackers was killed off. Cagius blew the whistle the second time, and the legions snapped back to the original position. The conscripts thrust forward again, and Cagius repeated the whistle system.

Repeating his orders two more times, the legate successfully broke the imperial charge. Sensing the tide had turned, Julius raised his sword.

"Forward!"

The legions broke formation, allowing the sprinting dwarves and Lurac to enter the fray for the first time. They brandished their axes and hammers as they leapt into swarms of retreating troops. The sight of sprinting, battle-crazed dwarves became too much for the broken and weary conscripts already suffering the humiliation of losing their fort to Cedric Rhone. The officers could no longer hold them in any cohesive formation. Retreating and using the Lake as a barrier was the only hope to avoid a devastating defeat. Julius joined Walker's cavalry and led a flanking charge against the shell-shocked troops. The imperial commander had no choice but to order his officers to wave blue and white banners.

"Signal the retreat! Fall back to the forest!" ordered the commander.

The conscripts were all too eager to heed the order, but the retreat was disorganized. Imperial troops were running all over the battlefield, which left them easy prey to alliance forces. Julius signaled with his sword to Amuro. She nodded and started to chant in the ancient elf tongue. Glowing in a faint red light, her sword enhanced the strength of her spell. The red magic circles on her gloves glowed in a fiery light and flames surrounded her body. Her final words came in the unified tongue.

"Explosion!"

Erupting from the core of the planet was a giant fireball. The impact of the explosion that followed sent enemy forces flying everywhere. The stench of burnt earth, grass, and flesh quickly filled the area. Cerwin put his hand over his eyes. Despite the smile on her face, a drop of sweat glistened down the left side of Amuro's face.

"She overdid it—again!" hollered Cerwin.

The ground shook in the area surrounding Arudin Forest, and what sounded like crashing thunder vibrated everywhere. The first waves of conscripts retreating to the forest put on the brakes as they watched Cedric and the Titan armada charging their way.

"Wedge formation! Close ranks!" ordered Cedric.

Cedric went to the pinnacle of a triangular formation with Horace and another knight filing in behind him. Dropping behind them were the remaining knights. Cecilia and the valkyries pulled to the flanks of the triangle with spears out. Civilia and the light cavalry, armed with bows, strode to the protection of the center, covered by knights on all sides. Cedric drew Ragnarok and screamed: "Titanus!"

Joining the chorus of "Titanus" was the entire armada. Those that had been the first to retreat to the forest were trampled and shred to ribbons. The imperial commander and officers of the conscripts pulled up in the center. They were trapped between the slow-moving alliance infantry and the hard-charging Titan cavalry.

"We have to break through!" shouted the commander. "Spear tips up! Archers! Fire at will! Kill the Marshal!"

The desert spearmen formed ranks. Bending low enough to put their spears in optimum position to dismount the charging armada, the imperial conscripts perspired heavily. Drawing their bows, all archers targeted Cedric. Anticipating the attack, he raised one of his hands and formed a blue magic shield. The arrows bounced off of it and fell meekly to the ground. Immediately there were murmurs of, "He can't be killed" among the frightened imperial troops. Many of the archers fled their positions and spearman followed suit. Calling from the sky above the charging riders, the raptor core dove into battle. Tearing at the hands and eyes of the front lines caused the remaining spearman to break ranks. Cedric swung Ragnarok upward and cut down the soldier in front of him. The Titans behind him followed suit. The knights chopped with mace and swords while the valkyries thrust their spears. Of course, the preferred method was simply to trample the enemy under the power of the closed horse ranks.

It was no longer a battle, but a massacre at Lake Cancer. On one side, legions marched in perfect coordination with shields and swords, now that the battle had shifted to close quarter combat. The elf battle mages used mace or swords while casting small spells that dealt damage to one foe at a time. Julius unleashed the enchanted holy power on Excalibur. The backlash produced by the swing of the sword killed five conscripts alone. Walker preferred the traditional method of the upswing of the sword from his horse as he commanded the cuirassiers speeding across the battlefield. As one soldier charged at him, Cagius jumped in the air and drove Dragonsbane into his foe as he landed. Colin tackled a conscript. Breaking his sternum with a single punch, he drew Deathbringer to confront two opponents at a time. Christian leapt from his horse and pulled a hood from his cloak over his head. He became invisible and moved in stealth to kill his enemies. Preferring a close-quarter approach, Valentine used martial arts maneuvers and his short swords. Often he licked the blood of an enemy from his sword in between kills.

The imperial commander drew his sword and charged for Cedric. The sword master saw him coming and caught the flat part of the sword below his armpit for no damage. Shocked at his foe's skill, the commander never saw Cecilia's thrust. Göttin-speer hurled the imperial from his mount. Breaking his leg in the fall, the commander lay helpless on the ground. The conscripts started to flee in terror. They threw off their armor, boots, and weapons. Jumping into Lake Cancer, many hoped they could simply swim to safety. Christian pulled down his hood. Holding his hand to his ear, he received the news he'd been waiting for. Rushing to his commander, Christian found Cedric busy driving conscripts into the lake.

"Cedric, we've got the Regional Army incoming and doing their interpretation of world-class sprinters!" exclaimed Christian. "ETA in ten!"

Cedric signaled to Bishop Arthur, who brought the rallying banner to the marshal. When Arthur started to wave the banner, the entire Titan armada rallied back to his position. Christian and Colin returned to their horses. Watching his play, Julius and Amuro similarly rallied their forces.

"We've received word that the Regional Army is sprinting through the forest and will be here in ten minutes," explained Cedric.

"We've got to give them orders, Julius," instructed Amuro.

"I think I finally understand you, Cedric," said Julius. "We'll never get another chance like this again."

"Did you ever think you'd live forever?" asked Cedric.

"I don't really think that's fair since you and I are immortal, Cedric," teased Amuro.

"Yet you are prepared to give up eternity and die here?" probed Julius.

"That's because there is no greater love than to lay down one's life for his friends," quoted Cedric.

Julius stared at his friend and could not believe the sincerity behind his words. He knew he'd never win the argument, so he started to twirl his sword over his head.

"Re-form the ranks!" ordered Julius. "Ready the charge!"

The Alliance Army snapped to attention. The infantry went to the middle, while the Titans pulled to the right flank. Archers filled in behind the two columns. The army used the lake as their second flank. Despite the fact they were just in a conflict, the alliance soldiers seemed hungry and eager for more. The warriors screamed and the horses snarled for battle. Julius seemed on the edge of his skin as he gripped his sword and shield. Three horn blasts signaled the coming of the four divisions of the Regional Army. Janissaries, Turkacon swordsmen, and Spahi cavalry made up the command. Arrows protruded from their armor due to the wood elf ambush ordered by Titanus. They stared in disbelief at the Alliance Army ready to engage them.

"Let's show them what we're made of!" screamed Julius.

The three marshals pointed their swords at the enemy. The entire Alliance Army followed them into battle. Despite their better discipline, the Regional Army could not match the fire and desire of their foes. Amuro used a charge technique on her mount. Protecting Maiden was a trail of golden light, and the winged unicorn could trample fifteen enemies. Cedric and Julius went in with swords blazing. The dwarves sprinted into battle once more, and the Turks were no match for their axes. Pasha Melmut of the Regional Army's knew he was outclassed by a superior army. In desperation, he staked a white banner of surrender in the ground to save his brave soldiers.

"We surrender!" shouted Melmut. "Yield!"

The Regional Army complied. Throwing down their weapons and raising their arms, the regional soldiers yielded. Alliance troops mercifully accepted. As he came upon Julius, Pasha Melmut held out his sword.

"My sword is yours, Marshal Imperia," offered Melmut. "I expect you to follow the proper protocols."

"You and your men will be given full quarter," explained a diplomatic Julius as he took the commander's sword. "We shall exchange you as prisoners as soon as possible. You may bury your dead and perform whatever rituals you see fit in the time being."

Cedric slowed Jericho to a trot and replaced Ragnarok behind his back. Removing his helmet, he reached inside his cloak for his flask once more. Taking a drink in one hand, the prince rubbed Jericho behind the ear.

The horse stared right at him as if it knew the outcome all along. Julius trotted over to him with Excalibur in its sheath and his shield slung over his back. He held Melmut's sword out to Cedric.

"You deserve this trophy more than I do. Had we followed my plan, we'd be at Orion by now."

"I don't need a trophy to hang in my den. You can thank me by buying me a drink next time we're in Verian."

Cedric pushed the sword back toward Julius. Filling the air was the sweet sound of an elf maiden's laughter. Amuro and Maiden joined for a final confab.

"All in a day's work. You two gentlemen were excellent as always."

"Well, we couldn't have done it without a lady's touch," praised Cedric.

"Still trying to flatter me, evil knight!" teased Amuro.

"Maybe I can . . ."

Cedric snatched Melmut's sword out of Julius's hand and gifted it to Amuro. Julius looked a little miffed at Cedric's actions, but Amuro was thrilled to receive the honor.

"Your good judgment is responsible for this victory, Amuro; the spoils are yours."

"Thank you, Cedric. I believe this deserves a place of honor in Brooke Run."

After calculating the battle statistics from each of the army captains, the vice marshals delivered status reports to the marshals.

"Looks like we've got a hearty prisoner haul—almost one hundred thousand," reported Walker.

"That's if we don't count the conscripts and their officers who are fleeing for the pass as we speak," joshed Cagius. "Lurac and his people are already scavenging the armor they left behind."

"It is logical to assume that Sultan Khan will have difficulty convincing more troops to march any time soon," stated Malcolm. "I expect an immediate offer of peace."

"Well, we've gone this far," noted Cecilia. "Why not finish this and cross the pass?"

"I would, but that pusillanimous wimp Richard Archibald would never rise up and give us the leverage necessary to win back Edenia's independence," described Cedric.

"Cedric, it really worries me that you answered that so quickly," opined Julius. "What's our status, brother?

"We took approximately 15 percent casualties," re-counted Cagius. "As I said before, we did pretty well today."

"What about us, Cecilia?" questioned Cedric.

"Two hundred souls will lead the way for the soldiers of the future!" exclaimed Cecilia.

"Two-hundred two-rank promotions; it's going to be a long night," said Cedric.

"Okay," stated Julius. "Well, there's little good that can be done by leaving the entire army here."

"Our vassals observed that the imperials are on the run; they're not coming," reported Cecilia.

"We should head back for Orion," suggested Amuro. "I think our soldiers deserve some much-needed R&R."

"Someone still has to play mother hen until the hover train arrives for the prisoner transport," proposed Julius. "Any volunteers?"

"We'll do it!" volunteered Cedric.

"Really?"

"Let's just call it a hunch!"

Walker turned to see the Acadian Templars, led by Jonas Marimon, rushing to the field of battle.

"I see what you mean," perceived Walker. "Good luck, Cedric! I'll make sure those transports should be here within the hour. Try not to go over the top!"

Julius, Cagius, Amuro, Malcolm, and Walker rode back to their commands. Cheering units, welcomed the news that they were finally heading homes. Jonas approached Walker.

"I'm glad to see you've come to the fight, now that it's over," taunted Walker.

"We all have our duties," retorted Jonas. "You are relieved, Lord Captain. Please take the cuirassiers back to Fort Orion. King Stephen wishes to bestow full honors on you and your knights."

"I accept his majesty's graciousness and will obey his orders."

The alliance forces began to fall out as the Titans remained behind. Horace, Civilia, and Christian approached the twins. Hanging behind his father Horace was Samuel Irvine. The young captain was dark-skinned with short black hair cut in a military style and hazel eyes. Horace pulled a cigar from his cloak and lit it with a stick match. Civilia's armor was covered in blood.

"What happened, Mom?" inquired Cecilia. "It looks like your streak of failing to be wounded in battle has come to an end."

"Actually, in his efforts to keep me safe, freigraf Horace managed to launch the brains of a conscript into my lap," narrated Cecilia.

"Of which I've already apologized for your highness."

"So why are we staying behind while the others are going home?" questioned Christian.

"The Templars arrived, and Jonas has that look in his eye," commented Cedric. "We're going to hang around until they leave. Order everyone to dismount."

"I see you got the same bad vibe as I did with the Templars hanging around here," concurred Horace.

"Freigraf, would you mind sending an officer with some of our better knights over to the conscript camp and see to the safety of the women that travel with the soldiers?"

"Absolutely, your excellency! Samuel, you heard your prince!"

"Right, Dad!" acknowledged Samuel as he signaled to his command to ride.

"A tad young for such responsibility—" queried Civilia.

"He is of considerable skill... and exceptional breeding, your highness," quipped Horace.

As Samuel's company made their way into the encampment, the templar army began to voice their complaints to Marimon. Riding at break-neck speed, Jonas intended to make Cedric answer for the insult.

"Here it comes!" observed Cecilia. "Want me to impale him with my spear?"

"Tempting, but I think we'll let diplomacy prevail this time," resolved Cedric.

"You're dismissed," screamed Jonas as he reared his horse in front of Cedric.

"You have no authority to order a marshal who outranks you!"

"What's with the stunt you just pulled?"

"I have no intention of letting you and your templars ravage the women, slaughter the wounded, and pillage the camp! A certain degree of civility must be kept even during war. You know the tribes have a name for you; in their tongue it means 'slayers of innocents.'"

"How dare you continue to interrupt my operations!"

"Jonas Marimon, you're nothing more than a butcher in the guise of a knight," taunted Cecilia.

"Woman, I am in no temperament to deal with your bitchery!" exclaimed Jonas.

Cecilia grabbed her spear to strike, but Cedric moved faster. He grabbed Jonas around his throat and began to squeeze tightly. Gasping for air, Jonas begged with his eyes to Civilia to defuse the tense situation. The queen responded by clearing her throat.

"My children can fight their own battles, but no mother can stand to have their loved ones suffer such insults! I will not bother to squeeze a false apology from you, but I warn you not to tempt my anger a second time. Cedric, release him and let him be on his way!"

Cedric released Jonas, and the templar still choked for air. Haughtiness had been replaced by outright fear of La Morte Angelus.

"You better begin to act with more civility," warned Cedric. "After all, my men are going to be watching you with greater scrutiny!"

Jonas sneered at the prince and rode away. The angry stare of his sister drew Cedric's attention.

"I can fight my own battles!"

"You would have killed him; I preferred to remind him about Titan honor."

"He deserves to die for his crimes!"

"It would have been a strain on our relationship to see the king's shield murdered," intervened Civilia. "Patience. We shall have our vengeance in time. We're not going to waste our time arguing about scum when Martha is sending us a trainload of steaks and beer."

"The armada will certainly appreciate it, your majesty," commented Horace.

"Where's Colin?" asked Christian.

The group turned to see Colin standing with a bloody Deathbringer slung over his shoulders.

"They were not worthy to dance with death," exclaimed Colin.

Verian, Central Acadia, Seat of the Stewardship of the Alliance

"King Stephen first took Sharon Fenidor of Evengard for his wife. He did this to appease the other rulers of the alliance at the time. However, it caused great distress in his country. The Acadian nobles hoped for a male heir to deny the claim of his daughter, Cassandra. Stephen was forced to marry a second time to the young and fertile Penelope Orpheus. However, Penelope also gave Stephen a female heir named Marie. Since neither daughter had a greater claim to the throne, the issue of succession had become a major point of contention among the alliance."

—On Succession, The Reign of King Stephen Acadia,
Royal Acadian Historian

The vast Lake Acadia stretched out for kilometers in all directions. On the southern shore was a long causeway bridge that stretched for a kilometer into a city built directly on the lake with canals and causeways connecting the different areas. The architecture of the city invoked a modern approach with the exception of three buildings built in the first part of the city—only walking distance from the main gate. On the right side of the road were the embassies of Titanus and Evengard, and on the left was the Napolitan embassy. The outside of each of these embassies was fortified with defensive walls. Soldiers and mercenaries patrolled the tops of the walls at all times. The flags and sigils on these buildings made them distinguishable from the different architecture around them. The defensive nature of such diplomatic buildings still showed the level of distrust the western allies had among each other. Centralizing the government and bureaucracy into a single city, the Acadians had built all of their administrative buildings across a five-kilometer stretch. Walking down the intersecting causeways, parents could give their children a lesson on the unified alphabet with all the acronyms. Gondolas remained the primary form of transportation from one section of the city to the next. Passing under high bridges and causeways, they were convenient, but only affordable to the elites.

Castle Acadia was a large, twenty-story building surrounded by four parapets at its corners. The parapets almost seemed out of place with the renovations of the main castle that occurred during the reign of Stephen's father, King Joseph Acadia. The grounds around the castle spread out in a five-kilometer radius. In front of the castle was a marble courtyard lined with red, white, and yellow roses. The rear of the castle had even more gardens, featuring mostly roses but also lilies, lilacs, gardenias, and poppies. There was also a giant hedge maze in this part of the castle grounds, though no one but the children of the nobles tended to use it.

On either side of the castle were two more causeways leading from the eastern and western grounds. Climbing into the sky was a thirty-story spiral building that curled at its peaks with a magic circle carved into the courtyard of the building. The path from the eastern causeway had a large sign denoting this to be the "Wizard's Guild." On the western causeway was a large forum that had the appearance of a circular-style temple. This senate served as the first attempt by the kingdoms at a unified government. Riddled with the shouts of endless debate, senators mostly grieved about the supposed "sins" of one kingdom against another.

Princess Cassandra Acadia sat on a stone bench in the rear castle gardens, directly opposite a yellow rose bush. The princess, approaching twenty revolutions of age, was extremely fair featured with high cheekbones, porcelain skin, and large green eyes that indicated high elf descent. She was rather tall, full-figured but without body fat, and though not as large as Cecilia, her cleavage was rather impressive. Flowing down her back was her waist-long raven black hair, held in place by a silver tiara with a garnet stone at its center. She wore a low-cut black dress trimmed with gold, white stockings, and black stiletto heels. Cassandra's makeup was heavy dark eye shadow, liner, blush, and purple lipstick.

At her side was her handmaiden, Felicia, who was stunningly beautiful as well. She was dressed in a blue uniform reminiscent of a maid with a white apron over it, white gloves, white stockings, and blue heels. She had long brown hair arranged in place by a white maid tiara that reached down to cover her ears. Distracted from needlepoint work, Felicia's blue eyes witnessed her mistress reading. She mouthed a sigh from her painted red lips, as Cassandra studied a very large tome with black bindings and gold lettering. Brushing against the pages, was the princess' most prized possession, a gold engagement ring bearing garnet and opal stones. Every once in a while Cassandra raised her gloved hand as she chanted a spell. A small fireball would appear in her hand before she chanted another spell to make it disappear.

Cassandra Acadia was a late bloomer. Nothing was particularly special about the girl when she was born. Tested at her fifth revolution, her aptitude suddenly measured off the scale. Confounded by these results, Stephen sent for her Uncle Cerwin Faulkner. After more tests confirmed his suspicions, the elf mage took particular interest in beginning her training as a spell caster. First born but not considered the true heir, Cassandra handled her delicate position with the dignity of a ruler. This behavior prompted many in Central Acadia and throughout the alliance to view her as the true successor. The princess had the innate ability to get whatever she wanted from her father, including the largest knight's tournament in the history of the alliance to celebrate her Quize. That fateful rotation allowed Cassandra to meet her true love, Cedric Rhone, who defied every Acadian tradition to crown her the "Queen of Love and Beauty." Shielding her talents from the outside world has been a priority of her father. Cassandra has only ventured outside the walls of Verian twice in her life.

"Are you going to make the bush burn again, my lady?" joked Felicia.

"You never let me live any mistake down," pouted Cassandra.

The two raised their heads at the sound of a commotion. Cassandra spotted her half-sister, Princess Marie, running down the steps into the garden. The sixteen-revolution-old princess had bright blue eyes filled with happiness and life. Long, golden blonde hair sparkled in the sunlight, as she cleared each step. Her golden tiara was set with a diamond. Marie was thin as a rail—not from lack of appetite—to the annoyance of Cassandra who constantly had to watch her weight. Seemingly more of a doll than a human, the younger princess had a kind and gentle heart. Running as fast as her heels would take and holding up the hem of her gold dress, Marie followed her mission faithfully. Cassandra closed her tome and stood to greet her.

"Cassie, I have wonderful news. The war is over!"

Cassandra's heart skipped a beat for a moment as she brought her gloved hands to the center of her chest. Noticing the look in her eyes, Marie dreaded what was coming. No one in the world could turn on the waterworks as quickly as Cassandra and no amount of tissues could ever hope to contain it. Her younger sister attempted to mitigate the damage by hugging her tightly.

"That means your fiancé is going to be coming home. I'm so happy for you."

Cassandra couldn't speak. She had spent almost three revolutions in vigilant prayer that Cedric Rhone would make it home safely from the war. Seeking an answer from her soul, she was sure that if the marshal commandant had been killed, the guards would be reveling in it.

"When do they expect the marshals to return?" asked Cassandra.

"The people are making preparations for a victory parade three rotations from now," replied Marie. "I've been secretly praying for Prince Julius as well. I'm glad he's coming home safe."

Knowing she wouldn't be able to concentrate on her work anymore, Felicia lifted her head. Eavesdropping on their conversations, her face fell when she heard the statements of the younger princess. The maid moved her eyes around the garden and realized her actions had gone unnoticed. Felicia pretended to return to her work. Cassandra took a deep breath and smiled.

"Well, this does call for a celebration. I'll get hold of the royal sommelier and have him bring up a reserve bottle of sparkling wine."

"I don't know, Cassie. Daddy doesn't like it when we drink alone."

"This is a special occasion, Marie, and what Daddy doesn't know can't hurt him," stated Cassandra subtly, as she brought her gloved finger to her lips. "Felicia, would you please handle the arrangements? We'll take it in my apartment."

Felicia stood from the bench, set her needlepoint down, and curtsied toward the princess.

"It will be done, your highness."

"Thank you."

Felicia left the garden as the two sisters could barely contain their excitement.

"I'll bet Daddy will have a ball for sure, Cassie."

"If there's a parade, they'll have to be a ball. I just hope three rotations is enough time for the royal seamstresses."

"Why?

"We haven't had a formal ball in over four revolutions. We're going to need new dresses."

"You're right. I'm glad I'm not going to have to wear that horrible outfit they made me wear at your Quize Ball."

"It was so cute. Of course, you were a kid then, so I can see where you would prefer something more elegant. I'll show you a few design patterns I have up in my room, and we'll send down the specifications after our little celebration."

Cassandra put her arm around her younger sister and they walked back into the castle from the gardens. She kissed her gently on the forehead as thanks for the news she had been praying for. Cedric was finally coming home to rescue her from her imprisonment.

Plains of Lake Cancer, Three Rotations Later

"The blood flows freely in the earth now, and the smell of death now permeates the once-fertile plains. We were once many, but now we struggle to maintain our way of life. Now our enemies demand that we choose our fate. One enemy claims to be a friend but speaks with a serpent's tongue. The other enemy we know to be honest, but do they offer more than slavery? In a choice of two evils... is there really a choice?"

—*Chieftain Aramas before the Great Council of the Tribal Confederation*

The sound of swift-beating wild horses boomed over the plains. On top of the brown-and-white-spotted horse was a girl in her late teens. Her long brown hair was pulled back in a ponytail and held in place with a headband sporting a bone carving of a wolf. Her outfit was made of hardened leather cloaked with gray wolf fur. The wooden shaft of her hunting spear was hooked to the back of her armor. The triangular spear head was made of steel and vanadium, thus the tip was remained red even when it wasn't covered in blood. Pulling up near Lake Cancer, her bright green eyes surveyed the area like a hunter. Upon spotting freshly dug graves, she took a moment to smell the air.

There's been combat again, the girl thought.

"Hippolyte!" echoed a voice behind.

Turning her horse, Hippolyte spotted a second rider closing on her. The girl on the horse was in her early teens with big, brown, innocent eyes and long brown hair tied up in twin pigtails. She wore the same leather armor with a wolf skin cape over her shoulders. A necklace made out of wolves' teeth was her main accessory, and a bow and quiver slung over her back. Running on the heels of her horse was a large, gray wolf with blue eyes and white feet.

The heir of the Wolf Tribe, Hippolyte was the granddaughter of Aramas, the leader of the Tribal Confederation. Though she had seen only sixteen revolutions, her natural abilities had proven invaluable and she had done much to unite the tribes in their opposition to the better-organized alliance. Hippolyte was extremely protective of her younger sister, Minerva, who had seen thirteen revolutions. Constantly daydreaming of a world beyond the borders of her tribe, Minerva wished that a handsome knight from the alliance would whisk her away. The sisters were the last remaining members of their village after the Acadian Templars, led by Jonas Marimon, slaughtered its inhabitants even after their father, Aegis, had surrendered. The girls were spared only when Cedric's armada drew their swords and drove the Templars from the Terrace River. Bringing them into the main encampment after those events, Aramas granted Hippolyte a wolf guardian named Stryker.

"You're too slow, Minerva!" shouted Hippolyte.

"You're too fast, sister!" retorted Minerva as she reared her horse.

The two sisters got off their horses and took them over to be watered. While the horses drank, the wolf went over to the kneeling Hippolyte. It licked her face as she scratched him under his chin.

"Are they steel-belly graves?" asked Minerva.

Prejudice had run rampant among both sides of the conflict between the alliance and tribes. The favorite pet names they had for each other reflected what they hated most about them. The alliance called their enemy barbarians because they refused to assimilate their culture. The tribes called them steel-bellies because of their powerful armor.

"There aren't enough markers. If there are mass graves in this area, they must belong to the cloth-headed troops," reasoned Hippolyte. "I'd bet anything that the Prime Eagle had something to do with this; I can feel it."

"You don't suppose he's still around," stuttered Minerva as she swallowed a lump in her throat.

"Not likely, but you know the legends. He flies in from behind and snatches away the weak with bloody talons that he has for hands. In fact, he might be behind you now!"

Minerva screamed and turned behind her. Of course, no one was there. When she did, Hippolyte grabbed her from behind and squeezed her tightly. Minerva got very angry as her sister started to laugh at her. Cedric Rhone had developed quite the reputation among the tribes in the last war despite his acts of good faith. He had become more legend than man among the Tribal Confederation earning the disdainful title of Prime Eagle.

"That was mean, Hippolyte!"

"You're so easy to tease! I'm not going to deny the fact that Prime Eagle is a great chief among the steel-bellies, but these legends are just tales to scare children."

Hippolyte stopped playing with her sister. Standing tall, her face was full of pride.

"In fact, I would stare the Prime Eagle in the face, not blink, and spit right in his eye."

"Really, sis?"

"Of course. Don't you think so, Stryker?"

The wolf gave off a short howl.

"You're amazing, Hippolyte! You're already the fastest rider and the best hunter in the wolf tribe! I bet you'll make a great chief someday."

"I think Grandpa can hold his own right now."

"I thought that Dad . . . well . . ." sobbed Minerva. "Grandpa is all we have left after the steel-bellies burned our home."

"Oh, Minerva," comforted Hippolyte as she grabbed her sister and hugged her tightly.

"I just miss them the most on these long trips out to the different camps. Those damn steel-bellies. Why did they kill them?"

"Mom and Dad died because war is not hunting! When an opponent is declared, everyone that battles takes a risk. For those reasons, what happened to Mom was unforgiveable; she died without a weapon in her hands."

"But why didn't we die with them? Why did they stop the attack?"

"I don't know, Minerva. I think another army arrived. So much of that day was a fog, but I think the steel-bellies started fighting one another. Now no more tears, okay?"

Minerva sniffled and stopped her sobbing.

"We should get back to the camp, Minerva. I'm sure Grandpa is waiting for us."

"I hope he's got a big feast ready."

"Always thinking with your stomach. You game, Stryker?"

Hippolyte gave him a last rub on his back while Stryker gave a snarl.

"That makes two. Let's ride, sis!"

The two girls leapt onto the back of their horses and took off across the plains.

VERIAN, CENTRAL ACADIA

"Angel of Death? It must be because his face was carved
by the angels."

*—Princess Cassandra Acadia upon seeing Prince Cedric Rhone
the first time*

L ining the streets, the citizens of Verian poured streamers and confetti on the pavement. Men put children on top of their shoulders so they could see the parade in front of them. The female citizens were throwing rose petals as the sound of the slow trot of horses drew closer. Cedric, Amuro, and Julius were honored with full regalia. Cecilia, Cagius, Walker, and Malcolm rode behind them, receiving their share of the honors as well. Welcoming a chance to remove their armor for the first time in five revolutions, the officers wore their everyday outfits. Julius was in a long green military coat over a white shirt with a white coif, green vest, and green pants. Cedric and Cecilia wore the Titan military officers uniform with some minor variations. Continuing the tradition started by his great-great grandfather, Cedric wore a kilt and had a large gold crucifix hanging down from his neck. Cecilia's hair was out of the braid and held in place by a thin gold tiara with wing barrettes and an opal stone in the center. Amuro wore a long blue military coat over a white shirt and white pants. Welcoming the opportunity for makeup, Amuro painted her eyes and lips in pink while Cecilia used purple to match her facial features. Malcolm was still in his ranger attire. Walker was dressed in a blue military jacket with a white tie, white pants, and blue cloak lined with rabbit fur. Cagius wore a blue military jacket with a white shirt and blue pants. A reporter was on the scene in a van with the initials "ANO" on it. Many photographers and cameramen were covering the event. The reporter continued her broadcast:

83

"We are here live in Verian at the victory celebration of the end of the Third Chinota-Alliance War. Alliance News Organization has confirmed that Count Luminas and Minister Saladin signed the Third Treaty of Deniva this morning, officially ending the war. The terms disclosed included the exchange of all prisoners and reparations paid to the alliance from the empire. The trade embargo in the independent fiefdom of Deniva has been lifted as well, and Margrave Dennis de-Milly has reopened the city to both sides. In a morning address, King Stephen bestowed full credit for the victory upon the three alliance marshals: Prince Marshal Julius Imperia, Princess Marshal Amuro Jenitzen, and Prince Marshal Commandant Cedric Rhone. Our cameras will now pan to the parade so we can give our viewers a better glimpse of the heroes."

The marshals and vice-marshals passed the three buildings on Embassy Row. Despising these parades, Julius was marred in depression. He never understood how his comrades were so adept at playing to the crowd. Two young women fainted after Cagius waved at them while Walker appreciated the chants of his name. Julius's one companion in wanting the parade to be over was Malcolm. The Napolitan centurion wished he could just gallop away to castle and end it. However, he remembered his duty to the people and faked a smile.

Observing a scene on the right hand side of the crowd lifted his spirit up. Two young boys and a young girl had setup some boxes with a few cans on top of them. They each held a wooden stick in their hand and one boy lifted a piece of cardboard like a shield. Raising his short stick in the air, the shield-bearing boy took command.

"Halt, Sultan Khan, and face your doom at the hands of the three marshals of the west! I am the dragon knight appearing courageously!" announced the first boy.

"And I am the unicorn maiden appearing beautifully!" boasted the girl.

"And I am the eagle master appearing honorably!" exclaimed the second boy, carrying a wooden stick too large for him.

Too eager to await an answer, the three proceeded to attack and knock over the boxes. Vanquishing the overwhelming danger of cans and cardboard, the children began to celebrate and cheer. Julius allowed himself a smile.

"See something you like?" inquired Cedric.

"Just a reminder of what Cagius and I did as children," recollected Julius.

"What's with the sour mood?" queried Amuro.

"Nothing," retorted Julius to shut down the discussion.

"My brother isn't really into these parades," said Cagius.

"I don't feel that the commanders of the Alliance Army are to be treated like clowns," stated Julius.

"It's not a bad thing to get such recognition every once in a while. After all, we're out fighting these battles so these people won't have it come to them," explained Cecilia.

"These aren't the Acadian noble elites standing before you, Julius," pronounced Walker. "These people represent what is great about my country. Their praise is genuine."

"So just smile and wave, big fella," teased Amuro. "Hopefully, we won't have to go through this garbage anymore."

A young boy ran out with flowers. Handing them to Amuro, she took them with a big smile on her face. She stopped to kiss the boy, who blushed deeply.

"Thank you. I am very happy to receive flowers from a true gentleman," acknowledged Amuro as she turned to Malcolm and stuck out her tongue. "That is how you treat a beautiful maiden, Malcolm!"

Malcolm continued to ride stoically as if he had not even heard her. Remembering the advice of Cerwin a few rotations ago and dreading the possibility of being a putz, he decided to secretly make note of it. Not satisfied, Amuro yelled at Cedric with anger,

"Cedric, please do me a favor and give courting lessons to Malcolm."

"I've tried many times, Amuro," responded Cedric.

"Well, can't you use that mind control power of yours to hypnotize him or something?"

"Amuro, please!" shouted a nervous Malcolm.

"I don't think lobotomizing Malcolm is good idea," chided Cecilia.

"Come on, Cecilia, you should be with me on this."

"I do agree with you that Malcolm doesn't know a good thing when he sees it."

"What does that mean?" said Malcolm.

"If you have to ask the question, then the statement is true," confirmed Cagius. "It means you need to act with more chivalry when pursuing the ladies."

"You mean like you?" asked Malcolm.

"Absolutely! It is our duty as knights of the realm to seek the favor of beautiful maidens and do as they bid. We will charge into battle screaming their names in the never-ending quest to destroy evil in this world. That is the sacred duty of every cavalier!"

"Sounds like a good way to end up dead," taunted Walker.

"Yes, but when a lady mourns your passing, it is worth it."

"I think I prefer Cedric's method of seducing every woman in the west better," jeered Julius.

"I believe courtship is the correct term," corrected Cedric. "I don't want to give myself a bad reputation."

"I'm sure it was only the first ten women that gave you such a reputation," ridiculed Cecilia.

Cedric gritted his teeth. However, his mood suddenly changed as he saw two black-and- red streamers fall in front of him. Looking up at a window in one of the administration buildings, he witnessed a black gloved hand with a red ribbon tied around it waving at him. Upon seeing Cassandra's face, Cedric gave her a salute and blew her a kiss. Cecilia simply shook her head at the window when she rode past it. Leaning against the window, Cassandra sighed lovingly as they passed. Felicia stood behind her, nervously staring around the room and windows.

"Princess Cassandra, I believe it would be wise for us to make our exit," recommended Felicia.

"Just a little longer, Felicia," begged Cassandra. "It's felt like an eternity since I've seen him."

Felicia was moved by the princess's emotions, as Cassandra began to well up when she saw that Cedric was still wearing her favor.

"He didn't lose it!" exclaimed Cassandra.

"Somehow, my lady, I didn't expect that he would. When you gave it to him, he took it as if it was a sacred relic."

"That's just his way; I love everything about him."

"Well, then, it is provident that your father arranged for you and him to be married."

"Provident? He practically had to prostrate himself in front of Civilia before she would even agree to his terms. Yet I still remember that big smile that came across her face when it was over. The Matriarch of Destruction— and my soon-to-be mother-in-law— wears the title proudly."

Felicia seemed lost in thought as she stared out the window directly at Julius. The Paladin took a gander toward the window as well but did not gesture as Cedric did. Rather, he simply brought his hands to his face to hide a large smile.

"Julius, your son has grown strong," whispered Felicia.

A knock on the door soon drew the attention of the two women away from the window. Felicia gathered herself and went to the door.

"Who is calling?" asked Felicia.

"Cerwin Faulkner. I'd like to speak with my niece," answered Cerwin.

Cassandra smiled brightly as Felicia opened the door. Not a moment after he entered, Cassandra jumped toward her uncle and hugged him tightly.

"Uncle Cerwin! It's wonderful to see you!" cried an excited Cassandra.

"Countless revolutions I have seen on this planet and many family members I have, but never have any of them shown as much affection toward me as you do, Cassie!"

"What did you bring me?" demanded Cassandra as she got a big pouting look in her eyes.

"Your father still spoils you, I see. Well, at least you admit that it makes you better than most. My gift to you is greater than any present I ever brought you. I cleared permission with your father to begin the final stages of your training."

"I can finally begin to train as a high sorceress?"

"Yes. It will be done strictly under my supervision. You are not to use these spells unless in my presence."

"Don't worry. I don't plan to do any palace remodeling anytime soon."

"That's good because we don't want a repeat of the fireball and tapestry incident when you nearly burnt the palace down," teased Felicia.

"Yes," said a frowning Cassandra.

"Or the time you made the ground swell during the Cuirassier Royal Review."

"That was a long time ago."

"What about your recent attempt to electrocute Lord Captain Walker during training?"

"All right, Felicia, must you be so frank? I am not the most capable high sorceress in the world, and that's why Uncle Cerwin is here to help me."

"You and Amuro casting spells—I don't know why I keep doing this. I'm just asking for trouble."

"We heard many rumors of your exploits during the wars with the tribes and empire."

"Really? Nothing bad, I hope."

"Did we almost lose?" asked a concerned Cassandra.

Sighing deeply, the joys of visiting his beloved niece gave way to memories of the horrible war.

"Yes. I'm not ashamed to say that all would have been lost if it hadn't been for your fiancé. It was not just the Istle Hills, Cassandra. He turned the tide in the war against the tribes, and his selflessness prevented us from suffering a tremendous defeat in the recent battle."

"Father has already decreed that the victory crown that belongs to Cedric will bear Julius's name."

"If Cedric was given the victory crown, the Nobles of Acadia would riot."

"The nobles pray to their false gods and make the coffers of Patriarch Javos rich while I spent nights in vigil to the Father."

"Despite your position, Cassandra, you need to mind your tongue. You have to remember that Verian is a dangerous place. The Temple of the Divine Saints is very powerful and will not tolerate someone born of such high blood to speak ill of them."

"I have my personal shield returned to me, and who is brave enough to dare challenge the wrath of La Morte Angelus?"

"I suppose you are right about that. How is your mother?"

"She seems content to reap in the darkness as always. She has little love or use for my father anymore, and I fear that his love for me has replaced any memory of her in his heart."

"I meant, how is she toward you?"

"She treats me as an outcast. It is not uncommon for her to describe me as a 'power whore' even to my face."

Cerwin closed his eyes and shook her head.

"I never trusted your mother, even in Evengard. It was a bad match, and she proved that very quickly. It is quite ironic that she uses such words to describe you. Well enough of this poison, let an doting uncle see his beloved niece."

Cerwin stepped back and stared at Cassandra.

"By the Father, when did you become such a beautiful young woman? Gone are the pigtails and baby fat. Cedric is very lucky to have you. That is, if you don't mind an old lecherous fool heaping such praise on you."

"Stop it, Uncle!"

Felicia stared at the clock and began to shuffle impatiently toward Cassandra.

"Mistress, what about our timely exit?" reminded Felicia.

"I think you should get back to the palace," advised Cerwin.

"Yes, Lord Cerwin. I feel that I'm going to need significant time getting the princess ready for this evening," said Felicia.

"Of course, I need to look my best," boasted Cassandra as she kissed her uncle. "Wait until you see the gown they made for me."

"I'm glad you finally have him home."

Cassandra and Felicia departed.

The marshals and vice-marshals arrived in the foyer of Castle Acadia. The castle interior was lined with many portraits of the different kings of Central Acadia. Prominently displayed was Marquis Nicholas Acadia, the first king, who joined with Frederick Rhone of Titanus in the First Alliance. The warriors marched up ivory steps that had a golden banister on either side. A pair of mahogany double doors opened in front of them that led into the castle throne room. The floor of the room was marble, lined with marble columns and a red carpet.

Seated on a gold throne above the marble platform, King Stephen reclined against the blue velvet backing. Deliberately placed two steps below him, sat his two queens on padded cedar benches. Seated below him on the right was Sharon Fenidor, a she-elf with long black hair and green eyes. Dressed as if attending a funeral, malice curled behind her red painted lips. On his left was Penelope Orpheus, a beautiful human woman with long blonde hair and blue eyes. Dressed in the traditional blue and white of her country, she played the part of the noble well. Hanging behind Stephen was the flag of Central Acadia and two banners of his house. Jonas stood before the marble steps of throne with his sword drawn while the remaining five bodyguards surrounded the king. As a subject of Central Acadia, Walker dropped to his knee before the king. Since each country was considered an equal in the alliance, the marshals and vice-marshals remained standing. Beckoning Walker to rise with a flick of his right index finger, Stephen stood to greet his heroes.

"I wished to honor the seven of you before tonight's celebration. As the steward of the alliance, one of my most cherished tasks is to bestow a victory crown."

Rushing to Stephen's side was a young squire carrying an olive crown on top of a velvet pillow. Summoned by the king's left hand, Julius stepped forward, to the disdain of Cecilia. She stared at her brother waiting for him to do something, but Cedric remained silent.

"Well done, Prince Marshal Julius Imperia," acknowledged Stephen.

An awkward moment arose as the much smaller Stephen tried to place the crown on Julius head. Seeing the discomfort in the king's face, Julius knelt down to grant Stephen easier access. A round smattering applause filled the galley of the throne room; most nobles seemed more disturbed than pleased that Julius was receiving his prize. Cagius rolled his eyes at the development.

"Thank you," said Stephen.

"It's my pleasure, your majesty."

"Prince Marshal Rhone and Princess Marshal Jenitzen, your sacrifices and skills are to be celebrated as well," noted Stephen.

"Thank you, your majesty," replied Amuro, but Cedric remained silent.

"I know its being a long time since we've had a celebration like this and I know everyone has preparations to make. I won't hold you any longer and once again convey my deepest gratitude for your service. I'll see you again this evening."

Turning on the heels of their boots, Cedric and Cecilia raced out of the throne room. The other warriors didn't waste much time in joining them. Acadian halberdiers closed the door behind them and everyone breathed a sigh of relief.

"You know, I believe those Acadians would rather have seen us lose to the empire," stated Cagius angrily. "Talk about walking into a lion's den!"

"Well, they're conflicted," said Walker. "They want to be independent but don't want to see anyone outside of Central Acadia get the credit for it."

"What fools!" exclaimed Malcolm as he shook his head.

"Well, we have a couple of hours," observed Cagius.

"Well that's because you're a guy," teased Amuro. "It takes me hours to pull this off."

"Anyone up for some drinks at the Golden Dragon Tavern?" recommended Julius. "I know I owe you a drink, Cedric."

"Cecilia and I actually have some business to attend to," retorted Cedric.

"Sorry, Julius, we'll need to take a rain check," Cecilia expressed her regret.

"I hope it's not too serious," fretted Amuro.

"I don't expect it to be, but we've been wrong before," said Cecilia.

The two departed. Julius, removed victory crown from his head, stared at it, and smiled.

"I hope he's not holding a grudge," teased Julius.

"I'm sure he is," quipped Amuro.

At the disappearance of the marshals, Stephen had the throne room gallery emptied. Ordering the shades to be lowered over all the windows, Stephen switched on the artificial lighting from the control panel on his throne. A secret passage to the right of the throne room opened, and a rather pale and distinguished gentleman emerged. Sweeping his long black and red cape over the shoulders of his tuxedo, the gentlemen focused his red eyes on the king. His black hair was shaped so a sharp widow's peak was prominent on the center of his forehead. His face was rather thin, and he had two white fangs curled under his lips.

"Count Maximilian Luminas, I expect good news," said Stephen.

Maximilian Luminas was a vampire with a reputation for being more trustworthy than humans. His immortality had allowed him to advise kings of Central Acadia for some one-hundred-fifty revolutions, and he had survived some of the worst of them. Maximilian had been very discreet concerning his personal life. However, there were rumors that his skill set as a warrior was similar to that of Cedric Rhone. Having a particular penchant for rich swine blood, the vampire abhorred the drinking of human blood.

"I have very good news for you," interjected a smiling Luminas. "The Tribal Council has sent back its preliminary communications. They are open to meeting with us to sign an armistice."

"Wonderful. I knew it was difficult negotiating with the tribes while fighting the empire, but it seems we cut off the Titans," declared an elated Stephen.

"Yes. Apparently the tribes hesitated when Civilia offered to make the Tribal Confederation a protectorate of Titanus. We've successfully curbed any future Titan ambition in the west."

"I am more concerned with fighting a war on two fronts. Too long have we had to deal with such enemies within our borders. Now we can solely concentrate on stopping the imperial encroachments."

"Yes, but as your chancellor, it was my duty to worry about Civilia's interference."

"Yes, but why should she be anything but emboldened!" interrupted Shannon.

"What are you implying?" questioned Stephen angrily.

"Civilia pulled her forces out of the Alliance Army when we first went to war against the tribes. She forced you to go to Rhinegard, offer your own daughter's hand in marriage, and a king's ransom in dowry to bring troops into the war that legally should have been ours."

"We desperately needed Titan intervention in the war against the tribes," argued Stephen. "I know I had to make a bad deal, but if not for Cedric's timely arrival and tactics, we would have lost the Battle of the Istle Hills."

"The Istle Hills was just dirt!"

"Had we lost that dirt, the tribes would have become emboldened to march on Verian," interrupted Penelope.

"Silence, wench!" bellowed Sharon. "Do not interrupt me when I speak!"

"You are in no position to speak to me in any such way!" retorted Penelope.

"It wasn't your daughter that was sacrificed to the Titan War Machine!" countered Sharon.

Rising from the benches, a confrontation between the two queens was inevitable. The two women had nothing but contempt for one another, but it had nothing to do with winning the affection of Stephen. If the elves had known the embarrassment Sharon would cause them, they would never have arranged for her to marry Stephen. The Acadians, on the other hand, despised Penelope for being unable to grant Stephen a son and ensure proper succession. Stephen stepped in between them and screamed.

"Enough! I tire of you bickering like harpies! A certain degree of civility must be kept in this difficult situation. To answer your question, Sharon, it wasn't just for the sake of the Alliance that I gave Cassandra's hand in marriage. You've seen the ways her eyes shine with love toward Cedric. She's had them ever since the day the sword master defied my orders and crowned her the 'Queen of Love and Beauty' at her birthday tournament. If I promised her to anyone else, Cassandra would hate me, and I couldn't bear the thought of destroying my relationship with her."

"We're going to have to break this news to the other members of the alliance," said Luminas.

"We'll do it tonight when they're off guard," decided Stephen. "The odds are Civilia and her spy network has found out about the tribe's intentions as well, and the Titans will not be happy."

"I don't see the reason for secrecy anymore either," advised Luminas. "We're going to have to figure out some way to compensate the Titans, but I'll have everything ready for this evening."

"Thank you, Maximilian. It comforts me that a vampire is more trustworthy than the endless stream of sycophants who corrupt my court."

TITANUS EMBASSY, CENTRAL ACADIA

"You are hereby banished from the kingdom of heaven. From this day forward, you shall bear the mark of both divinity and devilry. Your curse is to bear two pairs of wings, one to shed salvation's light and one as black as darkest night. You are permitted within the borders of creation to bring souls back to God, but you shall not have the power to save your own. From this day forward, Krystos, you shall neither be Sentinel nor Acolyte. Perhaps if you are deemed worthy, you may one day return to the Beatific Vision. May the grace of God be with you!"

—Lord Teman, reading the proclamation against Sir Krystos

The embassy of Titanus was built like a small fort surrounded by a nine-foot-high wall and gate. A giant stone cross and two House of Rhone banners hung from the roof. Despite the peacefulness of Verian, knights and valkyries diligently patrolled the courtyard. The first floor of the embassy contained a restaurant, a full-stocked lobby central bar, and the entrance to a twelve-story luxury hotel. The offices of the ambassador and staff were on the second floor, living quarters on the fourth and fifth floor, and an armory in the basement. The third floor was divided between a large computer tactical center and a strategy room. The hotel took all of the remaining rooms on the other floors. Perched like a mother eagle on the third floor terrace, Civilia followed her twins as they hurried up the stairs. Dressed in a uniform similar to Cecilia, the queen held the symbol of her office, a steel scepter, in her right hand.

"I hope King Stephen didn't keep you too bored," offered Civilia.

"It was rather disappointing," replied Cedric.

"It wasn't as if you didn't expect such a thing to happen," responded Civilia.

"As if Julius would ever have lifted half a finger to do what Cedric did during the war," interrupted an annoyed Cecilia.

"It's all right," said Cedric as he hugged his mother from behind. "Miss us?"

"You know I do, though I hate it when you grab me from behind."

"How about this then?"

Catching his mother off guard, Cedric scooped the queen up in his arms. The queen screamed. Cecilia started laughing hysterically as a few guards came out to check on the situation. She waved them off, and they returned to their posts when they saw it was nothing.

"Just practicing!" ribbed Cedric.

"You know what? Practice on your fiancé, not me!"

Cedric gave his mother a kiss and set her down. Civilia pretended to bash him with her scepter.

"Why are you so playful?" asked Civilia.

"The green-eyed monster was waving at him from the window during the parade," tattled Cecilia, not hiding her envy.

"Now I understand. Anyway, I called you both here because Duke Wilhelm von Angelhardt arrived in the capital this morning on urgent business."

"I was having a good morning, Mom," said Cedric. "Now my mentor returns to the capital, probably to give me notice of the next plot to bring about the end of the world."

"Cedric, the duke is always worried about the most trivial things," retorted Cecilia. "I'm sure it's just another one of his Demonkin problems that a few sword slashes will take care of."

"Since both the alliance and our ancient cousins the Kablisha refuse to acknowledge the Demonkin threat, it is our position to act in such matters," pronounced Civilia. "Therefore, we will heed any warning that

Duke von Angelhardt has. He has served the House of Rhone faithfully since its inception, and we know where he stands."

The three entered the doors to the soundproof conference room. His gold cloak resting over the titan officer uniform, Christian bantered back and forth with the Duke. Scratching his chestnut-brown hair cut in the same short military style as Cedric, Wilhelm focused his ancient brown eyes on the approaching family. Blemishing his otherwise youthful skin was a hideous scar under his right eye, which appeared to have been made by the talons of an eagle. Even though he was sitting down, the man was clearly tall and broad shouldered. Modifying the titan officer uniform slightly, he dressed in a long red coat and wore a white coif instead of a tie. As if preparing to present a case at trial, Wilhelm sat with his white gloved hands folded on the table. When Civilia entered, he promptly stood and bowed. When the three stared into his eyes, it was as if they were staring thousands of revolutions into the past.

"Duke Wilhelm, it's been some time," started Civilia.

Wilhelm von Angelhardt was the incarnation of the angel Krystos and had been on Terminus Mundus since life began. Wilhelm aligned himself with the Titan faction during the Schism of the Sentinels. He had come into and fallen out of favor with the kings and queens of Titanus throughout their long history. However, when Frederick Rhone came to power four Titan generations ago, Wilhelm was restored to full honors. Though he chose to no longer serve as Civilia's chancellor, the duke was invaluable to protecting the Titan Crown. Wilhelm had mentored all of the great rulers of Titanus.

"You've been distracted on two fronts with both the tribes and the empire," stated Wilhelm. "I did not wish to break focus in those matters, your highness."

Everyone took a seat. Christian whispered something into Cedric's ear. Seeming disturbed by the comment, he mouthed, "I'll deal with it later" to his friend as he slapped him on the shoulder. A servant in the room brought forward what appeared to be brandy for Civilia, Cecilia, Cedric, and Wilhelm and a glass of port wine for Christian.

"To what do we owe the pleasure?" asked Civilia.

"There has been much activity around the Kaiser Mountains in the caverns and passes where the Demonkin live," answered Wilhelm as he sipped his drink.

"What kind of activity?" queried Cedric.

"I have not yet been able to ascertain that information. However, I do know that after revolutions of hiding, the Nephilim are beginning to show their faces once more."

"Those are the fallen angels?" commented Cecilia.

"The Nephilim are descended of the Acolyte fallen angels of the prince, as the Divikin are descended of the Sentinel fallen angels," explained Wilhelm. "The Demonkin are beholden to their Nephilim masters. I know for a fact that Basarabas currently leads the Nephilim, and he's been seen in Verian recently. I fear that the noninterference of the Kablisha and the blissful ignorance of Edenia will leave us once again as the lone Divikin willing to take up this battle."

"I'll issue a writ," interrupted Cedric. "Colin can take care of him."

"I fear a simple assassination will not take care our problems, since our enemy is not entering the city through the normal channels."

"The only other way to get into Verian would be . . . Guild Guide. Wilhelm, are you accusing the Wizards Guild of bringing a Nephilim into Verian?" interrupted Christian.

"It's the only way," replied Wilhelm.

"What proof do you have for me to give to Stephen?" probed Civilia further.

"I assume the word of my contact will not be enough," said Wilhelm.

"Is your contact trustworthy?" demanded Civilia.

"She'd better be! I understand that you're familiar with my paramour Nadia," interjected Wilhelm.

"I'm sorry, Wilhelm. Nadia's testimony would never pass muster in Titanus, let alone Central Acadia," explained Civilia.

"Nadia has no reason to lie to me," countered Wilhelm. "Her knowledge of magic is very strong, and she can sense when transport magic is being used. The grace of God still flows through my veins and I assure you my magic has freed her from the controlling influences of Lucifer."

"Let's assume this is happening. Why would the Nephilim align themselves with the guild?" queried Cedric.

"I don't think it's the Nephilim that the guild is truly interested in," started Wilhelm. "I think it's what they're providing. Prior to the battle at Lake Cancer, a powerful energy signature registered on Terminus Mundus, one so strong my only conclusion is that it came from a celestial gate crossing. I know an angel of Lucifer has crossed into Terminus Mundus, and I have my suspicions."

There was a moment of silence among the four as Wilhelm sipped his drink before continuing his presentation.

"You are familiar with the rules. The Lord Father has chosen not to do anything that would interfere with the tenet of 'free will.' Therefore, angels that come from heaven must surrender certain powers before they can enter the temporal realm. Lucifer's followers do not have any of these restrictions. The Sentinels wiped out the Acolytes before the schism and we simply do not have the strength to contend with an Acolyte again. The stakes cannot be higher."

"So the Wizard's Guild aligns themselves with this angel and the Nephilim," reasoned Christian. "Guild members are human with traces of elf blood allowing them to use magic. That means they must have a short-sighted goal. Cassandra's betrothal to Cedric was not popular in Central Acadia. It could be for an assassination attempt."

"No organization would be foolish enough to target a crown prince of Titanus," interjected Cecilia. "It would mean war between Titanus and Central Acadia."

"Which is exactly the chaos this agent of Lucifer could be looking for," argued Wilhelm. "It's too early in the game to grasp motives; though I do not believe Cedric is a large enough target to warrant an Acolyte. My operative will continue to monitor the situation. The reason why I come to you with this is not to warn Stephen but to warn you, Civilia. We can't allow ourselves to become complacent because of our victories, despite how great they were. We were forced to expose your son to grant us victory, and there is now great fear among the alliance elites."

"I will heed your warnings, Wilhelm," declared Civilia. "Without your help, my throne would have never been secured. However, I'm going to need something more to go to Stephen with."

"Of course, your highness," acknowledged Wilhelm.

Wilhelm continued to stare at Cedric. The prince had fallen silent ever since Wilhelm had first mentioned the arriving Acolyte. The Duke couldn't tell if he was stunned or simply trying to formulate a plan.

"Now if you'll excuse me, we have a celebration to get ready for," said Civilia.

"Yes, the long-awaited celebration. You will give my apologies to King Stephen for not being able to attend. However, these matters deserve immediate attention."

"I will make up some excuse."

"With your permission, your highness, I would like to speak with Cedric privately."

Civilia held no objection as she and Cecilia left the room. Christian used Cedric's shoulder to help himself up. Cedric finished one drink and took another as they cleared out of the room.

"What's the situation?" asked Cedric.

"I want to speak with you about Cassandra privately."

"You gave me the birds and the bees talk already."

"The rumor concerning her birth is true. Stephen refused to bed Sharon after the wedding, but the need for an heir at the time was quite important."

"I thought we were the only ones with access to that technology."

"Yes, we were, but there was Virgus Tattenberg."

"He definitely could have done it."

"The temptation was overwhelming. The opportunity to match finest attributes of the elf and human race. I know you are not blind to the fact she carries tremendous power."

"The results of her tests have hardly been secret. Besides I doubt that Stephen would lock his daughter in the castle if he didn't fear for her safety."

"Cerwin Faulkner had his suspicions, and that elf knows something. I would never say it in front of your mother, but that angel is here for one purpose. He wants Cassandra."

Wilhelm could see a flinch of anger developing in Cedric's demeanor. The duke finished his drink and began again.

"There was a union of two forbidden worlds and that union produced a power soul—a soul the prince needs for his own diabolical purposes. I don't have the answers for you, but I do want you to know that you are the finest warrior I have seen since my days with the Powers choir. The time is coming where you are going to have to make a choice. It's not enough for you anymore to simply be a war hero. You must become the *Permaneo Eques Ordinares*."

Confused by the last statement, Cedric tried to interject. Indicating the conversation was over, Wilhelm simply stood. Walking over to Cedric, he playfully hit his former ward twice on the shoulder.

"If you love that girl with your whole heart as I believe you do, then you'll know what I mean when that time comes," said Wilhelm.

"We'll see," replied Cedric.

"Let's hope we don't. Have fun tonight! I know I will."

"Any secret rendezvous I should know about?"

"I fear that even I have given into the carnal cravings of the temporal realm. Nadia has invited me for dinner. I just hope what she makes is edible this time."

The two started to laugh as Wilhelm left Cedric standing by himself in the room. He walked over to the cart and made himself a third brandy. He stood there swirling it for a few moments before he took a drink.

"A fallen angel? If this is my burden, Father, then I accept."

Wolf Tribe Encampment, Southwest Acadian Plains

"Great spirits of the earth, heed our call; bless the fertile lands
and fertile game we hunt. May our children always remember
to keep the ancient ways. Grant us valor, temperance, and
brotherhood!"

—Prayer of the Wolf Tribe

In the sky above Terminus Mundus, red light was given off by Alpha
in its full phase, complimented by Beta and Gamma in their crescent
phases. Dancing high into the night sky, a huge bonfire raged in the center
of the wolf tribe main village. Concentric circles of huts built out of
wood and covered with canvas spread from the great longhouse of the
chief. Wolves were playfully tussling along the grounds of the camp or
chomping on bones. Men of the tribe brought deer and boars over to the
fire, while a cook cut choice pieces of meat for the men, women, and
children. Hippolyte and Minerva were seated on some rocks close to the
fire. They had a clay platter in front of them covered with rib and chop
bones. In between bites, many members of the tribe came up to them,
offering hugs and other forms of homage.

"I can't believe the feast they prepared for us," exclaimed Minerva.

"This makes those long trips worth it!" responded Hippolyte.

"It's just a shame we didn't get to see you in action on the hunt."

"It's good to reap the benefits without the work every once in a while."

The girls watched as Wolf Tribe members danced and sang around
the fire. Infected with the joyful mood of the camp, the elders continued
the oral traditions of the tribe. The girls watched a burly man wearing

wolf skin smeared with blood approach them. The blood guard of their grandfather obviously bore an urgent message.

"Kin of the chief, Great Aramas shall see you now."

"I'm surprised Grandpa didn't call for us right away," wondered Minerva as a woman collected her platter.

"Well, I know Reynard is visiting from the Myotis Tribe," stated Hippolyte. "Maybe he needed some time alone with him first."

"Of course, Grandpa could have just wanted us to get something to eat first."

The girls went around and bid individual good-byes to each of the members before heading into the great longhouse. When they entered, the girls saw nine other guards in the tent garbed like the original blood guard that came to them. Hippolyte focused her attention on her grandfather's bodyguard, Huskal. His head was shaved to the scalp and his piercing blue eyes were constantly hunting for threats. Representing his victories over the alliance, Huskal had twenty banded tattoos running up his muscular arms. He bowed in respect to Hippolyte as soon as she caught his eye. Reclining against a throne made of canvas, wood, and bone, the elderly Aramas was protected by two gray wolves.

Aramas had long, gray hair tied back in a ponytail and green eyes; wolf skin and leather armor covered his still hard body. He had his hands out and his palms down touching those of Chief Reynard, doing homage before him. The well-tanned Reynard had long, slicked, salt-and-pepper colored hair and gray eyes. Black leather covered his body. Josephine, a dark-skinned woman with blue eyes and long black hair, was his bodyguard. Her black leather outfit was tight to the skin, and around her waist was a black whip that had a sharp knife blade attached to the end of it. Upon seeing his granddaughters, Aramas stood from his throne and walked over to them. He gave Hippolyte a big hug.

"Welcome home, Hippolyte!" shouted an exuberant Aramas.

"Grandpa, it's so good to see you" replied Hippolyte.

"What is the word from the eastern tribes?" asked Aramas.

"It took some convincing, but they will fully support our plan to make peace with Central Acadia. They will send whatever help we need."

"Excellent!" said Aramas as he let go of his eldest granddaughter. "I knew my trust was well-placed to send you."

Aramas stared at Minerva slyly. The younger granddaughter had fear in her eyes when her grandfather grabbed her and threw her up in his arms.

"Well, Minerva, I hope you didn't cause your sister too much trouble."

"Why do you always assume the worst about me?"

"Actions speak louder than words; you've driven me crazy since you were an infant."

Huskal started to laugh as the chief put his wild granddaughter in her place. Minerva tried to slink into a corner away from her grandfather.

"Reynard, Josephine, you'll have to forgive the chief; he's very affectionate around his granddaughters," commented Huskal.

"It's quite all right, Huskal," retorted Reynard. "I'm expecting my first grandchildren shortly."

As Aramas was putting Minerva down, Josephine walked over to Hippolyte and bowed her head in respect. Her hand never left the handle of her whip.

"Josephine, it's been some time," said Hippolyte as she held onto a knife behind her belt.

"I hear you've been putting your skills to good use," challenged Josephine. "You know that you still owe me a rematch from the last festival."

"We'll be able to finally settle it soon."

"Yes, we will."

"We signed a temporary truce with the Alliance that ceased all hostilities," announced Aramas as he took his seat upon the throne. "Since the Alliance went to war with the Empire, we never truly negotiated the peace.

"We received offers from both the Acadians on behalf of the alliance and separately from the Mother Eagle in Titanus," commented Reynard.

Hippolyte and Minerva made a face as if they already knew what was coming next.

"The Titans have once again us asked us to become their protectorate. The Acadians want an armistice and a trade agreement," continued Reynard. "We know this will strain our relations with the Titans, but we simply cannot accept the Mother Eagle's terms."

"We've known the Acadians to speak with a forked tongue before, so we don't entirely trust their motives," countered Aramas. "If these negotiations are not spoken in truth, we know we can still turn to the Titans for aid."

"King Stephen is insistent that we send a representative of the tribe to Central Acadia." said Reynard. "Apparently they need time to prepare to answers our terms."

"I know you just returned from a long expedition, but Hippolyte, I need you and your sister to travel to Verian," commanded Aramas. "You will deliver the terms for our meeting."

Minerva tried her best to hide the excitement in her face and eyes but just couldn't. It took everything for her not to start jumping up and down. The more practical Hippolyte seemed very worried.

"Verian?" asked Hippolyte.

"I cannot go myself, and I dare not risk Huskal because they know him from the wars," responded Aramas. "I have to send someone who they will accept on equal terms. Stephen has two daughters, so he will not be offended if I send my granddaughters. This is a very difficult thing I ask you to do. However, we have to take the chance that we'll be able to obtain some form of peace."

"I guess with Minerva and Stryker . . . we can manage somehow," said Hippolyte, taking a few deep breaths.

"I always wondered how the steel-bellies lived," queried Minerva.

"Enjoy yourselves for this evening; you'll leave tomorrow morning," proclaimed Aramas, slightly disturbed by Minerva's comments and excitement.

"I will have the terms prepared by the time you leave," stated Reynard. "Aramas and I are still determining some final details. An escort will take you to the main royal road, but you'll be on your own most of the way. We can't risk any misunderstandings."

"Right," acknowledged Hippolyte.

The two girls left the tent. Removing his right glove, Aramas studied the tattoo of the cross carved into his hand.

"Do you honestly believe the Prime Eagle will keep his word and make sure they stay safe?" asked Huskal. "We just spit in the face of their offer."

"If I cannot trust the man who saved the lives of my granddaughters and my people when all hope was lost . . . who can I trust?" replied Aramas.

"The Titans do not handle rejection well," said Reynard.

"He won't let anything happen to them. He's proven that before."

Hippolyte and Minerva started back for the fire. Minerva ran around the front of her sister and grabbed her by the shoulders in excitement.

"I can't believe it—Verian!" interjected Minerva. "They don't let any tribal people into that city without a permit. I heard about so many wonders there."

"Yes... I just hope..." stammered Hippolyte, who couldn't hide her concern about the mission.

"We'll be fine, Hippolyte. I won't be able to sleep tonight at all. I wonder if I'll find one of those knights they are always talking about. It would great to finally fall in love."

"Don't get too excited; this is business, not pleasure."

"Spoil sport!" replied Minerva as she stuck her tongue out at her sister.

The two joined one of the folk dances with the other members of the tribe.

Castle Acadia, Royal Ballroom

"I hate aristocratic celebrations most of all. There is far too much a chance of the wrong word to be said or someone having a drink too many. We also never seem to make up the budget for the expenditures we make. If I had my way, I would end them all. However, I still do them for the little people."

—Diary Entry of Count Maximilian Luminas

The ballroom was located in the western wing of the castle and towered four stories high. The dance floor was immense; it could easily hold up to two hundred couples comfortably at a time. Flanking either side of the room were two large bars. In northern end of the room was a large dais set aside for the alliance aristocrats while circular tables occupied the southern end of the room for the nobility. In the northeast and northwest corners of the ballroom, spiral staircases allowed private access from the castle living quarters. An ivory staircase in the center of the room provided access to the main floor from the four levels of balconies.

Many decorations were set up around the room with the banners of the Four Great Houses of the west prominently displayed. Flowers were on each of the tables, with white roses representing Central Acadia, lily of the valley representing Napolitan, yellow tulips representing Evengard, and red poppies representing Titanus. The tables were lined with fine linens and enough silver utensils for seven courses of food. All of the servants were dressed in the finest silks of the east. The time was seven o'clock, and many of the invited nobility and burghers had already arrived. While many were engaged in conversation, most simply took advantage of the free liquor.

Walker escorted Cassandra down the northeast spiral staircase. Walker was dressed in a white tuxedo version of his military uniform with his same cloak over his shoulders. Grabbing the hem of her frilly black gown with her gloved hands, Cassandra's four-inch stilettos announced her arrival on every step. Felicia had prepared her for hours, arranging her hair within a silver crown. In addition to her engagement band, Cassandra wore a large golden necklace with three garnet stones, and her garnet earrings. Always two steps behind her mistress, Felicia followed the two down the stairs. Dressed in the same expensive silks of the other servants, her focus was on the princess at all times. The size of her corset was already becoming an issue for Cassandra. Unfortunately, she had gained a little more weight than she had hoped for before the ceremony, and Felicia had done her best to preserve her figure. Cassandra's presence caught the attention of many of the nobles in the room. They bowed and curtsied as she passed while others rushed up to greet her. The princess had heard them all before.

"Good evening, your highness!"

"You look lovely this evening!"

"Congratulations again on your engagement!"

"You'll make such a beautiful bride."

Cassandra smiled and offered the necessary, "Thank you." However, she had something else on her mind. Spying on the room, Cassandra was disappointed to see the Titans hadn't yet arrived.

"I don't know why, my lady, but for a race that prides themselves on punctuality, I have never actually witnessed the Titans show up on time for a party," joked Walker.

"I could stand to loosen myself up first anyway," answered Cassandra. "Let's get the necessary greetings over with Walker. I could use a martini."

"Of course, my lady."

Following their trail, Felicia was stopped suddenly by one of the pages.

"Miss Felicia, a pressing matter in the north corridor requires your urgent attention.

"All right."

Felicia followed the page into one of the back rooms. Upon her arrival, she saw Julius standing there, a smile on his face, and dressed in a black tuxedo version of his military uniform. Felicia smiled widely and immediately ran into his arms. Whistling, the page closed the door to respect their privacy.

In the Titan Embassy, Cedric was pacing back and forth along the first floor looking at an intelligence folder. Cedric wore a black tuxedo version of his military uniform with his kilt, crucifix, and his cloak over his shoulders. Despite the fact he was going to a ball, the marshal still managed to conceal Ragnarok under his cloak. Irritated as he turned every page of the report, Cedric reached his boiling point. Upon reaching the last page, he took the folder, threw it on the floor in disgust, and yelled a curse in the ancient Titan language.

"Someone must have gotten some bad news," teased Cecilia.

Cedric turned to see his sister and needed to do a double take. Transforming herself from warrior to royal princess, Cecilia had put on a tight-fitting red gown. The dress was cut to expose her plunging neckline and draw attention to her cleavage with golden trim. In addition to being set in her crown, a black bow ornamented with a red poppy flower was placed in the back of her hair. Long white gloves pulled the black fur wrap she carried tightly around her shoulders. Smiling brightly at the fact she was finally taller than her brother in her stilettos, Cecilia adjusted the opal necklace her brother had given her long ago.

"You know, it's been long time since I've seen you out of uniform," commented Cedric. "You really can be stunningly beautiful when you apply yourself."

"Don't tease me!" said Cecilia as she started to blush. "I was stuck in the beauty parlor for four hours today. They waxed everything!"

"I'm not teasing, sis. You are going to break a lot of hearts at that party tonight."

"Well, if there's one thing I'll say in my own defense, brother, it's that no one else can pull this off like I can! I just hope those nobles don't get any bright ideas and remember that I am both a princess and a valkyrie."

"You just prefer the prestige of the title of war goddess to princess any day. It is important that a Titan royal brings the same passion to their duties as an aristocrat and a warrior."

"Just feel free to keep quoting your book."

"It's as true today as I the day I wrote it. I don't see your spear, but how many weapons do you have on you?"

"Five!"

"I should have known."

"What did I interrupt?"

"Christian finally got me the intelligence I was dreading. While we concentrated on winning the war, Stephen moved behind our backs and negotiated a separate treaty with the tribes."

"I have a feeling that it didn't include our demand of vassalage."

"No, it didn't."

"Do we still have to go to the party tonight then?"

The two twins laughed. Just then Keiko, a sylph in Cedric's service, fluttered into the room. Unlike her fairy cousins, this sylph was approximately four feet tall but still had delicate, thin, fairy wings. The sylph had long golden brown hair and cerulean eyes. She wore a purple dress and had red ballet slippers on her feet.

"Master Cedric! Master Cedric!" exclaimed Keiko.

Cecilia looked annoyed as the sylph grabbed onto Cedric. She looked to be panic stricken and had tears in her eyes. Wilhelm had thought to forge an alliance between the magical creatures of Terminus Mundus and Titanus. The arrangement sent Keiko to live among and interact with the Titans. Keiko, unfortunately, thought the mission meant she was to dote upon the crown prince of Titanus any chance she had. In order to save her son's sanity, the queen gave her the distinguished position of running the Titan Embassy in Verian.

"What's wrong, Keiko?" asked Cedric.

"Master Cedric, I know you sent me to find Sir Colin, but I can't find him anywhere. I've checked all the normal locations."

"He must not want to go either," added Cecilia.

"Keiko, go find Christian; he'll know where to look for Colin," ordered Cedric.

"Right away, Master Cedric," acknowledged Keiko, who kissed Cedric on the cheek and went on her way.

"She is far too clingy, and you spoil her!" interjected Cecilia.

"What do you want me to do with her?" asked an annoyed Cedric. "It's not my fault that Wilhelm assigned her to me and she takes her job too seriously."

Cecilia put her hand to her forehead and shook her head as a playful and intelligent voice filled the room.

"Oh dear, my two favorite experiments are looking lovely this evening," stated Martha Heinrich.

Cedric and Cecilia turned to see a short and thin woman enter the room wearing a blue dress, white stockings, heels, and white fur wrap around her shoulder. She had long red hair which was set up for the evening and blue calculating eyes hidden behind very thin silver-rimmed glasses.

"You look nice, Doctor," complimented Cecilia.

"You're looking pretty good yourself, sister," praised Martha. "Then again, what did I expect, I am the greatest genius on Terminus Mundus, you know."

Martha looked over Cecilia for a second, causing her to blush. Trying to determine if it was only her inquisitive nature or if she was truly a lecherous man in disguise, Cecilia was at a loss for words.

"Yes, indeed, not only are you a physical specimen, but you also get high grades for your visual psychological tactics."

"Visual psychological tactics?" wondered Cecilia.

"Your sex appeal!" exclaimed Martha.

"I think you've embarrassed my daughter enough for the evening, Doctor Heinrich," said Civilia.

Civilia entered wearing a red dress, black stockings, and red heels. However, much of this could not be seen because of a long red and black cape that covered the whole of her body like a robe. It was fastened in place at her shoulders with two gold plates marked with eagle's heads and string of opals around the neckline. Although ornate, Cecilia appeared to be rather uncomfortable with it on. Her hair was set within her queen's crown, and she carried twelve red poppies in her gloved hands.

"You broke out the dreaded 'horse blanket'?" queried Cedric.

"It's unfortunately necessary for these occasions, though I must imagine that Queen Marion would have never worn something like this," sighed Civilia. "I will not, however, be the queen that breaks our traditions, as idiotic as they may be. Are we ready?"

"We're waiting on Christian," said Cedric. "He's on a special assignment."

The sound of grunting was heard. Christian, in a tuxedo and his gold cape, led Colin into the main room. Colin tugged at the collar of his tuxedo relentlessly.

"It wasn't easy, but I did threaten to use physical force if necessary . . . not like it would have done me any good," joked Christian.

"Master Cedric, I humbly ask to be excused," pleaded Colin.

"You're going, and you'll thank me one day when I make you a Freiherr. It's important that you learn to act among the nobility. You have nothing to worry about. Horace will take care of you."

"All right, Master," submitted Colin.

Cedric looked at his watch and noticed the time. Civilia caught the look in his eyes and began to hurry everything along. Standing outside the embassy waiting for them was Horace and his wife Shayla. Horace was in a tuxedo and Shayla wore a white dress that exposed her shoulders. Remaining at the entrance of the embassy, Keiko silently returned to her duties. Wood elf mercenaries spied the streets for any sign of trouble. Certain no danger would come to caravan they gave the all clear. The Titan royals entered a carriage surrounded by royal guards in the embassy courtyard. When they were all safely inside, Christian pulled out a PDA and started to examine it.

"What is our security situation, Christian?" asked Civilia.

"Your highness, in addition to the fifteen standard royal guards that we may bring, I have ten operatives infiltrating the party. The Acadia city guard has cleared the streets from the embassy to the castle, so the ride should go smoothly."

"That is what I wanted to hear."

"What are we going to do about the tribes, your highness?" questioned Christian.

"Don't worry, Christian. I will make Stephen pay dearly for this," stated Civilia with a flash of malice in her eyes.

Engaged in a deep kiss, time stopped for Julius and Felicia in the castle. When Julius pulled away, Felicia's red lipstick was smeared and her lips were swollen.

"I'm sorry I kissed you so hard, but I really needed that."

"Oh, Julius, I was so worried about you," said Felicia. "The daily reports we received were less than encouraging."

"I'd believe it. Felicia, it wasn't good out there. I'll tell you the truth, if we get hit again, we're not going to make it."

"You can't say things like that, Julius. The empire does not treat marshals with the same dignity as former rulers."

"I've read my share of history, Felicia, and I'm afraid nothing has changed," said Julius as he took Felicia by her arms. "I have plans for us. My time in the service is coming to an end and I'm going to tender my resignation as an alliance marshal. My father plans on abdicating in my favor next revolution and stay on as my 'Hand' while I learn the job. Is Cassandra going to keep her promise to you?"

"She intends to free me upon her marriage."

"If I support Cedric with Cassandra, he'll owe me a favor. If he can make you a Freifrau of Titanus, my father will no longer object. He won't insult Titanus by balking at a noble title."

"It's a dream, Julius."

"Yes, but now we're so close. No more hiding... no more deception... How's Joshua?"

"I think he's almost as tall as you now. He enjoys working down at the castle smith. A few of the cuirassiers even take the time to spar with him."

"I'm not surprised. I bet you he bests them, too."

"Lord Walker wishes to take him from the castle and send him to Deniva to train with the garrison there. It's a commission, Julius!"

Julius looked puzzled at Felicia's statement. He could see the tears in Felicia's eyes at the thought of losing her son.

"I'm sorry I caused the both of you so much pain."

"It cannot be helped. We understood the consequences when we began this relationship."

"I can't believe none have used this to my disadvantage yet. I'm certain Christian and Valentine know, but the others . . . well, I'll deal with that when the time comes."

Julius reached into his pocket.

"I have something for you."

Julius took out a sapphire necklace. Felicia looked at it in wonder as Julius fastened it around her neck.

"Cedric's friend in Deniva, Ethan, was able to get it for me. It's from the East."

"It's so beautiful, but it must have cost you a fortune."

"It cost us a few free trade agreements, but it was worth that look on your face. I'm sorry, but I have to return home for the Napolitan victory celebrations. I'll be back in the city first chance I get."

The two kissed just as a commotion took place in the ballroom. Julius smiled as he heard the sound of the chamberlain announcing the Titan royal family. Getting the necessary distraction, he watched Civilia staring down some very nervous dignitaries.

"You can always count on the Titans to cause a scene."

"We should be on our way."

The two left the room, Julius headed toward one of the bars while Felicia fixed her lipstick and went back to work. The Seneschal of Central Acadia was busy trying to calm an enraged Civilia. She stood there tapping her heel rapidly while her delegation filled the room with intimidation.

"What do you mean King Stephen isn't here to personally greet me!" shouted Civilia.

"Please understand, your highness," responded the Seneschal. "The king has many duties to attend to. As the organizer of this ball, it is my duty to handle the salutations."

"If this was Castle Titan, I would have met him at the steps!" screamed Civilia. "Does he think me some second-rate Edenian queen?"

"No, your highness. I would never think so less of you," said a smiling Stephen wearing his robes over a tuxedo and a crown on his head.

The two walked toward one another and kissed each other on each cheek. Embracing her beyond the normal greeting time, the king drew the attention of onlookers. The two finally let go and prepared to go through the normal protocols.

"I, Stephen Acadia, King of Central Acadia, and Steward of the Alliance of the Western Kingdoms do hereby welcome Queen Civilia Rhone of Titanus to Castle Acadia."

"I, Civilia Rhone, Queen of Titanus and Warden of the South do hereby accept your invitation for dinner and dancing this evening."

"I'm glad the formal greetings are out of the way. Now I can't tell you how happy I am to greet the mother of the man who's marrying my daughter."

"I am very proud to have a fine young woman like your daughter marrying my son. Duke Wilhelm von Angelhardt sends his regrets that he cannot attend this evening."

"It's a pity that the duke must miss this happy occasion, but I know that he has his reasons. Now where's my future son-in-law?"

Trying to deflect Civilia's anger, Stephen held out his hand toward Cedric. Despite his reservations, Cedric offered a firm handshake. Alerted by the firmness of his grip, the king prepared to receive the marshal's wrath.

"I'm pleased that I can see you on an occasion when I don't have to call you marshal commandant," greeted Stephen. "Is something wrong, Cedric?"

"The Titans are an honorable race, your highness," explained Cedric. "We do not appreciate it when our friends go behind our backs."

"I was hoping that this wouldn't come up before the whole alliance came together."

"You didn't think you'd be able to hide it from us all night," interrupted Cecilia.

"I won't inquire as to how you came about this information," said Stephen.

"It's as they say, 'the Eagle's Eye can see things very clearly,'" added Christian.

"I suppose this is where I plead for mercy," offered Stephen.

"I'm sure we won't make you pay too much," reasoned Martha.

"I figure six cases of premium wine would be sufficient compensation," negotiated Horace

"How about four?" countered Stephen as he reached into his pocket and pulled out a cigar. He handed it to Horace.

"It's non-negotiable."

Sniffing the cigar first, Horace reached into his pocket for a cutter and got rid of the tip.

"Very well. Queen Civilia, would you accompany me?" requested Stephen. "The other rulers are waiting for us."

"Of course. Martha and Horace, you will accompany me," commanded Civilia. "The rest of you mingle; that is an order."

Stephen took Civilia by the arm as she left with Martha, Horace, and Shayla. Horace struck a match, lit the cigar, and nodded in approval at the flavor. Whispering sweet words, Stephen made Civilia break out in laughter. Allowing himself a second to stare at what could have been, Cedric scanned the room. It took a few moments before he found Cassandra sitting at the bar on the far side of the room, eating an olive from the bottom of her martini glass. Winking at him, Christian put his hand on Cedric's shoulder.

"Your excellency, I do believe that you have some unfinished business to take care of, so we'll manage by ourselves."

"I appreciate that, Christian," replied Cedric as he noticed his sister turning her head in disgust. "Don't be too jealous, sis, they'll be lining up to dance with you tonight."

Concerned over the mood of his target, Cedric headed to the left end of the bar away from where Cassandra was seated. Dutifully waiting for him was Walker. The captain offered him a brandy of which Cedric happily took a sip.

"Marshal, welcome to Castle Acadia."

"That's what I call service. Now all I need is a gin martini and I can make my move."

"I anticipated your request," replied Walker as he handed him a martini as well. "I need to warn you that her highness has had two of these already."

"What kind of mood is she in?" said Cedric with a grimace.

"She is quite anxious to see you."

"Well, do I need to put up a magic shield, because if the fireballs start flying..."

"Personally, I watch out for thunderbolts. However, there is another matter we need to discuss."

"Walker, I've been back in town for a couple of hours and now you're the fifth person to bring an urgent crisis to my attention."

"You're reputation as a fixer is well-known. I think it would be prudent if we started training Felicia's son, Joshua, and I have recommended that he be garrisoned in Deniva."

"He would be a welcome addition, and your father would have approved. I'm really not in the mood for business right now, but I'll be in town for a while. Look me up at the embassy one rotation and we'll go through a bottle."

"Absolutely, Marshal."

Leaving Walker to his own devices, Cedric slowly brought the two drinks over to Cassandra's seat. The princess was keeping herself occupied by popping the heel in and out of her black stocking foot. Sighing, she finished the last drops of her martini. Leaning against her chin, she watched a full martini being pushed in front of her.

"I'd better not have another one, Walker," ordered Cassandra. "I don't want him to think I'm a lush."

"Guess again, Cassie..." countered Cedric.

A rush of excitement caused Cassandra to fall off her stool. Fortunately Cedric was standing right there to catch her in time. Blushing heavily, Cassandra pressed her lips against Cedric to make sure she wasn't dreaming. As Cedric held her around her waist, the princess rubbed her hands against her chest. Kissing him long and deep, Cassandra finally pulled back.

"Welcome back, Cedric!"

"I can't even remember how long it's been since I held you."

"Two revolutions, four lunar cycles, sixteen rotations, eighteen hours, forty-five minutes, and thirty-six seconds," answered Cassandra as Cedric stared in amazement at her preciseness. "I keep expecting to wake up, Cedric. It's so difficult to tell what is a dream and reality. I wanted you for so long, and now finally it's our time. Our parents just have to agree on a date, and then you're all mine, you evil knight."

"Let's not jump ahead of ourselves. I prefer to cherish this moment."

"Of course, but it is quite embarrassing for a girl of my age in Central Acadia not to be married. I still have my bridal fantasies to keep me company."

The two sat down and toasted with a *salud* before having their first drink. Watching Cedric murmur something under his breath, Cassandra wondered if he was praying or cursing something. The princess decided to change the topic of conversation.

"How's your family doing?"

"The same as always. Mom is thrilled that I'm marrying you. Cecilia, on the other hand, well, let's just say she hasn't quite warmed to you yet."

"She isn't going to throw her spear at me."

"She's not carrying her spear tonight, but don't underestimate my sister's ability to improvise."

"I'm not your ordinary damsel-in-distress-type princess, and I'm not completely defenseless."

"So Cerwin's told me. You know, you're quite the popular one, Cassandra. Every man that I approach who knows you, claims I'm not good enough for you."

"What can I say? I've got a lot of people that care about me."

"How's your sister doing?"

"Marie is bright and cheerful as always. She goes on constantly about how happy she is for me now that you're home. I know she's only my half-sister and probably will displace me on my throne, but . . . I can't get mad at her."

"It's better that she has a good heart. This situation is going to be difficult enough as it is."

"Will you indulge me for a second, Cedric?"

"It depends on what you're going to ask."

"Cedric, I heard a lot about your actions during the war. I know the truth about the Battle of Istle Hills, the Wolf Tribe Village on Terrace River, the way you took an imperial fort with fifty soldiers, and recently the Battle of Lake Cancer. The others can say all they want. I know it was you that saved us."

"Amuro has called me the 'riverboat gambler.' However, reciting that litany would make me believe that I either have the devil's luck or that God really loves me."

Taking his hands with hers, Cassandra stared him in the eyes.

"Have you ever heard of the prophecy of the Last Knight?"

"Is that an elf prophecy?"

"Yes. 'In Our Hour of Darkness; When Evil Infests Our World; When Courage Is No Longer a Shield; When the Hearts of the Bravest Lie Broken; The Last Knight Shall Take Up His Sword and the Prayers of the World and Inherit the Power to Destroy Evil.' After my prayers, I took time during the last two revolutions to read this prophecy. My conclusion, the Father placed you here to serve as the 'Last Knight.'"

Swallowing the lump in his throat, Cedric thought about what Wilhelm had said to him earlier. Immediately, he connected the term "Last Knight" with Wilhelm's *Permaneo Eques Ordinares*. The titan prince wondered if his mentor had been conspiring with to his fiancé to grant him a new title. Watching his mind wander, Cassandra thought she said the wrong thing.

"Cedric?"

"Sorry, I was just thinking about what you said. You mustn't judge the actions of enemies of our alliance as evil. Defeating the empire and tribes is mere swordplay.

"I've heard the tales of how you confront evil"

"I do not confront evil. I destroy it."

Welcoming a distraction from conversation, the band leader announced the first dance the "military two-step." Shaking his head, Cedric couldn't believe his luck. The majority of his life spent on the battlefield and even at a ball it doesn't escape him. Groaning voices throughout agreed with him on the bad joke. Realizing his worst fears, Cassandra curtsied toward him.

"It is customary that no knight may refuse the request of a maiden when made in Castle Acadia."

"I remember you used the same line on your Quize."

"It's still a very important custom."

"You know I'm bound to accept."

Taking her hand, Cedric and Cassandra strutted onto the dance floor. Sipping her brandy at the bar, Cecilia watched the two like a hawk. Accepting the task of guarding the princess, Colin remained disinterested but Christian was getting worried.

"Green-eyed monster!" muttered a jealous Cecilia.

"You know, traditionally that has been used as symbolism for 'jealous'!" explained Christian.

"I am not jealous of that witch!"

"You shouldn't be. After all, you have that knight from Deniva to fawn over."

A swift elbow to the ribs by the princess caught Christian off guard. Gathering his breath, the spy master rubbed his side to ease the pain.

"If you mean that parasite, then you are sadly mistaken, Christian!"

"I'm in no position to disagree with you, your highness."

Sipping what could have been milk, Colin heard the sound of a chair pulled back next to him. He noticed the white heels of a woman and checked her out. As he turned, Colin's mouth dropped open. Smiling at him with painted pink lips, Amuro adjusted her blue gown to fit in the seat. Her hair was fixed up in her crown. Uncontrollably drawn to her cleavage, Colin took a quick peek at a woman who had never been seen without her armor. The assassin finally just dropped his head in utter embarrassment.

"My deepest apologies, Marshal." offered Colin.

"You know, duelist, your face will freeze if your jaw hangs open like that," teased Amuro.

Cecilia shooed Colin out of the way to save him any further embarrassment. Greeting her friend with a kiss on the cheek, the two warriors burst out laughing at the duelist's expense. Christian ordered his friend something stronger.

"I see you've made a favorable impression, Amuro."

"I guess its okay for a test run. That's the first time I've ever seen Colin let his guard down."

"Forgive me, I've just never seen you look..." stammered Colin.

"What?" queried a primped-up Amuro. "Beautiful? Ravishing? Divine?"

"Actually, I was going to say feminine," replied a sheepish Colin.

Christian covered his eyes with his hand. Closing her eyes, Amuro dropped her head. Rapidly reaching for the duelist's head, Cecilia figured Colin was about to be strangled. Instead Amuro grabbed his head and playfully slapped him in the face. Colin had absolutely no idea what was going on or how to respond.

"Cecilia, I love this kid so much. He's so honest, he doesn't know any better than to tell the truth," teased Amuro. "Actually, Colin, this is my hunting outfit."

"I don't see how you could hunt anything in an outfit so frilly marshal," commented Colin.

"Well, I intend to capture one ranger this evening," retorted Amuro.

"I don't think he arrived yet," volunteered Christian.

"It would be just like Malcolm to waste my grand entrance on a pesky innocent bystander."

"I don't know why you even bother with him," stated Cecilia.

"Would you prefer I pursue your brother instead, Cecilia?" queried Amuro as she noticed a sneer forming on Cecilia's face. "No. Malcolm is my soul mate. I knew it from the first woman that I made break her engagement to him."

"That's more information than I needed to know," said Christian.

"Be careful, Christian. If it doesn't work out with Malcolm, you're on deck!" exclaimed Amuro.

"I'm flattered, Princess, but I'm afraid I'm already taken."

Amuro looked to Christian's hand and saw a vanadium ring that was designed with two flowers meeting one another. Questioning why Christian would wear an elven royal engagement ring, she noticed the court of arms on the ring was from House Landon, an aristocratic elven house that abandoned Evengard after the murder of Queen Gweyn Marisol. Snapping Amuro back to the reality was the commotion brought on by arrival of her younger sister. Fair skinned, beautiful, and perfectly proportioned, Saria Jenitzen's outward appearance was contrary to her inner meekness. Her long golden hair radiated like the sun, and her blue eyes entranced anyone who dared to look. Bewitching almost every suitor in the room, her personality echoed sweetness, mystery, and just enough of pout to drive the opposite sex wild. Swishing the ruffles of her golden gown adorned with sapphires, Saria glided across the floor on her golden heeled shoes. Unlike her warrior sister, the younger Jenitzen's talents were honed in the finest choral and vocal academies across Terminus Mundus. The demand for her performances made her father a very rich elf.

"Saria Jenitzen, no other woman has held the attention of so many single men on Terminus Mundus," sighed Amuro. "It's not easy being the responsible older sister at times."

Cecilia comforted her friend as the men in the room rushed past them for Amuro's sister. This made the Vanadis very angry.

"Hey, there are two beautiful young maidens over here too!" screamed Cecilia.

Trying to get through the crowd as quickly as possible, Saria was showered with praise and homage. She didn't spend more than a few courteous moments with each. Rather, the young elf maiden chose to approach Cagius, who got down on one knee before her. Noticing a pendant that recreated a golden dragon eye with a large blue sapphire jewel as its pupil on his tuxedo, the elf maiden swooned. Surprised, Cecilia turned to Christian who simply shrugged his shoulders. Amuro was impressed. Honeyed words formed in the pink painted lips of the maiden.

"My dear, brave cavalier, I have heard so much of thy exploits. I prayed thee would be safe all this time, and thou hast returned unharmed."

"It was my pleasure, my lady, to defend the lands in thy name. Would thou offer this humble cavalier a single dance as gratitude?"

Smiling, Saria curtsied, and the other suitors slinked away dejected.

"Oh yes, Sir Cavalier, you may have the very first dance."

Cagius stood and took Saria's hand. They joined the line in preparation for the dance.

"When did this happen?" asked Cecilia.

"Cagius is really amazing. Every man on Terminus Mundus lavishes her with gifts, and only he knows the right buttons to push," responded Amuro.

"Mother always said that he had a special way with the ladies," interrupted Julius. "Ladies, gentlemen, I see Cedric wasted no time renewing old acquaintances. I find myself in the middle of a drab and dreadful party, yet the stunning appearance of a beautiful young maiden has captivated my gaze. Would the vanadis do me the honor of a dance?"

Cecilia stared at Julius but was more annoyed than flattered.

"If you're teasing me, that is unforgiveable," exasperated Cecilia. "But if you're serious, it's even worse! Julius, don't waste your time on me. I know of your tastes."

"Appearances must be kept up, Cecilia. Besides, if I dance with you, these other ninnies will get up the courage to ask."

Slugging down a final shot of whiskey, Cecilia dropped into a deep Titan curtsey. Shocked by what they were seeing, her friends didn't move. Angrily, Cecilia remained in the curtsey, waiting for Julius to respond properly. After some mumbling from Christian, Julius finally bowed and lifted her with his hand. Taking pity on Amuro, Christian decided to fill in.

"Care for an opportunity to get Malcolm's blood boiling?" asked Christian.

"Why, thank you, Christian; however; I'm afraid Malcolm still wouldn't get it!" responded Amuro.

"Well, you could always try to get him drunk?"

"I may take you up on that offer."

Despite the fact they were late, Cassandra and Cedric made room for the last couples to stand next to them. Playing with a military flare, the band started the music for the dance. The complexity of the dance resulted in the partners dancing across the ballroom. Enjoying themselves, Christian and Amuro marched playfully towards each other. Julius on the other hand had problems. Unlike the spear carrying, gold-plated vanadis he was used to, Cecilia was the perfect model of feminine grace on the dance floor. As the eighth bar of the song played, Julius accidently kicked Cecilia in the shin instead of kicking around her. Gently slapping him in the back of the head, Cecilia shook off the pain. Observing from the bar, Colin watched as thirteenth bar of song transformed the movements from a line dance to a waltz.

While the dance took place, Stephen gathered the leaders and chief advisors of the four western Kingdoms in a soundproof room off of the main ballroom. Joining Stephen, Civilia, and Cerwin Faulkner, was the battle-hardened Constantine Imperia. The Napolitan Caesar's brown hair was turning gray but his green eyes remained youthful. Despite his growing girth, Constantine could take most young legionnaires in a fight. His brown-haired, green-eyed wife, Marguerite Draconius, was still attractive though middle-aged. Napolitan was also represented, with Constantine's two advisors: the battle-hardened and aged centurion, James Darius, and the refined well-spoken barrister, Judge Matthias Gravius.

Constantine, a distinguished aristocrat and former tribune, had led a coup against Napolitan's former caesar, Giovanni Draconius, who had robbed the country to line his personal coffers. In order to ensure a smooth transition, he married Giovanni's daughter Marguerite and sired two sons, Julius and Cagius. Darius and Gravius represented the interests of the conservatives and those calling for more liberal government.

"I've brought our final guests," announced Stephen.

"Well, I hoped you checked for weapons," joked Constantine.

Everyone seemed to get a good laugh at the Titan's expense. Horace grew angry at the tease but offered one of his cigars to James, who quickly took him up on the offer.

"Now that everyone is here, with your permission, your majesty, I'd like to begin," requested Luminas.

"Of course," said Stephen.

"As everyone in this room has been privy to, Central Acadia has been negotiating with the Tribal Confederation over a treaty," began Luminas. The purpose of it is to end the unnecessary conflicts that have befallen our two peoples. We all know the difficulty that we faced fighting a two-front war, and we hope to keep one of these fronts silenced permanently without resorting to genocide. The Tribal Confederation, after long negotiations, has agreed to meet with us and accept our terms."

"Where?" asked Constantine.

"The confederation is sending representatives to Central Acadia with the time and place of the meeting."

"So we're blind and deaf for now!" exclaimed Cerwin.

"It has taken many revolutions just to get to this point. We must accept their backward ways for now," continued Luminas. "We know for certain they will not meet in Central Acadia; our past actions warrant great prejudice among the tribes."

"Queen Civilia, you've negotiated with the tribes before," queried James. "Is there anything unusual about this behavior?"

"The tribes treat honest enemies with honor. Our cities and outposts have always been open to the tribes. Therefore, we receive certain liberties when we negotiate with them."

"That is what concerns our people," pronounced Cerwin. "Central Acadia has treated the tribes as second-class citizens, and Jonas Marimon's reputation among the tribes is well deserved. Are the tribes going to lump Evengard and Napolitan with the actions of Central Acadia?"

"It is difficult to determine in war whether certain actions were necessary," explained Stephen in defense of Jonas. "When we know the time and place, it will be important to send the correct delegation."

"I have advised the king that it would be prudent to send our brave war heroes," said Luminas. "Prince Julius Imperia would be the perfect representative to lead such a delegation, and we know the tribes fear Prince Cedric Rhone."

"My son will not attend this meeting to serve as an endorsement for these plans," interrupted Civilia. "We have signed our own peace treaty with the tribes and will not forgive the alliance for negotiating behind our backs."

"We should have expected nothing less!" interjected Sharon. "And you call yourself our ally! We had to bribe you to enter the war against the tribes in the first place."

"Bribed?" questioned an angry Civilia. "We were not the kingdom that initiated an aggressive war in the midst of trade negotiations because we felt that we were slighted at the bargaining table. Central Acadia attacked the Wolf Tribe; Napolitan and Evengard chose to honor that alliance. We were focused on a far more dangerous enemy to the east. After King Stephen's offer, I could not honorably refuse aid, knowing full well we would have to soon turn our attention from the tribes to the empire. You reward that service by insulting my honor! However, as we are still a member of this alliance, I have chosen to overlook such matters that demand restitution."

"While Titanus may have legitimate grievances against Central Acadia, Evengard will not object to any negotiations that bring about peace. I act with the full consent of the noble houses," announced Cerwin.

"I approve, but I suggest we make sure we send enough cohorts to protect such an important delegation," added Constantine with reservations.

"We offered six," replied Luminas.

"Six!" exclaimed James. "The tribes respect strength, and that is not enough cohorts for an effective scare tactic."

"Our marshals and well-trained forces will express a certain degree of superiority to the tribal rabble," countered Matthias. "Aramas would be a fool if he tried anything."

"The same tribal rabble who defeated us in three battles and nearly crushed our army at the Istle Hills prior to Titan intervention in the war," informed James.

The tension in the room was growing. Not only were the Titans visibly upset at these developments, but the Constantine and Cerwin started to doubt the wisdom in the negotiations. Intervening, Stephen moved the discussion along.

"Since we're all present, I'll assume that the kingdoms are in favor of such a delegation with a Titan abstention?"

"If we were to go strictly by the Alliance Charter, we would prefer to cast present with reservations," justified Martha. "After all, there may be issues we want to address later with the tribes in separate or continuing negotiations."

"There's no one here who would doubt your knowledge of the charter," said a smiling Luminas.

"That's why I am the greatest genius on Terminus Mundus!" boasted Martha.

"Well, Caesar, I'm sure you'll be more than delighted to tell your son he's been drafted once more," teased Stephen. "He shall be our lead negotiator in the matter."

"My son is a loyal servant of the alliance, and he will do what it takes to secure the necessary peace."

"Good, I know we have a party to attend, so if there is no more business..."

"What about the issue of the reparations paid to us by the empire?" questioned Cerwin. "We have not yet received any word on our share."

"We apologize, but as we previously discussed, the funds have been turned over to the senate to be used by Majority Leader Norville Warrington as he sees fit."

"It was the understanding of the wardens that those funds were going to compensate those soldiers' families who were lost in the last two wars," countered Civilia.

"I agree with my fellow liege," added Constantine. "I have suffering widows and orphans in Napolitan."

"There is much good that the Acadian bureaucracy can do with such a bounty," countered Penelope. "In the effort of fairness, our senate will determine how best to use the funds."

"We respect Central Acadia as an ally and we know of your financial difficulties," explained Constantine. "However, those debts were created by your nobility and their foolish experiments in social engineering. We have never agreed to comingle the funds that were rightfully ours."

"We can't settle this issue tonight. We'll discuss this at the next council session, and the senate shall debate it," mediated Stephen to his uneasy allies. "Perhaps this would be a good time to rejoin the party. May I do you the honor, Civilia?"

Stephen took Civilia's arm, to the disgust of both of his wives.

"Always the same!" begrudged Sharon.

"What do you mean?" asked Penelope.

"It means that you and I were quite down the list when it came to the woman Stephen would marry. Twice he pleaded with King Justin Rhone to marry his daughter Civilia, but she would not surrender the Titan name or her claims to Rhinegard."

"So they never married?"

"No!"

Filled with envy, they watched as Stephen and Civilia shared a laugh that helped ease the tension. Count Luminas took Sharon by the arm while Jonas escorted Penelope. In the main ballroom, the military two-step ended to a round of applause. Julius apologized profusely to Cecilia who laughed it off. Looking over at Walker, Cassandra gave her protector a signal. The knight winked and covertly walked over to the music director. He handed him some gold currency note.

"You know what to do unless you want to risk the wrath of Princess Cassandra," threatened Walker.

"Right away, Lord Captain."

The music director gave instructions to his musician, just as Cedric was starting to leave the dance floor. Hearing the chords of a tango beginning to play, he turned to face Cassandra. The young princess was bubbling with anticipation.

"Hey, evil knight, want to have some fun?"

Sighing Cedric dutifully put his heels together and bowed to Cassandra who responded with a curtsey. All of the other couples on the dance floor formed a large circle. Cassandra put out her hand to Cedric, who took her and spun her into his chest as Cassandra kicked one of her legs in the air. The two began a sensual tango with one another that may or may not have been entirely appropriate. Executing each step in flow rather than a mechanical style, is what made them perfect. As they neared a table, Cedric grabbed a rose and traced Cassandra's neckline with it. She grabbed it in her mouth and they continued. In the center of the floor Cedric stopped, and Cassandra proceeded to dance around him in a circle. When Cassandra twirled, her dress had a hypnotic effect on the crowd when it ruffled and bounced. Their movements were captivating and even caused Cecilia to chuckle.

"The ice queen is melting," teased Amuro.

"I have to admit, she's damn good!" agreed Cecilia.

"Hey, Amuro, showtime!" warned Christian.

Not bothering to give his card to the Chamberlain, Malcolm discreetly entered the room. Constantly shifting his shoulders in his tuxedo, the ranger was puzzled as to why there was a large circle in the middle of the ballroom.

"Oh... how do I look?" asked Amuro as she reapplied pink shadow and eyeliner.

"Just go!" shouted Cecilia as she sent Amuro on her way toward Malcolm.

Seeing his commanding officer approach, Malcolm tried to loosen the collar on his "monkey suit," but it wasn't working.

"Oh, Amuro, you look beautiful this evening," stammered Malcolm.

"Thank you, Malcolm. It's nice that they got you out of that ranger garb for once."

"Though my father has no problem with it, I deem it less appropriate for an event like this. Where is everyone?"

"Cedric and Cassandra are dancing."

"That would explain everything. Good evening."

Walking past a stunned Amuro, Malcolm took his seat at his place card on the dais. The elf marshal stood there, fuming at the ranger's behavior. Staring at the scene in disbelief, Christian and Cecilia enjoyed a shot of whiskey. The senior royalty entered from the opposite corridor and noticed the commotion. Walker stood at attention before the king.

"Lord Captain, what's going on?" asked Stephen.

"Her highness and her fiancé are dancing," reported Walker.

Martha and Civilia started to laugh. Walking toward the circle, they viewed Cedric lift Cassandra with one hand over his head. Cassandra nodded as he let her down. He twirled her out, and then the two seductively walked back together. Placing her back to his chest, Cedric grabbed her hand and walked in a circle. Cassandra twirled out again and did some ballet steps before she jumped into Cedric's arm. Catching her on her waist, he lowered her to ground as the song ended. Cassandra had one leg up in the air and her neck bent backward in a pose. Thunderous applause filled the room. Taking a pause for two seconds; Cedric lifted Cassandra up and gave her a big kiss. The applause was cut short when the crowd noticed the arrival of Stephen and Civilia. As the nobles and burghers bowed to the rulers, the king approached the happy couple.

"Well, Cedric, apparently you haven't lost any of your dancing skills," commented Stephen.

"I've always considered any sword fight a dance," quipped Cedric.

"Well, certainly no one in this kingdom can match your skills with a blade or on the dance floor."

"I may have something to say about that, your highness," interrupted Julius, drawing cheers and laughs from the crowd.

"I am blessed to have three powerful knights serving as marshals." said Stephen, drawing approval from Amuro as well. "Hector Reed was right, our military has never been stronger."

Civilia attended to Cassandra. Cassandra curtsied to her.

"Your respect is quite admirable," offered an appreciative Civilia. "I wish others your age shared such important values. Now give your future mother-in-law a hug!"

Civilia hugged Cassandra tightly. However, she felt awkward for a moment as Civilia ran one of her hands around Cassandra's waist. Feeling Cassandra's hips, she determined the princess would produce her many grandchildren. Civilia leaned over and whispered in Cassandra's ear.

"I'll share the same secret that I told my daughter. It is good to be strong, but it is important that a lady shows her strength with grace. That is, if you ever want to have children."

Civilia let the confused and slightly embarrassed Cassandra go. Amuro walked over to Cassandra and took her arm.

"Amuro?" asked a confused Cassandra. "Where are we going?"

"Cassandra, against my better judgment I have to take you over to meet someone," requested Amuro.

"Sorry I didn't come see you earlier, but I was indisposed."

"I won't take it as an insult if you were intent on spending time with someone you hadn't held in over two revolutions."

"I'm glad to see you're all right."

"It takes more than a few imperial curs to take Maiden and I down."

The two reached Cecilia, and a lump developed in the princess's throat. Slightly intimidated at the presence of the Valkyrie before her, Cassandra wouldn't allow fear to show in her face. Never having been formally introduced, Amuro attempted to heal the bad blood between them.

"Allow me to properly introduce the lady who will soon be your sister-in-law, Princess Cecilia Rhone, known affectionately as the vanadis, the goddess of war herself."

"I have heard much about your exploits in battle and your skills with a spear," complimented Cassandra, trying to be civil. "Cedric has spoken very highly of you."

"That is something you and I can agree on," replied an annoyed Cecilia. "So I hear you're a witch?"

"A witch!" exclaimed Cassandra angrily. "Sorcery and witchcraft are completely different areas of magic."

Cecilia got a smug look on her face. Crossing her arms beneath her assets, she proudly stuck her chest out.

"Forgive my bluntness princess," teased Cecilia. "I didn't mean to imply you to be a haggard old conjurer of spells."

Not ready to accept such an insult from anyone, Cassandra brought her open right hand to the left side of her face. Despite maintaining her prim and proper upbringing, she began to laugh slightly.

"Just as I would never seek to spread the wretched rumors of your 'big brother' complex!" taunted Cassandra.

Amuro spit her white wine back into its glass. Filled with murderous rage, Cecilia reached behind her back to the slip of her dress where a knife was hanging. Standing her ground, Cassandra focused her mental energy toward mana formation. Seeking to defuse this tense situation, Amuro grabbed Saria as she passed by her. The young sister had no idea what was going on, but as always followed her big sister's lead.

"Cecilia, Cassandra, I'm sure you remember my sister Saria," stammered Amuro. "She's an enchanting singer. In fact, I bet if you listen long enough, you'll both agree it truly soothes the soul."

"But sister, my talents won't work on a Divikin; they're immune to status effect magic," commented Saria honestly.

Upset at herself for forgetting such a fact, Amuro started yelling at her sister.

"Why are you always so useless whenever I need you?"

"I'm sorry." cried Saria.

Now she'd really done it. Not only did the elf marshal have to deal with two women scorned but her crying baby sister.

'Tis a far better thing I do, thought Amuro as she stepped directly in between Cecilia and Cassandra and did her best fake, over-the-top, nervous, laugh.

"What's a few digs between family members, right? Isn't it great to be a woman? Unlike the men, we can just laugh these little insults off. How about another drink? Right, Felicia?"

"Absolutely, Princess. The Mistress looks parched from her last exhibition," noted Felicia, taking her cue from the elf princess.

Staring deeply at each other, both princesses issued an apology. Amuro breathed a sigh of relief as Cassandra left with Felicia and Cecilia returned to her drink. Her display of heroism caused her younger sister to hug her tightly.

While this was happening, Julius walked over to Cedric and put his hand on his shoulder. Distracted by the events between his sister and betrothed, the Titan jumped out of his skin.

"That was quite an exhibition you put on before," commented Julius. "I'm not surprised that you found a way to be at the center of attention."

"What I did, Julius, I did for her. When we were born first, our lives were already laid out for us. I can't imagine what it feels like to be so powerless in your own country."

"Don't think me jealous, my friend. I think it's wonderful that you're finally back together with the one that you love."

"What do you need from me?"

"It's a shame that two friends cannot simply pass the time talking about the results on the pitch or the latest picture at the cinema. However, you and I do have business to discuss. I need you to meet me at the Golden Dragon Tavern this evening in the Napolitan Embassy. You can bring Christian because I'll have Valentine with me."

"Care to give me a sneak preview?"

"Sorry buddy but these walls have ears and too many belong to you."

"Yes. Just remember you owe me a bottle."

"I knew you'd be sure to remind me of that."

Business concluded, Julius left his friend to visit his brother.

"I saw you dancing with Saria," ribbed Julius. "Very good, Cagius!"

"I told you, the cavalier attitude works every time."

"But are you going to live long enough to see it come to fruition?"

"Details! Hey, where's Valentine?"

"He thought two young ladies were looking a tad lonely."

"Not again."

"Well, I guess if you have a name like Valentine. Maybe we should be thankful that he isn't spending his time in the brothel."

"Let's just hope it doesn't cost us anything this time. There are times that I wish our subordinates behaved more like Christian or even Wilkins, for that matter."

Approaching Christian from the corner of the room was a guard. Their conversation was inaudible, but Christian went to find Cedric. Seeking his target, the spy master was distracted when Felicia slipped him a note. He nodded and finally reached his intended target.

"Your excellency, it appears that Cassandra wants you to join her."

"Walk with me, Christian."

"Why me?"

"Did you think I wouldn't notice your little conversation with our operative? The look on your face says it all. Besides, Julius asked me to meet with him tonight. What do you think that was about?"

"I don't know, Cedric. My guess is it must have something to do with Felicia."

"What about our operatives?"

"Nothing concrete, but to tell you the God's honest truth, I've had a knot in my stomach all night. Something's not right."

"That isn't encouraging. I needn't remind you I received too many requests and warnings for one rotation. If anyone dares to pull anything tonight, I will literally pull the roof of this castle down on them."

"I should have something for you soon."

When Cedric approached Cassandra, she grabbed him tightly. Grateful for the few seconds that the world wasn't falling apart, he pulled her closer.

"What's the matter?" worried Cedric.

"Daddy said something about making a special announcement, so just in case he calls us up to formally recognize the engagement, I wanted to be ready."

The Titan prince knew better. Cedric took another drink from the bartender while Stephen approached the stage where the musicians were. Silencing the band and the crowd, he spoke from a microphone.

"I wanted to thank everyone for attending this gala tonight and once again for taking the opportunity to drink free samples of the best wine and liquor on Terminus Mundus."

Pausing for a few moments to soak up all of their laughter, Stephen signaled the guards in the room with his eyes.

"In all seriousness, I want everyone to raise their glasses and honor the heroes that this night is for—our brave soldiers living and also those that gave everything for our tremendous victories over our enemies from within our borders and the empire. I want to extend a special gratitude toward our brave marshals: Prince Julius Imperia, Prince Cedric Rhone, and Princess Amuro Jenitzen, who led us to victory when hope was lost. I believe they deserve a well-earned salute."

Everyone in the room started to clap heartily for the three marshals. There were also whistles and chants of "here, here."

"I am fortunate to bear further good news this evening," continued Stephen. "The Tribal Confederation has agreed to our terms and will hold a meeting very shortly with our representatives to give us true peace within our borders."

Loud cheers and catcalls were sounded at this announcement, though not from members of the Titan delegation, of course. Once again, they followed a policy of tentative acquiescence.

"The alliance has agreed this evening that the diplomatic mission is to be headed by Prince Marshal Julius Imperia."

Naming a military leader as an envoy shocked the nobles and burghers. Cagius and Julius looked at each other mouthing sighs.

"So much for the vacation," commented Cagius.

"I guess it's for the greater good," added Julius.

Staring down Malcolm, Amuro mouthed, "You are mine!" Malcolm looked a tad uneasy at the proposal.

"There is also a final issue I would wish to discuss this evening," concluded Stephen.

Catching everyone off guard with the surprise announcement, guards escorted Princess Marie into the room. Marie was wearing a long, flowing blue gown with a diamond necklace around her neck. Attending to their personal distractions, none of the aristocrats had noticed the younger princess hadn't made an appearance yet. Suspicions rose when she took her place at her father's side.

"The time has come to make the necessary preparations for the future of our kingdoms."

Rushing toward Christian, a servant whispered something in his ear. Caught off guard, the spy master dropped his head.

"The knot?" asked Cedric.

"It's worse than anything I could have imagined."

"The time for pretense is over. Tonight, I name Marie, daughter of Penelope Orpheus as the successor to throne of Central Acadia. My country formally offers Caesar Constantine Imperia a betrothal of Marie and Julius Imperia.

"Do you require it be matrilineal?" screamed Constantine.

"No," replied Stephen.

"Given the circumstances and the witnesses present in this room, I believe we have an oral contract. My terms have been met and I see no need to consult with my advisors. Napolitan accepts, may Houses of Acadia and Imperia reign."

The room burst with applause, with the exception of a few dissenters. Many of the young aristocrats took the news with shock and apprehension. Somehow, Felicia managed to maintain her composure. Staring at Julius across the floor, she observed the paladin about to mutter an objection. Cagius knew better and grabbed his left arm.

"Not tonight!" warned Cagius.

"Cagius, how could you? Do you really want me to get up there and destroy that girl!"

"If you embarrass Stephen here tonight in front of the nobles, it will be the end of everything we gained. We'll find a way."

Julius wore his best face of dignity. Constantine had already stepped forward, signaling to Julius to come join him. Knowing her handmaiden couldn't take anymore, Cassandra comforted Felicia.

"My eyes are burning Felicia. I need you to fix my makeup now."

Ten revolutions together had destroyed the master-servant relationship between Cassandra and Felicia. Her handmaiden needed a friend and the princess was more than happy to comply.

"Thank you Mistress."

Presented with the distraction, Cassandra brought Felicia to a private room. Felicia broke down first, seeking comfort in Cassandra's embrace. The handmaiden wasn't alone; the loss of her birthright struck the princess equally hard.

Leaning against the bar, Cedric folded his arms across his chest. Wondering if this was part of the warning Wilhelm had given him earlier, he felt Christian slide next to him.

"My apologies, your excellency. I seem to be having a very bad night."

"Minor blemishes on a flawless record, old friend; you can make it up by making a mental note of everyone who's not clapping."

"Shall I bribe them?"

"No, they are enemies we really have to worry about."

Interrupting their conversation, Cassandra returned to the room. The tears were gone from her eyes and obviously the princess had spent some time reapplying her makeup.

"I sent Felicia up to my room and used a sleep spell to calm her down for a while."

Reaching the stage, Julius was pulled up by Stephen. Getting the optic of a war hero endorsing his negotiation plan, the king eagerly posed for pictures.

"After your heroic actions, it is only fitting that you shall lead our alliance in the future."

"Thank you, your majesty."

Staring adoringly at her betrothed, Marie took Julius' hand. The paladin observed the joy in her face. Desperately pleading with himself to say something, Julius' heart hardened.

"I've dreamed of this moment for a very long time," explained Marie. "Just like my big sister, I knew the man I wanted to marry that day on the tournament field."

Flashing back in time, Julius had a much different recollection of the events. Helpless as a turned tortoise after Cedric had unhorsed him with his lance, the paladin could remember staring into the crowd. Next to the fifteen-revolution-old Cassandra, was a young girl enjoying a bag of sweet candy. Julius remembered the compassion she had for him in defeat.

Returning to the moment, Julius remembered Cedric's words from earlier that evening. Sometimes, a true knight simply did what was best for a maiden. Taking Marie by her shoulders, Julius bent down and kissed her. He pulled back quickly, many in the room assumed from nervousness. Utterly disappointed, Marie had assumed her first kiss would be as exciting as what her sister described. Reasoning Julius was overwhelmed by the moment, she allowed the slight to pass.

"If you would, ladies and gentlemen, please take your seats and enjoy the wonderful dinner our marvelous chefs have prepared this evening." announced the Seneschal.

Finishing his brandy, Cedric escorted Cassandra to the dais. A place of honor had been setup in the middle of the table for them. In light of the recent announcement, a place was setup for Julius and Marie across from them. King Stephen assumed his place at the head of the table and Civilia took her seat at the opposite end. While Christian and Martha were allowed to sit at the dais, Horace and Colin sat at a circular table with the titan nobility. Overwhelmed by the pieces of silverware, Colin wondered what he was going to do.

"Is all this necessary?" questioned Colin. "I didn't expect to be served so much food."

"No, but it makes them feel good," replied Horace. "Just work outside to inside on every course they bring you. I hope you didn't bring your appetite."

Nodding Colin was served a half-ounce of caviar as his first course. Prodding at it with his outer spoon, the assassin gave up, swallowing it in a single bite.

"Don't worry, we'll eat later," teased Horace.

For the next few hours, servants brought seven courses of food with the appropriate wine or aperitif pairing. However, Colin never received a course suitable to his taste.

Caverns of the Demonkin, the Griffin Mountains

"The Demonkin were once human but were seduced by the Nephilim with promises of power. They allowed their souls to be bound to fell spirits. Over the revolutions, these fell spirits would scar, twist, and mutilate the flesh and structure of these humans until they resembled nothing more than the terrors of nightmare. They are bound to the Nephilim and, as a result, are treated as slaves. They come in many classes, including the lowest ranking members: simple-minded goblin footmen, orks, ogres, and trolls. There are the shape-shifting and cunning duco-mutatios, and most deadly, the wise and powerful lich. The Demonkin inhabit the caverns of Kaiser Mountain and, with the Nephilim, are the sworn enemies of the Divikin."

—Von Angelhardt's First Report

A baddon and Basarabas walked into the large hollow-mouth entrance to a cavern off a ridge in the mountains. Descending down artificial pathways, they reached a city of stone. Festering with the stench of blood, iron, and death, few dared to enter the ancient Demonkin hideaway. Orks toiled endlessly at the bellows producing weapons and armor. Lugging heavy materials, trolls and ogres were whipped into shape by hobgoblins and imps. Feared throughout the world were the mysterious Duco-Mutatios. Though they couldn't assume the form of a specific person, these shapeshifters could take on the characteristics of any race. Passing by these lower forms, Basarabas approached the elder lich. Skeletal hands emerged from his black-and-red robes. The necromancer's face was mostly bone with some remnants of flesh remaining, including two blue eyes. Anticipating a conversation with Basarabas instead of a fight, he placed a wizard's staff with a skull at its top on his back.

"Welcome, Basarabas," greeted the lich. "We've been expecting you."

"I trust my message was received," said Basarabas as Abaddon stood silent.

"Yes. We have been informed of the contract, but we were surprised at the quantity necessary."

"Terminus Mundus is about to become a war zone, and we're going to need every able Demonkin."

"Very well. How would you prefer to structure the payments?"

"I am under orders to provide you with no compensation."

Unable to believe his ears, the lich didn't know whether to chuckle or banish Basarabas. The silence of Abaddon began to concern the wizard. Yet, he dismissed these concerns as greed took hold of him.

"Basarabas, we have worked together before," castigated the lich. "You know that we will not be called to battle unless there is compensation."

"Trust me, what you are working for is the moment we've all dreamed of. I'm not just speaking about revenge on the Divikin and Titanus."

"I tire of your promises."

"I do not exaggerate this time. The weapon of our glory has been placed in our hands. The emissary that we waited for has arrived."

"I have no time for games."

Ending the negotiations, the lich walked away from the two. Frustrated with the insubordination, Basarabas pleaded with Abaddon to do something.

"Wait," commanded Abaddon as he pulled out a gold necklace and threw it to the lich.

Despite the lack of flesh of his hands, the wizard managed to catch the necklace in his bony fingers. Carefully inspecting the necklace, the lich noticed a pentagram hanging from the end of the chain.

"Yes, I know this to be a symbol of the Nephilim. A minor trinket like this is hardly enough to buy our services."

"Who said anything about compensation?" sneered Abaddon as he gripped his hand.

Black fire erupted all around the lich. Lack of flesh did not matter to the wizard. The hellfire scorched his bones. Screaming in agony, he witnessed Abaddon remove his cowl

"Lord Abaddon, I beg your forgiveness!" pleaded the Lich.

"I have patiently bided my time in my castle on the sixth plane," explained Abaddon. "Now I have been given the opportunity I have waited for since my exile. The Prince's granddaughter has become known to us. We will bring her to him even if the planet must be torn down to its very core. I have dreamed of wiping the smug look from Camael's face. The angels will cower in terror as gates of heaven crash to the ground. Revolutions in these caverns have made you weak, but now you have purpose. The way I see it, you have two options. Either your will or your life belongs to me . . . is that enough gold to satisfy your appetite now?"

"Yes, my lord," groveled the lich. "The Demonkin are yours to command."

"Excellent," said Abaddon as he snapped his fingers.

The black fire subsided and the lich stood up once more.

"What do you wish?" asked the lich.

"Gather the Demonkin and be prepared to move; final negotiations are underway with our other allies. We must be ready before the Divikin get wind of our plans."

"It will be done, my lord."

Hurrying into the city, the lich ordered his taskmasters to crack their whips. The mindless demonkin stopped what they were doing to pay homage to their new master. Satisfied Abaddon and Basarabas noted the size of the army.

"That went well," commented Basarabas.

"Once the Prince gets hold of your soul, it becomes bound for all eternity. Gather the Nephilim together; there is much to do now."

"At once, but how are we going to deal with Krystos?

"I will handle Krystos personally. That fallen angel is wild card I may have to deal with before this is over. The Prince still believes him to be a loyal ally, but I will not share any glory with a twice-turned traitor. Where can I find him?"

"We usually contact him at Nadia's hovel; she's his women."

"Nadia is here?"

"Yes. She's been hunting Teman and Eva ever since they escaped from Hell."

Basarabas noticed Abaddon's eyes filling with rage. He didn't understand if this had to do with Nadia herself or Krystos's relationship with her.

"The Nephilim and the Demonkin stand ready," announced Basarabas. "Now only the Divikin stand in our way."

"Where are they concentrated?" asked Abaddon, regaining his composure

"The Kablisha Tribe has locked themselves away behind a force field so we can afford to deal with them later. Divikin rule the royal houses in the nations of Edenia and Titanus. The kingdom of Titanus has longed used its power to battle our kind when all others show weakness."

"Yes, Titanus will have to be dealt with sooner than later. What about infiltrating their capital?"

"Not possible; we believe there is a sentinel among them, who assumed the name Duke Wilhelm von Angelhardt. This angel had snuffed out every plot we've tried. Nadia came close to killing him in her pursuit of Teman. Alas, that army was destroyed and she was forced to seek Krystos's protection.

"I didn't realize Daddy had not yet recalled all of his beloved sentinels. Come, Basarabas, we've lingered among the pawns far too long, and we need to pay Lady Nadia a visit," announced Abaddon as he left the caverns.

Castle Acadia,
Royal Ballroom

"The Sword Master is a class with the ability to enchant a blade with the four elements of the earthly realm: fire, ice, earth, and thunder and the four elements of the celestial: holy, darkness, lunar, and nature. Celestial element mastery is what makes this class so deadly, because of the unique power of restoration and absorption drawn from the lunar and nature element."

—Warrior Classes, the Elf Scholar Demetrius

Reclining at the dais after the final course, the aristocrats enjoyed after-dinner cordials, cigarettes, or cigars. Smiling, Stephen decided to bang his fork against a water glass, inviting the others to join.

"I was expecting dinner and a show provided but that I wouldn't be providing the entertainment," joked Cedric.

Everyone laughed. Turning to his betrothed, Cassandra gave him a nice, full kiss. Realizing he was next, a solemn countenance befell Julius. His brother nudged him in the ribs, and Julius kissed Marie, to a round of applause.

"My intention is to stagger the marriages, if you don't object," announced Stephen. "Cassandra has been waiting far too long, so I would like to have her married to coincide with the start of solstice cycle."

"It has to be after Easter Sunday. She must complete RCIA first before the marriage can take place," interrupted Civilia. "The traditions of Titanus demand that she will be married in Archangel Basilica, though we will cede the honor of the reception to Castle Acadia."

143

"Very well, and for the new revolution, we'll have Marie's marriage."

"Yes, it will be lovely in Napolitan that time of year," commented Constantine.

"Wait, Constantine, the reception must be here," joked Stephen.

"I'm sorry, but I'm hiring my caterers at my expense."

"Well, that should help ease the burden of paying for two weddings."

"No, you're not," countered Civilia. "If the basilica is to host the mass, it is not honorable to allow a guest to pay in the host's country."

"I forgot about your religious fanaticism and your adherence to that antiquity of an honor code," interjected Sharon.

"Fanaticism?" questioned Cecilia. "We aren't the ones that light candles to show how great we are."

"Humanity has come a long way over the revolutions," explained Penelope. "Is it not right to proclaim our individual good deeds?"

"Secular Progression is not a religion," argued Martha. "You should be acting on behalf of others because it's right."

"A wise man once said to avoid unnecessary fights at the dinner table. Avoid talk of politics, religion, and the Western Champions Final," interrupted Luminas.

"FC Aufgabe Rhinegard and Port Talus Internazionale are meeting for the third straight time!" exclaimed Martha.

"Thank you for proving my case."

"Politics, religion, and football—three areas haunting us since Titanus was admitted into the Alliance," argued Sharon.

"Sharon, this is not the venue," demanded Stephen.

"Have any of you been listening to conversations we had this evening," continued Sharon. "While they continue to lecture us on the virtues of honor and trust; they secretly conspire to gain as much power as possible to be used against us."

Figuring this was too great an insult, Constantine started to sweat. Oblivious to her words, Cedric continued to sip his brandy.

"Titanus loves its freedom as much as any of the kingdoms in the west," lectured Cedric. "My great-great grandfather, Frederick, organized the First Alliance and did what no one thought was possible—win victory over the Chinotal Empire. My grandfather, Justin, invoked the alliance when the empire came back two of our generations later. Its member states refused to join him to battle, recommending we negotiate a settlement where we gave the empire hostages. They even had the audacity to ask him for a share of spoils when the war was won. When Central Acadia foolishly provoked the empire into a third war, he did not show disdain for his allies; rather he charged fearlessly to drive back the empire. I will not apologize for what I say next—I witnessed the near defeat of the alliance at the hands of the empire. The Chinota Turks are a proud and determined people. The Walls of Edenia held back the Imperials three times before they collapsed, and Palacio Magnifico was taken without a battle. The empire always wins because they do not bicker over trade rights, minor slights, race, or politics. I say before you tonight, unless we join with the tribes on equal footing, we will not repel the next attack."

Licking his lips, Luminas consumed the rest of the swine blood in his wine glass.

"And I suppose you are the one we should crown emperor?"

"I will not say that I have not desired such a title, and if a consensus among the kingdoms and tribes would offer me the opportunity, I would not refuse. Rest assured, I will never win that position by force."

"Well then, what say you, Prince Julius?"

"Sorry, Count. The Napolitan philosopher Cicero spoke of the soldier's prerogative involving such a matter. That is to say, don't let the military comment on matters of politics."

Intoxicated by the amount of liquor, the safe answer drew a round of applause from the table. Believing the conversation had ended, Stephen was about to dismiss his guests.

"All the more reason my whore of a daughter has no business marrying such a brute," interrupted Sharon.

Stephen slammed his fists into the table to stop her, but it was too late. Pulling off her glove, Civilia slammed it down on the table.

"Sharon, perhaps it's time you took your leave for this evening," commanded Stephen. "I will not sit here and let you insult my daughter and our guests. Queen Civilia you have my most sincere apologies for the behavior of my wife. However, this is a personal matter and I do not need you to fight a duel to defend my daughter's honor."

"What a laugh, a daughter you were so eager to toss a crown from!" exclaimed Sharon.

"Mother, you've said enough," screamed an extremely angry Cassandra.

"Perhaps I've held my silence for too long," admonished Sharon. "You're so stupid to see you're just being used by that power mad warmonger sitting next to you. He has no love for you; he's incapable of it. All he sees in you is a stepping stone to his empire. In fact, I wouldn't be surprised if he discarded you like the slut you are once he obtains his objective!"

"Silence, Mother!"

Pushing back from the table, Cassandra's eyes started to roll back in her head. Frost formed on all the glasses on table and the flowers wilted. Fear gripped the faces of the aristocrats as a projection of light blue energy surrounded the princess' body. Cerwin recognized the danger right away but had no way to stop it.

"By the Father, Sharon, what have you done?" shouted Cerwin. "Cassie, you have to focus; stop it!"

Deaf to her uncle's pleas in the trance, Cedric had the only solution. Standing, the knight pulled Ragnarok from behind his cape. Horrified, the aristocrats screamed for the guards to come.

"Cedric, No!" shouted Stephen.

Jonas and the others rushed for their swords, but Walker cut them off.

"Stand down," ordered the protector.

"Move, Walker!" yelled Jonas. "As her bodyguard, you should draw your sword!"

"Wait and watch!"

Cedric began to chant in an ancient elf tongue. In a blast of frozen air, he uttered nature at the end of his chant. Rose petals surrounded Ragnarok. Gently tapping the shoulders of his fiancé with the blade, Cedric absorbed the powers controlling her. Falling temperatures signaled the danger was over, and Cassandra fainted into Cedric's arms. Christian couldn't help but snicker at Cedric's self-satisfaction with a beautiful damsel resting peacefully in his arms. Settling the princess down gently in her chair, Cedric returned the sword to the clip on his back. Seated once more, he ordered a brandy as if nothing had happened. Sharon stormed from the table in anger. The saints retook their positions, but Jonas shook his head in disgust.

"What just happened?" asked Marie.

"Cassandra went into a magic trance there for a second. It happens during times of severe arousal," explained Cerwin. "My guess is the alcohol consumption caused her to lose control of her powers. Cedric, even to my surprise, recognized the problem immediately and used the nature saber magic ability to drain Cassandra's magic reservoir before she turned this ballroom into a glacier."

"Well, that's a relief," stated Cagius as he sipped a glass of wine with a smile. "I do admit, though, that this dessert wine tastes divine since it's been chilled, so it's not a total loss."

"Thank you, Cedric," apologized Stephen. "It would seem I owe you my gratitude once again."

Sipping his brandy, Cedric's focused on Cassandra's recovery. As she came to, Cassandra stood and bowed to the guests.

"I apologize for my inappropriate behavior. Father, with your permission, I would like to retire for the evening."

"Of course, Cassie," granted Stephen.

"I think we should all follow suit on that suggestion," recommended Civilia.

"Typical. As soon as one person asks to leave, everyone joins in," joked Constantine.

Cassandra grabbed Cedric as he pushed away from the table.

"Thank you for everything this evening."

"My pleasure, Cassie. I have some business that will keep me in Verian for a few rotations, so if you would like to go riding some afternoon . . ."

"It's a date."

Rewarding the prince with a long kiss good night, Cedric lifted the princess up in a proper hug. Dutifully, Julius paid his respects to Marie.

"I had a wonderful evening," said Marie.

"Yes."

"It's a shame you have to head out again so soon. I was hoping we could spend some time together."

"Perhaps we will when I return."

"I do hope so," said Marie with a big smile.

"Good evening," uttered Julius as he kissed Marie good night.

Standing at the entrance of the room was Valentine. He wore a smug look on his face, suggesting he had been lucky in his earlier endeavor. The paladin wasted no time reaching him.

"Get me a private room at the Golden Dragon Tavern. Cedric and I have much to discuss."

"Of course, Sir."

TAVERN OF THE GOLDEN DRAGON, NAPOLITAN EMBASSY, VERIAN

Wake the Dragon and you shall face its rage.

—*Coat-of-Arms of House Imperia*

The lobby of the Napolitan embassy was decorated with columns, a fountain in the center of the lobby, and open air passages to aid with the climate control of the building. Similar to the Titan embassy, the Napolitan embassy hosted offices and a luxury hotel. The legions had a private barracks attached to the right side of the building. The royal families expended a small fortune turning the upper floors of the embassy into a retro nightclub. The Tavern of the Golden Dragon, consisted of six restaurants, two bars, and three clubs. Legion officers frequented the Exclusive Officers Club in the late evening hours. Weapons, coats-of-arms, standards, and a huge, winged, dragon adorned the walls of the club. Climbing the stairs, Cedric and Christian could hear the zealous atmosphere through the closed door.

"We could have taken the lift!" argued Christian.

"If we took the lift, every single person on there would be constantly saluting me," explained Cedric. "Besides, we still have the element of surprise."

Christian shook his head and opened the door of the club. The legions were certainly having a ruckus time inside, and it wasn't surprising to see many had the company of a "lady of the night." As soon as Cedric entered, one of the officers shouted, "Prince Marshal Commandant Rhone!"

The legionnaires in the room snapped to attention, stopped what they were doing, and saluted. The prostitutes in the room looked hungrily at the handsome prince and his companion.

"At ease, men," ordered Cedric.

The legionnaires went back to what they were doing. An officer at the bar pointed Cedric toward one of the private, soundproof rooms in the back. Kissing a woman, Valentine stood guard at the door. When he saw Cedric and Christian arrive, he stopped what he was doing. Dismissing her with a slap on the rear end, Valentine slipped some money down her dress.

"We've been expecting you," said Valentine.

Valentine allowed Cedric and Christian to enter before signaling for two Praetorian guards to watch the door. Well aware of the high value of two crown princes in a public place, Valentine made sure the door was sealed. Poking a fire, Julius watched Cedric intently.

"I don't like to sound like a pyromaniac, but I do love a good roasting fire on a cool night," commented Julius.

Retiring to a couch in front of the fire, Julius offered the seats across from him to Cedric and Christian. Watching Valentine's moves, Christian took his seat.

"I know I owe you a brandy, but I'd like to share one of my favorite libations," said Julius. "We add in a drop of port wine to ease the harshness."

Julius poured brandy into four glasses and then placed a drop of port wine into each. He passed out the glasses. Cedric swirled his and took a sip as Valentine stood behind Julius.

"What is this about, Julius?" asked Cedric. "I'm missing a hell of an after party at the Titan embassy."

"I need to know, as a friend, if you're going to sabotage these negotiations."

"The alliance's business with the tribes is not the concern of Titanus. I didn't come here to play games, Julius. Why did you insist on talking to me?"

"I can't marry Marie. I don't know what would be worse for her, finding out I have a son with Felicia or the issues of succession that would arise from it."

"If you're looking for sympathy, Julius, I'm not going to give you any. You chose your bed, and you're going to have to lie in it."

"I'm looking for advice."

"My advice is simple, Julius. Marry the girl and disavow your son with Felicia. The line of succession will be maintained and Marie will pardon you for your past indiscretions."

"Just like that!" screamed a disappointed and angry Julius. "I thought you were a man of moral character."

"Do not lecture me on morality, Julius! I was disappointed when I found out you compromised your integrity. You knew this was going to be an issue and you didn't prepare. As a friend, I've giving you the best advice I can."

"We're walking on thin ice as it is already, Julius," reminded Christian. "There are already whispers of a civil war brewing. The Acadian elites and socialists feared that Titanus was going to form a personal union with Central Acadia upon Stephen's death."

"That's why the betrothal of Marie came so quickly," argued Valentine. "There are many outside of Titanus that would have been very happy to see Cedric as monarch of both Titanus and Central Acadia."

"Were you part of this chess match?" asked Christian.

"Though I do appreciate Luminas's schemes from time to time, I had no part in this game," countered Valentine. "However, it's not too hard to follow the breadcrumbs."

"The problem is that Stephen is becoming more and more unpopular with the Acadian Nobles," argued Cedric. "He has completely eroded their former base of power, and talks of rebellion are no longer whispered in dark corners. How many kings can claim they are more popular with people outside their country?"

"I've got the place covered, and my ladies are constantly feeding me information," noted Valentine. "There is no talk of a coup yet."

"Only along the channels we can monitor; it's not like we have the wizard's guild or the temple bugged," said Christian.

"You believe the wizards are fomenting rebellion?" queried Valentine.

"Nothing that we can yet confirm," answered Cedric.

"However, many of the nobles and wizards in attendance tonight were not applauding when you took the stage with Marie," explained Christian.

"Perhaps I should send them a card," jested Julius.

"You don't understand," argued Cedric, "Stephen and Luminas figured out that I was an unacceptable match, so they turned to a more palatable choice for the Acadians to embrace."

"A paladin and a war hero!" exclaimed Valentine.

"Not to mention a man that is perceived to be able to contain Cedric Rhone," interjected Christian. "I guess we can allow them to dream."

"The ninnies still couldn't help but object," interrupted Julius as he sipped his drink. "Yet they claim the elves in Evengard are a 'stiff-necked' people."

"You and I have effectively ended the Acadian line of kings," explained Cedric. "Verian will no longer be the stronghold of the alliance. This is a very dangerous time."

"I will not abandon Felicia to fulfill foolish ambitions," said Julius. "Why should you get to marry for love while I'm trapped in a false relationship?"

"In the end, she was only a dream, Julius; as an aristocrat, you have a duty," bellowed Cedric. "If our positions were reversed, you would counsel me the same way."

Julius shook his head as Cedric sipped his drink.

"Isn't there an alternative?" asked Julius.

"You and I will become enemies," replied Cedric coldly.

"What do you mean?" questioned Julius, now sounding of fear.

"Without your marriage, Titanus will claim a personal union with Central Acadia. If so, the Acadians will look to someone to lead their faction in the resulting civil war. You will be that choice, and brother shall be turned against brother in every nation."

"The empire will surely take advantage of such an opportunity," echoed Valentine. "In the end we'd all have to bend the knee to either Julius or Cedric and crown the victor emperor."

"That's why you warned us about your goals of an empire this evening," reasoned Julius. "That wasn't idle banter or philosophy; you've already taken a side."

"Even if you marry Marie, we're going to have to settle this one day," warned Cedric. "It is destined that either you or I will rule a western empire."

"A part of me knew the first time that I met you it was going to come to this. However, I must speak to my father about this marriage."

"You know his answer," chided Valentine.

"I must speak with him!" repeated Julius.

"You do what you have to do" explained Cedric. "I know what I have to do. Forces are right now at work beyond both of us, Julius."

"Cedric, I want to thank you for being honest with me."

The rival stood. Grabbing Julius, Cedric gave him a firm hug. In spite of everything that transpired between them, the bonds of brotherhood in warfare burned in their hearts.

"You take care of yourself out there in the wilderness," ordered Cedric. "I'll hold down Verian and find out what I can."

"You're making it sound like only the marshals are going to be able to stop some mass conspiracy," worried Julius.

"What if we are, Julius? Watch your back and heed this warning. If things remain as they are, the night Cassandra and I marry, we can longer be friends."

"I understand. Don't do anything to bring about the end of the alliance while I'm gone."

Breaking the embrace, the knights participated in an old tradition. Grasping the right hand of the other as firm as they could, one tried to bend the other to his will. Faces red from the energy expended, Julius finally surrendered. Shaking the pain from his hand, Julius spoke once more.

"I never could compete with you in strength. You were always luckier with the ladies as well. Have you ever heard the 'Legend of the Last Knight?'"

Three times was too much for Cedric. Ignorant of the prophecy, the sword master had heard three people as different as could be speak of it in a matter of hours.

"Yes but why?"

"The way you describe what may come to pass, we may need him before this is over," reasoned Julius. "I always believed an idea can be greater than a man. Perhaps I may be this last knight and not even know it."

Approaching Christian, Valentine issued his own warnings.

"Spy to spy, I will have my girls keep their ears open as well."

"Every bit helps, Valentine!"

"I'll be in Verian if you need me."

Cedric and Christian finished their drinks, leaving Valentine and Julius behind. Sinking back into the sofa, Julius covered his eyes with his hand.

"What the hell am I going to do, Valentine?" asked Julius.

"Cedric speaks the truth, but I would suggest a good night sleep," counseled Valentine. "We travel to Napolitan and Port Talus in the morning. You know your brother will be anxious to get home."

"I may hold the honor of centurion, but my brother is the true legate and people's god. He has always been home at Port Talus."

Hustling down the stairs, Christian and Cedric made plans.

"Christian, I know you've got a lot on your plate with the special package arriving in Verian. However, I am going to need you to get me all the information you have on the *Permaneo Eques Ordinares.*"

"Why?

"I don't believe that three people mentioning the same prophecy to me is only a coincidence."

"My people will look into it. As soon as the package is secured, I'll get back to Verian."

Meanwhile, in the royal palace living quarters, a teary-eyed Felicia prepared Cassandra for bed. Her apartment reflected her prim and proper nature, yet the stuffed lion toys gave it an hint of immaturity. Having her hair set for bed, Cassandra alleviated her headache with medication and an ice pack.

"My head is killing me," commented Cassandra. "I know I can't keep up with Cedric. Why didn't I take my own advice to stop myself?"

"I warned you about drinking so many martinis, my lady," teased Felicia.

"Well, we both had a bad night."

"Yes, we did. What time shall I wake you tomorrow?"

"Uncle wants me to practice, but there is no way I'm getting up before mid-morn. By the Father, I hope he doesn't call the whole thing off based on my behavior tonight."

"I'll have your breakfast prepared. I think pancakes might help you with the hangover. "

"Chocolate-chip, please."

"Your highness, remember your diet."

Placing the comb down, Felicia helped Cassandra into her soft, feather bed. Pulling up the silk sheets around her, the handmaiden playfully tucked her in and kissed her on the forehead.

"Good night, your highness."

"I hope we both feel better in the morning."

"If you need me, your highness, I'll be with my son."

Felicia shut out the lights.

"Good night, Mom," teased Cassandra, causing both girls to laugh.

ENCAMPMENT OF THE WOLF TRIBE, THE FOLLOWING MORNING

"You saved my granddaughters. Why? You owed me nothing. From this hour forward you and I are blood brothers. Though our war continues, I end the curse that my ancestors placed on your kingdom. A time will come when the poppies bloom white again!"

—*Chieftain Aramas to Prince Cedric Rhone after the Battle of Terrace River*

Hippolyte and Minerva prepared riding satchels for the journey. Packing weapons, traps, tribal herbs and potions, the girls readied themselves for every danger possible

"I couldn't sleep a wink last night," exclaimed a very excited Minerva.

"I know; you kept me up all night talking about going to Verian," teased an annoyed Hippolyte.

"I'm sorry,"

"Do you have all your gear?"

"Is all this really necessary?"

Hippolyte slid two daggers behind her back and another on the side of her boot. Minerva, seeing her example, placed a dagger behind her back as well. She also checked her quiver to make sure she had plenty of different types of arrows.

"We don't know what we're going to be up against, and its better that we're prepared. We are literally riding into the lion's den and you'd better not slow me down."

"I'm ready!"

"I'm actually surprised; you're always in tears before you leave."

"But this is so different, sis. We're going on an adventure! Who do you know that's been in Verian among the tribes?"

"I guess you're right. Let's go!"

Pulling back the canvas of the longhouse, Hippolyte and Minerva observed an image beyond their wildest imagination. The villagers of the nearby wolf and myotis tribes had come to bless the girls before the journey. Forming a small walkway for them to travel, Hippolyte and Minerva were treated to shouts, handshakes, and congratulations. Stryker wagged his tail beside two horses prepared for them. Huskal was mounted with Josephine and twenty members of both tribes to serve as an escort. Aramas and Reynard awaited them on foot before the horses.

"Did you sleep well?" asked Aramas

"As best I could, Grandpa, with Minerva chatting me up all night," replied Hippolyte.

"I understand."

Reynard handed Hippolyte a bag marked with the Seal of the Tribal Confederation. Taking the package with trepidation, the girl awaited her final orders.

"These are the terms for the negotiations and the site of our meeting place," described Reynard. "You must understand that these terms are not negotiable. Should King Stephen refuse them, you are to return immediately. It will be our signal not to move our armies."

"Yes."

"You've become quite strong, Hippolyte, and on this mission I hope that you will learn the other necessities of being a chief," complimented Aramas as he careful examined his granddaughter. "Be careful and make sure you watch after your sister; she'll need it."

Pouting at the remark, Minerva watched her sister get scooped up in a big hug by her grandfather. Despite her size, Aramas resembled a big old bear crushing his prey.

"Great Spirits of the Earth, heed my call. Bless this young one on her quest. May she keep the ancient ways, and grant her the valor and temperance necessary among our enemies," blessed Aramas.

Letting his elder granddaughter go, Aramas turned to her smiling little sister. Minerva scampered like a ground squirrel trying to escape a predator. Struggling for air, she was forced to endure her grandfather's grasp.

"Great Spirits of the Earth, heed my call. Bless this young one on her quest. May she keep the ancient ways, and grant her the valor and temperance . . . especially make sure she maintains her temperance among our enemies. Who am I kidding? Great Spirits, I just ask you to give me a break with this one for once."

Upset that Aramas had changed the ancient blessing, Minerva stuck her tongue out of him as he let go. Her little act of rebellion was cut off quickly as she watched the tears in her grandfather's eyes. Hippolyte put her hand to her sister's shoulder and finally understood the gravity of her mission.

"You should be on your way," announced Aramas.

"Please go with the blessings of the Tribal Confederation, and we wish you the best," blessed Reynard.

The two men helped the girls up on their horses. Listening to the villagers sing an old tribal song for the girls, Huskal moved his horse toward Hippolyte.

"Josephine and I will stay with you until we reach the main highway to Verian," asserted Huskal. "We dare not cross any farther."

"For what it is worth, the Titans have guaranteed you safe passage, but the other kingdoms have not been so forthright," added Josephine.

"We'll manage," chimed an excited Minerva.

"I hope so," stated a reserved Hippolyte, staring at the package again.

"You girls are in for a treat," interjected Josephine. "I've bet you've never seen a city float before."

"Really?" asked Minerva.

"Indeed, young one!" replied Josephine.

"I can't wait!" exclaimed Minerva.

"This is business, Minerva," corrected her older sister.

Minerva let out a sigh as Huskal and Josephine started to laugh.

"We'd best get going," ordered Huskal.

Aramas stared at his granddaughters one last time.

"Be strong!" cautioned Aramas. "Under no circumstances should you draw your weapons against the Acadians. Trust in yourselves and our noble enemies to defend you."

Nodding, the girls followed the rest of the company. Stryker hung on the heels of Hippolyte's painted horse. Breathing a sigh of relief, Aramas stared at the tattoo on his hand.

"I'm sure he'll keep his promise, Aramas," reassured Reynard.

"If it was any other man, but he is my blood brother. It was after the Battle of the Terrace River, the rotation, my son, Aegis, was killed. It wasn't enough to kill every last man in battle, that butcher Jonas and his friends moved into the village. Not satisfied with raping the woman to death, they turned their swords on the children. The last thing I could have ever imagined was the Prime Eagle clashing swords with his own allies. He owed us nothing, yet he still saved Hippolyte and Minerva. I won't doubt his word."

"Did you tell them?" asked Reynard

"How could I? How could I tell them that an enemy they've been indoctrinated to hate actually saved their lives? However, I cannot hide the truth from Hippolyte any longer; she must know who she can trust."

"Do we trust the Titans? The Mother Eagle's wrath will be horrible. I'm sure her advisors are already claiming we did not behave honorably."

"We have to take our chances but I doubt the Mother Eagle will harm us over such a small slight. I'm worried about Minerva. She is young and already quite worldly for her age. We may lose her to Verian's seduction."

"Either that or a handsome young knight," chuckled Reynard.

"Perhaps that is my greater concern. As long as it's not Hippolyte, my heart should be able to take it. I've called Posha of the Syrus Clan and Adnar of the Nordice Vikings to join us for a full assembly of the Tribal Confederation. We need to strategize on how to deal with the meeting.

Reynard bowed his head and opened his arms submissively to the great chief. Watching until the company completely disappeared from the road, Aramas retreated to the silence of the longhouse.

Cottage, Griffin Mountains

"There you are, sweetheart. I heard you were handsome, but never did I expect this. Alas, like tragedies of old, ours must be a forbidden love. So please don't be offended, but you must die."

—*Nadia, preparing to deliver the deathblow to Wilhelm*

Nestled within the mountainous landscape was a two-story cottage; from the outside its white brick outlays and tiled roof screamed nothing out of the ordinary. However, behind the redwood door the cottage told a much different story. The inside of the house was carpeted in red with oak panels all around. The entire downstairs consisted of a massive study with books and shelves from one wall to the next. There was a large alchemy set in the middle of the room, and two pedestals for the purposes of making spells and enchantments. Tapestries hung from the walls with rather gruesome depictions of skulls, gargoyles, and other bestial familiars.

In a large, plush, and comfy chair sat a beautiful, well-endowed, and sinister-looking female. Clothed in a skin-tight, purple leotard, the woman had most of her skin exposed. She wore a necklace with three skulls on a gold chain, purple gloves, purple boots, and a gold band on her right arm. Her long black hair was set within an obsidian circlet marked with a ruby stone at its center. Closing her crimson red eyes, Nadia was falling asleep from the monotony of her reading. Slipping out of her hands was a red, leather-bound tome with golden runes etched in an ancient language. Nadia snapped to attention when the owl on one of her tapestries screeched. Taking out a small compact she fixed her dark eye shadow and lip liner to match her olive-colored skin and smeared blood-red lipstick. Satisfied with her appearance, Nadia moved her right hand and the door opened.

"Come in, lover!" teased Nadia as Wilhelm entered the cottage.

161

"I'm sorry, Nadia, I couldn't get away any sooner," apologized Wilhelm.

Jumping to her feet, Nadia threw herself into Wilhelm's chest. The Duke smiled and gently rubbed her shoulders.

"Thank God; there's been so much talk lately. I know I summoned you, but you mustn't stay long."

"What's the matter?" asked Wilhelm.

"Abaddon is here!"

"I observed that someone crossed over from beyond the temporal and I suspected it might be him. The prince is going all out if he's sent one of his chief lieutenants."

"Yes."

Waving her hand, Nadia called a scroll from the eastern bookcase. Wilhelm noticed it was marked with a pentagram and the writing was in blood.

"Basarabas sent this three rotations ago. All of the Nephilim are being called into service."

"What about me?"

"The prince wants you involved in the mission, but Abaddon doesn't trust you."

"That boy is smarter than I thought."

"From my investigations it has nothing to do with your true mission. Rather, Abaddon doesn't want to share the glory of his victory with one whom he perceives to be a traitor. Of course, there are also personal reasons, if you get my meaning."

"What does he know about me?"

"The Nephilim continue to believe that you and Krystos are two separate entities. Since I am a daughter of the prince and I vouched for Krystos, the agents of hell have no reason to suspect anything. Wilhelm, sooner or later Abaddon and the Nephilim are going to realize that you've been playing them for fools. My dad isn't going to happy about that."

"I can't leave Titanus and Prince Rhone blind, even if it costs me my life."

"You can't say that! Wilhelm, you've fought so hard to bring so many of us back; if you die, your soul will become the property of my father."

"I know my fate. Every sentinel that came down from Heaven had to give something up. I just gave more than most. I am still an angel of the Powers choir. I will not stand around and do nothing."

"But why die for Titanus?"

"Titanus is the only place left in this world where there is strength and fervor to survive what is coming. Besides, I believe I've found the man that can stop this."

"Prince Rhone?"

"Yes."

"Is he strong enough to protect our daughter from Abaddon and my father?"

"His love for her is strong; it may be enough in the end. I don't know what it is, Nadia. I taught the Titan prince well, but his style is beyond that of any being in creation. He fights like an angel!"

"I thought you told me that Divikin only possess such powers when they're at death's door!"

As he was going to responded, a gargoyle let loose a frightening howl. Nadia's face filled with fright.

"The Nephilim are coming!"

"Basarabas and Abaddon, no doubt. I'm sure they picked up my signature here. We'd better get our game faces on."

Masking him in the body of a Nephilim, the markings under Wilhelm's eyes began to sprout tribal tattoos on his face. His Titan royal uniform was exchanged for a long black trench coat, black vest, long black pants, and black boots. Radiating in otherworldly light, small horns and black wings sprouted from Nadia's body. Reverting to her succubus form, her assets expanded and her red lips curled in a seductive manner. As they anticipated, Basarabas entered the room with Abaddon in tow.

"I knew I would find you here, Krystos," said Basarabas.

"I'm here quite often," taunted Wilhelm as he noticed the rage begin to form in Abaddon's eyes.

"I wanted to bring over a mutual friend while we had a spare moment," announced Basarabas. "Allow me to introduce Abaddon, locust king of the sixth plane."

Blatantly ignoring Wilhelm, Abaddon greeted Nadia properly. He took her right hand, and bowed before a daughter of the Prince.

"Forgive me for indulging in your beauty, but I have missed your radiance for quite some time," flattered Abaddon as he kissed her hand.

"I reject no flattery from the lord of the sixth plane," responded Nadia, smiling seductively.

"Your highness, I did not want to believe that the rumors are true. Are you really the woman of this pathetic fallen angel?"

"She's not anyone's woman Abaddon." challenged Wilhelm. "She chooses to remain with me."

"Well, at least you and I share the same taste in the fairer sex."

Satisfied with his opening blow, Abaddon turned his attention to the bookcases. Perusing the various sections, Abaddon allowed a smug smile to cross his face.

"This is a very impressive collection, my dear."

"Terminus Mundus is a very large and important planet," lectured Nadia. "The opportunity to gain knowledge is vast if you know the right places to look for it. Besides I am still in process of hunting down a large quarry and I must discover any place they could go."

"I've heard," answered Abaddon as he stopped and stared at a specific book bound in red with black lettering. "This is a title that interests me. *The Titan Battle Manual* by Prince Cedric Rhone—an ancient warrior who shares the same name of the current prince, perhaps?"

"Actually, that is the current crown prince of Titanus," stated Wilhelm.

"Quite pretentious to write a memoir at such a young age."

"It's not a memoir. It's a book of strategies, commitment to a code, and various commentaries on faith."

"Would you mind, you highness?" requested Abaddon.

"Please, with my compliments," replied Nadia.

"Thank you, I always believe that it is wise to know the ways of one's enemy. Someone, pretentious enough to take the title 'La Morte Angelus,' should be thoroughly studied. The way the Nephilim speak of Titanus, I believe our paths will cross eventually."

"When did you arrive?"

"What is the word?" started Abaddon. "You treat rotations as days and revolutions as years. Thus, I arrived a few rotations ago. I would have hoped for more of a grand entrance, but the circumstances did not permit."

"Care to let me in on the plans?" asked Wilhelm.

"Sorry, friend, this is my show. There will be a time when I will require your help; be ready at that point."

"The rumors of your distrust with me are quite true."

"You have disappointed Prince Lucifer far too many times, my fallen friend. Actually, though, there is something you can do for now. Are you familiar with Duke Wilhelm von Angelhardt?"

"His deeds are known to me," replied a nervous Wilhelm, fearing his cover blown.

"According to Basarabas, this is the last of the sentinels on Terminus Mundus. I want him eliminated before my plans can take shape. Kill him, and maybe I'll let you in on what I'm doing."

"Take down a member of the Titan royal court? That's ambitious, but I've always enjoyed a good challenge. I'll take the job."

"Excellent. Well, I'll have to bid you adieu for now; there is much that still needs to be done."

Abaddon bowed to Nadia once more, who reveled having her enemy eating out of her hand.

"Thank you, my lady. I will try to endure without your radiance. However, if you ever feel like taking your rightful place among the Nephilim, I welcome you with open arms. Your father has a message for you: 'Suspend your pursuit of Teman and Eva for now, the only task at hand is the retrieval of my granddaughter.'"

"I understand."

Abaddon and Basarabas left the cottage. Nadia spit on the glove that Abaddon had kissed.

"I don't know whether I should break out the disinfectant for my hands or my ears. Can you believe trying all of those honey words on a 'daughter of the Prince'?"

Transforming back, Wilhelm and Nadia embraced each other, shaking from the events thrust upon them.

"Answer me this riddle, Nadia. How does one destroy oneself?"

"You're not serious."

"I'd love to know what his plans are."

"You know there are other ways."

"Don't go spoiling everything I've earned for you!"

"Don't worry about me, sweetheart, you just make sure you don't end up at the end of one of his swords."

"I was a master-of-arms, you know."

"Yes, but he is among the finest swordsman in the celestial realm. My father spoke of the greatness of Camael and Cassiel but never of you."

Disappointed his enemies in hell had no appreciation of his skills, Wilhelm focused on the task at hand.

"Nadia, find out what you can. Cedric needs to be warned."

"Don't worry about me. You just make sure that Prince Rhone can keep our Cassie safe, or else we're all done for. And for the love of God, try not to get yourself killed."

Nadia wrapped her arms around Wilhelm and kissed him good-bye. Knowing his departure was imminent, both Wilhelm and Nadia were filled with pain.

"I'll get back as soon as I can," ordered Wilhelm. "You keep that door locked and the warning systems in place. Be ready to flee at a moment's notice."

"Yeah, I know, the same precautions as always. I can take care of myself, you know."

Wilhelm held her one more time tightly before disappearing from the cottage in a cloud of feathers. Nadia allowed herself to wipe tears from her eyes for a few moments before settling in. She waved her hand over a crystal orb in the center of the table, revealing an image of Princess Cassandra.

"All right, sweetheart, for you it's time to get to work! God, you do work in mysterious ways. I mean what a messed up fairytale, we're counting on a knight embracing the light and darkness to save us all. The only way it could get any worse is if Cassie completes her sorcery training."

Nadia waved her hand, closing the orb. In her other hand she called a book over from the shelf. She went back to her chair and started to read.

Dragon's Rest, Port Talus, Napolitan

"Rexus Populasque Napolitanus."

—Inscribed on the entrance of the gate of Port Talus

Contrary to the architecture of Verian, the designs of Port Talus invoked Terminus Mundus's past. A well-developed cobblestone road system divided the city into square blocks. Aesthetic and practical, the buildings were constructed with stone and marble. Two large aqueducts connected into the city from the north and east. The main source of income for the city came from its east end. Inhabiting the Sea of Serenity, trade cogs arrived from every port on Terminus Mundus. Protecting these trade routes, a large navy consisting of frigates and brigs guarded the port. Eager brokers busily traded their commodities to every merchant in the city, while investors traded business secrets outside of the marble Napolitan Exchange. A large circular building with ionic columns rested in the center of the city—the Forum, home of the Napolitan senate.

On a hill above the city rested the royal palace, Dragon's Rest. Spread out like a grand estate, the construction of the palace focused on length rather than stories. Buildings were spread out over five hills with the lavish main estate in the center hill. Marble dragons lined the entrance to the gate. Poplar trees and lilies lined the palace grounds with marble stone for its outer wall linings. Residing in the central courtyard of the royal estate was a large fountain with dual spiral staircases flanking it. The room was decorated mainly with spears and murals of dragons. The Praetorian Legions, dressed in black tempered armor, guarded the palace and royal family. In full view of the citizens of Napolitan, Constantine and Marguerite waited on the steps of the palace for the return of their sons.

The Napolitan Imperium was a merchant republic up to the time of the War of the First Alliance. Placing their fate in a noble concept, the people elected senators to represent their interests in the government. When called to fight in the First Alliance, the senate selected one of its most prominent members, Phillius Draconius, to serve as First Consul, a military dictator during the war. The decision proved fatal since, after the war, Phillius seized power from the senate and took the title of caesar from the ancient Napolitan. The Draconius family would rule the Imperium until Giovanni Draconius brought the kingdom to the edge of bankruptcy. A popular legate and war hero, Constantine Imperia wrested the throne from his control. In order to seal an uneasy peace, Constantine married Draconius's daughter Marguerite, uniting the families. Napolitan, like Titanus, was very conservative when it came to protecting their ancient traditions, the most important being that Dragon Legions, the standing army of Napolitan, could not enter Port Talus. Thus, they remain stationed at Fort Dragonstone due to an inherent fear of a military coup.

Dutifully watching from the tower of the entrance to Port Talus, a soldier spotted the praetorian escort of Julius and Cagius. Taking out his horn, the soldier signaled the entrance of the two princes. When he replaced it, he screamed in an echoing voice,

"Caesar, the sons of Napolitan have returned!"

The gates opened, and the sound of loud cheering from the streets was heard. Boarding dual chariots at the gate, Julius and Cagius began their parade to Caesar. No longer feeling the role of the clown, Julius proudly passed under the seal of the Golden Dragon and the words "RPQN." Following marching bands, and displaying the spoils of conquest, honored officers of the legion joined the princes. Constantine smiled as Julius dismounted his chariot before the entrance to the estate. Caesar took a victory baton from his side and handed it to his conquering paladin before embracing him. Cagius stopped abruptly and kissed the floor, causing Julius to shake his head.

"I didn't know you meant that literally," teased Julius.

"Hey, I'm just happy to be home!" replied Cagius.

"Welcome home, my sons!" exclaimed their jubilant mother.

Marguerite went to Julius first and kissed him. Julius seemed slightly embarrassed by his mother's public display in front of the others.

"My brave Paladin!"

Julius had no answer. Marguerite went to Cagius next, who seemed much more cordial with his mother. Kissing him, the younger brother picked up his mother and hugged her.

"My noble legate and cavalier!"

"How's my number one gal?" teased Cagius.

"I'm your mother, Cagius," scolded Marguerite. "You need not use your talents on me."

Cagius let her down. Returning to the comforts of the estate from the cheering crowds, Constantine playfully hit Julius on the shoulder twice.

"You have exceeded every one of my expectations, Julius!" admired Constantine. "Valor in battle, nobility at the court, and now you will become the leader of this alliance. Thank the saints, these halls will no longer tell of the glories of Constantine. My son, from this day forward all glory is to you. I know now that I will rest peacefully because all I have sacrificed for is in safe hands."

"Thank you, Father," answered Julius. "However, some of the glory must be reserved for Cagius as well. He has shown tremendous skill in his ability to command the legions, and they have nothing but respect for him."

"I suppose legates serve a purpose as well," rebuked Constantine, who looked at Cagius with some disdain, despite Cagius's happy disposition. "I am more concerned, however, at your brother's exploits of playing the fool quite well."

"Constantine!" shouted Marguerite, who was livid at having her son insulted.

"It's worked for me so far," quipped Cagius.

"It is good you have returned alive and uninjured, but then again your brother was probably looking out for you."

"Cagius is more than capable as a warrior," interrupted James Darius.

"If I want your opinion, centurion, I will ask for it. Now, we are celebrating your return this evening. I know you're not going to be able to stay for long because of the negotiations, so let us cherish what little time we're going to have together. You are free until dinner; savor the relaxation!"

"Father, wait!" interjected Julius. "I must have a word with you."

Constantine sighed and closed his eyes as if he knew what was coming. Signaling for the room to be cleared, he allowed only his wife, sons, and chief advisors to remain.

"Julius, I wish not to discuss such a matter," commanded Constantine.

"It matters greatly to me," argued Julius. "How could you arrange for my marriage without telling me?"

"Because there was nothing official until the past evening, I cannot explain why Stephen suddenly approached me with such an offer. However, I had to accept it. Julius, you met with Cedric that night in Verian, and I'm sure you know of the potential civil war that is coming. I wished not to have to choose sides in a war between Central Acadia and Titanus. You, my son, were the only individual acceptable to all sides."

"I'm in love with Felicia, you know that."

"Yes, I do. She is a mere peasant servant!"

"A handmaiden of a princess; there is a great difference!"

"She is not even of noble blood. How can you accept such a denigration of your aristocratic duties?"

"My duties?"

"Julius, please understand, your father and I shared nothing but our adherence to duty when we were married," pleaded Marguerite as she walked over to her husband and kissed him. "However, over time there was love. Right now it's going to be very hard for you to accept the shattering of your dreams. Princess Marie is a gentle and loving soul; over time you will come to love her."

"You can't understand my pain! There are other reasons. I have a son."

"What?" screamed Constantine, clutching his chest.

Closing his eyes at the statement, Cagius figured you could hear a pin drop. Watching his father's face fall, the legate was crushed.

"How old?" asked Constantine.

"He's seen ten rotations," responded Julius.

"Ten?" questioned a surprised Marguerite.

"I had been seeing Felicia before, and I got very drunk after the convocation ceremonies," recollected Julius. "We met with each other at the tavern later that evening. It was in the time before you gave Valentine to me and Cagius was still training at Dragonstone."

Floored by the disturbing revelation, the Caesar began to think long and hard. The look in face showed that even though Constantine had formulated a plan, he wasn't pleased with himself.

"Well, he's only a bastard," said Constantine. "Civilia is honorable but a well-placed favor could probably get him enrolled at the Titan Military Academy. Since he is your son, the boy will have no difficulty excelling in school and maybe he'll even earn himself a landed title. It will be less messy that way."

"Just like that!" screamed Julius.

"You know he has no chance for a life in Napolitan. The people will never accept a bastard caesar. Stephen has little choice and must remain bound to the terms, but he must know."

"Father!"

"In time, it will be like this had never happened. With the marriage, Felicia will be heading to Titanus. You'll never have to worry about her or your bastard son again."

"How dare you!"

Julius, at the peak of rage, stormed out of the room and up one of the staircases. Constantine, with anger in his eyes, stared at Cagius.

"You knew of this!" cried Constantine.

"Yes, he confessed it to me some time ago."

A smile crept across Constantine's face.

"I would never ask you to go against your brother. Do not fail Julius in these negotiations or else I will strip you of every privilege. Now centurion Darius, getting the boy out of the palace and into the wilderness may be good for him. Select our finest men for the cohort; nothing is going to happen to my sons."

"Don't you have any symbol of victory for brave son here?" pleaded Marguerite.

"Must I reward every legate that diligently and exceptionally performs their duties in the service of the caesar?"

Understanding smirks came across the faces of Constantine and Cagius, as the Caesar retired to his study.

"Your father does love you, Cagius," said Marguerite.

"Mom, trust me that back-handed compliment is the only praise I need from my father."

"A right attitude!" joked James Darius. "I remember this hot-headed legate who seemed pretty damned cavalier when it came to rushing off to fight the empire. You and your father are so alike it's scary."

"An interesting observation, my centurion friend," reasoned Matthias Gravius. "Since Julius is going to assume the throne of Central Acadia, Cagius will become the rightful heir to the Napolitan Imperium."

"That's way too far down the road for me," deflected Cagius. "Mom, if you'll excuse me, I think I'll just try to calm down Julius."

Cagius walked up the staircase, and Marguerite also departed, leaving Darius and Gravius alone in the room.

"I expect no opposition from you on this," argued James.

"What makes you think I would stand in your way?" countered Matthias.

"I know your mind and how you sometimes place your own interests ahead of the caesar's, especially at the senate."

"I am nothing but loyal to the caesar. We both seek the same goal, centurion, just by different means."

"I wonder what that goal truly is."

"We will see in time, but we both support Julius's ascension, and that is what matters for now."

"Then I'd better make sure he stays safe on this mission or else it will be both of our ends."

"Precisely."

From the shadows of the room above the corridor, Valentine watched the two men leave. A serving girl stood there. He mouthed the words, "Follow him," pointing in the direction of Judge Gravius. Bowing to the spy master, the girl pursued her target.

Cagius found his brother in one of the training rooms. He was assaulting the training dummy with a sword he had picked up. Despite his rage, his technique was still flawless. Knowing it was the only way to draw his brother's attention; Cagius ripped out his trident and struck the dummy.

"Julius, what are you doing?"

"Anger management!"

Intensifying his blows, Julius spun and sliced the head off of the dummy.

"I can see that... perhaps you would take some brotherly advice. Of course, I would prefer if you would put the sword down first."

"And?" demanded Julius as he sheathed his sword.

"You're in a horrible dilemma, but you have a mission to take care of."

"I know, brother, this is my opportunity."

"What opportunity?"

"Political capital, my dear legate. Father is right. I cannot get out of this marriage contract with Marie. However, there is precedent in Central Acadia for the taking of a concubine."

"Julius, you don't think you could..."

"It's all based on political capital, Cagius. Succeed in this mission, and I can buy anything I want. Let the marriage to Marie be as fake as the Acadian Nobles; Cedric has already said he won't draw swords against me. I have the backing of Napolitan and Evengard. Who would dare move against me? "

"Bro, this is a terrible idea. You can't share love between two women. Look what happened to Stephen."

"Who said anything about sharing? I will take my wife to be my concubine and I will take my concubine as my wife. I must only put a son in Marie's belly and the technology is ahead of the curve in that area."

"Julius," pleaded a crestfallen Cagius, "you have to promise me that you're not going to do anything stupid. Right now, I'm afraid you're blinded by love and that blindness is going to cause you to do something you'd never do. Remember, bro, I am not going to let you become something you're not."

Sympathetically, Julius put his right arm to his younger brother's heart. Staring at him with his green eyes, Julius eased his brother's fears.

"Cagius, I don't know what I did to deserve a brother and legate as loyal as you. You have to nothing to worry about. You and I are always going to stand on the same side."

"Okay, Julius. It's just that I'm a history buff and Phillius Draconius commentaries on political capital sound an awful lot like the arguments you just made."

"James always griped about you reading those history texts when you should have been relaxing. Cagius, you are awfully smart; it's a shame you spend all your time on chivalry."

"You have to measure the important things in life—love and virtue are extremely important."

"You kidder!"

Julius punched his brother in the arm. Not too keen about being hit, Cagius launched a retaliatory punch. Staring at each other with playful rage, the two boys wrestled each other to the floor. The noise caused Marguerite to enter the room with a smile on her face.

"It's so nice to have you boys home once more," observed Marguerite. "Too bad nothing ever changes."

She separated the two of them by grabbing them by their ears.

Titan Embassy, Central Acadia, Three Rotations Later

"Whether by elf or kin, there shall be no unsanctioned training of magic beyond the guidance and direction of the guild."

—The fourth tenet of the Wizards Guild

Exuding the same meticulousness that accompanied his military style, Cedric's office in the Titan Embassy served as his base of operations. A vast array of military novels, journals, and periodicals were stocked in bookshelves around his desk. A wet bar faced the opposite direction of his desk near the door where a large decanter of brandy was present along with some other liquors. Blocking whoever entered, two royal guards stationed themselves across from his desk. Cedric's desk was completely clear, save for a small computer on the left side. Sitting at his side, Keiko watched her master scribble a writ of assassination. Colin Wilkins walked past the guards and saluted.

"You wished to see me, master?" asked Colin.

Cedric said "yes" without lifting his eyes from the parchment. He scribbled his signature at the bottom of the page before tightly rolling up the scroll. Removing a black and red case from the bottom drawer, the prince carefully placed the scroll inside. He put his signet ring to the edge of his desk where a wax well was located. With the wax affixed, the seal of Titanus would absolve the carrier of the crime of murder. Raising his eyes, he handed the case to Colin.

176

"Another writ?" questioned Colin.

"Wilhelm discovered another one of the Nephilim hiding in the city," explained Cedric. "There is business that might be related to this current infiltration. I won't risk more Nephilim loose in this city. I want him disposed of; Christian says he can be found near the Wizards Guild. While you are at the guild, investigate for any unusual happenings."

"I'm not exactly comfortable with spying."

"Christian is right now seeing to the safety of an important package that is being delivered to Verian, so I need you to do some double duty. Can you handle it?"

"The enemies of Titanus shall breathe their last in the talons of the lunar falcon," quoted Colin as his bowed before leaving the room.

"I always get chills when he's in my presence," shivered Keiko.

"I trained him to be intimidating. Acadians think twice about their plots against me, knowing I have an able bodyguard and someone who would be more than willing to avenge my death. Now, since I have been nothing but magnanimous since I've come home from the war, what can I do for you, Keiko?"

"Lord Cedric, I believe it is time to discuss my role pending your final vows with Princess Cassandra," cried a teary Keiko. "I do not wish to leave your service or remain at this embassy without you."

"If you wish to return to your people, Keiko, I understand. If you desire, I am willing to have you serve as seneschal during my reign due to your extensive experience here at the embassy."

"My lord, I humbly beg not to be thrust from your service. I will gladly accept such a post when the time comes. Master, I'm so happy!

The sylph happily kissed Cedric on the cheek. Noting the time on his pocket watch, Cedric put on his jacket and cape.

"Time to make my grand entrance. Keiko, please go down to the kitchen and arrange a picnic lunch."

"Are we heading over to the castle?"

"Shortly but I have to pick up a package at the city gates first. Meet me in the embassy courtyard in five minutes, I may need some backup."

Approaching the city from the Royal Highway, Hippolyte, Minerva, and Stryker finally arrived at their destination. Observably weary from their long and dangerous journey, Stryker stayed stalwart as their defender.

"Verian, we've finally made it," said a relieved Hippolyte.

"You have to admit, it was nice of that Titan patrol to put us back on the right road when we got lost," interjected Minerva.

"Grandpa always called them honorable enemies. I still suspect it was a little convenient that they happened to show up after we got lost for a few hours."

"Well, we made it this far, sister!"

"Let's go finish our mission."

The two girls rode for the city gate with Stryker on their hooves. Two halberdiers guarded the entrance to the city. Snapping to attention, the guards suspected trouble was on the way. The young, confused first halberdier turned to his more grizzled fellow sentry, wondering what he should do.

"Wolf Tribe..." observed the young halberdier.

"Could be trouble; stay on your guard," ordered the older halberdier.

The halberdiers crossed their halberds at the entrance to the gate of the city. Pulling up short of the gate, Hippolyte was irritated by the rude reception.

"Halt!" shouted the younger halberdier. "No members of the tribes may enter the city of Verian without the king's permission."

"We are expected; my sister and I are the official delegation of the Tribal Confederation," answered Hippolyte.

"Sorry, little girls, we're not buying that one," said the older halberdier.

The halberdiers positioned their weapons into a fighting stance.

"What do we do, sis?" asked Minerva.

"I don't think grandpa intended to have us fight our way through, and we can't just go home."

Gritting her teeth, Minerva hadn't expected her impressions of knights to be shattered before she entered Verian. When she started to shout, Hippolyte worried about the consequences.

"Stupid steel bellies! Why don't you just check your orders!"

"We know our orders!" retaliated the younger halberdier.

The older halberdier turned back to the city and saw Cedric approaching on an unarmored Jericho with Keiko in tow. Breathing a sigh of relief, he figured the tribes fear of Cedric Rhone would end the standoff without violence. The guard pulled his younger companion aside.

"What a break! The marshal commandant is here."

Cedric rode over to the gate. Presented with the sword master in his civilian attire and indoctrinated with stories of a wretched monster, Minerva and Hippolyte only observed a handsome prince approaching them.

"Marshal, you're just in time. We're having problems with these girls from the tribe," explained the older halberdier. "They do not understand the laws of Acadia and the city of Verian. They refuse to leave."

"Perhaps your sword would teach them some much-needed manners!" boasted the younger halberdier.

Dismounting, Cedric walked toward the girls and looked them over. He smiled and slightly nodded his head. The girls had never seen a "steel-bellied" noble take such action before.

"You match Colonel DeVries's descriptions perfectly—two teenage girls in wolf skin protected by a large gray wolf," greeted Cedric. "Hippolyte and Minerva, daughters of Chief of Chiefs Aramas of the Wolf Tribe, I bid you welcome to Verian."

"But they... they are of the tribes!" yelled the younger halberdier.

"They are the official representatives of the Tribal Confederation and have urgent business with the king. Deny them entrance into the city no longer, and offer your apologies for your rudeness."

Perceiving a flash of malice in Cedric's eyes and words, the girls thought that the guards were going to relieve themselves. Before he had turned around, the guards bowed before Hippolyte and Minerva.

"We offer our sincerest apologies for our ignorance," pleaded the younger halberdier.

"We need to be careful, but that is no excuse. We welcome you warmly into Verian, Lady Hippolyte and Lady Minerva," regretted the older halberdier.

"Lady Minerva. I like the sound of that," boasted Minerva.

"I'll provide you with an escort to the castle," declared Cedric. "I don't want any more 'accidents' to happen."

"Thank you, sir knight," said Hippolyte, remembering her protocol.

The two girls crossed into the city. As Stryker passed the two guards, he gave a sudden growl. It caused the guards to fall over, and the wolf snickered as he entered into the city. Cedric smiled as he straddled Jericho. Incredulous stares followed the girls as they rode through the causeways of Verian. Uninterested with prejudice, Minerva had her undivided attention on the gondolas ferrying people through the canals. Every once in a while she would wave at the people in the boats. Sometimes they would wave back, encouraging Minerva to do it more. Hippolyte was more focused on Keiko.

"I thought the sylphs remained in the deep old forests?" queried Hippolyte. "I never heard of one serving in the capacity of a guardian."

"I am for the master," exclaimed Keiko, laughing cutely.

"She's very good at running an embassy and very helpful in a fight," stated Cedric. "You'd be surprised at her hidden talents.

"Against the tribes?" asked Minerva.

"Yes, and against the empire as well."

"You shouldn't be so rude to his lordship," chided Keiko.

"Steel bellies are steel bellies!" exclaimed Minerva.

"Steel belly?" asked a puzzled Keiko.

"A term of affection from my people for your people," joked Hippolyte.

"It sounds more flattering than barbarian," quipped Cedric.

"Right!" agreed Minerva. "You know you're a lot nicer than most steel bellies we meet."

"Minerva!" scolded Hippolyte.

"Well, how many have you truly met?"

"My sister and I were refugees in the last war, moving from one village to the next. There was one alliance warrior who saved our lives at the Terrace River, but we never saw his face."

"Well, we also know about the Prime Eagle by reputation, but that's about all," added Minerva.

"That's true, but it's difficult to get such a monster out of our minds."

They have no idea who I am, thought Cedric. He merely mustered a grimace and a sigh.

"You're Titan, aren't you?" inquired Hippolyte.

"Affirmative."

"It figures that you would be the only one willing to escort us," reasoned Hippolyte. "No matter how hard I try to avoid you, I keep bumping into your people on this trip."

"Well, allow me to offer you some friendly advice: make sure you stay clear of the Temple of the Divine Saints and the Wizards Guild. They don't take kindly to the tribes. If you need supplies or anything else, we'll be happy to offer you such hospitality at the Titan embassy in the southern end of the city. If you wish, we could also provide hospitality for your guardian."

Looking at Stryker, Hippolyte realized a royal castle was no place for her wolf. Despite his whelps, the wolf knew he was never going to get his way.

"That may be a good idea. I don't think you'd fit in well at the castle, boy. Be good and wait at the embassy."

She dismounted and bent down to Stryker. Grabbing her companion around his collar, Hippolyte hugged him tightly. A final lick to face was greeted with a final rub, Stryker obediently pranced into the embassy courtyard.

"We appreciate the kindness," said Minerva.

"It's all part of the sacred laws of hospitality," replied Keiko. "We hold them dear."

After Hippolyte got back on her horse, Cedric and the girls broke for the castle. Servants waited for them to arrive, so they could take the horse. Realizing their time together was over, Hippolyte prepared to say her goodbyes.

"You didn't have to come out this way for our expense."

"I have my business at the castle as well," explained Cedric. "It was no trouble. Besides, I prefer to keep conflicts in this city to a minimum."

"I hope the hosts of this castle are as nice as you are," said Minerva

Surprising Cedric, the young wolf tribe girl grabbed him around the waist. The sword master laughed at her affection and gave her a pat on the head. When she let go, Hippolyte bowed before him.

"Thank you, and can we know your name so we can kindly speak to our grandfather about you?" inquired Hippolyte.

"I am Prince Cedric Rhone, the Prime Eagle in your tongue. As you can see, the legends about my height are greatly exaggerated."

Awkwardly laughing at first, the girls stared at the sincerity in Cedric's face. Realizing he was serious, a pale Minerva took a step back in fear and Hippolyte blinked.

"No... you can't be..." stammered Hippolyte.

"Please wish my blood brother Aramas long life and prosperity by his custom. Good day, ladies, and good luck. It was an honor to meet and escort you. If you need anything, do not hesitate to impose on the hospitality of the Titan embassy."

Cedric bowed his head to the girls, turned on his heel, and entered the castle. Keiko smiled and bowed as well, floating with him.

"Hippolyte!" screamed an excited Minerva.

"No, I won't believe it!" denied Hippolyte.

"We just met the Prime Eagle and lived... no one in the tribe is going to believe this story."

"He was so nice to us... but the legend... He wasn't tall enough!"

Minerva looked slyly at her sister.

"Don't tell me you're in love with him!"

Hippolyte got very angry and defensive.

"You were flirting with him, too!"

"I'm not the one who blushed!"

"I'm not the one that hugged him!"

Hippolyte and Minerva were nose to nose. Breathing deeply, the girls composed themselves. Blushing heavily, they shook off the embarrassment of not only flirting with the enemy but at getting into a screaming tirade in front of bewildered servants.

"Stop it! We have a job to do," ordered Hippolyte.

"Right."

The girls walked to the entrance of the castle. Hippolyte grabbed her sister around the shoulder and the two started to laugh.

"He was really handsome," joked Minerva.

"Nothing like the legends at all."

Walker was standing at the entrance waiting for them. As they reached him, he clicked his heels together and bowed to them in a full salute. Quickly forgetting about her first knightly escort, Minerva focused all her affections on Walker.

"Lady Hippolyte, Lady Minerva, I bid you welcome to Castle Acadia; we've been expecting you," greeted Walker. "My name is Jonathan Walker, Lord Captain of Central Acadia. I trust Prince Rhone provided a gracious escort."

"He did," responded Hippolyte.

"Excellent. If you would follow me, please, I will take you to meet with Count Maximilian Luminas. We can proceed to King Stephen Acadia from there. Do you have any questions?"

"Are all Acadian knights as handsome and nice as you are?" asked Minerva.

Walker blushed slightly at the question.

"MINERVA! STOP IT!" interjected Hippolyte.

"Sorry, sis, I couldn't help myself," apologized Minerva.

"Please lead the way, Lord Walker."

In the east wing, Cassandra was standing in the middle of a large room. Holding her uncle's staff in her hands, Cassandra was observed by Cerwin from above the danger zone. Working on her needlepoint behind him, Felicia passed the time until the training was over. Cassandra was dressed in a black leotard and stood barefoot. Moving his hands like a puppeteer, the master-mage created eight targets that had the shape of three dimensional diamonds in front of her. They began to move perfectly with the movements of his hands.

"Now!" screamed Cerwin.

Closing her eyes and chanting, Cassandra formed spirals of fire around her body. Upon opening them, her green irises sparked with fire. Yelling the elf incantation "blaze wall," waves of fire flowed in four directions, incinerating he targets. Not satisfied, Cerwin waved his hands and more targets formed, but these diamonds had small eyes on them that could fire ice projectiles. Using her magic barrier to deflect these icy spikes, Cassandra performed a series of gymnastic maneuvers to get herself into a better position to attack. Cassandra shouted the incantation for "icicle" first, which fired sharp ice projections at some of the targets. A second incantation, "air blast," produced a wind attack that blew the remaining targets into the walls.

"Time!" shouted Cerwin.

Spinning the staff into an upward position, Cassandra calmed the magical rage burning inside of her.

"Very good. The use of the level three fire spell is a great improvement," observed Cerwin. "I'm glad to see your hangover hasn't affected your spell casting either."

I've practiced night and morning even when you were gone," retorted Cassandra. "Uncle, just because I couldn't practice two rotations ago, didn't mean that I wouldn't be ready this morning."

"I have something for you."

Using a simple levitation spell, Cassandra floated up to the balcony where her uncle stood. Cerwin waved his hands. He created a large book that floated into Cassandra's hands. It was bound in silver lining with blue rune markings etched all over the covers. It didn't take a master-mage to realize the book was old and precious.

"I've never seen a spell book like this," observed Cassandra.

"This is a special book, child, the *Book of Rune*," lectured Cerwin. "It is used in the training of Rune Mistresses, the most powerful of sorceresses. In this book are a series of spells that will not only inflict damage but also severely cripple your opponent's abilities. Only the most disciplined magic users can obtain this class, but you are special, my dearest. Only when you master these techniques will I reward you with your own staff."

"Thank you, Uncle," said Cassandra as she hugged her uncle tightly.

"Of course, there does remain one small issue, a growing concern about the partnership that is about to be formed," joked Cerwin. "It's bad enough that your fiancé has embraced a dark path but an evil sorceress as well—what terrors have I unleashed on this world?"

"Cerwin, I hold the light and the darkness in my heart," countered Cedric.

Cerwin turned to see Cedric standing in the alcove of the room with Keiko.

"Good afternoon, darling. Come to see me practice," asked Cassandra.

"Unfortunately I only made it in time for the grand finale; I've been having a busy morning."

"Want to spar?" Cassie playfully teased.

"I'm afraid you'd have me at a disadvantage, since white magic is primarily used for defensive purposes," explained Cedric. "Actually, I've come by to ask if you are available to go for a ride and picnic lunch."

Pleading with her eyes, Cassandra turned to her uncle.

"Am I?"

"We've trained enough for today. We'll start again early tomorrow. It's very important that you don't get drunk again today!"

Pretending to weep, the princess hung her head. Still the thought of rising so early without breaking her fast was not an attractive proposition.

"Can't I sleep-in one day?"

"We have two revolutions of catch-up to work on."

Setting down her needlepoint, Felicia interrupted the conversation.

"My lady, I have anticipated the prince's arrival. Your riding clothes are laid out behind the screen for you."

"Thank you. No peeking you two!"

Gathering her riding clothes, Cassandra walked behind the dressing shade. Slightly perturbed by accusation of peeping, Cedric turned his attention to Felicia. The handmaiden had dreaded this moment and one look in his eyes showed the sword master's thoughts were weighing heavily on him. Felicia tried to steer the topic of conversation away from what he was going to say.

"Mistress has been very happy since your return, my lord."

"I don't want you to be coy with me, Felicia. I am well aware of your pain."

"We must all deal with our pains."

"Don't think me a fool. I know exactly who you are. I can see the drawn bows of hundreds between you and Julius. I want to help you."

"I fear the path I have chosen has brought me beyond salvation."

"I can't save you. However, I've heard some very positive things concerning your son. We would be honored to have him at the academy."

"It is a generous offer, my lord. However, I must speak with him first about this."

"You are as wise as I expected to mention the son and not the father. I expected you to take your time, but know right now that forces are moving against you quickly. I don't have a heart made of out stone, and I want to save your boy. When you were pressed into this service, you never expected to fall in love. Now I'm afraid the truth of it will plunge us into full civil war."

Felicia began to well up but kept her composure. Suspecting that Christian DeVries might have something to do with Cedric's knowledge of her situation, she refused to press him further on it."

"I appreciate your kindness, my lord."

As they finished their discussion, Cedric slipped her an envelope. From behind the dressing shade, Cassandra emerged in a black riding outfit as if she were headed out for equestrian events with her crop under her left arm. The grin of her face proved she was not privy to heartbroken conversation between her fiancé and handmaiden. Devotedly, Felicia rose and fixed the princess's hair underneath her riding helmet.

"Are you ready, Cedric?" asked Cassandra.

Felicia's face suddenly turned to panic. She put her hand on Cassandra's shoulder.

"Oh dear, I had nearly forgotten," said Felicia. "Your highness, I am needed in the castle, and Lord Walker is detained. There is no one who can serve as your chaperone!"

Her beaming smile turning sour, Cassandra beseeched her Uncle to follow them. Not wanting to get involved, Cerwin faked a limp on his left leg. Flutteringly proudly, Keiko bowed the princess.

"Your highness, I am more than capable of handling such a duty,"

"Mistress Keiko, you are Lord Cedric's loyal servant," argued Felicia. "I'm not sure if you will serve as an appropriate defender of virtue."

Keiko began to cry and sag at Felicia's comments. She was very hurt and couldn't understand why the princess's handmaiden distrusted her so. Fearing she had hurt the poor fae's feelings, Felicia silenced her tongue. Acting as intermediary, Cerwin reasserted himself.

"Felicia, Keiko is more than capable as serving as the young couple's chaperone. She even carries a missile spell, a large burst of a white magic discharge. It is very effective as both an attack and as a blinder."

"Besides, I'm almost twenty now, Felicia. I don't think a chaperone is necessary anymore. Do you think I really have anything to worry about with Lord Crusader the Pure over here?"

Everyone laughed at Cedric's expense. Taking Cassandra by one arm and having Keiko latch onto the other arm, Cedric left the room.

Walker provided his escort in the west wing of the Castle. Forced to stop at every picture and suit of armor, he waited patiently as Hippolyte and Minerva took a personal tour of Castle Acadia.

"Are all these people chiefs of Central Acadia?" asked Hippolyte.

"Despite our relatively short existence, many have sat on the throne of Central Acadia," added Walker. "We are going to be entering the room of the king's advisor, Count Maximilian Luminas. I think you ladies should be warned ahead of time that Count Luminas is a vampire."

Hearing the heels of the girl's boots no longer clicking the ground, Walker turned and comforted the young wolf tribe princesses.

"Don't worry. Everyone in Central Acadia has only ever seen him drink animal blood. He seems to have a certain penchant for swine. It's a good thing too; the cabal the Titans might raise against the count would be very unpleasant."

Breathing a sigh of relief, the sisters followed Walker into the Count's private office. Drawn shades over two small windows near the ceiling, necessitated a large chandelier in the center of the ceiling. Lavishly decorated with the tribal and imperial spoils of war, the sisters found themselves biting their tongues in disgust. A dignified portrait of the count hung on the northern wall just above the desk of Count Luminas. His desk was as neat as Cedric's desk, though he refused to use a computer at all.

"Count Luminas, I've brought our visiting dignitaries," announced Walker.

Count Luminas stood from his desk. Walking over to the girls, he bowed to them deeply. Despite his courteousness, the girls were made uneasy by his red eyes. They reacted as if he were digging into their very minds.

"Aramas's granddaughters, I've been expecting you," greeted Luminas. "I believe you have a package for me."

"I was instructed to give this to King Stephen Acadia," countered Hippolyte as she gripped the pouch tightly.

"I am the king's advisor. I will take whatever documents you provide me to him."

"I'm sorry, but I must give them to him personally. It is the way of our people."

Luminas continued to be patient and calm in his tone. Use of his powers of persuasion on Hippolyte would get him what he wanted; however with Walker present, the Count decided that the diplomatic route was his best option.

"You seem to misunderstand," reasoned Luminas. "Here in Central Acadia, I am in charge of the tribal negotiations. Thus, all matters pertaining to the documents will be handled by me. I assure you that I have no intention of betraying your grandfather before the king."

"Misunderstand?" shouted an angry Minerva. "We understand enough to know that if we were at Castle Titan, Queen Civilia would be meeting with us herself!"

Hippolyte shot an angry look at her sister.

"Stop it, Minerva!" shouted Hippolyte.

Minerva shirked down in her sister's presence and remained silent. Hippolyte turned back to Luminas. Boasting a large smile, Walker put his hand on Minerva's shoulder. Even Luminas had to admit his defeat.

"I think she's got us," joked Walker.

"Yes, a very worldly child indeed," praised Luminas. "Since it would be fruitless to argue with you further, I believe I have no choice but to honor your wishes."

Luminas walked over to his desk and pushed an intercom button.

"Your majesty, it appears I have two guests who insist on seeing you."

Luminas released the button and walked back over to the girls. He made eye contact with Walker, who nodded and sighed. The girls knew there was going to be trouble. Walking in front of the girls, the lord captain spoke in a conciliatory tone.

"I'm sorry, but as a security precaution, I'm going to have to ask you to give up your weapons before I allow you to see the king."

The girls groaned at first but knew there was no other way. Minerva stared at Walker and was immediately ready to trust him. Both girls reached behind their back and in their boots to surrender their daggers. Minerva gave up her bow and quiver of arrows while Hippolyte, with great reluctance, surrendered her spear. The runic letters engraved into the shaft caught the sharp eye of the knight.

"I was unaware the dwarves made weapons for the Wolf Tribe." commented Walker.

"Its name is Gungir," explained Hippolyte. "My grandfather gave it to me less than year ago. He said King Frederick Rhone presented it to our tribe as thanks for our participation in the War of the First Alliance. I think the king hoped it would end the violence between our peoples."

"Really? I didn't know that," said a puzzled Luminas.

Recounting the stories his father had told him, Walker remembered the tales of strange ore that had been found deep in Lion's Peak after the end of the Great War. The dwarf kingdoms that were allowed to live were forced to forge this material into what would be known as the legendary weapons. The known legendary weapons were the swords: Ragnarok (Cedric),

Excalibur (Julius), Sigmund (Walker), Enhancer (Amuro), Deathbringer (Colin); the daggers: Orichalcums (Christian), Dawn and Dusk (Valentine), the spears Göttin-Speer (Cecilia), Dragonsbane (Cagius); and the bow Apollo (Malcolm). Rumors persisted that the dwarves still had some of this mysterious ore available to forge. The four waited as King Stephen arrived, surrounded by Jonas Marimon and the other "saints." His temper raging, Jonas refused to give the girls quarter.

"Get up against the wall so I can pat you down for hidden weapons."

"They surrendered their weapons freely, Jonas," countered Walker.

"And you know this for certain, Walker?"

"I'm not going to allow you to conduct an investigation to satisfy your own ego. We should receive them with the proper respect we gave all foreign dignitaries."

Stephen sighed as he watched his two best knights at each other's throats.

"That's enough. Jonas, I thank you for your concern, but, if Walker got them to surrender their weapons peacefully, it is enough for me. Ladies, I am King Stephen Acadia. I believe you have some information for me."

Hippolyte nodded and bowed in the presence of the Acadian King.

"I am Hippolyte, daughter of Chief Aramas of the Wolf Tribe, Chief of Chiefs in the Tribal Confederation. I present you with this packet."

Hippolyte went to give it to the king. Forced to stop by Jonas' grabbing her arm, the tension in the room rose.

"What do you think you're doing, barbarian!"

"Leave her alone!" shouted Minerva.

Just as Minerva was going to intercede, Walker stepped in and shoved Jonas away from Hippolyte. Minerva looked and noticed his left hand clutching the hilt of his sword. More infatuated then before, she decided then that Walker was the knight of her fantasies.

"Have you no respect?" asked Walker.

"Not for barbarians, you worthless bastard!" cursed Jonas.

"Jonas!" screamed Stephen with an edge on his voice. "I believe I've had enough of your antics for one afternoon. You will treat these dignitaries with same respect as you would an Acadian."

Jonas just grumbled as Hippolyte handed the package to Stephen. Breaking the tribal seal, the king took the documents. After handing them to Luminas, Minerva rolled her eyes.

"These are the negotiated terms—they ask us to settle in three moons time at... the Ruins of Istle Hills," read Luminas.

"The Istle Hills?" questioned Stephen with shock and fear in his voice.

"My God!" prayed Walker.

"I should have known those barbarians would perform a stunt like this," taunted Jonas, staring at the girls coldly.

The girls were surprised at the reaction of the Acadians in the room. Stephen shook his head.

"I assume we don't have a choice," pleaded Stephen.

"I am instructed to leave immediately if you do not agree to the terms as a whole," responded Hippolyte.

"I guess we don't have a choice, your majesty," reconciled Luminas. "I recommend we agree to the terms as stated or we risk Titanus returning to the table."

"Very well," agreed Stephen. "We will attend your meeting. I'll have the castle servants prepare quarters for you."

"If it's all the same, King Stephen, if you just give us some fresh supplies, we'll be on our way back," stated Hippolyte. "I think we've caused enough trouble."

"Didn't your grandfather tell you?" asked Stephen.

"Tell us what?"

"You are to remain here at Castle Acadia as our guests until the negotiations are complete," explained Luminas. "Your grandfather fears that someone may wish to take advantage of this situation."

Minerva hung her head as Luminas handed Hippolyte the documents. The heir to the Wolf Tribe confirmed her fears.

"Minerva, it looks like we're stuck here."

"I give you my word that you will be treated the same way we treat all of our foreign dignitaries," affirmed Stephen. "If you have any special needs, please don't hesitate to ask one of my daughters, Cassandra or Marie. They will be more than willing to assist you with clothes or anything else you need. Well, I have much work to do. Count Luminas, I'll trust you to deliver the necessary information to Fort Orion."

"I will leave with Captain Walker when Julius and Amuro arrive at the fort."

"Excellent, I wish to do a troop review on the morning of your departure. We could use a good morale boost."

"I'll make sure preparations are made."

"Hippolyte, Minerva, it was a pleasure to make your acquaintance." Thank you. Ladies, I hope you will enjoy Acadian hospitality. Good day."

Stephen left the room with the saints. Jonas remained behind for a moment and confronted Hippolyte, once more poking his finger toward her.

"Watch your step, barbarian. In Verian, I decide who lives and dies!" said Jonas before he turned and left.

"Geez, what an asshole," commented Minerva.

"MINERVA!" shouted Hippolyte, as Luminas and Walker started laughing.

"She's right; he is an asshole," quipped Walker. "All right, ladies, I'll show you to your quarters; you can take your weapons with you now. Count, I'll make preparations for our departure with the cuirassiers."

"Thank you, Walker. I want to pour over these documents some more."

The three left the room. Laughing as he started to read the documents, Luminas enjoyed his favorite swine blood.

"The Ruins of Istle Hills. My dear Aramas, you are a shrewder tactician than even I gave you credit for."

Far away from the politics of Castle Acadia, the bustling city of Verian conducted its midday business. People of all classes returned from midday services at the temple. Watching them like a falcon, Colin Wilkins leaned against the Wizards Guild target targeting his prey. Bored with the duty, he recited his daily litany.

"I am death incarnated on Terminus Mundus. I am not burdened by emotion. I feel no remorse for what I do. By the power of my blade, I serve my master. I am death incarnated on Terminus Mundus. I am not burdened by emotion. I feel no remorse for what I do. By the power of my blade, I serve my master."

Target approaching, the assassin silenced himself. Even though he wasn't a divikin, Colin had been trained to recognize duco-mutatios and other agents of hell through their disguises. What surprised Wilkins was the fact that this particular Nephilim agent made no effort to hide himself. Wiping the sweat from his copper skin, he moved about the city in brown tattered robes. Slowly at first, Colin matched the foot movement of his prey. The Nephilim's eyes widened when he knew he was being followed. Taking a deep breath before he turned around, he watched Colin unlatch his sword and put down his mask.

"So the wretched 'La Morte Angelus' sends his favorite dog to kill me. I guess I should be honored. My only concern is that you found me so quickly."

"It wasn't hard since you chose to stick out like a sore thumb. Anyway, you know what's going to happen here, so do yourself a favor and don't run. I can't grant you a quick death when I'm angry."

"I won't run from you. I was sent here because I have a message for your master."

"Really?"

"'La Morte Angelus' cannot prevent the storm that is coming! The fate of the west has been sealed! Brothers shall spill their own blood! Neither God nor prophecy can save this world. The Ragnarok has come to its end!"

"Master Cedric will not be defeated. As sure as I cut you down here, he will destroy your plans. You have been judged!"

Colin drew his blade and sliced without hesitation or emotion. Despite knowing he was going to die, the Nephilim hadn't anticipated the speed and power of the attack. Horrified innocent bystanders started crying 'murder' at the sight of the body cut in half. Nonchalantly, Colin went about cleaning Deathbringer on the tattered robes. Guards rushed to the scene but the assassin had the writ waiting for them.

"Stop! You've violated the law," ordered the first guard.

"The writ will explain everything," said Colin.

"Don't bother... its Colin Wilkins..." identified the other guard.

"Sorry, Sir Colin. I got carried away."

"I take no offense, you have a job to do."

"I just wish your boss would give us a heads up when he plans something like this," pleaded the first guard.

"As per alliance law, the writ is sufficient," explained Colin. "There seems to be a lot of security here today."

"The Wizards Guild is having a conference today," announced the second guard.

"Indeed, well, if you gentlemen don't need me for anything else, I will be on my way," said Colin as he handed the writ to the guards to make it legal.

"Of course, sir."

Watching Colin disappear into an alley, the middle-aged guards stared at one another.

"You don't suppose that the marshal thinks there's something going on?" nervously questioned the first guard.

"My family is already packed. I think you should get your family out of Verian too. I don't know but ever since 'La Morte Angelus' returned I've got this feeling of inevitable destruction," prophesized the second guard.

Lost in thought, the guards returned to their posts. After discovering he wasn't followed, Colin Wilkins opened a briefcase in the alley. Inside the briefcase was a portable computer and transmitter. Colin took a pair of headphones and put them over his ears.

What are these wizards up to? thought Colin.

The inside of the guild hall reflected a huge, circular room securely locked from all sides. Banners hung from corners of the room representing the black magic disciplines: Elemental Destruction, Summoning, Alteration, Mysticism, Enchantment, and Alchemy. Carved into the columns of the room were the symbols for white magic, tribal magic, and necromancy. Wizards, sages, witches, and sorceresses numbering 118 gathered inside of the halls of the guild. Descending down the spiral staircase of the upper library, Celius was greeted with applause. The guild master had gray hair, a long gray beard, and was dressed in dark blue robes lined with gold trim unique among his colleagues. Filled with knowledge, his deep blue eyes made sure that all of his subordinates were present.

"All hail Arch Mage Celius!"

"Greetings, my fellow guild masters. Since the arrangement of the marriage of King Stephen Acadia's two daughters to outsiders, we in the guild have sought a means of an open rebellion," announced Celius to the cheering mages. "Our long wait has finally come to an end. Too long have we allowed our so-called 'allies' to control the destiny of Central Acadia. Select people, elites are the only ones who should shepherd the flocks to a greater Terminus Mundus. Too long have we been forced to swallow the unsanctioned training of magic by those outside the guild. Under our own noses, we have watched the daughter of the king herself being trained by an elf. No longer shall we endure such insults! I would like to introduce you to an individual who will make our dreams reality. May I present the leader of the Nephilim, Basarabas, and his associate, Abaddon."

Casting a spell, two mage guild guides created a star-shaped portal in the middle of the guild hall. Freely transporting into the guild, Basarabas and Abaddon were greeted with silence. Celius did not share the trepidation of his fellow mages; instead he warmly welcomed them with firm handshakes. Impressed by the powers of his new allies, Abaddon's mood improved.

"It's good to see you in this hall once more Master Basarabas." greeted Celius. "May I present to you the other guild masters from across the provinces of Central Acadia. Lord Abaddon, I am pleased to finally meet you in person."

"Charmed," replied Abaddon.

"The guild is quite pleased with your proposal and know that you have our complete support in the matter."

"It's easier than having to destroy all of you," taunted Abaddon.

"How do we know this individual can do for us what he says he can?" challenged a wizard who stepped forward.

"Mind your tongue!" shouted Celius.

"I would prefer to see a demonstration of this one's power."

Chanting, the rogue wizard made a fireball appear on the top of his staff. Unconcerned, Abaddon signaled for Basarabas and Celius to move away. The wizard ended his chant by shouting, "fireball." Lifting his right hand, Abaddon stopped the launched attack in its track. Satisfied the fallen angel could deliver on his powers, the guild members in the room applauded.

"Amazing, you dispersed the attack without a spell. What kind of a mercenary are you?" asked the challenging wizard.

"The type of mercenary that you need," boasted Abaddon calmly as he began to generate dark energy in his hand.

"What are you doing?" questioned the wizard with fear in his voice.

"I do not suffer fools. You asked for a demonstation of my prowess and I intend to leave you satisfied. Your ignorance and arrogance have no place in my army."

Tendrils of dark energy emerged from Abaddon's fingers. To no avail, the challenging wizard threw up a magic shield. Tearing through the shield like tissue paper, the energy ripped his chest and disintegrated his heart. There was mumbling and screaming among the other members as their dead associate fell to the ground.

"Let that serve as a warning to all those who would doubt my powers," challenged Abaddon. "Your guild will now be my eyes and ears in Central Acadia. I'm relying on you to deal with problems as they arise. Basarabas will be your contact."

"I need you to make sure the guild guide remains open to us," requested Basarabas. "I will not risk entering this city by conventional means with the agents of Titanus watching."

"Yes," agreed Celius as he stroked his beard. "La Morte Angelus remains in the city, and while the Lunar Falcon prowls the streets, no one is safe. May I inquire as to your next move, Lord Abaddon?"

"Yes, I have some business in the wilderness that demands my attention. You will provide me with Acadian armor and weapons. If any of your colleagues are skilled in mind manipulation, I have use for them in the telecommunications building here in Verian. As my plan unfolds, I will require much more of you."

"As you wish, my lord," said Celius.

"We don't wish to overstay our welcome; let's get out of here," suggested Basarabas. "Also, we'll take the dead wizard's body, the demonkin necromancers are always looking to experiment."

Abaddon nodded. Preparing for the departure, the guild guides sent their new allies on the way. Outside the guild walls, Colin was shaking his head and banging on the computer.

"A dampening field . . . damn, those wizards are clever," cursed Colin as he packed up his equipment. "Maybe Martha can pull something off of it."

Grassy Knolls surrounding Verian, Central Acadia

"You can imagine my surprise when my first experience with a Titan picnic included linen table cloths and silverware."

—Colin Wilkins

Racing their horses up a grassland hill, Cedric and Cassandra were enjoying themselves. Adhering to her preference, Cassandra rode side-saddle. As they approached the top of a hill, Cedric pulled Jericho up to the horse's dismay. Easily winning the race, Cassandra suspected nothing. Angrily turning his head to Cedric, Jericho stared at his master in disgust. Bending down to his ear, the Titan prince pleaded his case.

"Easy, Jericho, sometimes you have to lose a battle to win the war."

Unappreciative of his reasoning, Cedric knew that only an apple would quell Jericho's rage. A slap to the neck and two apples from his bag caused the mighty horse to forget the earlier slight. Keiko stayed right behind him as he walked up to Cassandra on her horse. Allowing Cedric to help her from the horse, Cassandra removed her riding helmet to let her hair down.

"That felt great! I hadn't gone riding since the wars began."

"Glad you enjoyed it, Cassie!"

"Well, dearest, now what?"

"I thought you'd never ask."

Taking his fiancé by the arm, Cedric led Cassandra to the eastern end of the hill. Shocking her with a full view of Lake Verian and her beloved city, the princess turned on the waterworks. Titan servants had set up a table in a gazebo on the hill with all the compliments of fine dining. Anticipating a picnic, Cassandra couldn't fathom the difficulty Cedric had gone through to set this up. A stable servant took the horses to be watered as the happy couple was helped to their seats. A servant came by and dropped napkins onto their laps while a sommelier poured a white wine in glasses. The embassy chef and his assistant were busy working on grills and trays nearby. Keiko spotted something down by the river and went over to Cedric.

"If you'll excuse me, my lord, I have some friends that I wish to catch up with," quipped Keiko with a wink. "Please do not do anything to dishonor yourself, master."

Keiko fluttered away to converse with some nymphs. A waiter came over with a plate that appeared to be quail with an herb seasoning stuffed with cornbread.

"May I serve your highnesses?" asked the waiter.

The two nodded, and the waiter placed one quail on Cassandra's plate while he placed three on Cedric's plate. Another servant came over with a plate for each diner that appeared to be some kind of Caesar salad. Blushing at the attention, Cassandra listened to the soft music of three violins playing in the background.

"Cedric, you didn't have to go through this much trouble for me," said a slightly embarrassed Cassandra.

"You love being pampered; besides, I haven't gotten a chance to spoil you in the past two revolutions. I guess we'll have a toast."

"What words did you mutter at the ball?"

"It's a Titan blessing, we toast the heroes of the past and the soldiers of the future. God bless the warriors because sure as hell knows no one else will."

"Simple, yet filled with meaning. I know a few soldiers in Central Acadia that deserve such praise. Salud!"

The two tapped their wine glasses together and drank.

"A fine acadian pinot this early in the rotation, a girl could get use to this treatment," commented Cassandra. "I didn't know you were on such good terms with the castle Sommelier."

"Even your people cannot deny a request like that while I'm in your country."

"I'm just surprised to see you not sniffing and sipping a fine brandy. I can't believe you can stomach that. So, any particular reason you came riding over to the castle today?"

"I was on escort duty today."

"The delegation?"

"Yes. Aramas's two granddaughters, Hippolyte and Minerva, arrived. I hadn't seen them in almost three revolutions. The eldest daughter has certainly matured into a fine and strong woman. The Wolf Tribe will be in good hands. The younger one is certainly a spitfire. All-in-all, I guess they're still traumatized by that battle because they didn't recognize me."

"Amuro was right. You truly have tried to seduce every single woman on Terminus Mundus."

"Don't be jealous. They just happened to be two of the villagers I saved from the sword of Jonas Marimon on the Terrace River. Praise be to God that I did because if they had died, Aramas would have never ended the war, and we'd be fighting on two fronts right now."

Cassandra shook a little bit when Cedric said that. Despite her age, Cassandra had grown up quickly in terms of the affairs of the world, as her father spared no expense with her tutors. She was well-versed in politics, war, and economics. After a few moments, she returned to her food. Dainty and proper, Cassandra used her utensils to eat the quail. Cedric gave up. Removing his gloves, he started to eat the quail with his hands, picking the flesh to the bone like a ravenous predator.

"Those two tribal girls are going to be staying at Royal Castle during the negotiations," commented Cedric. "I would ask a personal favor that you would be extra nice to them."

"All right, but only because you asked so nicely. Actually I've heard quite a bit about this she-wolf of Fenrir. I wonder how much is true. Then again, she can't be more difficult to deal with than your sister."

Cassandra bit her tongue before the last word. Embarrassed with the slip, Cassandra anticipated the worst but Cedric let the comment slide.

"You don't have to apologize; Cecilia is big enough to handle a few insults. My sister can make a very imposing enemy. Believe it or not, she has matured greatly. You should have seen her when we were younger."

"Cedric, I don't want to pry, but she is of marriageable age."

"You sound like my mother," laughed Cedric. "There is one knight that may be strong enough, but, well, let's say that his courtship so far has met one disaster after another. He's persistent, though, so I haven't given up hope yet. I would be honored to have him as a brother-in-law."

"I hope so because I think our only chance for happiness is if we get her married."

"Give my baby sister some time. Don't worry about it, Cassie; she'll accept you."

"Why are you so sure?"

"My sister knows better than to make me her enemy."

Used to dealing with people who held everything to their chest, Cassandra sat in disbelief of the bluntness the Titans spoke with. Deciding it was for the best, she changed the topic again.

"Now that the delegation has arrived, are you going to be headed home?"

"I can't say for certain what my next move is going to be. I hate to say this, but you may wake up one morning and I'll be gone without a good-bye."

"Cedric, please be honest with me. Is something wrong?"

"Right now, Cassie, I have no answers for you. The facts are that when your father gave Marie's hand to Julius, it was greeted with anger rather than rejoicing."

"My handmaiden was one of them. Please tell me that you aren't planning a coup, though. My father is good man and he is trying his best. I don't want to have to choose between the two of you."

"Your father and I share the same vision. If things stay the way they are now, I have no intention of moving against him."

"That makes me feel so much better, darling," said Cassandra as she drank her wine. "I know I'm being selfish, but three revolutions was too long for me, Cedric. I don't think I can stand being separated from you again. I wanted to apologize to you for the other night. It was probably the alcohol giving me false courage but I shouldn't have mentioned my feelings concerning the *Permaneo Eques Ordinares*.

"The Divikin, despite all of our blessings, are cursed with the duty to drive out the demonkin. We don't get to have normal lives. I made that plain to you from the beginning. Even with all this, Cassie, I promise that no matter what the battle, I'll live for you!"

From a combination of the wine and words, Cassandra lost it. Taking out her handkerchief, she began to well up.

"Why are you saying these things to me now, Cedric? You never said these things when you came to court me. Instead you spoke of the beauty of the world and goodness of people. Was that a lie?"

"There may be events that are coming to pass that go beyond the things I was speaking of the other evening. I cannot say more, not out of distrust, but simply because I am currently ignorant of all of the facts. I believe in the goodness of this world and the power of God if we take the right path."

"Uncle Cerwin does not speak highly of Duke von Angelhardt."

"I'm not surprised because they have known each other for a very long time. What he chooses to believe is his business. I trust my mentor with my life."

"Three revolutions and I sit here crying. I'm terrible company."

"On the contrary, Cassie. There were many nights I've longed to even see you crying."

"You have an awkward way of making a girl feel special, like she's the only girl in the world, even if your words are those of a fatalist."

Standing from her seat, Cassie walked to Cedric, plopping herself down in his lip. Flushed with red in her cheeks, the princess kissed him for a long time. The sight caused Keiko to fly at break-neck speed to the table. Staring intently at what was going on, only the nonchalant wave of Cedric's hand gave her comfort.

"Despite whatever ill tidings passed between us today, we're finally back together," said Cassie, as Cedric returned her kiss.

"Espresso and dessert?" asked Cedric.

"I don't know, Cedric. We've had a lot of food."

"The chef made chocolate lava cake."

Cassandra's eyes lit up, and she immediately returned to her seat, ready to eat again. Everyone there shared a laugh as the servants served coffee to the happy couple.

Fort Orion, Sixty Kilometers South of Verian, That Evening

"My first order of business as king of this new realm is to commission this Grand Fort. I have learned much from the War of the First Alliance, and Central Acadia will be defended. It is my privilege to name this Fort Orion."

—*King Nicholas Acadia on the dedication of Fort Orion*

Fort Orion was an imposing four-wall fort in the middle of the flat plains. Automated siege weapons were stationed on the top of each of the parapets. Acadian archers lined the top of the walls, staring at the surrounding area. The front of the fort bore banners of the House Acadia and the flag of Central Acadia at the top of Fort Citadel. Inside, the fort became more like a castle that had separate rooms featuring a full armory, a main conference room, and a larger grand meeting room that could host more than ten thousand guests. Julius, Cagius, Amuro, and Malcolm waited in the conference room at Fort Orion. Manned by ten technicians under a single supervisor, the control room served as the eyes and ears of the base. Placed in the center of the room, was a grid map of the whole of the western plains with the key country divisions and forts clearly marked. A second map showed the country of Central Acadia in a grid, and third map showed the immediate area around Fort Orion. Real-time video showed the slow approach of a carriage with Walker and his cuirassiers surrounding it. Jumping out of his skin, Julius crossed his arms and paced.

"Julius, the count will get here when he gets here," said Amuro.

"They should have been here by now. How does the count expect us to deploy in the morning if we are briefed at this ungodly hour?"

"Well, that's the problem with placing a vampire in such a high position of power," commented Cagius sarcastically. "Of course, he can't take the hover train because that would be beneath a person of his stature."

"I'm sure Walker is as concerned as we are and is doing what we can to move the Count along," reasoned Malcolm.

"Worrying about it won't do us any good until they get here," reinforced Amuro.

No calm came to Julius as a thousand thoughts ran through his head. Debating the merits of keeping Felicia, gaining political capital and most importantly proving to the Alliance that he didn't need Cedric backing him up, the paladin had no comfort.

"What do you think about Talus's chances?" asked his brother trying to calm him.

"Please don't talk about the championship; it's too depressing," remarked Julius. "I am sick and tired of Rhinegard hoisting that damn trophy every single revolution."

"Come on, Julius, we all know that the team is backed by the Titan Crown!" teased Amuro.

"I just wish we didn't always play so defensive," grumbled Cagius. We shut them down for seventy minutes, think we have them trapped, and all the sudden they come rushing in from the flanks."

"Sounds just like their military strategy," noted Malcolm.

"Malcolm, everything Titanus does is based on their military strategy," argued Amuro.

Hearing the door suddenly open, the four commanding officers were more relieved than startled. Entering first, Walker gave the heads up with his face that the news wasn't going to be good. Count Luminas entered next flanked by two unrecognizable, young lord knights.

"I'm sorry, but weather conditions made my traveling quite impossible, so we were unfortunately delayed," pleaded Luminas.

"Obviously, you know my only concern," said Julius.

"Yes, the representatives arrived today at the castle," stated Luminas. "King Stephen has agreed to meet the terms of the Tribal Confederation. They asked to meet us at the Ruins of Istle Hills."

"We didn't agree to that!" screamed Cagius.

"Surely that's madness!" retorted Amuro.

"There's no choice; the terms were absolute," explained Walker. "We are forced to deploy there."

"Just wonderful . . . they did that on purpose!" reasoned Julius.

"Why are you so sure?" questioned Luminas.

"Can't you see? We lost that battle to the tribes. I was ready to signal the surrender until the Titans arrived. The confederation wants us to remember how weak we are without the help of Titanus."

"The thought was not lost on me," countered Luminas. "However, we did not have a choice. We need to leave early tomorrow morning so the party will get there in time for the meeting. King Stephen wants to perform a troop review beforehand."

"Fine," agreed a sighing Julius. "Our cohorts will accept the king on time."

"In addition to the men that you are taking, I would like to present Lord Alwein and Lord Cambridge," announced Luminas. "They are knights assigned by the senate to accompany you."

"No way," exclaimed Cagius. "We're not taking two green-behind-the-gill knights on a mission of this importance."

"The senate insisted Acadian interests be taken into account," countered Luminas.

"What's Walker, chopped liver?" asked Cagius.

"Apparently two daddies wanted their little sons to share in the glory," taunted a sneering Walker.

The two knights were visibly upset with Walker's comments. Assuming an aggressive posture, they went for the swords on their waists. The marshals and vice-marshals retaliated by moving for their weapons as well. Determined they were outclassed, Alwein and Cambridge returned to a submissive posture.

"We both graduated at the top of our class and are eager to show our skills," boasted Alwein.

"We each bring a cohort of Acadian cuirassiers with us," said Cambridge.

"A ragtag bunch of mercenaries either plucked from the streets or the prisons," explained Walker. "None of the cuirassiers hold title."

"Count, I strongly protest these conditions," argued Julius with an edge in his voice. "Military decisions should be left to the marshals."

"That's not your decision, Prince Julius," commanded Luminas. "This is not a military action, so the authority of the steward and the senate take precedence over the desires of the marshals. You are nothing more than a mere ambassador in this circumstance. I am providing you with all of the necessary documentation. I will not see you off, as I must return before daylight. I wish you all good luck."

Luminas turned and left the room. Lord Alwein and Lord Cambridge followed suit.

"This is just wonderful!" said Amuro.

"They come from very powerful noble houses sworn to the king," described Walker. "I doubt we had little choice in the matter."

"Dammit... those two better not screw this up!" cursed Julius. "I hardly think my father ever agreed to such demeaning terms."

"Walker, are you going to be okay with this?" queried Malcolm. "We all know what happened to your father."

"I have to face the Istle Hills sometime. It might as well be now rather than in battle."

"I know we're limited to six cohorts, well, four if you count the Acadians we're playing nursemaid for," joked Cagius. "Did anyone notice what is conspicuously absent is the number of cohorts our tribal friends are bringing. If we're up against the entire army, we might need more than luck."

"Since we're going to be heading out early in the morning, I think we should all get a good night's sleep," recommended Amuro.

"That's a wise decision," added Malcolm. "All of our problems will still be here in the morning."

"Hey, whose turn is it to cook breakfast tomorrow?" asked Cagius.

"I think it's mine," volunteered Walker.

"It can't be any worse than Cedric and Cecilia last time," recollected Amuro. "I had to run my mouth under that faucet for an hour."

"Those two love their food very spicy," commented Walker.

"That deep-fried cinnamon toast they served with it, though, was to die for," said Cagius. "I think I had four or five helpings."

"At least we won't have to worry about heartburn again," stated Julius. "I wonder, since Cedric took that fort that next rotation, if it was all part of a master plan to put us out of commission. Well, I'll see you at dawn."

Julius hugged his brother before leaving the conference room to a chorus of "good nights." He walked up two flights of stairs to the private rooms of the marshals. Vincenzo was standing outside of his door.

"All is prepared for you, sir," said the squire.

"Gratzi, Vin, we've got an early call tomorrow."

"I'll set the alarm and be ready to wake you, sir. Good night."

Vincenzo saluted Julius and left. Playing with the knob on the door three times, Julius entered the room and quickly locked the door behind him. A hooded figure in a long robe was waiting for him. Removing her hood, Felicia ran into his arms.

"Darling!" exclaimed a smiling Julius.

"Cedric delivered your message."

"Bless his soul! Felicia, I didn't know what was going to happen that night. I am so sorry, I just couldn't…"

"I know this is not your doing, Julius, but it still hurts."

"I'm still trying. I have a plan."

"It's a fool's hope; you know that."

"I won't stop trying."

"Julius, there is something else you should know. Cedric formally offered to take care of Joshua."

"What do you mean?"

"He wants to place him in the Titan Military Academy."

"I'm not going to treat him as a bastard, Felicia! Apparently my father and friend have been conspiring behind my back."

"Do you realize the opportunity he's been given Julius? It is the finest military school in the world. They take so few outsiders."

"I can't believe Cedric would do this to me! I thought I explained my intentions to him."

"I don't understand."

"You said yourself that Joshua is very impressive with a sword. He'll make knighthood in Titanus for sure. That means land and title! He wouldn't be my son anymore. He'd be Joshua of some highland fife."

"Perhaps Cedric realizes the consequences of our actions. I believe he is sincere in looking out for Joshua. There are personal reasons for myself as well."

"Felicia, I promise you I am never going to renounce my son."

"I know, Julius, but right now that's irrelevant," cried Felicia as she dried her eyes.

"It's been so hard. I know what is best for all of us. I know that I should accompany her ladyship to Titanus and remain there. That way you would not be burdened."

"No."

Putting her delicate fingers to Julius' lips, Felicia smiled. The calming influence of her eyes set Julius's rage at bay. Felicia put her finger to his and smiled.

"However, your sincerity and integrity make it impossible for me to ever say good-bye to you."

"That made my night," said a smiling Julius. "You won't believe the garbage I have to put up with, Felicia. I got two rich boys in shiny mail without the slightest clue of the history and carnage of the Istle Hills. By the saints, I bet they never marched before."

"Fifteen revolutions in Central Acadia, and I've come to expect nothing less. I know you have your troubles. However, you must know as a mother, I need to look at the best interest of my son. My choice is Titanus over the garrison in Deniva."

"We'll talk about it more when I come back."

"Julius, you're treading into dangerous waters. There are many back in the capital who would not mind seeing you come home in defeat."

"You're not the first person to tell me that, but I've got a lot of people here protecting me," said Julius as he started to unlatch his cloak. "When I come back, it will be better. Are you needed back at the castle?"

"No, Mistress is covering for me."

"Then we have some time. I guess I won't be taking Amuro's good advice after all."

Fumbling to remove their clothes, the lovers prepared for bed.

ENCAMPMENT OF
THE WOLF TRIBE

"Accept thy honor, Alpha of the blood guard of the Wolf Tribe.
Your fealty and service is to the chief of the tribe alone. All
other interests are secondary. May the spirits steady your hand
when the time to use the sword is necessary, may the spirits
counsel you with wisdom when your chief seeks your advice,
and may you perform all that is asked of you with wisdom,
strength, and love. Arise, Alpha Huskal! "

—*Chieftain Aramas during the Ceremony of Alpha*

The Wolf, Myotis, and Syrus Tribes were standing around the great fire
of the Wolf Tribe encampment. Reynard and Aramas were joined by
the middle-aged Posha of the Syrus clan. Her black hair was hidden under
a hood of white with brown markings along its edges. She wore a one-
piece woven brown-and-white dress. Shuffling her sandaled feet against
the dust, her blue eyes stared past the fire. Approaching from the north
were four rather large and burly individuals wearing hauberk mail with
bearskins over their shoulders. These men were wearing horned helmets
and carrying axes and war swords. Their leader, Adnar, had a long red
beard and blue eyes.

"There is no word from Hippolyte and Minerva," announced Aramas.
"The Titans communicated their safe arrival. The Acadians have acquiesced
to our terms."

"I can't say that I'm not too surprised," said Reynard. "What do you
say, Posha?"

"The Syrus clan has prayed many moons to the spirits; we expected them to accept."

"Yes," bellowed Adnar. "The alliance is nothing but a mere school of fish without the Titans herding them toward a goal. I trust we are not altering from the original plan."

"The final preparations have been made," described Aramas. "We will send the Tribal Confederation army as well, in case they have decided to lay a trap for us. Under no circumstances are more than the agreed six cohorts to approach the site of the negotiations."

"The important question is who among us will go," suggested Reynard.

"Since King Stephen will not expose himself, I shall be the one that remains behind," pronounced Aramas. "Huskal will go in my place."

"Great Chief, I'm a warrior, not a diplomat," offered a surprised Huskal.

"Would you not agree it is your duty as the Alpha to serve my needs?"

"Absolutely, I remember my vows."

"Then you will fulfill your vow for me. I want the tribes to know that their commander will be with them. I remain here with the blood guard and those that cannot travel. The remaining members of all tribes will fall back to the mountain encampment."

"You still distrust the motives of the Acadians," added Reynard.

"The blood guard and I can handle ourselves within the encampment. I will not let King Stephen appear superior to me and run."

"I believe that is wise, Chief Aramas, but I worry about your granddaughters," argued Posha. "They are technically hostages."

"I have faith in Titanus and the honor of the Prime Eagle," retorted Aramas.

"Allow me at least to send some of my Nord warriors to help defend your camp," offered Adnar. "It's too inviting a military target to remain here alone."

"The Acadians will do nothing that jeopardizes this peace," countered Aramas. "It would instantly mean war between our people."

"What must I do, my chief?" questioned Huskal.

"Use your discerning eyes, search them for weakness, and ensure the future for my granddaughter," ordered Aramas. "You must serve Hippolyte as you served me."

"I swear by the spirits."

"You'll be fine, Huskal. You'll know what to do when the time comes."

Content with the counsel of his fellow chieftains, Aramas prepared to address the tribal contingent. Standing before the tribal army and villagers, all would fall silent before the Chief of Chiefs.

"People of the tribes, long have we suffered at the hands of the alliance. With the blessings of the spirits, those times are coming to an end. The alliance king has offered to negotiate a treaty with us. No longer will we suffer the wars and famines caused by the brutality of the steel-bellies. Finally, we have a chance to achieve peace. However, it has been our experience that the alliance speaks with the tongue of a snake. Thereby, all peoples that can should move immediately to the mountain encampment; all that cannot travel will remain here with me and the blood guard. This will be done in the morning. May the spirits protect us all!"

The traveling members of the four tribes broke out into a chorus of resounding cheers, along with shouts of, "May the spirits protect us!" Breaking into singing and dancing, the tribes celebrated the chance for peace. Aramas, however, remained troubled.

"Hippolyte, may the spirits grant you the peace I never had."

Titanus Embassy,
the Next Morning

"When fighting the unbeatable enemy, do not fight with emotion. Rather, you should fight the enemy with your whole mind. Only through careful coordination and calculation can you determine the weakness of that foe. There may be times when extraordinary measures must be taken in war. It is important, however, that you make those decisions based on the best information available. In the end it is better to make an intelligent mistake rather than rely on false prudence."

—excerpt from The Titan Battle Manual, *Prince Cedric Rhone*

Cedric sat at his desk with his computer running. Focusing on a map of the Istle Hill terrain, the sword master clicked on a particular hilly area in the north. Taking a break, he poured himself a cup of tea from the pot on the desk. Roused by the sound of footsteps, Cedric was greeted by Wilhelm.

"I could use some good news, Wilhelm."

"It's worse than I thought, your excellency."

"Have you discovered the face of our enemy?"

"Yes."

Pulling up a seat, Cedric offered Wilhelm a cup of tea. After a single sip, he furrowed his brow.

"That's strong."

"An eastern blend, it is supposed to have certain medicinal properties. Cecilia is on a bit of a health kick and insisted I try it."

Cedric watched as Wilhelm started putting sugar in the tea. Nine scoops later he was finally done.

"What are we up against?" asked Cedric.

"It's the king of the locusts—Abaddon, the lord of the sixth plane of hell," described Wilhelm. "This isn't an ordinary fallen angel; it's the angel that led the assault on the gates of heaven. The Prince was grooming him to be one of his Sefiroth once he took his place on the throne."

"So he's one of the nobles?"

"Yes. He is an extremely skilled swordsman and an excellent statesman. In other words, he's a lot like you."

"Why am I not reassured by that fact?"

"He has plans for Terminus Mundus, and I know they involve Cassandra. Abaddon is cunning, he won't simply walk into Castle Acadia or send his minions on some fool mission to kidnap the girl. These negotiations that are coming up, you have to get there."

"You know the official position of Titanus is not to attend. We gave our word to the Acadians that we would not interfere."

"I warned you that the protocol and decorum of this alliance is too small for this enemy. Abaddon is going to make sure those negotiations go sour! Mark my words Cedric, when Abaddon strikes, we will need divine providence."

Licking his upper lip, Cedric returned to his computer screen.

"I'll see what I can do."

"I'm heading out into the wilderness to see what I can find myself. It's likely you won't be able to contact me. Don't worry, I'll find you."

"I understand."

"I do not know whether the seer Garrett Greensage can help us, but we do not have the time to consult him either way. The time has come that I warned you about—abandon the path of the marshal and become the Last Knight. You can't work within the system anymore; you must rise above it."

"Wilhelm, you know my goal. I will protect Cassandra with my life, if necessary."

"Yes, between the two of us we may be able to pull this off. Needless to say, it's very important right now that you don't die."

"Self-preservation is my primary goal."

The two stood and exchanged a hug.

"Good. Stay safe and I'll find you." soothed Wilhelm as he left the room.

Cedric shut down his computer and stood before the mirror in his office to perfect his appearance. Staring in the mirror, the sword master challenged himself to dissuade the slightest semblance of doubt. Cedric left the room, opened a pocket watch to check the time, and locked the door behind him as he walked quickly down three flights of stairs. He entered a large conference room that prominently featured a large LED screen that served as a transmitter and a communicator. Ten computer terminals were in the room, each manned by a technician. Two supervisors covered the room. Seated at a large table in the center of the room were Cecilia, Christian, and Colin. Appearing via conference, Martha and Civilia communicated on the main screen. Disturbed by the look on Cedric's face, Christian and Cecilia made mental notes to get to the bottom of it.

"I trust I haven't missed anything," said Cedric.

"ANO just started the broadcast of the troop review," offered Christian.

As they watched from the safety of Verian, cohorts began to parade in front of King Stephen at Fort Orion. The marshals and vice marshals were grouped at the back of the review. Julius was very focused at the task ahead, much to the discomfort of the others with him. Amuro tried to keep things light.

"Walker, you really surprised me!" praised Amuro. "Those crepes were delicious!"

"I'm glad you liked them. It's an old family recipe."

"Well, I'm stuffed, but considering the rations we'll be eating for the next few rotations, that might be a good thing," joked Cagius.

Amuro made a face. Looking at a bundled package on her shoulder, she read a note scribbled to her: *Amuro, hope this helps. Christian.* The she-elf marshal silently thought to herself that if it didn't work, nothing would. Spying on her comrades, she looked past a distracted Malcolm to a familiar piece of cloth tied to Cagius's Dragonsbane. The material didn't escape the keen eyes of her elf vice-marshal.

"Excuse me, Cagius, but are you wearing a favor?"

Surprised that Malcolm had the courage to make this observation, the commanding officers stared at their dragoon comrade, who grinned from ear-to-ear .

"I don't believe it," commented Julius.

"Saria came by this morning to wish me luck," said Cagius.

"You mean Princess Saria Jenitzen, the girl who's been courted by almost every eligible noble in the west."

"She likes his cavalier attitude and his devotion to chivalry," explained Amuro.

"How do you know?" asked Malcolm.

"I read her diary."

"Then my efforts have been worth it," boasted Cagius.

"You are amazing," remarked Julius.

"Thanks, Julius."

The brief moment of levity came and went with the passing breeze. Staring at the review stand, Julius witnessed Princess Marie standing next to her father. Shivering in the morning cold, she pulled a white mink fur coat over her body. The paladin wasn't prepared to deal with this and his slumping shoulders were observed by Walker. Walker noticed this immediately and went over to check on the marshal.

"Are you all right marshal?"

"I'm fine . . . I'm just . . . I'm not too happy about bringing those two Acadian knights with us."

"I understand what you mean. This isn't the first time that the senate has chosen to do something like this. My guess is the two of them are up for appointments in the Ministry of War and needed a battlefield commission before that happens."

"Damn Acadian politics as usual! I would prefer to conduct one military operation without bureaucrats undermining my authority."

Reaching the review stand, Julius dismounted and climbed the steps of the review podium. Snuggled warmly in her coat, Marie nestled her body next to Julius as Stephen addressed the troops and officers.

"One of the greatest privileges of a monarch is the opportunity for a troop review, especially under circumstances that do not necessarily involve a march to war. Prince Julius Imperia, marshal of the Alliance Army, I need not remind you of the importance of this mission."

"I am well aware, your majesty."

"Good, our trust is in you, and I have no doubt that you will succeed in your mission."

Despite her trembling hands, Marie interlaced her fingers with Julius. Frightened a servant had blabbed about his midnight rendezvous, the paladin sensed timidity in the princess's movements. Marie presented a favor of blue and white with a symbol of a lion on it. Figuring the younger princess had seen older sister present a similar favor Cedric, Julius breathed a sigh of relief. Returning his thoughts to political capital and the sword master's warning of civil war, the paladin let Marie have her moment.

"I humbly ask that you wear the colors of Central Acadia on such an important mission."

"Yes, my lady."

"I'm glad you didn't make me quote the traditional statement my sister has to use on her fiancé," kidded a smiling Marie.

Marie reverently tied the favor around Julius' waist as if she was dressing the god of war himself. Taking the time to tie and retie the sash, Julius decided he wouldn't embarrass the princess or her father. Swallowing his pride and pretending it was Felicia, the paladin gave Marie the benefit of a full kiss. When he pulled away, he saw what he perceived to be a young, naïve, and innocent face. Marie was a deep shade of red and bubbling over with joy. It was the kiss she had dreamed of since she first saw Julius at Cassandra's Quize. Julius knew in that moment the threat that those around him spoke of. Laughing at his own disgrace, he wondered what kind of Paladin would so willingly tear the heart out of a sweet princess. At a loss for words, Julius could only sputter out one thing.

"I'll see you upon my return."

Returning to his horse, Julius got in the saddle and returned to the marshals.

"As a commanding marshal, don't I get a favor and a kiss too?" chuckled Amuro playfully.

"Let's go!" ordered Julius displeased at his comrade's jest.

Traveling at a nice and easy pace along the Gold Highway, the marshals left Fort Orion with the remainder of the caravan. Marie stood there waving good-bye until the group disappeared from site.

Shaking his head with his hands over his eyes, Cedric watched in horror from the Titan Embassy.

"If he continues torturing that sweet girl, I'm not going to be able to take much more of this."

"When are you going to accept the fact, brother, that you are better than Julius?"

"It's not a question of who is better; it's about doing what is right!"

"Julius's actions notwithstanding, I'm not used to seeing you this anxious. What's wrong?"

"I don't know yet. Colin, what did you find out?"

"The Nephilim was a bit of braggart, but he wanted himself destroyed once he was found out. I happily obliged him and surrendered what little of the recording I got out of the Wizards Guild."

"I've got my people working on it, but the filtration process is very difficult," chimed in Martha via teleconference. "This isn't an ordinary dampening field caused by magic; someone designed this."

"The Acadians don't have that technology, so apparently our list of enemies is still growing," remarked Christian.

"Thus the hour of darkness encroaches upon us again," worried Civilia. "Since Titanus has yet to be attacked and we're still alive, we may still have some time."

"What time?" screamed Cecilia. "I just watched a delegation get sent off into the wilderness that might as well be a funeral convoy. Five senior officers with only six cohorts of troops as an escort, why don't we just put a giant bulls-eye on the caravan!"

"Not to mention agreeing to meet the tribes at the Istle Hill Ruins, it is as if we would have asked the tribes to negotiate with us at Eagle's Gate," added Christian. "Then again, I doubt that Aramas would object since he's already agreed to hand over his granddaughters to the Acadians as hostages."

"There are just too many negative factors surrounding this encounter," interjected Martha. "The desire for peace at any cost seems to have clouded the judgment of all parties involved."

"There is no way out of those ruins if something goes wrong for the caravan," said Civilia. "Even if I station the armada at Eagle's Gate, we could never get to the ruins fast enough to organize a relief column."

"Doctor Heinrich, can you bring a map of the surrounding region?" asked Cedric, who sat back in his chair.

"At once, your highness," answered Martha.

Martha typed on her end of the conference. On the main view screen, the area surrounding the Istle Hill Ruins was brought up. She started to zoom out little by little until a diamond-shape building appeared south of the ruins. Cedric put his hand up, and Martha stopped what she was doing. When Cedric walked up to the screen and touched the shape, the words *Fort Capricorn* appeared. Christian started to laugh.

"If you can still call it a fort," described Christian. "It was commissioned originally to be western twin of Fort Orion. However, the senate has never funded the dilapidated structure and it's on the verge of collapse."

"Do they keep it manned?" questioned Cedric.

"Yeah, they station about sixty Acadian soldiers in there, mostly those that would wind up in debtor's prison. I think they'd rather the fort killed them."

"The last war showed that there were deficiencies in the ability of the Acadian fort system to adequately defend Verian against tribal raids," lectured a smiling Cedric. "I believe that it would be in our best interest to conduct a fort inspection and some war games while we're there."

Cecilia smiled widely. Jumping from her seat, she embraced her twin brother and kissed him on the forehead.

"Big brother, I'm sorry. I thought you had gone soft on us!" she playfully teased. "However, you just totally redeemed yourself. My valkyries will be ready to march."

"Let's not get too far ahead of ourselves," reminded Cedric. "We've got to make our actions look completely legal. Christian, what's the maximum number of troops I can travel with at any time in Central Acadia and not arouse any suspicion?"

"You can have thirty thousand as an escort, per your rank as marshal. The princess may also have twenty-five thousand as an escort."

"It's not much but it's enough to break a line if we run into trouble!" said Cecilia.

"Mother, with your permission, I'd like Martha Heinrich to come to the embassy in Verian," requested Cedric as he turned back to the screen. "I require that Captain Samuel Irvine be sent with a division to take over the embassy duties in Verian. In addition, Marshal Irvine should come with our best forty thousand riders to the junction of the Gold Highway and Royal Highway as soon as possible."

Despite sensing concern in her son's voice, Civilia could not fully grasp her son's master strategy. Her maternal instincts were enough in this matter to trust in what he was planning on doing.

"You have my blessing, my son," said the queen. "However, you're short by fifteen thousand."

"No, I've already sent messengers to Valentine in the Napolitan embassy and Sirius in Evengard," explained Cedric. "I'm asking them to bring soldiers from each country to participate in our little deception. We need to make this war game look real, in case we have to defend ourselves later."

"Very well. Marshal Irvine has kept the armada stationed at Fort Hawkeye since Wilhelm's meeting with us. I sent a message to them as we spoke."

"I'll load up a hover train with a mobile command center just in case Fort Capricorn is in the shape that Christian believes it to be," added Martha. "My team will continue to work on the message, and I guess I'll start packing to come to New Verian."

"Is there any word from the duke?" asked Civilia.

"The duke is following leads out in the wilderness as well," responded Cedric. "He believes our enemy is going to be there and his only doubt is when they will strike."

"We can only prepare," said Civilia.

"Let's just hope it's another intelligent mistake," stated Cecilia.

"On the contrary, it's about time I had some fun," said Colin.

"Okay, let's not waste any more time," ordered Cedric. "We've got to get ahead of that caravan and make it to Fort Capricorn tonight."

"Cedric, Cecilia, perform your duty but exercise caution," warned Civilia. "This is not the time to create an international incident. My prayers are with you."

Cedric and Cecilia provided a simultaneous, "Thanks, Mom" causing everyone to laugh. As the queen and her chancellor ended the transmission, Martha gave a cute "peace sign." Moving to the control screen, Cedric pressed a few buttons. A few seconds later, Cerwin appeared on the screen.

"To what do I owe the pleasure, Cedric?" asked Cerwin.

"Something important has come up. Can I count on you to keep an eye on Cassandra for me while I'm gone?"

"What's the matter? Are you afraid she'll find another beau? Don't worry, I have many 'lessons' with the princess for the next few rotations. You just do what you have to do."

"I appreciate it."

"Temple Services are starting soon; the heretics will be gathering. If one was to sneak out of the city then, I don't think they'd be noticed."

"Thanks for the advice," said Cedric as he signed off and ended the transmission. "Keiko!"

Fluttering in absentmindedly, Keiko crashed into a few soldiers. As she approached, Cedric pulled out note from the inside pocket of his jacket. Taking a moment, the sword master sealed the wax with his ring. Signaled by her master, no order was too great for the sylph to fulfill.

"Yes, Master Cedric."

"I need you to do me a favor. Wait a few hours and deliver this to Cassie."

Cedric handed her a sealed note. Taking the note as if it was a sacred treasure, Keiko bowed to Cedric. Raising her eyes, she hastily kissed him.

"Of course, my lord. Please be careful." Keiko kissed him and fluttered off.

Filling his lungs with air, Cedric turned to his only comfort. Taking his rosary beads made from the relics of the Istle Hills, the sword master began his daily prayers as he prepared for the journey.

"Holy Mother, be with us and watch over Cassandra."

Border of Central Acadia and the Wolf Tribe, That Evening

"My existence in hell has given me perspective on many things.
The first is that I knew that once I betrayed God, I had no hope
for redemption. I can never accept the fact a race so fatally
flawed can receive so many blessings from on high. The second
is that I must temper my arrogance so not to underestimate an
adversary again."

—Excerpts from Abaddon's journal

Abaddon was sitting in a tent reading *The Titan Battle Manual*. The three moons of Terminus Mundus were full and bright in the night sky. So focused on reading the book, Abaddon hardly noticed Basarabas enter the tent. Deciding to interrupt, the Nephilim leader cleared his throat twice.

"My lord, the ones that you requested have arrived."

Lifting his head, Abaddon watched twenty duco-mutatios enter the tent. Dressed in a simple outfit of green and black, the uniform kept the silver bodily skin devoid of any blemish. While most could only maintain the transformation for short periods of time, masters were able to maintain their transformations for revolutions. Duco-mutatios did have a weakness. Immune to magic that affects the mind and body, Divikin can see through the shape shift. Recent attempted infiltrations of western nations have resulted in nasty ends for these stealth demonkin.

"Why did you ask only for duco-mutatios?" asked Basarabas. "A goblin or a troll would be more effective for the task."

"Basarabas, you disappoint me," chided Abaddon. "Duco-mutatios are necessary for my designs. Just make sure that the wizards are ready with their end of the bargain."

"Why are you taking such a gamble?"

"I'm concerned about this Duke Wilhelm. The assassination of our agent in broad daylight, made me believe that the duke is on to us. Basarabas, under no circumstances are the other Nephilim to know about this stage of the plan. There are other matters that they will be needed for very soon."

"Are you sure you don't want me to accompany you?"

"I prefer to work alone. Don't worry; there'll be plenty of Divikin for you to kill soon enough."

"Very well, my lord."

"Have you read this, Basarabas?" asked Abaddon, holding up the manual.

"No, we don't keep many Titan books stocked in our locations."

"I just can't put this book down. This Titan prince continues to pique my interest. I'll have to pay him a visit in time. I'm sure we'll get along famously."

Fort Capricorn, Forty Kilometers South of the Istle Hill Ruins

"Therefore, stay awake, for you know neither
the rotation nor the hour."

—*Scriptures of the Christ, Evengard Evangelist 25:13*

Fort Capricorn was everything that Christian had described. Part of the north wall had collapsed, leaving a gaping mess of wood and stone. The other walls had stones chipped away and loose ramparts. While Fort Orion was built by the Titans as a gift to Central Acadia, Fort Capricorn was the Acadians' first attempt at a defensive fort. The senate had cut costs, and graft was not uncommon in its construction. There was no ceremony to open the fort, and no effort was ever made to correct its mistakes. Occupying space rather than performing their duties, the soldiers were sprawled across the courtyards. Lacking the discipline to drill or keep watch, they sat around fires and played cards. The soldiers in the fort certainly didn't have the professional look of the halberdiers that guarded the city of Verian.

A lone sentry stood on top of one of the fort parapets. Drooping eyelids caused to soldier to continually stomp his feet to keep awake. Eventually succumbing to the allure of sleep, the watchman closed his eyes for a few minutes. Upon opening them, he witnessed cloud of dust kick up from the road leading to the fort. Caught between his dreams and reality, the soldier blinked repeatedly until the trail was clear. The Titan armada breached the perimeter. Forty thousand riders strong led a hover train across the plains. Panicked, the sentry started to ring the alarm bell. Ignoring the call at first, the soldiers went about their business. It wasn't until the first column entered the fort that threat was taken seriously. Encircling the occupants within moments, the terrified fort defenders huddled together for protection. An officer made it out of the interior of the fort, distinguished from the regulars only by the four bars on the side of his uniform. Seeing his soldiers handing over weapons, the officer wondered what happened.

"What's going on? Are we under attack?"

The riders stood still and silent, carrying only the banners of Cedric Rhone and the country of Titanus. Resting a hand on the hilts of their weapons, the Titans were prepared in case the Acadians resisted the occupation.

"I'm in charge here!" shouted the officer. "I demand to know what's going on!"

"Not anymore!" retorted Cecilia.

The voice of the vanadis was enough to make the officer's blood run cold. He stared as Cedric, Cecilia, and Horace entered through the column of riders. Swallowing hard, the officer at once bowed submissively.

"Marshal... vice-marshal... I had no idea," stammered the officer. "If I knew you were coming, I would have prepared a reception."

"What's your name, son?" asked Cedric.

"Cole, Sir."

"You are temporarily relieved of your command duties by my personal authority as marshal commandant of the Alliance Army," ordered Cedric. "Do you have an operational control room?"

"Sorry, Marshal, but it broke down about three revolutions ago and we're still waiting for funding from the senate to get it repaired."

"Well Cole, you're going to have a long wait," teased Cecilia. "Don't worry about it, we brought our own."

"Marshal, bring up the Mobile Command Center, and let Martha's men get to work on it," commanded Cedric.

"At once, your excellency," answered Horace as he lit a cigar.

Cedric turned his attention to the distraught soldiers in the fort. The soldiers stopped going for their weapons and, likewise, the riders went to an at-ease position. Clearing his throat, Cedric barked out some orders.

"I am Prince Marshal Cedric Rhone. The alliance command staff has decided to conduct war games at Fort Capricorn over the next few rotations. Representatives from Napolitan and Evengard will be arriving tomorrow. As Acadians you are expected to be active participants in these war games. Sleep well tonight, for tomorrow you belong to me!"

Terrified at the presence of "La Morte Angelus," the soldiers obeyed and headed into the barracks. Clearing the courtyard of the rabble, Christian's commando unit was free to enter. Carrying large black suitcases, they approached Cecilia for orders.

"All right men. I want you to go with the CO and find out every single thing wrong with this fort. Don't leave a single stone unturned; we have to make this look as official as possible."

"Absolutely, ma'am."

Two commandos grabbed the officer and gently encouraged him to show them around the fort. Cecilia tapped her ear in order to listen to a communication. She turned back to her brother.

"The perimeter is secured. The hover train has been docked and our engineers are working on a temporary command center and barracks as we speak. Horace figures it may take about two hours."

"We caught a break with that radio being out. I figure we'll get about half-a-rotation before anyone realizes we're missing. Of course, then all hell is going to break loose. Damn, I should have left Christian and Colin in Verian."

"Do you care to let your sister in on your secret plans?"

"I think this fallen angel that the duke is warning us about is going to hit the negotiations."

"It's a plum target. Now I know why you wanted the military presence."

"You can read me like a book, sis."

"How do you want to handle the riders?"

"I want everyone to get a good night's sleep. We had a long and hard ride. Those horses need some rest. Keep a skeleton watch only once the mobile command center is up. As early as tomorrow we may need to go two to a horse."

"Right away, Marshal," acknowledged Cecilia as she went to relay the orders.

Cedric dismounted Jericho and took out his flask. Taking two slugs, he savored the test as Christian approached him.

"Well boss, we made it without a hitch."

"What good will it accomplish?"

"You've never been good at second guessing, yourself.

"I can't shake the feeling that I'm missing something."

"That's hard for me to believe, since you've pulled us out this far. Don't worry, boss, I trust you."

"Then do me one favor. I want you and Colin packed and ready to head back to Verian at a moment's notice."

"No problem. I've already taken the liberty of charting the fastest route back to the city avoiding all contact with the main roads."

"Now let's go see if we can give Martha's crew some help."

"Right with you, friend."

Joining in with the engineering crews and other riders outside the fort, the Titans worked together to establish the mobile command center. Steel plates were bolted in on four sides; inside the building, technicians setup a table with four computers and large view screen. While not as technologically superior as other permanent command centers, it would do the job.

Istle Hill Ruins, Midday

"Fellow Sentinels, our civilization will begin in these hills. Maintain a watchful eye on the elves and dwarves, but under no circumstances are you to interrupt the development of the human race. If they are to come to our Lord Father, they must do so of their own free will. Let these hills be known as the Istle because they are where Sentinels came down to the temporal realm."

—Apocryphal Book of Sentinels 2:1–3

Standing on a grassy hill, Julius and the military party awaited their counterparts. In the valley below was a series of roads and structures that were now nothing more than marble ruins. Vines and grasses had grown out of the ruins of what was once a magnificent city. The Istle Hills had been the original home of the first Sentinels when they descended from heaven to earth. However, over the revolutions, a deep divide split the descendants of these first Sentinels, the Divikin into three separate factions. The factions eventually divided into the Titans, the Edenians, and the Kablisha. The Edenians would abandon the city for the eastern side of the Kaiser Mountains and form the Edenian Empire. The Titans moved to the more defensible southern Griffin Mountains, forming Titanus. Last, the Kablisha would move north to a fortress city known as Antiquity defended by a magical barrier in the current age.

A few tents had been set up by an archeological team studying the remaining buildings. However, they had long abandoned the site with news of the coming of the two delegations. In the center of the ruins was a large monument bearing the Central Acadian coat-of-arms. Upon entering the ruins, Walker removed his helmet and walked over to the monument. He bent down on one knee and said a silent prayer. A plaque on the monument read "Here fell Lord Marshal Hector Reed, in a heroic defense to save the Alliance from tribal aggression."

"I hate this place," commented Cagius. "I hate this place more than any other place on Terminus Mundus."

"I remember it as if it were yesterday," recounted Walker as he turned back to his companions. "Jonas Marimon charged the Templars forward into the enemy trap. The Lord Marshal had to come to their aid in order to spare them from being slaughtered. The Templars showed their gratitude by turning tail to run. The last I saw my father he was surrounded by enemies. Yet, he suffered a single sword wound from behind, and that was the end."

"The command was devastated and in panic. Julius and I did the best we could to pull them together, but there was no hope," added Amuro. "We were ready to raise the white banners in the hopes of just keeping the rest of our measly forces alive."

"Then came the miracle: Cedric and the armada broke the enemy lines with a single charge," interrupted Julius.

"Aramas is one of the greatest generals the tribes have ever had," praised Malcolm. "Yet even he is afraid of fighting Cedric on the battlefield. It saved us that day."

"It's all in the original home of the Sentinels," stated Amuro, visibly shaking. "Why would such a holy place give off such bad vibes?"

"If you believe in those legends," countered Julius.

"They're not legends, Julius!" retorted Amuro. "It's an important part of our elf history."

"The Sentinels gave rise to Titanus and Edenia, right?" asked Cagius.

"Yes," lectured Malcolm. "A majority of nobles from the major houses of each kingdom can trace their descendants back to the Sentinels. In addition, the Kablisha also can trace their origin to the Sentinels. Whether or not you believe the tribe simply disappeared however, is debatable."

"They didn't necessarily disappear," countered Amuro. "A legend says they erected a barrier around their last remaining stronghold in the City of Antiquity when the Chinota Turks crossed the Kaiser Mountain

Pass. I would think that our Titan friends would know more about it since it is rumored that King Justin Rhone was the last to encounter them."

The sound of the ram's horn brought the debate to a screeching halt. Turning their attention to the south, the marshals and vice-marshals witnessed the approaching tribes.

"We'll have to save our intellectual discussions for the dinner table," joked Julius. "I believe our guests have arrived."

"How should we approach this?" asked Malcolm.

"We proceed with caution and hope they aren't carrying weapons," quipped Cagius.

Walker took out his scopes. He watched a group that consisted of Reynard, Josephine, Huskal, Posha, and Adnar. Cagius's concern was soon realized as each of the command staff spotted the weapons that the members of the tribal delegation were carrying. Walker allowed himself a slight chuckle.

"They're carrying weapons."

"Well, so are we," refuted Julius, a smug look on his face.

Laughing, the alliance officers greeted the tribal leaders. Julius and Reynard were the first to step forward. Looking over the hills behind the tribal delegation, Amuro and Malcolm used their keen eyes to search for any sign of tribal ambush. Watching Reynard first put up his hands, Julius unlatched his sword and handed it to Vincenzo.

"Greetings. I am Chief Reynard of the Myotis Tribe."

"Prince Marshal Julius Imperia of Napolitan. I represent the Alliance of the Western Kingdom in these proceedings."

"Ah yes, the Dragon Paladin. Your reputation precedes you, my friend. I am Adnar, the leader of the Nordice Provinces."

"Allow me to introduce my right wing commander Josephine, Alpha of the Wolf Tribe Huskal, and High Priestess Posha of the Syrus clan," introduced Reynard.

"Allow me to present Princess Marshal Amuro Jenitzen, Prince Vice-Marshal Cagius Imperia, Prince Vice-Marshal Malcolm Fenidor, and Lord Captain Jonathan Walker," the paladin responded in kind.

"We give thanks to the great spirits for allowing us to come together," prayed Posha.

"We praise the virtues of the saints who walked before us," invoked Julius.

"And we give thanks to the Father of all!" blessed Amuro.

"I have to admit that originally I was uncomfortable with the idea of meeting with a marshal," pronounced Reynard. "I would rather the delegation to have been led by a diplomat or an interested party."

"My fiancé is King Stephen Acadia's daughter," said Julius. "Thus you can understand my desire for these proceedings to move forward as diplomatically as possible."

Cagius turned his head around to mutter something under his breath. Annoyed that his brother had openly offered so much information, the dragoon wondered if his brother had even heard the advice he gave him at Dragon's Rest.

"I understand," replied Reynard.

"I believe the terms that were given to you ahead of this meeting were sufficient."

"We do understand them."

"We have certain concerns that we insisted upon when we agreed to meet with your people that were not addressed in the treaty," interrupted Huskal. "We are especially disappointed that our people will still not be allowed to enter your kingdoms without passes. Our people have moved freely in Titanus for some time now."

"These are preliminary negotiations," rebuked Amuro. "An armistice between our people will not include such specifics yet."

"We grow weary of being treated as uncivilized barbarians," stated an angry Huskal.

"We grow weary of going to war," admonished Cagius.

"Wars your people have been responsible for," chided Josephine.

"I think we're all willing to agree that mistakes have been made on all sides," countered Malcolm diplomatically.

"Well-spoken, my elf friend," agreed Posha.

"The most important thing we can do now is end the violence between our peoples," mediated Julius.

"If we don't, we all risk the empire using their war machine against us," added Walker.

"It has taken extraordinary measures for the tribes to trust the kingdoms in the past," said Reynard.

"Our people strongly supported the First Alliance!" challenged Huskal. "King Frederick Rhone proved to us that your kind can be trusted. The greatest regret of our chief is that his father refused King Justin's call for aid. However, the Acadians have proved that your kind can speak with forked tongues."

"I am not here to deny the crimes of my country," beseeched Walker.

"But you're Acadian?" countered Josephine.

"Thus I have perspective on the treachery of my own people."

"We all expect that we are going to be traveling down a long road," instructed Julius. "I've said this before, but peace must be the first step. If we can learn to trust each other, not to raise our blades against one another, then all of the petty differences we have will start to fade away. I am tired of fighting, and I'm sure you are as well."

"We are tired of fighting," said Huskal. "We have suffered too much death, including the loss of the chief's heir at the Terrace River by that butcher who guards your king. Titanus has offered us a proposal as well, but many of us find this unacceptable. We shall not kneel."

"We're not asking you to kneel," addressed Julius. "We want to treat your people, after time, the same way that Titanus does. Look how far we've been willing to come already. The alliance chose to meet with you on your terms. Surely you must understand the importance of this."

"We do appreciate your words and kindness, Prince Julius," acknowledged Reynard. "The alliance appears to have some honor. Our tribal confederation has labored over your terms with discerning eyes. It was our judgment that if your kind appeared sincere, we would be more than willing to acquiesce to the peace treaty. Though we will not sign any trade agreements or further negotiations at this time, we will sign the armistice."

"I thank you."

Disturbed by the ease of the tribal conciliation, Cagius almost had to be ordered to signal to the soldiers behind him. The soldiers set the table down in the middle of the field along with the necessary documents. Julius went first and bound his name to the document. Once again, Cagius couldn't believe what his brother was doing.

"If you have any final reservations or wish to review the document again, this would be a good time."

"Will this stop your raids on my people?" asked Adnar.

"There is reciprocity to be considered. Adnar, if you raid our ports, Napolitan reserves the right to retaliate."

"Looks like we'll be going back to hitting Imperial Ports again," bellowed a laughing Adnar. "The weather's nicer anyway."

Adnar stepped forward first and put his name on the document.

"I believe the spirits sent a man like you to us to end this needless violence," prayed Posha as she signed the document next.

Intently focused on Huskal, the paladin tried to gauge the mindset of the wolf warrior. Julius was well aware of his reputation on the battlefield and believed he had crossed swords with the commander. Huskal closed his eyes.

"It is my duty to fulfill the will of the Chief Aramas."

"I know for a warrior this must be hard for you."

"It's not, Prince Julius. I am charged by my chief to look at this document with great scrutiny. A man's word has much meaning for our people! Words are backed up only by actions and honor. The Prime Eagle has proved time and again what his word means. Do you truly speak on behalf of the alliance?"

"I am authorized to act in the name of the king. I will rule as king of Central Acadia and sit as steward of the alliance when Stephen dies or abdicates. You have my word in these matters, and will find my integrity second to no man."

"All right, give me your hand!" commanded Huskal.

Despite some trepidation, Julius acquiesced to Huskal's demand. As the tribal warrior grabbed his wrists, the alliance officers went for their weapons. Raising his hand to dismiss their concerns, the paladin agreed to Huskal's ceremony. Streams of blue light began to flow out of Huskal's fingertips. The paladin reacted surprised as he saw the head of a wolf engraved in his right hand. The wolf tribe commander proceeded to engrave his own hand with the same magic. As Julius was of Napolitan, a dragon's head was tattooed on Huskal's hand.

"Let this serve now as the bond between our peoples, just as my chief is bound as blood brother to the Prime Eagle. You Julius Imperia are bound to my blood."

"Prime Eagle?"

"That is what my people call the Titan prince."

"That's actually pretty funny," quipped Amuro. "We call him the 'Angel of Death.'"

"Then he is both feared and respected by your people as well," declared Reynard.

"Sometimes more feared then praised," added Walker.

"You have the word of the Wolf Tribe," said Huskal.

Huskal signed the document. Passing the pen to Reynard, the Myotis clan chief signed the document and affixed the tribal seal. Reynard extended his hand to Julius.

"Peace!" shouted Reynard.

Julius shook his hand. Tension dispersed, both delegations allowed for a moment of levity. They exchanged hugs and handshakes now that a declaration of peace had finally been obtained.

"Perhaps you would come back to our campsite and enjoy a celebratory drink," offered Julius.

"No," decided Huskal. "Your drink does nothing for us. If you would indulge us, however, we could have a toast here."

"That's fine," warned Julius. "Just so you know, we'll be heading back for Central Acadia in the morning."

"Yes," praised Reynard. "You will be the bearers of grand news."

"Yes, but you don't know how good," said Julius.

Members of each camp carried wine to the hill where the delegation was positioned. Pouring a glass of each other's wine, Julius and Huskal crossed their arms under one another, and drank a toast.

FORT CAPRICORN, EVENING

"The minds of Demonkin and Nephilim do not work like those of creation. They are cunning and full of deception. No matter how much time you devote to studying them, there is still more to learn. I have not pretended that I can guess their plans, and that is why I exploit my cursed form whenever I can. The only way we can truly stop them is to guess correctly and hit them will full power. Either that, or rely on pure luck."

—Duke Wilhelm's Second Report

Nestled just outside Fort Capricorn, Duke Wilhelm nodded in approval of the establishment of the mobile command center. Walking past the overworked technicians, the duke took his place at the strategy table with the Titan command staff. Staring directly across from his seat, Cedric read utter frustration in his mentor's countenance. Cecilia and Horace sat on either side of Cedric with looks of boredom and depression. Horace's only comfort was the cigar that he was working on. The only entertainment was Christian and Valentine yelling on the other side of the room over the results of the war games and who had the better intelligence system. The jovial nature of the two rivals showed it wasn't really much of an argument.

"Look what the cat dragged in," exclaimed Cecilia. "The Sentinel who drove us out to this God-forsaken fort for absolutely no reason!"

Wilhelm paid no heed to the comment but rather stared at the decanters on the table. Accepting Cedric's hand gesture, the Sentinel took a brandy.

"Anything?" asked Wilhelm.

"Thanks to Valentine's camera, we observed the whole meeting," commented Cecilia.

"Spying on your own commanders, Valentine?" questioned Wilhelm. "You're a man after my own heart."

"I figured we needed a bird's-eye view of the proceedings," declared Valentine.

"If not for his absolute disregard of the natural law, Valentine would have made a perfect Titan," offered Christian.

"Dare I ask how the meeting went?" teased Wilhelm.

"Let's just say the alliance and the tribes will be holding hands and skipping through the fields soon," quipped Cecilia.

"They bought it?" inquired Wilhelm.

"Only the armistice, but our hopes for vassalage are all but gone," chimed Cedric.

"We could have stayed home for this," scolded Cecilia.

"An intelligent mistake?" pleaded Wilhelm, shaking his head. "We all saw the same intelligence."

"I know," reassured Cedric. "Oh well, it was only a forty-kilometer wild goose chase, so it wasn't too bad."

"At least we got some good training in today!" exclaimed Cecilia.

"That's the spirit, your highness!" interjected Horace.

"It was hysterical trying to watch those Acadians try to keep up," recollected Cecilia. "Cedric riding up and down their lines trying to get them into battle shape as they fell on their asses. It almost made the trip worth it."

"I just don't understand why Abaddon didn't hit the negotiations," mentioned Wilhelm as he sipped his drink. "Two marshals and the four tribal chiefs—the target was just too inviting."

"Three tribal chiefs . . ." corrected Christian.

"Three?" questioned Wilhelm, a slight panic in his face.

"Aramas sent Huskal to attend the meetings in his place," said Valentine.

"The tribes are all about symbols," explained Christian. "Since Stephen didn't attend, Aramas wouldn't lose face."

Standing from his seat, Wilhelm banged his hands against the table to the shock of everyone in the room.

"Oh, God . . . what have I done?" exclaimed Wilhelm, gathering his things. "Abaddon isn't targeting the meetings! He's going to assassinate Aramas!"

"Get ready to ride!" ordered Cedric.

Everyone made haste to leave before Wilhelm interceded.

"No, Cedric! You'll never make it there in time; at least I'll have a chance. Stay here with the armada. You may be needed yet."

Wilhelm ran out. Concerned, every warrior and soldier in the room looked to their commander for orders.

"Cedric, if Aramas dies, all bets are off," counseled Cecilia.

"The tribes will immediately retaliate," reasoned Horace. "Six cohorts against the entire tribal army; it will be a slaughter."

"Then the tribal envoy is dead!" cried Cecilia.

Wiping the sweat beading off his brow, Cedric pulled out his rosary beads. Though it seemed like an eternity to those in the room, the sword master offered up a silent prayer. Inspired by divine providence, the titan prince's open eyes were focused and determined.

"Christian!" barked Cedric.

"Yes, sir."

"Walk with me! Cecilia, Horace, muster the riders and our reinforcements. Load our armor and weapons onto the hover train and have it follow us. Night-riding clothes only. We need to form a quick encampment and close the gap on the ruins."

"Shouldn't we just go right in now?" questioned Cecilia.

"I don't want to make the tribes nervous and think we've broken the deal until our friends need us. This dark angel's plan may anticipate us causing greater chaos in a blind charge."

"Understood."

Cedric winked at his sister before he walked out the back door with Christian. Staring at the stairs in the night sky, Colin chomped on a piece of sugar cane behind the building.

"Perfect, on your feet, soldier," commanded Cedric.

"What is it, master?" asked Colin.

"Christian, do you trust me?" questioned Cedric.

"Cedric, you don't need to ask that question of me."

Grabbing him on his soldiers, Cedric stared his friend in the eyes. Not unused to this treatment in the past, Christian tried to read his commanding officer.

"Do you trust me Christian? I need an answer."

Christian returned the stare. In that moment, he knew what was being asked of him and knew he had to respond.

"You are my prince and my friend. I have vowed to serve you with my whole heart and soul. I would follow you anywhere you asked, even into the gates of hell themselves. Cedric, I trust you and I put my life in your hands."

"Ride back to Verian, and on my signal, I want you to extract Hippolyte and Minerva from the castle."

"Master Cedric, do you hear yourself?" roared a panicked Colin. "The legal consequences to you are far too great! You'll be charged with treason."

"Don't worry, Cedric, I'll take care of it," responded a nodding Christian.

"Godspeed!"

"Just don't do anything stupid out there while I'm not here to watch your back!"

"I've got my sister here; I'll be fine."

Cedric gave Christian a quick hug. He hit Colin on the shoulder and smiled. Putting on his riding gloves, Christian vaulted himself onto his saddled horse. A confused Colin trailed him, wondering what the spy master was thinking.

"Christian, why didn't you try to talk him out of it? He'd listen to you! These orders!"

"Are you going to shut up? Or am I going to have to leave you behind?"

"Christian!"

"You'd better learn something if you want to be an officer some day and not just an assassin. There are some orders you receive that you don't question. You just follow them."

"It's treason under Acadian law!"

"I find no duty in following an unjust law! In fact, I find a duty in opposing it. Now, are you coming?"

"Well, I'm not leaving you by yourself," said Colin as he straddled his horse.

"We have to ride quickly. We must be in Verian before first light."

"God, when we snuck out of the city, I didn't think we were going to sneak back in."

"One of the many ironies of life! I'm warning you this isn't going to be an easy mission and maybe by the grace of God we'll execute it. Let's ride!"

The two took off at breakneck speed for the Gold Road and the path back to Verian. Returning to the command center, the prince's younger sibling cornered him.

"I know what you're doing."

"Cecilia, if you want to relieve me of command, you'd better do it now."

"Never! You know everyone else in this alliance talks about doing the right thing. You, brother, actually do it!"

"Time will tell if it does us any good. Let's just pray Wilhelm was wrong."

"He may exaggerate but he's never wrong."

Sharing a sense of the unavoidable consequences, the twins saw Horace speaking to one of the other officers. Preparations were already being made outside for transport. The war master reported back to Cedric.

"We picked out a suitable location to make camp. We can bring in the train with little suspicion as long as we keep the train nice and slow. Since no one knows we're out here, it shouldn't be too hard."

Cedric nodded before he walked over to one of the technicians.

"You keep this channel open and receiving. If you need to talk to me, use my emergency frequency only. If you get a message from Marshal Julius, relay it to me pronto."

The technician acknowledged Cedric's order with a, "Yes, your excellency." The command staff left the tent and walked out into the fields in front of the fort. They watched as Acadians with "eyes filled of sleep" marched mindlessly to the hover trains among the more professional infantry from Evengard and Napolitan. Riders were busy loading their gear into the rear cargo holds of the train. Once their gear was loaded, the Titan riders began to change into outfits that gave them the appearance of rangers. The scarlet riders simply grabbed the edge of their cloaks, and their capes transformed into hooded green cloaks. Cedric walked to Jericho and Cecilia to Myst. Mounting their steeds, they pulled up the hoods. A quick hand signal from Cedric was all the riders needed to surround the train. Forming blue paths of light below, the hover train began to glide. The riders flanked it in a due-north direction. Turning to his sister, a smile returned to Cedric's face.

"Well, you said you were bored."

"It gets me wondering, brother—we were already too late to save Aramas. Are we too late to save Stephen as well?"

"I was thinking the same thing, sis."

Cecilia could see the rosary beads in her brother's hand as the riders continued their methodical pace in the night.

Wolf Tribe Encampment

"Hippolyte, by the grace of the spirits, I bestow upon you the sacred blessing. In the event of my passing, I name you chief of the Wolf Tribe. Normally you would have had many revolutions to learn our ways, but you're going to have to learn quickly. You must perform the tasks I assign to you and gain the wisdom and temperance necessary to become a chief. I have no choice left. My son is dead, and you are all that I have. I know that when my end comes, I leave the tribe in good hands."

—*Aramas, on the naming of Hippolyte as his successor*

Aramas sat on his tribal throne surrounded by his blood guard and his two wolf guards. Interlacing his fingers, the chief contemplated a million thoughts. He imagined that the peace treaty must have been signed by now. However, he also wondered what was keeping Huskal from sending him some sort of signal that the negotiations had concluded. Only then would his beloved granddaughters be able to come home. As he pondered these facts, a strong wind began to blow all over the tent. Sensing danger, Aramas stood from his throne and drew a long curved sword from the scabbard sitting on his lap. The two wolves around him sat up and growled. Upon seeing the actions of their chief and the wolves, the blood guard drew their swords and formed a phalanx around their chief. Positioned a step above them, Aramas made sure he could see the entrance to the longhouse.

"This wind is not natural," remarked Aramas. "All I can sense is darkness."

A dark gate opened in the middle of the tent as the blood guard put up their hide shields. Abaddon strutted out of the gate, grinning from ear

242

to ear, as if he were going for an evening stroll. Cloaked duco-mutatios, followed the dark angel out of the gate. Twirling his finger in the air and bowing, Abaddon mocked the stature of Aramas.

"Chief of Chief Aramas, I am truly awed to stand in your presence."

"Who are you?" asked Aramas. "Why do you defile my people with your malevolence?"

"I have you at a disadvantage since you don't know me. My name is Abaddon. I am a warrior like yourself; we just don't share the same goal."

"What goal is that?"

"You want to create peace in this world. Very noble, but it simply interferes with all of my plans. You see, in order to accomplish my mission, it would be much easier to have the tribes and the alliance at each other's throats. Therefore, I concluded the only way I'm going to achieve my objective is with your assistance. "

"And what makes you think I would assist you?"

"You're not going to have to do much—just drop dead!" taunted a laughing Abaddon.

"What in the name of Terminus Mundus are you?"

"Do not insult me by thinking of me as another common human of this world. Your race has always been so narrow in that thinking. No, friend, my origin is of a much different location!"

Abaddon tore the robes from his body. Revealing his armor and spreading his wings, had the intended objective. Though they would not fail in their duty to the Chief, the blood guard faces were laced with terror.

"You are one of the dark ones the ancients and the legends spoke of!"

"Legend? Do you doubt your own eyes, Aramas?"

"Even if you kill me, what good will that do?"

"It's truly naïve to think that killing you was the only part of my plan. You'll love this next part."

Abaddon snapped his finger. Shifting their appearance, the duco-mutatios transformed into humans. Pulling off their robes, ornate Acadian armor and Acadian blades adorned their bodies. Aramas knew the implications.

"Duco-mutatios! You demon!"

"You can now decide what will be worse! Your own death or the thought of your tribe's retaliation! Huskal is too hot-blooded for the situation you left him in. The delegation from the alliance is as good as slaughtered. As soon as they attack, your granddaughters will already be dead!"

"NO!"

Pointing his finger forward, Aramas commanded his wolves to tear Abaddon to pieces. Anticipating the retaliation, Abaddon fluidly drew the curved swords behind his back. Abaddon kicked the first wolf under his chest and drove his sword into the back of his neck. The second wolf went for Abaddon's throat, but the angel grabbed him and stabbed him quickly in the side of the neck. Charging fearlessly drown the steps, the blood guard attacked the dark angel as one. Abaddon stabbed the first one in the stomach, then spun and sliced him with his second sword. He killed the second one by striking up with his sword, cutting him from groin to neck, while at the same time striking a third member of the guard deep in his chest.

Abaddon spread his wings and jumped back to give himself more room as seven more opponents attacked him. Even with their superior numbers, the finest warriors of the Wolf Tribe were no match for Abaddon. The dark angel was simply too fast. Moving from one opponent to the next, a blood guard would die before he struck the fallen one. Staring in horror, Aramas witnessed the utter butchering of his blood guard by Abaddon's swords. Tormented by the sight of blood and organs splashing all over the tent, he could hear the screams and cries of his people as the duco-mutatios slaughtered them outside the tent. Abaddon licked his lips as he loped off the head of the second-to-last blood guard standing.

The last guard was kneeling and nursing a wound he had already received. As he stood to attack, Abaddon drove his blade deep into his midsection. Laughing heartily, the dark angel ripped out his guts as he pulled out his swords. Snapping at the sight, Aramas jumped from his throne and gripped his sword with two hands. Knocking Abaddon off balance with the jump attack, Aramas sliced at Abaddon's left arm, breaking through his armor and drawing blood. The dark angel stared down at his wound and managed a smile.

"Pretty good, old man!" saluted Abaddon. "It looks like I'm going to have to get serious."

Attacking in rage a second time, Abaddon prepared for Aramas. The two hit their swords together, but the stronger Abaddon was able to shove Aramas at will. Outside of the tent, the duco-mutatios performed their farce brilliantly. They mercilessly killed anyone they came upon, driving spears and swords through them. Parents bravely fought the tormentors so their children could escape. Running for safety, a group of nine children managed to make it to the cornfields behind the encampment. Two of the demonkin took off after them on horseback. Appearing as if they were going to run them down with the horses, a second mystical gate burst open in front of them. Knocked off balance by the impact of emerging white-and-black feathers, they witnessed Wilhelm von Angelhardt step out of the gate. Dressed in Titan steel plate bearing the insignia of house Rhone on his chest, the duke held a long spear in his right hand and a tower shield in his left hand. A crossbow was strung across his cloak in the back while a glowing red long sword was clasped to his side. As the feathers touched the faces of the duco-mutatios, the false transformation disappeared and the silvery skin returned.

"I thought so," boomed Wilhelm before he turned to the children. "Run! I'll hold them off!"

The children needed little coaxing to heed Wilhelm's words. They took off as the two face-dancers sneered at him. Staking his spear in the ground, Wilhelm drew his blade, Devilslayer, from his side. The duco-mutatios attacked him, but Wilhelm knocked the first away with his shield. The other came upon him, and Wilhelm used his sword to block the attack. Striking at the Titan duke in unison, they could not overpower the veteran warrior. Managing to watch the children escape with one eye, Wilhelm fended off the attacks.

Inside the longhouse, Aramas and Abaddon continued their battle. It took everything Aramas had just to defend himself against the fallen angels' sword attacks. His exhaustion was showing because Aramas's attacks became wilder by the second. Toying with the chief long enough and sensing a bizarre power, Abaddon decided to finish him off.

"Pretty good Aramas, but not good enough!" said Abaddon.

Abaddon knocked Aramas's sword away. Driving his lead sword into the chief's neck, Abaddon pierced his midsection with his other sword. Aramas's mouth filled with blood as Abaddon slowly removed his swords, gutting the old chief. Impressed with his work, Abaddon managed a slight laugh.

"This end was inevitable. All of your efforts have gone for nothing, but know that you are only the first."

Aramas fell to his knees before collapsing on his face. The fallen angel surveyed the room, much to his delight. Replacing his swords behind him, he opened a portal and left.

Outside, Wilhelm watched the village children escape to safety. Focusing his full attention on the duco-mutatios now, he drove his sword into the neck of the lead attacker. As this one lay dying, Wilhelm rolled back to his original position and grabbed his spear. He aimed and caught the other face-dancer in the chest with his throw. In one motion he pulled out both weapons and replaced them. Sprinting into the village proper, the duke knew he was too late. The remaining duco-mutatios had completed their performance and were in full retreat. Reeking with blood and the smell of death, Wilhelm angrily drew his crossbow. Fruitlessly firing shots into the distance, the duco-mutatios were already done. The full retreat made Wilhelm realize the gravity of the situation.

"Aramas!" screamed Wilhelm, hoping against hope that the chief would emerge.

Wilhelm ran into the longhouse and witnessed the slaughter. Covering his mouth to prevent him from gagging, the duke bowed his head and blessed himself. Scanning the room, he detected movement from one of the bodies.

"Oh, no,"

He went over to Aramas's body and turned him over. Closing his eyes, the duke murmured a prayer and placed his hand over the chief's heart. A read of his vitals, however, told Wilhelm that he was beyond any craft he knew to save his life. The chief strained to open his eyes as he felt warmth upon him.

"I'm truly sorry, Chief Aramas," pleaded Wilhelm. "I can do nothing for you."

"Tell them, Titan!" a struggling Aramas stammered. "Speak truth... of what happened here.

"I know who did this, Aramas. This crime will not go unpunished."

"Tell your prince... make him honor his vow to save my granddaughters..."

"Rest assured old friend, your trust is not misplaced."

Aramas died in his arms. Placing his hands over Aramas's eyelids, Wilhelm closed them and spoke the final blessing over his body.

"Eternal rest grant to them, O Lord, and let perpetual light shine upon them. May their souls and all the souls of the faithfully departed rest in thy divine presence. In nomine patri, filia, et spiritus sanctus!"

Setting the body of the great chief down, Wilhelm beat his hand into the ground.

"I was such a fool. My prince... how I failed you!"

Somberly walking out of the tent, Wilhelm turned his head to the night sky. In the mountains he perceived smoke signals rising into the sky.

"It's already begun. Right now, I have to try and keep those children alive. When Abaddon founds out his demonkin failed, there won't be any quarter."

Examining the slaughter one last time, Wilhelm finally understood the nature of the enemy he was facing. Determined to stop him, the duke followed the path the children took in order to ensure their safety.

CASTLE ACADIA, VERIAN

"Everyone complains that Cedric has a drinking problem, but I think we all have addictions; mine is chocolate ice cream."

—*Princess Cassandra to Felicia*

Despite their reputation to the contrary, the Acadians certainly didn't skimp on the accommodations for Hippolyte and Minerva. The apartment they had received was spacious with a sitting area, private baths, and an adjoining bedroom. Hippolyte was lying down on a very large and comfy bed with her hands behind her hair, staring at the ceiling. Grabbing her stomach, fear and panic gripped her.

"Grandpa?" cried Hippolyte.

"Did you say something, sis?" asked Minerva's from one of the bathrooms.

Walking into the room, Minerva dressed for bed in silk robe over a silk negligee. Hippolyte thought of this as just another incident of Minerva taking full advantage of Acadian hospitality. Minerva had taken to eating all of her meals in the Acadian royal dining room rather than in her room like her sister. She had also taken full advantage of the generous donations from the wardrobes of both Princess Cassandra and Princess Marie. Hippolyte worried, however, that her sister was simply being treated as a court fool by the Acadians.

"No . . . just had a weird feeling there for a second . . . it's gone now," replied Hippolyte.

"Good," said a smiling Minerva before she jumped onto her bed and sprawled out among the pillows. "I could so get used to this. This is so much better then sleeping on the ground with a root in your back."

"Just remember, it's not going to last forever. You should start distancing yourself from the luxuries of this place."

"I know. I just wish I could see that handsome captain one more time before we pulled out."

"Keep dreaming; let's just pray to the spirits that the negotiations went okay today. I'd hate to have to deal with the consequences."

"I was thinking about that. I figured they would have made some announcement. Isn't that something the Acadians would broadcast?"

"You may be right. It might be worth snooping around a little bit."

Sitting up from the bed, Hippolyte put her boots on and laced them up.

"I'm a little hungry. I'm going to head back down to the kitchen. Do you want anything?"

Hippolyte looked to see her sister was already passed out with the same dreamy smile on her face. Headphones plugged in her ears, Minerva was oblivious to the world.

"Grandpa was right about you."

Like the good sister that she was, Hippolyte tucked Minerva in and kissed her good night. Quietly opening and closing the door, Hippolyte strode the long, silent hallway corridors. The only presence was the night crew of royal guards, but they gave the tribal girl her space when they saw she was unarmed. It took her a good fifteen minutes before she finally walked down a back staircase to the castle galley. A single chef was on duty at this time of night.

"Well, look who's here!" greeted the chef. "Hippolyte, right?"

"Yes."

"In my line of work, you learn to remember names and faces. What can I get you?"

"A late-night snack would do me good. Do you have any ice cream left?"

"Of course, we've got to make it by the carton here with all the sweet tooths that we have. I was just making some now. If you would take a seat next to her highness, I'll bring some right out."

"Her highness?"

Pointing to a single table in a room adjacent to the galley, the chef directed Hippolyte's attention to the princess. Seated at table, Cassandra was dressed in her black nightgown, robe, and slippers. Tugging at the ponytail she had her hair set in for sleep, Cassandra waved toward the wolf tribe princess.

"Hi."

Hippolyte walked over.

"Hi, I don't think we've had the pleasure. I'm Hippolyte."

"Cassandra Acadia. It seems like we both had the same craving. Just don't talk too loud or my diet will know what we're doing."

"I was a bit hungry."

"My problem is that when I get depressed, I bury myself in ice cream."

"And why are you depressed?"

"Because I'm worried about my fiancé. He had to leave rather abruptly."

"Anyone I know?"

"Probably by reputation alone, it's Prince Cedric of Titanus."

Grimacing at the name, Hippolyte blushed slightly. She thought back to the incident a few rotations ago and realized what the handsome prince had meant when he had business at the Castle.

"Oh?"

"I understand that reaction," laughed Cassandra. "I just didn't expect a tribal girl to be so envious of me."

"I didn't know he was engaged."

"I'm sure they don't tell too many tales of Stephen's eldest daughter out in the wilderness. However, you do have a bit of reputation. They call you the she-wolf of Fenrir!"

"I like that title," boasted Hippolyte as she stared at an envelope in Cassandra's hand. "Late-night reading?"

"My Cedric left me a note explaining his departure and a poem. I don't have the heart to tell him that his poetry is terrible because he tries so hard."

"A warrior writing poetry?"

"Among our people it is a custom for a warrior to embrace a classical education. Cedric is a master of many trades, just not writing poetry."

The chef brought two dishes of ice cream out to the girls.

"Here you go, ladies," said the chef, bowing to Cassandra. "Your highness, I'm heading up to bed, but I left more in the freezer if you need it. Good night."

Cassandra nodded her head slightly to answer the courtesy of the departing chef. Joining her new found friend in a late night indulgence, the ladies preferred to enjoy it differently. Cassandra was dainty as usual, scooping a little at a time and bringing it to her mouth. Swirling it together with her spoon, Hippolyte gobbled large bites. At one point she finally grabbed her forehead, much to Cassandra's delight.

"Ha!" teased Cassandra. "Brain freeze!"

"What?" questioned Hippolyte.

"It's what we call the headache you get if you eat frozen food too fast."

Hippolyte started to laugh at Cassandra's teasing but knew that she had an ample opening to come back at her.

"Sorry for laughing, but I would have never guessed that an older woman from the steel-bellies could be so fun."

Cassandra was taken aback by the last comment and Hippolyte's laughter. Abruptly ending her laugh, the princes adopted a serious tone.

"I am not an older woman! In fact, at most I might have seen three or four more revolutions than you have. I'm just very mature for my age; it happens to run in my family."

"Can I ask you a personal question?

"So bluntly... well, I guess it can't hurt too much..."

"I didn't realize that Acadians had pointy ears."

"I'm half-elf on my mother's side, so the trait is dominant. It is very rare for a half-breed not to have the ears."

"If you're an elf, that means you can use magic."

"I would prefer if you would call it sorcery. I don't pull a rabbit out of my hat or anything."

Hippolyte looked at her blankly, wondering where this sudden haughtiness came from. Frustrated by the moment, Cassandra struggled to entertain her blunt guest. However, she felt herself big enough to put up with a few insults since Cedric had asked this of her.

"Forget it."

Cassandra smiled after she ate another bite. In the hope of breaking the tension, the princess changed the subject.

"Do you have anyone special waiting for you?"

"Well, I'm the daughter of the chief so many warriors like to give me things. I really haven't had the time... there are certain approvals that need to be made."

"I see. What kind of guy would you prefer?"

"Well, he'd have to be strong of body and spirit, cunning, but still have a gentle heart."

"Well, that's pretty subjective."

"Now you know why I don't have anyone waiting for me."

"I only asked because I've had some long conversations with your sister since she's been here. She seems to be quite certain about the type of guy she wants."

"I hope she didn't cause any trouble."

"She's a doll. I know she was quite smitten with my shield the first time that she saw him, so I was curious about you."

"Your shield?"

"Lord Captain Walker is my personal bodyguard when he is on duty at the castle. When I was a little girl I kept forgetting his name so I called him shield because of the big ornate shield on his back. I still use it as a term of affection."

"That isn't much different than Huskal, who serves my grandfather."

"I guess some similarities can transcend cultural differences. We both like strong men, can protect ourselves, and enjoy chocolate ice cream."

"Common ground, no doubt."

"Well, I do hope that everything works out at these negotiations."

"That's two of us, but it's been hard for my people to accept. I lost both my parents to templars of Central Acadia."

"Though I didn't personally know him, I know my grandfather was killed by renegade members of your tribe."

"I wish we didn't share that."

"Agreed."

"I wish we could do this more often, Cassandra."

"Please don't keep doing it over ice cream, I have a hard enough time maintaining this figure as it is. Am I correct to assume that you must be pretty good on a horse?"

"I'm one of the best."

"Would you like to ride tomorrow?"

"You ride?"

"I'm good enough to stay on the horse. I used to ride a lot more, but I started doing it again recently. It helps to have a cavalry officer as a companion."

"I was tired of being cooped up in this castle anyway. I'd love to go for a ride."

"Invite your sister and I'll take you around the grounds. Afterward we can come back for high tea with my sister Marie."

"You have a younger sister too?"

"Yes."

"Are all younger sisters cute and impertinent?"

"Well..."

As Cassandra contemplated Hippolyte's statement, an image of Cecilia wielding her spear kept returning to her mind. Clearing her thoughts, she pictured the vanadis blushing, wearing a frilly dress, and speaking in proper decorum. The thought was utterly horrifying to her.

"There are always some exceptions. Well, meet me about midday; I have some training to take care of in the morning."

"I'm glad we'll get one more chance to talk before we leave. Maybe this will be the start of a friendship."

"I hope so. Without the help of the tribes, we'll never be able to stop the empire. Cedric once talked about a time where the kingdoms and tribes fought side by side. Now would you like seconds?"

"I'd thought you'd never ask."

"Follow me."

The two girls walked back to the galley.

"By the way, how do you keep your hair so straight in the wild?" asked Cassandra.

"There are actually some herbs that, you ground them together with some rose water."

"I'll have to try that in the summer. My handmaiden is simply working too hard to get all the knots out."

Laughing, Cassandra opened the refrigerator.

Ruins of the Istle Hills

"Any good marshal needs to keep a journal of the events recorded in his tenure. It makes it easier to dispute the facts from fiction when determining his legacy. I will allow history to determine whether or not I was a good general, but I shall leave an undisputable record of truth."

—*Page one of the journal of Prince Marshal Julius Imperia*

Julius was sitting by a large fire, a thin necklace around his neck and a felt-tip pen in his hand. Scribbling in a large book, a lock hung down from the side of it. Despite the light mood of those around him, Julius remained in his armor with his sword and shield lying next to him. He was busy noting all of the conversations that took place between the delegations. When this was completed, the paladin left some room to make his own personal notes on the incident:

"Finally on this rotation, I have achieved my goal. I've done all that has been asked of me, and now I finally have the necessary political capital I need to get what I want. No one is ever going to take this one from me. Sorry, Cedric, but I can do it on my own after all. You're the better soldier, but I am the far better diplomat."

Julius had just dotted his period when Walker came up to sit next to him by the fire. Closing his journal, Julius locked it with the key around his neck. Easing the cold of the night, Walker put his hands right in the fire. The paladin observed Walker was wearing his armor, and also had his sword and shield attached.

"You look like a man who's troubled," observed Julius.

"Call it the cold or just simply a gut feeling, but in my heart I know that something isn't right."

"Like what?"

"I picked up smoke signals coming from the Griffin Mountains in the south."

Pulling out his scopes, Julius focused his attention on the mountains. The dragon paladin wasn't taking any chances of anything ruining his victory. Observing the same smoke signals, Julius pondered the meaning.

"I don't know what those mean, but they're definitely tribal. Damn, Valentine is the only guy I know that can read tribal signals, and he isn't here!"

"What do we do, Marshal?"

"I don't know if we should jump to military conclusions. For all I know, the signals are communications between the delegation and the tribe that the meeting was a success."

"I've tried very hard to believe that at first."

"If they were going to hit us, Walker, they would have done it by now."

"No. If I were them, I would wait. They know they've got all of the advantages in this place and we're outnumbered. I wouldn't risk a night attack."

"Your concerns are noted; we're out of here at first light. I had my men dig in with a proper stockade, so we're going to have some protections. We'll have the officers take two-hour shifts, but make sure you sober up some of our men and post them as guards."

"Yeah. I think I'll do that."

"Make sure you reign in those two Acadian bucks as well. I don't want any incidents after a victory like this."

"You and me both," agreed Walker as he stood and walked away.

"I wonder where the hell Amuro is. She should be helping me. I guess I can understand why Walker would be so paranoid in this place, but now I can't shake the feeling that something is wrong."

Amuro walked gingerly outside of the stockade dressed in her cloak over an elf ranger outfit. Held in her hands was the bottle Christian gave her and two long-stem glasses. She moved with a purpose and didn't have the normal cheery expression that she showed toward her peers. Spotting her target, she observed Malcolm sitting on the limb off the bough of a large and old oak tree at the front of treeline just before the ruins. Presuming the ranger was meditating since his eyes were closed, she tapped her foot impatiently. Amuro took two deep breaths to calm herself, but she jumped back slightly when she noticed Malcolm opening his eyes.

"Good evening, Amuro."

Amuro blushed and was surprised at the gentlemanly tone that Malcolm was using toward her for once. Malcolm stared at his commanding officer with genuine surprise as well. He wasn't used to seeing Amuro so timid and meek. Malcolm jumped down from the limb.

"Would you mind if we sat underneath this tree for a while?" asked Amuro. "I'd like to talk with you."

"As you wish."

Dusting off a spot on the ground, Malcolm allowed Amuro to take seat with her back against the trunk. The ranger took a seat next to her.

"Would you care for a drink?" offered Amuro.

"I don't prefer human libations."

"I brought an elven one with me."

"Really? I didn't realize that any wares from Evengard had reached Verian or Fort Orion."

"It was a gift from a friend."

Opening the bottle with a little magic, Amuro poured two glasses. The liquid was much thicker than most alcohol with a deep red color. She passed a glass over to Malcolm, who sniffed it as he took it.

"Sweet wine . . ." queried a puzzled Malcolm. "I don't know which friend gave it to you, but it must have cost them a good bit of gold."

Amuro and Malcolm hit their glasses together and took a drink. Tasting it, Malcolm nodded his head.

"This is a very difficult bottle to come by; it's a reserve from one of the finest vineyards in Evengard. You said a friend gave this to you?"

"A very good friend, well-versed in elven traditions."

Taking a moment to gaze at the sky, the elves observed the reddish Alpha was full this evening while the orange Beta was waxing and the yellow Gamma was waning. Amuro nudged herself a little closer to Malcolm so her head rested on his shoulder.

"It's a beautiful night," commented Amuro.

"Yes."

"That's all you can say?"

"What do you want me to say?"

"Something a little more romantic. You know it's proper for elves to be chivalrous."

"What's with this obsession with chivalry? I'm never going to be Cedric Rhone, so you might as well stop wishing for that."

Intentionally distracting him with the conversation, Amuro tried to fill Malcolm's glass again. Malcolm didn't miss a trick and put his hand up to say "no more."

"Malcolm you're a great guy, but you're stiff as a board. Do you know why I'm so aggressive with you?"

"Sadism?"

"Sadism, are you insane! I tease you because I don't know what signals you're giving to me."

"Signals?"

Amuro closed her eyes. She opened them quickly so they were big and bright in front of Malcolm.

"Do you think I'm beautiful?"

Malcolm took a long drink first before answering. Dreading the voice of his mentor Cerwin Faulkner screaming 'putz' at him, the ranger composed himself for a moment before giving an answer that seemed to be with him for a long time.

"Yes, Amuro. I've always thought you were extremely attractive. I didn't think the other elves were right when they called you tomboy. They just never saw your true grace and beauty."

"You thought this all along!"

Malcolm nodded. Grabbing him by the collar of his uniform, Amuro pulled Malcolm close to her. Not knowing if his commanding officer was prepared to strike, the ranger prepared to dodge the attack.

"Why didn't you ever say any of this before?" demanded Amuro.

"You never gave me half a chance!" pleaded Malcolm. "You were always so flamboyant in your displays, and I just don't think it's proper to say these things in front of soldiers during combat. I just thought you were trying too hard."

Amuro pushed her lips forward and kissed Malcolm very hard. The elf prince was quite shocked but wasn't resisting. Tipsy from the booze, the elf marshal lost her balance and actually knocked the two of them over. The two elves started to laugh when they broke their kiss on the ground. Amuro looked dreamily at the smile on Malcolm's face as if she'd been waiting for an eternity to see it.

"Come here, you!" said Malcolm.

Wrapping his arms around Amuro, Malcolm made out with his commanding officer in the moonlight. While the two elves were fooling around, Julius walked along the camp. He spotted a few of the legionnaires on duty and relayed Walker's concerns to them. Julius watched Walker do the same before he joined his legions soldiers at one of the tapped barrels. His brother was busy joking with the legions and reliving past war stories. Though he would never admit it, Julius was envious of his brother's relationship with the army. Spotting his brother, Cagius had a mug of ale ready for the triumphant paladin in one hand and held up Julius' drunken squire in his other. The older brother took the mug and had a long swallow.

"You rascal. What have you done now?"

"I was trying to found out how good a drinker the judge's son was. I guess even at law school, Matthias must have been a lightweight."

As soon as he said that, Vincenzo fell over and threw up. Cheering and hollering, the legion soldiers picked up the squire and tossed him in the air. Even Julius couldn't help but laugh at his brother's antics, still he felt duty-bound to warn Cagius about what was coming.

"Cagius, Walker picked up some smoke signals coming from the Griffin Mountains."

"From the mountain encampment?" asked Cagius.

"That's what we think."

"Looks like it's time to break up our party. I knew we should have brought Valentine with us."

"Just keep an eye out for anything suspicious and use your instincts. Walker's taking the first watch. You relieve him, and I'll relieve you. Where the hell is Amuro, I need to tell her what's going on."

"Trust me, I don't think Amuro going to be too much help tonight. Do you we think we should signal back for reinforcements?"

"If we bring in more troops, the tribes will think that we broke the treaty. I'm afraid we're alone here. We ride early and hard."

Nodding, the brothers clinked their mugs before taking a final drink. Five kilometers from the alliance encampment, the tribes were singing and dancing in front of a large fire. A scream brought the celebration to a sudden halt.

"SIGNALS!" screamed one of the guards.

Hush fell over the camp as Huskal and Josephine emerged from their tents. Two tribesmen began to record the message on tanned skins before handing the message over to Huskal. The wolf tribe commander didn't need to read them to confirm the horror in his mind. Josephine gasped.

"No," cried Huskal.

"They can't be right," stammered Josephine as she stared at the note. "It must be a mistake."

"Reynard!" screamed Huskal. "Posha! Adnar!"

The three leaders of the tribes emerged from their tents. Adnar seemed to still be in a drunken stupor while Posha was wiping sleep from her eyes. Reynard snatched the note from Josephine and scanned it. There was no reaction in his face save for two tears streaming down from his eyes. Posha and Adnar both looked at the note in disbelief.

"I need your counsel," demanded Huskal. "We cannot afford to make a mistake."

"I recommend I use the tribal magic to summon your spirit beast," suggested Posha. "You will be able to travel the great distance in no time and see what you must with your own eyes."

"I agree," concurred Reynard.

"All right," agreed Huskal.

Posha drew a magic circle in the dirt with her staff. Beckoning Huskal to enter the circle, the tribal chief priestess began to chant in a barely audible language. Members of the Syrus clan spread their incense and torches around the circle. Huskal took five deep breaths.

"Ancient spirits, heed my call," chanted Posha. "Return this brave soul to his ancient route. Open the path for the journey of the traveler!"

Huskal felt smoke and yellow light form around him. Even though his body did not transform, Huskal could feel the changes to his very soul. His sense of sight and hearing strengthened. Smelling blood hundreds of kilometers away, he felt comfortable in the enveloping night. It was then when he lost consciousness. When he woke again, Huskal was racing along the plains in the body of the wolf. The scent of his home penetrated all of his senses. As he closed on the target, the scent changed from his home to blood and death. Shuddering from the horrid smell, Huskal pursued the quickest path. Everything was as Wilhelm had left it; the grounds and tents were littered with dead bodies. A group of tribesmen had arrived from the hills to take the bodies. In his spirit beast form, Huskal could move unnoticed in the encampment. Bounding into the chief's tent, the wolf whelped at the sight of swords marked with lions' heads—Acadian swords—scattered all over the place. Evidence clearly planted by Abaddon and the duco-mutatios but totally foreign to the blood guard of the chief. Howling in sadness, Huskal nuzzled the butchered body of his beloved chief Aramas. The same thought ran through his mind again and again.

"My chief . . . how I have failed you . . ."

The broken heart and howl of the spirit beast reverberated across the plains. Wolf packs picked up the sound and continued it straight to the heart of the tribe encampment in the Istle Hills. Huskal's wolf spirit closed his eyes and growled. His thoughts echoed through his mind once more.

"There is no word for the treachery that the Acadians have performed this night. I promise you now, my chief, that Hippolyte and Minerva will not suffer your fate. I will ensure that they are returned safely and that Hippolyte rises to her rightful rank among our people. Then we shall have our revenge! We were such fools to trust the Acadians. We should have gone with the Titans!"

Huskal bounded out on the tent at full speed. He knew exactly what he wanted to do, and at first light he would hold the Napolitan prince accountable for his treachery.

Titan Encampment, Ten kilometers South of the Istle Hill Ruins

"I'm glad I enjoyed the victory party at Castle Acadia. It was the last peaceful night we ever had."

—*Reflections of Antonio Valentine*

The rays of Primus were just beginning to break through the darkness of night. Awakened early and standing at the ready, soldiers in the Titan camp simply awaited Cedric Rhone's order to mount and ride. Cedric and Cecilia, each with a cup of coffee in their hands, were standing side-by-side. Horace came over to them and saluted.

"There are no reports of any tribal activity moving along the road, your excellency. We have to assume that means the tribes already had their full army standing at the ruins."

"We're vastly outnumbered, but that's nothing new," counseled Cecilia. "It's my duty to inform you that if we are going to retreat, now is the time."

"No," decided Cedric, shaking his head. "We've come this far. If something is going to happen at those ruins, I may be the only mediator that can diffuse the situation."

"Do you still intend to use those girls as a bargaining chip?" asked Cecilia.

"As you mentioned... we're vastly outnumbered."

The three walked over to the technician working at a portable communication device. The technician seemed to be having difficulty with the devices.

"What's the matter, soldier?" asked Cedric.

"Your excellency, for the last hour we've had difficulty reaching Fort Capricorn," explained the technician. "It's as if some form of a dampening field suddenly enveloped the area."

"Your excellency, didn't Colin Wilkins make a similar report with our equipment concerning the Wizards Tower?" reminded Horace.

"My God," ordered Cedric. "Saddle the riders! Boost the power to that device as much as you can. We've got to know if there is an attack."

"Yes, sir," accepted the technician as he went back to work.

Julius Imperia and Walker paced around one another at the Istle Hills encampment. All around them, soldiers were finishing disabling the stockades and loading the equipment to depart. Searching the surrounding area with their scopes, the two officers were concerned with more than just the disabling of the camp.

"Any sign of them?" asked Julius.

"Nothing," screamed Walker. "I am going to kick some ass when those two get back to the encampment. This insubordination can't be tolerated."

"Easy, Walker. I can't imagine what they expected to hunt around here anyway. They can't have strayed that far from the encampment."

"You'd be surprised. I don't like it, Julius!"

"You don't like a lot of things. You kept me up half the night convinced that a night raid was happening on the camp."

"We heard noise from that camp, and then all of a sudden it fell silent. I don't think everyone turned in that quickly! Do you deny that the smoke and light show we were treated to was natural?"

"No. We couldn't risk a night ride. If they were planning an ambush, we would have been ducks-in-a-row."

"It would have been prudent if we departed when I recommended."

"We could not afford to insult the tribes after the ceremony. Calm down, Walker. I'll figure something out."

Shielding her eyes from Primus's rays, Amuro staggered out of her tent. Passing soldiers packed it up to her amusement.

"Do you mind keeping it down? Some of us are still hung over. Am I being punished by not even being offered a cup of coffee?"

"Walker didn't want to light any open fires this morning to give away our position," explained Julius. "You're going to have to endure. What happened to you anyway?"

"Elven sweet wine... if I knew the consequences, I wouldn't have asked DeVries for help!"

"And?" asked Julius.

Watching Malcolm walk out of his tent with a smile on his face, the officers wondered if Amuro finally had had Cedric lobotomize him. The ranger gave Amuro a kiss good morning and held her tightly to his chest.

"I see," observed Julius.

"I worked out a lot of issues last night... I'm getting better," said Malcolm. "Perhaps I have finally shed the reputation of being a putz."

"What's with Walker?" queried Amuro.

"Our two little knights decided to go hunting at dawn despite the fact there was an order not to leave the camp!" yelled Walker. "They haven't come back yet, and we can't get out of here until they do!"

"Walker suspects that something is wrong at the tribal camp and we shouldn't wait to find out," described Julius.

"Walker may be on to something," reasoned Amuro. "I felt a different kind of magic coming out of the camp, at first I thought it was hangover, but I can't be sure anymore."

"Good morning all!" announced Cagius.

"Not again... not this morning..." declared Amuro.

Cagius joined the other officer as if he hadn't drunk a single thing all last night. For a moment he held onto Amuro, who looked incredibly depressed that Cagius was feeling no ill effects of either the drinking or standing on watch. Her eyes betrayed a sense of disdain for the legate, who gave her a peck on the cheek in return.

"What is wrong with you? Are you some kind of Divikin separated from birth? The only guy I've ever seen drink as much as you without a hangover is Cedric."

"It's one of my many secret techniques. I wouldn't be much of a cavalier if I was sloshed all the time. Julius, our boys have got everything packed up, and we are ready to march."

"We're still short two knights,"

"Leave them!" shouted Walker.

"Nobody gets left behind," retorted Julius.

"Want me to organize a roundup?" asked Cagius.

"Walker, gather your men, go with my brother and find those idiots. When you do, confiscate their horses and weapons; they're walking back to Verian."

"Right away, Marshal," answered Walker.

Walker and Cagius went to get their horses. The sounds of horns giving the alert stopped the two in their tracks.

"What now?" demanded Julius. "Five horns signal an attack by the tribes."

Sprinting to the front of the camp, the marshals joined the cohorts gathered to depart. A circle formed around a cuirassier bleeding badly, who had obviously fallen off his horse. Amuro put her hands together and started to chant. Opening them over his wound, she chanted the phrase in elvish meaning, "Heal, light." Amuro put her hands directly to the wounds. The bleeding stopped and the wounds started to close.

"I can stabilize him for now, but he will need more treatment."

Julius bent down to the cuirassier, looking for answers.

"What happened?"

"I was in Lord Cambridge's guard for the hunt," explained the cuirassier. "They surrounded us out of nowhere. They appeared to be of the Wolf Tribe. They didn't say a word. They just started killing us. Lord Alwein and Lord Cambridge ordered us to charge and break through their ranks. Only I survived to tell the tale . . ."

"Then they are dead... that's really bad news for us..." said Walker.

"Are you certain it was the tribes?" questioned Malcolm. "That pattern of attack does not mesh with their tactics."

Holding up his right hand, the cuirassier brought forward an arrow with an obsidian head marked with a wolf sigil. Removing the doubt from the officer's minds, the command staff looked to Julius for orders. Tribal horns sounded in the distance. Cagius grabbed his scopes and looked out. The entire tribal army was moving toward their position with Huskal in the lead. Battle wolves, Nordice vikings, and Myotis infantry had taken up the center behind Huskal while Wolf Tribe light cavalry surrounded them on both sides.

"They're coming in force!" shouted Cagius. "It's the whole damned army at least three hundred thousand strong. Huskal's leading the coalition into battle."

"Call to arms!" ordered Julius. "Defensive positions! Into the ruins! Turn the wagons over once we dig in!"

"We're going to fight?" asked Amuro.

"I don't know, but I'm not going to stand around with a bulls-eye on my back," directed Julius. "Get a radio signal going; see if you can reach Fort Capricorn."

"I don't even know if they have communications at Fort Capricorn," retorted Walker.

"If you've got a better idea, Walker, I'm willing to hear it," demanded Julius.

"I'll see what I can do."

"Double time, people!" shouted Julius back to his men.

The paladin directed the wagons where he wanted them to go. Cagius and the legions were busy digging defensive trenches. All of the officers soon joined in, but something was troubling Amuro.

"I can't believe that the tribes went through all of this just to get us to fall into a trap,"

"That wouldn't be like them at all," observed Malcolm. "They're taking actions we've never seen before."

Deciding the digging was taking too long, Amuro used some of her earth magic to make to some holes. The alliance convoy found a good defensible spot in the ruins by the worn-out shells of an old temple and a large mansion. Turning over wagons, the legions setup defensive barriers Malcolm took his archers on top of a series of steps for a better vantage point. Climbing to the top of the tallest building, a technician desperately tried to get a better signal.

"Emergency line alpha-beta-theta, copy Capricorn over... Emergency line alpha-beta-tango, copy Capricorn over..."

A voice came over the transmitter to the relief of the troops. Everyone started to breathe a little easier.

"This is Capricorn, omega-delta-epsilon... barely reading over..." said the voice over the radio.

"Ruins of Istle Hills... tribal attack... need emergency relief... over!"

"Relief column in area... approximately ten to fifteen minutes away. Over!" answered the voice on the radio.

Arms crossed, Cedric stood behind his technician working the transmitter. Holding a headphone tight to his air, the technician picked up the signal he wanted.

"Your excellency! The tribes attack!"

Signaling to his sister, Cecilia hurried to him. Behind the twins, the Titans had gone two to a horse with members of the infantry sitting behind knights.

"Take five thousand single riders with you and head five kilometers due west of the ruins," ordered Cedric. "Our operatives report that you'll find the tribal encampment; it will be unoccupied save for those that travel with the camp. Kill no one, but detain them and burn the camp to the ground! We need to create an illusion of a larger force. When you're done, ride back to my position. I'll leave my signal locator on. Godspeed, Cecilia."

"I'm on it. Godspeed, Cedric."

Leapfrogging onto Myst, Cecilia signaled to a five-thousand rider command of Valkyries. Breaking before them, the winged riders followed her lead. Cedric took a device in his hands and pushed five buttons on it. Slipping the device into his cloak, he pulled himself up on Jericho. Horace rode up to him.

"Armada ready to ride, your excellency! Valentine and Sirius are here as you summoned."

Riding on the back of another rider's horse, Valentine and Sirius were brought to Cedric.

"Orders, Marshal?" asked Valentine.

"Follow the plan as I diagrammed it last night. I hope Julius would have had the sense to duck into the ruins to buy some time to assess the situation. We'll drop your men off at the southern hill, hide behind it until we ride around the ruins. Legions and halberdiers should protect the archers. I'll signal you when we're ready for the attack."

"What will be the signal?" asked Sirius.

"Trust me; you'll know. My friends always say I have a flair for the dramatic. Now come; we need to create a new definition for Godspeed."

Cedric raised his arm in the air and dropped it quickly. He and Horace led the rest of the knights out as they rode north for the Istle Hill Ruins.

"How are you going to give enough time for Cecilia to accomplish her mission?" questioned Horace.

"I have an ace-in-the-hole I can play. I figure if Wilhelm's right, all hell's broken loose in the tribes right now. They're probably just as confused as us, but we've got to get there in time to make a difference."

"And Christian?"

"If Christian fails in his mission, we will achieve the sum of all fears," commented Cedric with a voice sensing an impending doom. "Then he's fired!"

Huskal had led his army forward to hilltops just above the ruins. Reynard and Josephine were armed and ready behind him. Adnar stood before his warriors inciting them into a frenzy. Filled with rage and vengeance, the tribal soldiers needed little incentive. The warriors decked out with their full regalia and war paint were desperate for battle, but Huskal was holding them back temporarily. Posha and priests of the Syrus Clan were burning incense in front of the troops and administering final blessings before the battle. Posha seemed torn between the loyalties to her people and her desire to barter a peace.

"Is this the only way, Reynard? Can't you calm Huskal's storm?

"If the Wolf Tribe calls for aid, the Myotis Tribe will answer," replied Reynard stoically.

"They're sitting ducks down there waiting for us!" shouted Adnar. "Why do we delay?"

"They're still holding Hippolyte and Minerva," reasoned Huskal. "We're going to take our time and capture them. They're all alone; no one can come to their aid in time."

Stationed in his semi-protected corridor, Julius and the officers waited for Huskal to make his move. Waves of anxiety flowed over the soldiers; Amuro tensely rubbed her hands together while Cagius couldn't stop tapping his foot.

"Estimated time?" asked Julius.

"If it was accurate, five minutes until help arrives," estimated Cagius.

"This is the longest fifteen minutes in the history of fifteen minutes!" cried Amuro.

Walker kept shaking his head to the dismay of those around them.

Forty kilometers south of the ruins? thought Walker. *Even if they had a hover train they couldn't make it here that quickly. Even if they could, it can't be more than sixty halberdiers and maybe forty cuirassiers stationed at Capricorn. That sure as hell won't break these lines.*

"Something's fishy about Capricorn. That relief was all too ready to go when we called for help," reasoned Malcolm. "When have Acadians ever been that determined?"

"In all honesty, Malcolm, we've got bigger problems to worry about," retorted Cagius.

The tribes looked down at their adversaries.

"They dug themselves in pretty well," observed Josephine. "It's going to be difficult to launch a full assault into the ruins."

"I shouldn't have expected an alliance marshal to have been so stupid," said Huskal. "This Julius is cunning, but he can't wait us out forever. Send a wave forward. I want a head count!"

"Right!" acknowledged Josephine.

Josephine signaled to some tribal cavalry behind her. About one hundred riders broke down the hill at full speed toward the ruins. The marshals witnessed this.

"A first wave?" wondered Walker.

Malcolm signaled to his archers to draw their bows. The elves took aim without breaking a sweat but held their attack.

"Hold your fire Malcolm! They're only counting us!" ordered Julius.

"Well, they know now how bad off we are," said Amuro.

The riders did one pass and swept back up the hill. The lead rider reported back to Huskal.

"Approximately five hundred steel-bellies consisting mostly of legions and archers; they have limited heavy horse!"

"Thank you," acknowledged Huskal before he turned to the chiefs. "It's as I thought. Unless you have any objections, I'm going to deliver terms for their surrender."

Reynard and Posha agreed immediately, but Adnar's silence was seen more as a grudging consent. Huskal rode forward and screamed.

"JULIUS IMPERIA, I DELIVER YOU THE TERMS OF THE TRIBAL CONFEDERATION! WE DEMAND YOU ANSWER FOR THE ACTIONS TAKEN AGAINST US! YOU ARE HOPELESSLY OUTNUMBERED! SURRENDER TO US! YOU WILL BE SAFE FOR NOW! YOUR LIVES HAVE GREAT MEANING TO US! DON'T BE FOOLS! YOU MAY KILL SOME OF US, BUT ALL OF YOU WILL DIE!"

Knowing the severity of being called out by name, Julius pondered his next move. Every word Huskal spoke was true; they would never defeat the tribal army with five hundred men.

"They seem to be much more considerate of our situation than they were with Cambridge and Alwein," observed Amuro. "It just doesn't add up."

"Time!" shouted Julius.

"Maybe two minutes," guessed Cagius.

"What do you think, Amuro?" asked Julius.

"We know we've got some relief coming. If it's not enough, I think surrender might be the best option."

"If Huskal wanted us dead, he would have sent the whole army into the ruins by now," reasoned Malcolm. "Why give us the option? This is not about vengeance... at least not yet. I say surrender today; live to fight tomorrow."

Huskal was growing impatient on top of the hill. Not anticipating that the marshals would be debating his terms like politicians, the wolf tribe commander offered them some incentive.

"MY PATIENCE GROWS SHORT! I WANT A DECISION OR WE CHARGE!"

Julius closed his eyes as the remaining officers knew what needed to be done. Cagius and Walker seemed the most opposed to the matter, but Julius, Amuro, and Malcolm agreed this course of action was best.

"I'll go," volunteered Julius. "Huskal called me out."

"Julius!" protested Amuro. "I am a marshal, and it is my duty to offer the surrender as well."

"I gave them my word and something happened. Maybe if I go alone I can bargain the rest of you to safety."

"I don't think that's a good idea," interrupted Cagius. "If anything were to happen . . ."

"There's no hope left."

Bouncing against the grounds, rocks and unpacked dirt skipped around the Marshals. Thunder sounded from a cloudless sky. Anticipating an earthquake, the tribal soldiers felt the ground but their worst fears had been confirmed. A jubilant Walker took out his scopes and stared to the south. Resounding cheers from the soldiers echoed in the ruins.

"It can't be rain, and only one other thing makes that sound!"

"That sonuvabitch is going to save us again!" laughed Cagius.

On the southern hill, Titan riders emerged. Cecilia was missing with her division. Executing his plan stealthily, the Titan riders had dropped off the infantry before making themselves known to the tribes. Cedric and Horace were at the front of the riders. The Titan prince had his rosary intertwined with the reigns of his horse.

"Is that going to be enough riders to break the tribal lines?" asked Amuro.

"I don't know," concluded Julius.

The otherworldly presence displayed by *La Morte Angelus* was too much for his foes. Losing their focus, tribal soldiers felt their rage being displaced by fear. Warriors retreated backwards and the wild horses had become uneasy. Psychological warfare was trumping numbers on the battlefield. Cedric reached into his cloak, took out his flask, drank, and replaced it.

"Horace, if my plan falls, I want you to close our ranks and form a wedge. We're going to have to punch a hole through their lines to escape."

"Yes, your excellency. I understand, but I beg you not to do anything foolish and get yourself killed. I don't think this is going to be a good time to die and I dare not bring your mother the bad news."

Cedric called for a rider to bring his banner. Tying a white cloth to the top of it, Prime Eagle edged Jericho forward. He crossed a silent field alone as everyone on both sides wondered what his true plan was.

"Is he surrendering?" asked Malcolm.

"I hope not," prayed Cagius.

Riding toward the tribal army, Cedric positioned himself only fifteen meters away from the enemy. The soldiers retreated a few meters as the prince staked his banner into the ground. Removing his right gauntlet, Cedric proudly exposed the wolf tattoo on his hand, the indication of his blood brother pact with Aramas. This caused great disbelief among the members of the tribes. There were murmurs everywhere, wondering how their greatest enemy could be blood brother of the late chief.

"I come to treat with the members of the tribal confederation," pronounced Cedric. "I stand before you only as the crown prince of Titanus. Let your commander come forward to present his grievances."

Reynard and Adnar looked at one another but didn't make a move. Staring at the fear in the eyes of his army, Huskal shouldered the burden upon himself. Huskal inched his horse toward Cedric. The two stood with little distance between them, and Huskal didn't bat an eye.

"Prime Eagle, I did not expect to see you here," started Huskal.

"Huskal, Alpha of the Wolf Tribe, my honored enemy; I came here because my friends are trapped in those ruins."

"You seem to know a great deal about many things. Do you know why we approach them like this?"

"Yes, and by your appearance it is as I feared . . . Aramas is dead then."

"You also know of the betrayal of our tribes by the Acadians!"

"Huskal, listen to me. The evidence is probably overwhelming that this was done by Acadians, but believe me it wasn't."

"How could a man of such honor take their side?"

"There are diabolical forces at work that wish to see chaos happen between our peoples. The leader of these forces is a very powerful mercenary. He was the one that orchestrated the attack and murder of your chief."

"No. I have seen the scene myself. I saw the Acadian weapons that were used to butcher my people! Julius in the ruins gave us his vow! He swore to us that there would be peace! Yet in his other hand, he had a snake ready to strike. The Acadians will pay in time for their crimes! Yet that is not the reason why I am here. I have a greater concern right now."

"You speak of the safe return of Hippolyte and Minerva."

"Chieftain Hippolyte now. I need to have hostages to exchange for their lives."

"You have no need for hostages. The Acadians will never make the exchange. Besides, any bargaining with them would be fruitless. I took actions this morning to ensure the safety of your new chief and her sister. They are now under my protection."

Huskal's confidence faded from his now pale face. The thought of the chief of the Wolf Tribe and the only heir in the hands of his greatest enemy was too much.

"They are in the castle of the enemy!"

"They were until my agents extracted them. Huskal, I don't want a war; it would play right into the enemy's plans. If you lead this army from the field and allow me to take my friends to safety, I will ensure that Hippolyte and Minerva are returned to you."

"I've made my decision! I'm sorry. I want to trust you, Prime Eagle, but I simply cannot. I never understood why Chief Aramas spoke of you the way he did."

"I'm putting my life and honor on the line for them, Huskal. All I demand in return is some time!"

"I've heard you out. You came to us under truce as a prince of Titanus. We have no quarrel with you nor do we wish to wage war with your kingdom. If you depart from the battlefield now, no harm shall come to you or your men."

Huskal turned his back on Cedric and returned to his lines. Fuming and dissatisfied with Huskal's arrogance, Cedric screamed in rage.

"I can be ruthless if you force me!"

Cedric ripped Ragnarok from behind and chanted "darkness." A wave of dark magic surrounded his blade, inciting terror in the tribal soldiers before him. Slicing the white cloth from his banner, he urged Jericho to trample it under his hooves. The shockwaves from the swing knocked over some of the front lines of the tribal infantry and all cowered behind their shields. One of the priestesses screamed, causing Huskal, Josephine, and the chiefs to turn around. On a hill behind the tribes, Cecilia and the valkyries that had journeyed with her prepared to charge. A sadistic smile formed across Cecilia's ash-covered face as billows of smoke from the now burnt-out tribal encampment climbed to the sky. The attention of the tribes was drawn to a third hill now as legion and archer units formed ranks. The legion was making a lot of noise by bashing their spears into their shields. Wondering if they were about to confront the Alliance Army, the tribes staggered aimlessly. Even the marshals in the ruins looked on with amazement.

"He's deceiving them into believing that he has a much large army," observed Amuro.

"Let's hope the riverboat gambler draws an ace," commented Walker.

The tribes were now in total chaos. They ran from one flank to the next, wondering where they should attack first. Foolishly firing an arrow at Cedric, an archer watched in horror as it merely deflected off of his shield. Convinced their foe was immortal and invulnerable, the morale among the tribal army dropped. Reynard grabbed Huskal in desperation, looking for an exit strategy.

"The entire Alliance Army may be mustered already. I doubt the Prime Eagle would have come here alone."

"It can't be... but perhaps they were watching... this Prime Eagle... he has the devil's luck!" stammered Huskal.

"We can't risk this, Huskal," said Josephine. "We're no match for all of their forces if we're exposed like this. I believe him when he says that he'll keep Hippolyte and Minerva safe. Why save them on the Terrace River to betray them now."

Returning his full attention to the Prime Eagle, Huskal's confidence had been shattered. Cedric pressed his high-handed negotiations.

"My offer still stands, Huskal. Will you give me peace?"

"We need a chief. If you deliver Hippolyte and Minerva to me unharmed, I will wait to settle my grievances with Central Acadia. We will wage no war this hour."

"I thank you."

Huskal waved his spear in the air. Calling for a retreat, the sense of relief in the faces of the tribal army could not be measured. They hid their heads in shame as they retreated past the Prime Eagle.

"Withdraw to the mountain encampment!" ordered Huskal.

The tribes started to march slowly away from the scene. When the last of them had finally marched away, loud cheers emerged from the many soldiers. Taking a deep breath, Cedric couldn't help but chuckle as his sister rode to his position. Cecilia put her forehead to his and joined in his laughter.

"After that performance, it's a wonder you didn't go into show business," teased Cecilia.

"Well, we're not out of the woods yet; there's still more work to be done. By the way, I like the touch of the ash on your face."

"Don't get me started on that! The conflagration spread a little too quickly and I had to save an old woman from being burned alive."

"You've got too good a heart sis. Of course, if DeVries failed me, well even the might of Eagle's Gate won't save us from tribal wrath."

"I guess that will be the real miracle. Well, let's go meet with the grateful survivors."

Cedric and Cecilia rode down to meet with the marshals coming out of the encampment. Dismounting, Cedric was met by a tight embrace by Amuro.

"Thank the Father you were here!" celebrated Amuro.

"Got to admit that was one hell of trick you pulled!" admired Cagius.

"Then again, considering what we've seen you do, we shouldn't have been so surprised," commented Walker.

"Is what the tribes spoke of true?" asked Malcolm.

"Chief Aramas was murdered last night in his own tent," explained Cecilia.

"By whom?" asked Amuro, sharing the same shocked expression as her comrades.

"Nephilim duco-mutatios disguised as Acadian soldiers," described Cedric. "Duke Wilhelm arrived too late to stop them. He said they were led by a fallen angel."

"Nonsense!" shouted Julius to the surprise of his comrades. "A fallen angel, Cedric? Aren't you a little old to believe in fairy tales? The tribes set us up!"

"Do not doubt the powers of evil, Julius; it is their greatest strength," retorted Cedric.

"Why kill Aramas?"

"To start a war between the tribes and the alliance, and plunge the entire west into Chaos!"

"That doesn't absolve the tribes for the murder of Alwein and Cambridge."

"The two Acadian Lords are dead?"

"They were attacked outside of the encampment this morning by members of the Wolf Tribe. They killed them right where they stood."

Cedric's face turned pale. Attempting to formulate what happened, he and his sister looked to one another.

"Oh God, Cedric, duco-mutatios disguised as tribesman. It will send all of Central Acadia into a bloodlust."

"Aramas died first, and now the two Acadian lords that accompanied the delegation. Blood has been shed on both sides, and it's only the beginning. We have to return to Central Acadia as quickly as possible and stop any further response."

"Cedric, no one is going to believe your story," said Walker.

"I have proof, but I need the support of everyone here," pleaded Cedric. "Only if the marshals stand together can we counter the power that breaks against us!"

Julius looked to have serious doubts concerning Cedric's story. Studying the armada carefully, he probed for further information from the princely friend.

"If we are to trust you, we need to know some facts first," said Julius. "What were you doing out here?"

"We were here because we had good intelligence that this mercenary fallen angel was going to strike. However, we thought the target was going to be the negotiations, not Aramas. We stationed fifty thousand riders at Capricorn and staged a phony war game."

"A war game, that's creative even for you."

"It's a good thing, or we'd all be in chains bound for the wilderness." teased Cagius.

"Yes, well I guess we should saddle up and head back," recommended Amuro. "It will give us some time to get our story straight."

"I have one last question," interrupted Julius with his eyes burning with rage. "Where's Christian DeVries?"

Cedric didn't answer, but the others looked on with some curiosity. They stared at the Titan contingent, and he was nowhere to be found, nor was Colin Wilkins for that matter. Anger growing by the moment, Julius flexed his fists.

"Don't give me that look! You don't go anywhere without him, Cedric! Where is he?"

"Christian was ordered to carry out a mission of life or death."

"Traitor!"

The paladin lunged at Cedric, grabbing him around his waist and tackling the stronger knight to the ground. Cedric's helmet came off in the struggle. Landing two punches, Julius gained the early upper hand until Cedric put his boot under the paladin's stomach. Flipping him over, Cedric straddled Julius and delivered a blow with his forearm to the Napolitan prince's jaw. Stunned for a moment, blood dripped from the paladin's mouth. Cedric pressed his gauntlet down into Julius' throat and cut his air off.

"How dare you," warned Cedric with an edge in his voice. "After all this time, after what I just did for you, is that what our friendship meant?"

Cecilia grabbed Cedric from behind and pulled him off of Julius. Free of the grip, Julius went to lunge at Cedric, but Cagius got him from behind. Stepping in between the two, Amuro put up her arms, knowing neither of them would try and punch while a lady was in the way. Applying her healing magic to Julius, the elf maiden used some of her calming magic as well. Cecilia whispered something into her brother's ear and he started to cool off. Content, he adjusted himself and his sister let him go. Fearing rage still consumed his brother, Cagius maintained his grip. Despite her treatment, Julius still seemed eager to tear Cedric apart.

"Julius, what are you doing?" demanded Amuro.

"He couldn't stand it!" shouted Julius. "Cedric couldn't stand that I was going to get all the glory for once! These negotiations were mine! They were based on my word!"

"You were such a fool, Julius! Every word spoken to these people has great meaning! When you gave the tribes your word, you put your reputation on the line, not anyone else in the alliance. They are going to make you answer for this. Your name and reputation isn't worth spit among the tribes anymore. The Alliance and Tribal Confederation will be plunged into war the rotation you begin your reign!"

"I did what I had to do! I needed this, Cedric! I needed the political capital!"

"I warned you that remaining with that girl is going to get you nothing but trouble. You blatantly refuse time after time to do your duty!"

"Who are you to lecture me! Why don't you tell the others what you're doing? You want to know why Christian isn't here! It's because Cedric is having him extract Hippolyte and Minerva from Acadian custody!"

Amuro's face turned pale. She turned back to Cedric for some sign of denial. However, she saw none.

"Cedric . . . you didn't . . ." stammered Amuro. "The nobles want to crucify you, and you're handing them the nails! Please, Cedric tell me that you just didn't commit an act of aggression against a fellow member of the alliance."

"My brother is well versed in Acadian law and how it violates the natural law," explained Cecilia. "This was before we knew of the treachery against the Acadian lords."

"They're right," added Walker. "With Alwein and Cambridge dead, they'll be looking to lop off the heads of Hippolyte and Minerva at twilight. If he didn't get them out of the castle, their heads are going to be on pikes when we get back."

"You want to live with that, Julius?" asked Cedric. "You want to see two teenage girls die for nothing?"

Julius calmed down. Ashamed by Cedric's reasoning, Julius held back his tears. Thinking back to his brother's advice, the paladin knew he was acting out of character.

"I'm a soldier, not a butcher. However, I am also a marshal of the Alliance Army. I have to ask you for your sword based on your admission of an act of treason."

"There may be an ethical duty not to follow an unjust law, Julius!" professed Cedric. "I will not surrender my sword to you or any man that comes to me asking for it. I am prepared to face the consequences for my action, but we have to end this war before the Nephilim and Demonkin swallow us all. In order to do that, we have to get Hippolyte and Minerva back to the tribes. I need you to stand with me against injustice!"

Walker did not hesitate for a moment and walked over to Cedric's side. Perhaps this was his act of personal defiance against those destroying the country he loved. Cagius looked at his brother and shook his head. He went over to stand with Cedric, much to his brother's dismay.

"Cedric, we're with you!" agreed Cagius.

"Definitely, life is too precious to have destroyed for petty vengeance," reasoned Malcolm.

Amuro pleaded with her eyes toward Julius to stand with Cedric and forgive him. Julius gritted his teeth and hung his head. Deciding he had been defeated by the Titan for the last time, Julius knew his friendship with Cedric was over.

"I'm not going to apologize for what I did," said Julius. "Those words you spoke to me in the embassy that night haunt me even now. I am no longer your friend, Cedric Rhone."

"I'm prepared to go down that road. However, before you do, answer the question of 'what would you die for?'"

"Why, Cedric?"

"Because Julius you are my friend and there is no greater love to lay down one's life for his friends!"

Castle Acadia, Concurrent with the Events at Istle Hill

"As soldiers, we will face the unenviable task of killing our enemy. If we were to simply die for our country, we would surely lose. However, there are times when we are called to go beyond our oath to monarch and country. It is at this time that we must remember our commitment to faith and the Natural Law. In these times, our duty as a soldier is to protect and promote peace above war."

—*The Titan Battle Manual*

In the early morning hours, Minerva and Hippolyte were getting ready for the promised ride with Princess Cassandra. Lacing up her boots and gear, Minerva noticed a smile on her sister's face that she hadn't witnessed since they arrived in Verian.

"You looked better this morning, sis," observed Minerva.

"I had a nice long conversation with Princess Cassandra last night," said Hippolyte as she tightened the straps on her armor. "Let's just say that it wasn't the encounter that I expected."

"I knew you'd get along with her. Princess Cassandra is so nice. Wait until you meet her sister Marie; she's even nicer."

"Well, we'll find out later. Cassandra has invited us to go riding, and then we're going for something called 'high tea' with her sister."

"'High tea'? What does that mean?"

"I don't know. It must be a steel-belly thing."

"I hope they have some of those desserts available. It'll feel so good to get a ride in . . ."

As her sister put up her right hand, Minerva silenced herself. Crawling on the ground, Hippolyte put her ear to the door. She could hear the sound of armor clanking against the floor at a fast pace. The concern in her face drew her sister's attention. Minerva spoke to her in a low tone.

"What is it?"

"Knights . . . at least thirty of them coming toward us."

"Do you think they're coming for us?"

"Yes!"

Hippolyte crawled back toward Minerva.

"We've got to get out of here," ordered the older sister.

Hippolyte ran to the window. She opened it to find they were pretty high up in the castle. Looking down upon the area, she began to spin, nearly fainting into her sister's arms. Since she had been a young girl, Hippolyte had always had problems with heights. If she had been in the kingdoms, she would have been diagnosed with vertigo. Minerva guessed that they certainly weren't going to be getting out that way.

"Hippolyte!" worried Minerva.

"It's too high," said Hippolyte. "I don't think we're getting out of here."

The sounds got closer. Just then, the door to the room was kicked open. Armed palace halberdiers were standing in the doorway and staring down the Wolf Tribe girls. Parting the waves of troops, Jonas Marimon entered the room with his sword drawn. The smugness of the templar commander disgusted the two tribal girls.

"Well, if it isn't the two little traitors now. As of this morning, your people attacked the alliance caravan set to meet them. You two are under arrest and will be held for questioning. Of course, if you resist, I can kill you right now. I haven't gotten a chance to kill a barbarian in a long time; I'll make it nice and slow."

"What are you talking about?" demanded Hippolyte. "My grandfather would never order such a thing unless he was provoked."

"I don't appreciate being called a liar, girl!"

"What do we do, sis?" asked Minerva. "We're really outnumbered."

"I doubt seriously that Grandpa would have wanted us to start a battle in the heart of Central Acadia. Give up your weapons nice and slowly."

Resigned to the fact their was no escape, the girls began to hand over their weapons to Jonas. A slight creaking in the ceiling drew the attention of everyone in the room. A vent popped open just above Jonas. Hair frizzing out from a sudden charge of static electricity, the tribal girls heard Christian DeVries issue a warning.

"Hippolyte, Minerva, cover your eyes!"

The girls complied. Watching Christian move his hands in series of odd but deliberate motions, Jonas heard him shout, "Thunder jujitsu!" Landing in front of the Acadians, a bright flash blinded all of the knights including Jonas. The Templar commander held his hands over his eyes and seethed with rage.

"DeVries, if that was you, there'll be hell to pay!"

Cracks formed on the ceiling, weakening the structural integrity. Hippolyte and Minerva jumped back to the safety of the outer walls. After a few moments, the whole middle of the ceiling gave way, dropping plaster and metal on the Acadians as Christian and Colin fell to the ground. They were both in full armor and grimacing as they got to their feet.

"Colin, you've got to stop eating those donuts," teased Christian.

"Trapped for three hours in full armor with an elf in a ventilation shaft, if anyone wants to see my breakfast, it will be on display in two minutes," quipped Colin.

Minerva and Hippolyte sought out each other for guidance. They both had a look of utter disbelief on their faces over what had just happened. Closing her eyes, Hippolyte put her fingers to her forehead.

"Are they here to save us?" asked Minerva.

"Honestly, Minerva, I hope not," responded Hippolyte.

Christian bowed slightly to the girls.

"Bonsoir, mademoiselles. I am Colonel Christian DeVries of His Excellency's Intelligence Agency, the Eagle's Talon."

Christian elbowed Colin in his ribs, causing the young man to lift his protective mask.

"This is my partner-in-crime, Colin Wilkins, affectionately known around here as the Lunar Falcon."

Colin and Hippolyte locked eyes. Blushing at first glance, both of them turned away from one another to save further embarrassment. Colin tried to whistle while Hippolyte pushed her two index fingers together. Staring at the scene in disbelief, Christian was at a loss for words. Though it wasn't the first time he had experienced love at first sight, it was the last thing that he had expected to happen. Minerva grew a little jealous.

"Sis!" pleaded Minerva.

"This is a tender moment, but we really need to make our escape," reminded Christian.

"How are we going to do that?" asked Minerva.

Christian nodded to Colin, who shook himself out of his daze. Moving to the large window, Colin pushed out the pane and glass. Christian took out two grappling hooks and put them on the window. Christian and Colin attached ropes from the hooks to their waists.

"You're going to have to forgive us, but rappelling down the wall is our only chance at escape," described Christian.

"I can't!" cried Hippolyte. "I get dizzy."

"Vertigo!" shouted Christian. "That's just what we need."

"Don't worry," offered Colin as he took Hippolyte's hand. "I'll take care of you."

Hippolyte turned a deeper shade of red now. It was the first time in her life that a man had ever made such an offer to her.

"You will?"

"Hang on tight!"

Witnessing that Jonas and his men started to recover from the blinding; Christian wished they'd move their love affair along. Minerva was just getting sick at the sugary moment. She took one look at Christian and decided at that instant he was no Captain Walker. However, she didn't have much of a choice.

"Oh brother, well I guess I'm stuck with you," quipped Minerva.

"Oh joy," teased Christian.

Colin strapped Hippolyte around his back while Christian did the same to Minerva. The two jumped on the ledge of the windows with the girls hanging behind them. Looking at one another, Christian and Colin determined they had lost their sanity participating in a mission like this. Resolved to complete Cedric's orders, Christian counted off.

"Three . . . two . . . one . . ."

The two jumped back as they released the ropes on the grappling hooks. Both girls started to scream as the two hit the castle wall and continued their rappel down. Screaming louder, Hippolyte, grabbed Colin around his neck with both arms. Gasping for air, the assassin had difficulty getting enough into his lungs due to her grip. When they hit the wall the second time, Minerva put her arms out and screamed like she was having the thrill of her life. They hit the castle wall a third time, and that provided enough momentum to hit the ground. Christian cut the two grappling hooks as Jonas ran over to the window.

"Alert the city guard!" ordered Jonas. "The barbarians have escaped with DeVries and Wilkins! Stop them before they reach the embassy!"

Christian noticed halberdiers and archers running from behind the castle walls.

"All right, ladies, I hope you are pretty good sprinters. We've got to make a run for it,"

The four took off at breakneck speed. Consternation filled Colin's face as he noticed the castle courtyard gate was closed. Turning to Christian for guidance, the spy master waved the group on. Christian focused on one of the parapets near the gate. Cassandra and Felicia were chatting idly and pretending to be nonchalant. Discreetly, the princess entered the codes for the gates. As they opened, Cassandra winked at the spymaster. The half-elf operative gave the princess a quick salute before bolting for the city beyond the gate. Putting her left hand over her mouth, Cassandra laughed. Felicia joined her by snickering as she bent over slightly with her eyes closed. The princess's little rebellion made it a pure foot race with Verian city guards chasing down the political prisoners and their escorts. Civilians stared in awe at the race taking place before them. Yelling "make way," the city guard cleared a path to their quarry. This did not stop them from shoving civilians either to the ground or into the canals if they didn't react fast enough. Slightly out of breath, Hippolyte tried to bleed some information out of her rescuers.

"Where are we going?" asked Hippolyte.

"The Titan embassy... it's sovereign soil," said Christian.

"You expect me to run right into the teeth... of my greatest enemy?"

"Hey, lady, this hasn't exactly gone as planned so far. Right now the choice is between who's trying to save you and who's trying to kill you. This way!"

Resigned to follow her rescuers, Hippolyte allowed Christian to lead them down one of the alleys heading toward embassy row. At the far end of the street, Samuel was standing outside of the embassy gates on horseback with his scopes over his eyes. Sweating heavily from his brow, the young captain could hear the sounds of bells and sirens played throughout the city. Samuel wiped the sweat away as he remembered the orders he had received from his father. "You cannot venture outside the embassy to protect Christian and the others. Once they clear the gates, hold that embassy as if it were Eagle's Gate itself." Firming up his resolve with two deep breaths, Samuel put the scopes up to his eyes once more. He spotted Christian and his companions cutting past the Evengard Embassy alley just as Acadian city guards turned down the main street. Samuel turned his horse toward the courtyard where two companies of cavalry waited in the courtyard with him.

"Form ranks!"

Snapping to attention, the riders took their positions. Two Titan landsknechts ran to the computers on either side of the gate to get ready to close it when necessary. Drawing their bows, mercenary bowmen took up their position along the embassy walls. Samuel rode before his line and reminded them of their rules of engagement.

"We've got four coming in and coming in hot! Do not engage unless engaged, as per the orders of the queen! If anyone sets foot on our sovereign soil, charge and break their lines!"

The riders answered with an emphatic, "Yes, sir!"

Samuel rode back outside and saw the four closing on the embassy gates fast. Putting up his hand, the young captain signaled frantically for Christian and the others to hurry. Minerva turned back quickly and saw that the city guards were almost on top of them. Entering the embassy first, Samuel ordered the landsknechts to be ready. The fugitives and rescuers dove straight past the embassy gates. The landsknechts worked the computers, and the reinforced steel gate slammed shut within two seconds. Running forward with two steels beams, other landsknechts reinforced the gate in case the Acadians tried to ram it. Christian, Colin, Hippolyte, and Minerva lay in the courtyard completely spent of breath and energy. Minerva turned over and dry heaved a few times as Christian sat up and held her hair back. Ordering servants to come over with water, the fugitives gladly welcomed the sustenance. Colin looked over at Hippolyte and winked; the Wolf Tribe heir blushed and giggled. Samuel rode over to Christian so he could debrief him. Pushing himself up by his hands, Christian answered the captain's salute.

"You had me worried there," commented Samuel.

"Well, this rescue operation wasn't one of my finest," explained Christian, trying to catch his breath. "I didn't know the Acadians were renovating the East Wing. We had to double back around through the ventilation system to get to the girls; hence, the uninvited guests standing outside our gate."

"Looks like someone is in need of their seasonal physical," teased Martha.

Yawning and stretching, the Titanus chancellor walked down the stairs of the embassy. She had a smile on her face pointed directly at Christian. The good doctor was wearing a skirt suit over a white blouse, giving the appearance of politician rather than scientist for once.

"I see Civilia had you trade your provost outfit for your chancellor outfit," joked Christian.

"Queen Civilia thought someone who knows the alliance charter like the back of her hand better be here to defend our actions. I thought I'd dress appropriately for the part."

"I'm obliged for that. However, I think we have a formality we should settle first before we go quoting the charter."

Martha walked over to Hippolyte and pulled a card out of the pocket of her jacket. Handing the card to the wolf tribe heir, the good doctor put her hand on the girl's right shoulder.

"Princess Hippolyte, my name is Martha Heinrich. I am the chancellor of Titanus and Queen Civilia's most trusted advisor. I'm going to have to ask you to read this."

"Why?"

"Titans are sticklers for rules and can't appear to be dishonorable around the other kingdoms. This is going to make everything we've done here ethical. Except for the slight part of Christian starting a full-scale war with the Templars, we're not going to be able to cover that up so easily."

Hippolyte stared at the card and read it. Watching her expression, Christian believed Hippolyte had doubts about what she was about to read. The spy master wondered what was so difficult to understand when he and Colin had gone through so much to help them. Though but a few moments, it seemed like an eternity before she muttered the important words.

"Oh divinely ravishing and beautiful Doctor Heinrich, the smartest and most brilliant scientist on Terminus Mundus, I, Hippolyte and my sister Minerva humbly implore you to use your brain power and grant us sanctuary," recited a confused Hippolyte.

Christian and Samuel just shook their heads while Martha beamed with a smile.

"Martha, that's too much!" bellowed Christian.

"What's 'sanctuary' mean?" asked Minerva.

"It means that you are now under the protection of Queen Civilia and the nation of Titanus," explained Martha. "It also means that the Acadians can't do a blessed thing to you while you remain behind these walls."

"I guess that's good," said Minerva.

She turned to her sister, who seemed to still have doubts. Gritting her teeth at being beholden to her greatest enemy, Hippolyte realized she didn't have any other option. However, she did acknowledge that this was the second time that Prince Cedric had gone out of his way to help her.

"Now that our formalities are settled, Colin, why don't you see our guests inside," said Martha. "We have rooms ready for them at the hotel."

"Thanks, Doctor Heinrich. Ladies, if you would please follow me," offered Colin.

Colin took Hippolyte by the arm and led her into the embassy. Minerva took a second to turn to Christian and bowed her head slightly in thanks for saving her. Quickly turning on her heel, she bounced up the steps to catch her sister up. As the girls entered the embassy, Keiko was standing there ready to greet them.

"Lady Hippolyte, Lady Minerva, I bid you welcome to the Titan embassy. As mistress of this embassy, I hope I have made everything comfortable for you. I'm just glad that Sir Christian and Sir Colin were able to help you."

"I just wish it didn't involve running for my life," quipped Minerva.

"I'm sorry. I didn't get a chance to ask you under the circumstances, but are you all right?" asked Colin.

"I'm fine," replied Hippolyte.

"Good. I'm sorry our first meeting had to be so eventful."

"I'm not."

Clearing his throat and blushing, Colin looked to Keiko to get him out of this. The sylph gladly interceded on his behalf.

"Actually, Lady Hippolyte, we have someone dying to see you."

One of the servants brought in Stryker. Playfully leaping into his caretaker's arms, the wolf licked her face as she held him tightly. Eyes welled up with tears, Hippolyte kissed and rubbed the wolf on the neck many times. Rubbing his fat belly, she surmised that the Titans hadn't been starving him..

"Boy, how are you? They certainly have been feeding you well."

"Titan beef certainly seems to agree with him," said Keiko. "Actually, many of the riders have grown quite fond of him."

"I wouldn't doubt it," said Hippolyte.

"If you ladies would follow me, I'll take you to your rooms," announced Colin.

"I hope you guys treat us as well as the Acadians did," remarked Minerva.

"You've never experienced hospitality until you experience Titan hospitality."

The girls and Stryker followed Colin to the hotel. Upon their arrival, the concierge at the desk worked to make them as comfortable as possible. Spying the cameras, Keiko witnessed Jonas Marimon approaching the embassy with his Templar knights in tow. Jonas relieved the city guard commanders who bowed to him. Samuel got off his horse and walked up the steps to the embassy wall. He dared not use the gate because of the Acadians' intentions.

"Who's in charge here?" shouted Jonas.

"I am! Captain Samuel Irvine of her majesty's armada!"

"Of course," bellowed a laughing Jonas. "Well, boy... open these damn gates now! You're harboring two fugitives, and I have orders from King Stephen himself to bring them to justice."

"I take no orders except from that of the queen and his excellency. You have no power to order an officer of Titanus on his sovereign soil."

"You're trying my patience, boy! I will not hesitate to use force to get what I want."

"Oh, Jonas, why can't we all just get along," teased Martha as she walked up the steps to the gate wall. "Don't you have something better to do than bully us with your idle threats?"

"I should have expected the queen to send her mad scientist to the embassy," retorted Jonas.

"Jonas, I would prefer if you would not intrude in situations that do not concern you. You know I prefer evil genius to mad scientist."

"King Stephen Acadia has signed an order that the two Wolf Tribe girls be taken in immediately for questioning. If you comply with this order, I will overlook the events of early this morning."

"Let's see, that's going to be a problem now. The Titan embassy is an extension of the kingdom of Titanus; therefore the soil of this building is the same as the soil under Castle Titan. Therefore, under page sixteen, paragraph six, clause four, King Stephen will have to negotiate with Queen Civilia over their extradition."

"What? Your agents smuggled them into the embassy! They had no right to be here in the first place."

"Titanus was not made aware of any crime that Hippolyte or Minerva committed. I was under the impression the girl was here to play with her wolf. They entered the embassy of their own free will, asked for sanctuary, and as such we are under no compulsion to release them. We will begin our own investigation into the matter before determining a proper course of action."

"Sanctuary! This is Cedric's doing, isn't it? I've warned your people many times not to cross the line. This action is unforgiveable! Your prince liberated two prisoners from custody, trespassed on our soil, wounded Acadian soldiers, and in turn committed an act of treason against the alliance."

Martha hid her concern over what Jonas had said by flashing a grin that showed calculated anger behind it. However, Jonas was speaking the truth, and there was a clear distinction in this case between what was legal and what was ethical. No marshal in any army in the history of the west had ever committed such an act of treason before.

"The matter that's unforgiveable here is your unquenchable thirst for blood. Did you honestly believe that we would sit idly by while you murdered two girls?"

"The tribes have defied the alliance for the last time! Do you understand the gravity of what is going on? We are at war, Martha. Two Acadian knights were murdered by the Tribal Army this morning. We're going to make them pay for those sins."

"We shall see. We've received radio contact that the marshals are returning to deliver their report. I'm sure it will enlighten us all to the situation at hand."

"Your actions here have forced me to change my tactics. I'm not going to be gone for long, Doctor. Before this rotation is out, it would grant me great pleasure to see all of you traitorous Titans with your heads on pikes."

"I'm sensing a lot of anger coming from you. I happen to be skilled in many disciplines, and one of them is psychology. I should schedule you for some appointments and maybe we can get to the root of your male impotency."

Jonas sneered at Martha and turned to the halberdiers.

"Captain Graves! Keep your men stationed here. If those girls so much as set foot outside the embassy, arrest them."

"Yes, sir," acknowledged a halberdier who stepped forward.

"I'm returning to the castle with the templars. The king will wish to hear of this."

Mounting his horse, Jonas turned and rode back toward the castle. Martha and Samuel watched him intently and made sure he had ridden off before making their way back down into the courtyard. Christian stood there waiting for them.

"That was fun," quipped Martha playfully.

"I did like the impotency line," commented Christian.

"It's one of my favorites."

"Where's the queen?"

"She'll be here shortly. However, we really don't have anything we can use legally against the Acadians. You really made a mess of things Christian."

"I know. Did you get anything off the recording?"

"Nothing good. I can prove Basarabas was there. However, there's nothing incriminating. I did an analysis on the tape itself. The reason we couldn't get a listen was because someone put a dampening field around the room you were in."

"Dampening field? The Acadians don't have that technology."

"I know. However, my mentor, Virgus Tattenberg isn't dead, and I suspect he needs to make a living somehow."

"If Virgus is working with the Nephilim, then none of our technological secrets are safe."

"They might even be ahead of us. I've never been able to successfully expand on my mentor's work. How about Cedric or Wilhelm?"

"We have no evidence. Cedric can get up and talk all day about honor and the natural law, but it won't do us any good."

"We're in a world of trouble, but at least we did the right thing."

"That's one way of looking at it."

"So my mobile command center came in handy?"

"Yes, but then again you are the greatest genius on Terminus Mundus."

"I know, but it sounds some much better when someone else mentions it. Let's get to the command center and monitor everyone coming in."

The two went inside as Samuel approached his soldiers, yelling at them to "stand down." The riders finally got a chance to relax and dismounted.

"First round on me," offered Samuel to the cheers of his soldiers.

The commotion from earlier in the rotation had caused screaming and confusion in the royal throne room. Yelling back and forth over what was to be done when Jonas brought the girls back, the nobles of Central Acadia divided themselves into multiple camps. The majority were clamoring for the girls to be put to death immediately. Another camp made demands for a trial. A small minority even wondered why they were arresting them in the first place. No one truly knew what was going on, and that greatly disturbed King Stephen. Sitting on his throne, the king pondered his next move, resting his chin on his fist on the right side of his throne. Count Luminas walked over to the different parties across the room, trying to keep some semblance of order. The two queens were on their benches as well. Penelope showed grave concern at the events, while Sharon simply sat there stoically with her hands folded across her lap. Marie sat on a wood bench behind the steps to the throne. Focusing her gaze on Sharon, she was concerned over the whereabouts of her sister, who the guard could not locate. Marie was supposed to break her fast with Cassandra but she hadn't been seen all morning. To her relief, a door behind the thrones finally opened. Cassandra walked into the room nonchalantly with Felicia in tow as if it was a normal morning. She curtsied before her father.

"I apologize for my lack of immediate attendance, Father. I simply had some pressing duties that needed my attention."

Not prepared to discuss the matter further, Stephen nodded to accept his daughter's explanation. As Cassandra sat on the bench next to her half-sister, she stared at the fear in Marie's face. Consoling her, the older girl took her around the shoulder and embraced her tightly.

"Have you heard?" asked Marie. "I can't believe they've had those girls arrested."

"I would bet on that," commented Cassandra with a devious smile creeping across her face. "I can't believe all of the commotion I've had to deal with this morning. I'm sorry I missed our appointment this morning, but my apartment was in the area placed on lockdown."

"There are bad rumors for both of us as well. There's talk of Julius being held accountable for the deaths of Lord Alwein and Lord Cambridge."

"Why doesn't that surprise me?"

"But Julius couldn't!" cried Marie.

"Nothing is going to happen, Marie, because the marshals won't let it happen. Just look at these sanctimonious wimps in this room, their faces are filled with terror over two teenage girls. They don't have the guts to confront a real warrior."

"The nobles want Cedric detained for treason."

The news hit Cassandra like a ton of bricks. She had treated her part in the escape like a game without recognizing the consequences. Turning pale, the older sister now had to be comforted by Marie. Well aware that the threshold for proving treason was very low under Acadian law, Cassie had no doubt from the actions she had witnessed; her country had a strong case against him. The sound of Jonas Marimon storming into the room startled her so much she almost screamed. Stephen sat up in his throne and silenced everyone with a wave of his hand.

"Lord Marimon, I would have hoped you could have handled your duty with grace. Have you done as I asked?"

"My liege, I demand the authority to lay siege to the Titan Embassy."

"Jonas, are you asking me for permission to start with a war with Titanus?"

"My liege, Christian DeVries helped the two prisoners escape the castle and has taken them into the Titan Embassy. They are claiming that the barbarians have asked for sanctuary and will not turn them over for the sake of justice."

The room exploded at this sound. Phrases such as "death to the Titans," and "we've put up with them for too long" were clearly being shouted. Sensing a riot about to start, a worried Luminas pleaded with the king for action. The more moderate nobles were silenced and some left the room in protest. Stephen stood from his throne and cleared his voice. He spoke with a very deep edge.

"Silence!"

"My liege's pardon, if they are on Titan soil, we cannot make any move against them," commented Luminas.

"I am aware of that, Count."

"I would also inform my liege that normal extradition procedures may be less than effective in this matter. The Titans have refused to honor our extradition procedures since we crucified that mason many revolutions ago."

"They'll never give them up," pronounced Sharon. "It's probably a plot to sign some secret agreement with the Wolf Tribe."

The disgraced queen found herself the most popular person in the room. Searching for a scapegoat, the nobles and elites agreed that Titanus planned in secret against them. Perhaps they only had hours to prepare a defense of Verian.

"I fear then we have no choice in this matter," retorted Luminas. "Thus, with his majesty's permission, I request that we hold an inquisition at the senate for the command staff of the Alliance Army."

The nobles cheered on Luminas's suggestion. Staring at the angry mob before him, Stephen determined all sanity in his castle was lost. He knew he had to give into the arcane and foolish process that the law demanded of him. Still, the king had questions he wanted answered, namely why had his future son-in-law invaded the sanctity of his castle?

"What charges do you wish to bring to hold an inquisition?"

"The marshals that accompanied the caravan should be charged with dereliction of duty, failure to comply with orders, and irresponsible handling of inferior officers, specifically the deaths of Lord Alwein and Lord Cambridge," stated Luminas. "In light of the recent events performed by his inferior officers, I believe Prince Marshal Cedric Rhone should be charged with treason.

Stephen nearly sunk in his throne as a resounding cheer rose up among the nobles. Cassandra swallowed a deep lump in her throat but refused to cry in front of them. Felicia put a hand to her left shoulder in order to offer support and comfort.

"Count Luminas, you may proceed with preparations for an inquisition and send out the necessary messages to all that must attend," commanded Stephen. "If at all possible try to arrange for Caesar Constantine and a noble delegation of Evengard to attend."

"My liege, my men will take the marshals into custody as soon as they arrive in the city," offered Jonas.

"You'll do no such thing, Commander Marimon. I wonder sometimes if you ever have a sane thought in your head. If you attempt to arrest the marshals, alliance soldiers will spill their own blood in the streets of Verian. Diplomacy will remain supreme in these matters. Inform the embassies of Napolitan, Evengard, and Titanus that we request the presence of their officers at the Senate."

"I do this with a heavy heart, my liege. It will be prepared," responded Luminas.

"Finally... some backbone!" remarked a laughing Jonas under his breath.

Standing, Stephen strode behind his throne to the private apartments. Not wasting any time, Cassandra and Marie followed him down the hall. The king did all he could to ignore them but Cassie would be heard.

"Daddy!" shouted Cassandra.

Stephen stopped and closed his eyes. Cassandra was seething while her younger sister's eyes were still red from tears. Understanding the gravity of the charges against the men they loved, the princesses pleaded their respective cases.

"They are accusing the man who has selflessly saved this alliance on numerous occasions of treason," charged Cassandra.

"What can I do, Cassie?" said Stephen. "Cedric is a war hero, but he has to learn that he cannot simply act in complete disregard of Acadian law just because he disagrees with it."

"They're looking for a scapegoat!" shouted Cassandra.

"Daddy, Julius would never have let those men die," sobbed Marie.

"I'm sure neither of you has anything to worry about," comforted Stephen after a deep sigh. "We don't go around destroying war heroes here. However, I'm going to ask that you do not attend the inquisition."

"Father, I must be there for him!" demanded Cassandra. "I know you understand!"

"No, Cassie!" bellowed her father angrily. "Not this time! Please go to your rooms! I will speak nothing further on this."

Feeling badly over his outburst, Stephen stopped and turned to his daughters. The king walked back to embrace them as a symbol of his sorrow for what he planned on doing. When he reached Cassandra, the raven-haired princess turned on her heel and left him. Stephen stood there dejected for a moment as he watched her leave. Embracing Marie for a moment, his younger daughter returned no warmth to him before leaving. When Cassandra reached the door of her apartment, Felicia stood waiting for her.

"I need orders, mistress," commanded Felicia with a devious smile.

"I want you to order my guard to clear the senate gallery."

"You plan on disobeying your father?"

"Daddy forced my hand. Observing from the gallery, I intend to keep my eye on the proceedings. I think we all can agree something isn't right here."

"Of course, mistress."

"Besides, I think you wish to be there as well."

Felicia nodded, and the two walked away.

CAVERNS OF THE DEMONKIN

"The difference between myself and other Titan scientists is that I am not a hypocrite. They claim to pursue only the purest forms of ethical research, but in reality they show the same propensity to test their theories on humans. I simply don't pretend and would advocate outright human experimentation to achieve my goals."

—*The lectures of Doctor Virgus Tattenberg*

Abaddon sat reading *The Titan Battle Manual* in a well-furnished room. Making notes with a pen inside the book, the dark angel found himself nodding in agreement with the written word. Despite the fact it was penned by an enemy, Abaddon thoroughly enjoyed reading the book. An exasperated Basarabas ran into the room.

"My lord, the Acadian wizards have disappointed us."

"In what way?"

"They have failed to secure the two granddaughters of Aramas."

"I give them the simple task of murdering two teenagers and they couldn't even do that right. I warned them to use duco-mutatios and not Templar knights but that Jonas Marimon is so self-righteous. What happened?"

"Rumors persist that agents of the Titan prince extracted them from Acadian custody this morning."

"His antics are no longer amusing. It's as if he is anticipating our every move."

"I warned you that he has long been a formidable enemy to my people."

"Either that or someone on the inside cannot be trusted. All that planning gone to waste, but then it was my fault to trust in the humans. Well, Doctor Tattenberg, it would seem that your services are going to be needed after all."

A man entered the room. Half of his body was replaced with robotic components; he had a single blue eye and long silver hair where skin was left. Despite all this, his lips and mouth were still flesh and he wore a large smile.

"Well, you don't keep me around for my charming personality Lord Abaddon," quipped Virgus.

"I assume that you are prepared."

"I would like the opportunity to run a final test. However, it will be ready in plenty of time for your designs, my lord."

"Good. What is going on in Acadia now?"

"They're holding an investigation into the incident with the tribes," explained Basarabas. "The marshals are being blamed."

"Perfect; it never ceases to amaze me how gullible mortal man can be. Then again, they did crucify their own savior. In light of recent events, we're going to have to tigthen our security. If this *La Morte Angelus* suspects our role in the death of Aramas, our contacts in Acadia must do everything they can to belittle him. Basarabas, is everything prepared for the movement of operations?"

"The Wizards Guild has prepared the way for us. The Demonkin and Nephilim are ready to start teleporting into Verian. I estimate that in a rotation or two, we can have all of our divisions in place.

"Good," said Abaddon as he returned to the book. "We'll let them have their little trial, and then it will be time to strike. Let me continue my research into how our little 'nestling' will handle this next crisis."

TITAN EMBASSY, AFTERNOON

"Blessed are they who are persecuted for the sake of righteousness, for theirs is the kingdom of heaven. Blessed are you when they insult you and persecute you and utter every kind of evil against you because of me. Rejoice and be glad, for your reward will be great in heaven. Thus they persecuted the prophets who were before you."

—*The Evengard Evangelist 5:10–12*

Acadian halberdiers and guards remained stationed outside the embassy. The sound of the steel gate opening caused them to snap to attention and get their weapons ready. Riding out the gates, the Titan delegation made their stand. Civilia was in the lead with Cecilia on her right and Cedric on her left. Horace, Martha, Christian, and Bishop Arthur accompanied them as well. Cleaned up, dressed in full regalia, and riding proud, the Titans followed the ancient philosophy of the first King of Titanus Ulysses Rhone: "Look your best for you never know if you fight your final battle." Civilia had called her four main bannermen: HerrGraf Curtis Stillwell, HerrGraf Otto Johnstone, FrauGraf Kerry Flynn, and FrauGraf Dorothy Gerhardt to join the delegation, along with twenty-one other high-born aristocrats and nobles that served in the Titan armada. Carrying the banners of Titanus, House Rhone, the great houses of Titanus, and sigil of Cedric Rhone, the Titans looked ready for war. The gate closed quickly behind them, and the Acadian guards grudgingly had no choice but to let the delegation pass. Civilia remained in full command as the delegation rode very slowly and cautiously toward the main Verian roads.

"Freigraf, did you relay my orders to Samuel?"

"He understands fully the rules of engagement, your highness. He also knows to signal for us should the Acadians try anything. We have some of our best knights and valkyries defending the embassy. We'll give them a beating they'll never forget."

"If this is going to be the end of everything, at least our people won't have to dress us for the funeral."

This drew smiles from most of the delegation, but Cedric was silent. Watching her brother pray the rosary interlocked in his reigns, Cecilia searched for words of comfort. A simple smile was all she could offer her twin and for Cedric knowing his sister had his back was enough. Martha was more direct, specifically riding next to Cedric and tapping him on the shoulder to get his attention.

"I'm sorry, your excellency, the tape is no help. I fear we have no direct evidence to put forward in our defense."

"It was fool's hope to believe our enemies would make such a grave mistake. I was fully prepared last night when I gave Christian his orders that I would have no evidence to put forward."

"How are you going to defend yourself?" asked a desperate Cecilia.

"I am guilty under the laws of Central Acadia. There is no defense."

"I won't let you admit to treason."

"I have no intention to. I am going to lay out the truth for those at the inquisition. We have to put our faith in the fact that our allies and men of goodwill can decide whether I acted in accordance with that truth."

"There isn't much hope in that," commented Christian.

"Will you two quit worrying? Do you realize this is the biggest show trial ever put on in the history of the world? The inquisition has no authority to bind a Titan to any Acadian law. Stephen is merely throwing a bone to the Acadian nobles so they can rant and scream—the same arrogance that got those morons killed in the first place."

Civilia listened to these words and wished she could share her son's faith in humanity. However, Cedric's self-righteousness was always his crutch, especially when it came to human life. She hoped that Stephen would do the honorable thing but wondered if the nobles of Acadia had already bound his hands. She prayed that the man she loved could find sympathy for her son. The Titans weren't the only ones making their way through the city. Marching through the city, Cagius and Julius led an army of both regular legionnaires and praetorian guards. The two lords of Napolitan were dressed in full regalia as well. Valentine stood behind them and focused on the streets for any sign of Acadian treachery.

"Well, we're royally screwed now," commented Cagius. "I knew this whole adventure was a bad idea."

"Shut up!" shouted Julius.

"Hey, Julius, you'd better not make me mad. After this is over, you and I are probably going to spending a lot of quality time together since no one is ever going to talk to us again."

"This isn't the time for jokes!"

"I'm serious."

"I agree with Cagius; you'd better be careful in there," warned Valentine. "The nerve of Count Luminas, how dare he claim that they couldn't get a hover train to your father in time. Julius, the Acadians treat these inquisitions very seriously. You'd better not open yourself to any liability."

To the anger of the Napolitan spy master, Julius nodded as if to dismiss Valentine. He wondered how the marshals would ever be viewed again after this disgrace. Julius was an enemy of two worlds now. The tribes had lost all respect for him and would never fear him as an enemy again. Now the Alliance, who had embraced him heartily but a few rotations ago, wanted to rake him over the coals. It left the paladin pondering how his life had completely fallen apart in a matter of hours. Paranoid by the whispers of his men, he contemplated if they truly thought Cedric had more control over the situation then their beloved first tribune.

Amuro and Malcolm filled in with a delegation of elf lancers as they waited for the others at the bridge leading toward the alliance senate. Dismounting before the bridge, the Titans allowed the squires to return the horses to the embassy. Dealing with Julius's solemn face and Cedric's seething rage, Amuro smiled brightly to lighten everybody up. The marshals noticed Walker walking up to the group in his full royal regalia as well. The delegations of all four nations took a few moments to go over to each other and embrace everyone. The same sense of foreboding filled all of their thoughts, that it might be the toughest battle they had ever faced. However, when Cedric went over to Julius, the Napolitan prince refused to take his hand. Cedric nodded his head slightly in understanding. Amuro interjected and took both of their hands for a moment.

"I don't pretend to understand what goes on in the male mind. However, we better stick with each other now because when the three of us have fought together, the alliance never lost a battle."

Squeezing both their hands tightly, Amuro's elf empathy flowed into both Julius and Cedric. Inspired by their comrade's words, Julius managed to pull off a smirk, and Cedric's rage calmed for a moment.

"Oh well... let's show them what we're made of," commanded Julius.

The three delegations and Walker let out a loud scream that shook the will of the Acadian guards surrounding the senate. Purposely walking over the bridge, a Napolitan Senator Marcus Polonius greeted them. The former war hero turned politician had very neatly cut gray hair, a gray beard, and green eyes. He was rather muscular for a man his age, though he was dressed in the outfit of a noble. He wore the coat-of-arms of Napolitan on his jacket lapel. Valentine walked over to him and immediately started to rib him.

"Well, Senator, shouldn't you be inside?"

"Considering the mood inside the chamber, I felt it best that I meet you outside. I think you should know that our senators are deeply divided and the majority party is siding with the Acadians. The few elf senators are sitting in silence, and Queen Civilia could have done me a favor by at least having one senator show up. I need more conservative voices. I've been holding the floor for a few hours in order to prevent any more votes; my party is giving me a break right now. It's just a regular rotation here in Verian."

"Wonderful," stated Julius.

"You shouldn't be too upset, Julius. After all, they'll be so intent on raking me over the coals you'll probably get off with a slap on the wrist," joked Cedric.

Clearly ready for a battle, the Titan prince walked right up to the stone doors and pushed them open. The moment the delegation stepped in the room, all that could be heard was screaming by the various senators. It was just as Polonius had warned them. The large majority of the Senators now stood on the left side of the room while a clear minority remained on the right including some elves, who simply had their heads down. Civilia was growing clearly irritated that she was not recognized by the senate Augur.

"Marshal... if you please..."

"It will be my pleasure, your majesty," responded Horace as he took a deep breath and screamed.

"HER ROYAL HIGHNESS QUEEN CIVILIA RHONE, RULER OF THE KINGDOM OF TITANUS, LORD PROTECTOR OF THE DWARVES AND WOOD ELVES, WARDEN OF THE SOUTH!"

The room fell silent, and everyone's attention turned to the marshals entering the room. Walking to the center of the senate floor, Senate President Norville Warrington waited for them wearing the lapel of Central Acadia on his long blue coat. He had long gray hair, blue eyes behind gold-rimmed spectacles, and utter disdain for the marshals entering the room. Warrington was seated at a wooden desk, the normal position for the senator of his office.

King Stephen was seated with his two wives on a step above the senator. Maximilian Luminas stood at a wooden podium next to Senator Warrington's desk. The Acadian nobles and the Wizards Guild made sure they had front-row seats at the inquisition. Focusing their attention on Celius, the Titans observed the guild master seated in the front row with a smile.

"Pretty smug for a guy who's planning a coup," observed Cecilia.

"He doesn't know we're on to him yet," replied Cedric.

The marshals stopped in the center of the forum. All eyes in the room were fixed on them. Civilia was escorted to a throne set aside for her. She refused to take her seat until she was recognized.

"Queen Civilia, do you have a matter to discuss before this body?" asked Warrington.

"I believe that under the Alliance Charter, Titanus is allotted twenty-five senators in this body."

"Yes, under the current rules of the senate. However, as you do not see fit to send senators to this body . . ."

"The twenty-five men and women with me will serve as our senators."

Collectively dropping their jaws, the body of the senate sat in silent horror. Polonius had to cover his mouth to prevent his laughter from being heard too loudly throughout the room.

"How and when have these men and women been elected?" asked Warrington.

"The Titan Magna Carta does not call for elections in the matter of representation. All matters concerning international relations rest in the sole jurisdiction of the sovereign. You will seat these men and women as per my request."

"I fear I have no choice. I recognize these men and women as senators. I assume they prefer to remain on that side of the aisle. Do you have any further objections concerning senate business?"

Civilia took her seat. Warrington turned back to King Stephen.

"My liege, the senate is honored by your presence. I hereby turn control over this body to you."

King Stephen nodded to Warrington. Staring at the Marshals, he witnessed Walker standing with them. It disturbed the king greatly that his daughter's personal bodyguard could be brought up on charges.

"Lord Captain Walker, you do not stand accused," stated Stephen.

"My liege, am I not a vice-marshal of the Alliance? If they are accused, I prefer to stand with my friends."

Clicking the heels of boots together, the lord knight made a dramatic salute to the king. Stephen slumped back in his throne, knowing the finest soldier in his country was prepared to accept his fate. Luminas stepped forward.

"With his majesty's permission, I formally bring the inquisition to order.,"

"Proceed, Count Luminas!" ordered Stephen.

Luminas licked his fangs and walked to the podium.

"Prince Marshal Julius Imperia, Princess Marshal Amuro Jenitzen, Prince Vice-Marshal Cagius Imperia, Prince Vice-Marshal Malcolm Fenidor, and Lord Captain Jonathan Walker, you are called here to answer for, not only failure of the mission, but also for the death of two knightserrants entrusted to your service. As per custom, you will surrender your weapons and enter your plea."

The marshals were shocked by such a demand. Cagius was grinding his teeth.

"I was not under the impression that this inquisition was, in fact, a court martial," countered Julius. "If so, I demand that I am tried before the appropriate military commission and am subject to the Uniform Alliance Military Code."

Luminas took a deep breath, realizing that he had overreached and the marshals were well aware of the lack of power the inquisition had. Throughout the room, the legionnaires nodded their heads in agreement at the showing of some spine by their first tribune. The Count regained the calm demeanor on his face and nodded.

"I did not mean any offense. You may keep your weapons, but I am afraid that I must ask you to plea."

Julius turned to Polonius for counsel, who shook his head no.

"I will not enter a plea until I am subject to Uniform Alliance Military Code," answered Julius to Luminas's further frustrations.

"Prince Marshal Commandant Cedric Rhone, this morning your agents extracted two prisoners who were ordered into custody by King Stephen Acadia himself," dictated Luminas, turning his attention to Cedric. "We deem you to be responsible for their actions. It is an act of treason to free political prisoners from a kingdom in the alliance. Men were also injured in this raid, and thus you are responsible for these actions as well. How do you plead?"

"Titanus does not recognize the legitimate authority of Central Acadia to conduct such proceedings," noted Cedric, displaying his extensive legal knowledge. "There is no regulation either within the laws of the alliance or in the Alliance Charter that allow for one nation to formally charge members of another nation without procedural due process. I will acquiesce to your questions where I deem necessary for the sake of the investigation."

The Acadian senators stared with great contempt. Senator Warrington gritted his teeth.

"You dare defy the customs and traditions of Central Acadia?" challenged the senator.

"The last I time checked, Senator Norville Warrington, we are an alliance of four nations, not Central Acadia and three vassals!"

"Continue with this arrogance, and we will hold you in contempt!" shouted Warrington.

"I challenge any man here to put me in custody."

Cedric's brilliant defense strategy and he hasn't even started drinking yet, thought Christian as he rolled his eyes.

"I was unaware that in addition to being a soldier you were also a barrister," taunted Luminas.

"Well, it was either that or economics; I took the easy way out."

"I'll place the question to you this way. Were your agents acting under your orders?"

"I find it insulting that any member of this chamber would believe that I do not have control over my agents at all times. They indeed acted under my orders."

In the gallery above the senate, Cassandra and Felicia were trying to keep a low profile. Growing concern crossed the face of the princess with each passing minute.

"Cedric, be careful," pleaded Cassandra. "I'm sure you have a plan..."

"I don't see how antagonizing the senate is going to help his cause," stated Felicia.

The two looked on as Luminas proceeded.

"It has come to our attention that you, Marshal Rhone, were not in Verian the past few rotations. Where, in fact, were you?"

"I was conducting war games at Fort Capricorn,"

"War games?" scoffed Jonas Marimon. "You can't be serious!"

Eagerly ceding the floor to his sister, Cecilia stepped forward with three disks in her hands. She threw them down on the table.

"These are documented records of the war games conducted by Titanus, Evengard, Napolitan, and the Acadian soldiers stationed at Fort Capricorn.

We simulated an attack on two fronts from both tribal and imperial forces. The officers on duty make the following recommendations for immediate spending for Fort Capricorn. The fort is undermanned, has been stripped of all technology, and is literally falling apart."

"It is well within the Alliance Charter and established Alliance Law that any nation may lead a war game as long as it includes troops from each member," interjected Martha as Cecilia ceded the floor. "Also, both the marshal and vice-marshal conducted the exercise with the appropriate number of troops based on their rank and command."

Luminas simply tore up the piece of paper he was using for that line of questioning. The senators in the room appeared to be growing restless. Conducting personal business was a petty matter, they wanted to hear more about the tribes and Cedric's actions in Verian. Luminas thought it best to move on at this point.

"That was a longer answer than I anticipated, but I believe it answers the question, your majesty."

"It does," chimed in Stephen.

Luminas readied his next card but looked toward Cedric and Cecilia who were instructing members of their staff on key points they should be writing down. He wondered exactly what they were doing for a moment before turning back to his questioning of the marshals.

"Let me then turn my attention to you, Prince Marshal Imperia. Please describe the events leading up to the tribal attack."

"Everything proceeded according to plan. The tribes inspected the documents we presented to them at the set time and place. Chief Reynard and Josephine of the Myotis Tribe, Huskal of the Wolf Tribe, Chief Priestess Posha of the Syrus Clan, and Adnar the Bold of the Nordice were present at the meeting. They expressed great reservations over the lack of movement and trade agreements; however, they agreed to the armistice. All papers were signed and documented that rotation. Since we were familiar with tribal traditions, we knew we could not simply pack up the camp that evening and depart. During the evening, Captain Walker and I noticed smoke signals coming from the mountains. However, no one in the command staff is an expert in such signals and we still have no idea what they meant. The encampment was heavily stockaded, and we posted an extra watch. When we woke at first light, the command staff discovered that Lord Alwein and Lord Cambridge had disobeyed my direct orders and left the encampment to go hunting.

"Why did you issue the command?" asked Luminas.

"The smoke signals made me uneasy," stated Julius. "The marshals decided that we needed to strike camp at dawn and make it to the relative safety of the Gold Road."

"And none of you saw either of them in the morning?" continued Luminas to be met with vertical head nods. "May I see the documentation that the tribes signed?"

Julius gave the folder bearing the documents with the alliance seal to a page. Delivering the page to the Count, Luminas opened the packet and reviewed the Armistice Treaty.

"My liege, all of the papers here are in order. It is clearly signed by the tribes. There was no dereliction of duty by Prince Marshal Imperia concerning these proceedings."

"It is so noted; you may proceed, Count. I'm curious to learn more about the demise of Lord Alwein and Lord Cambridge.".

"Very good, your majesty. How did you learn of their deaths?"

"A wounded soldier arrived at the camp just as Captain Walker and Vice-Marshal Imperia were heading out to find them," recounted Julius. "Marshal Jenitzen treated the soldier's wounds with magic and he told us what had happened. Members of the Wolf Tribe surrounded the knights and attacked them. The knights chose to try and break through the lines. The soldier relayed that this is how they were killed, but I did not witness this. The soldier is currently being treated in a hospital and we received nothing more out of him. The unit that retrieved the bodies of the two knight-errants found spear and bow wounds in both knights consistent with tribal weaponry."

Cries of "death" and "blood" sounded now from the senate. The senate was certainly riled up over the actions of the tribes, and Julius's account only made it worse. This made the marshals very uneasy at the events around them. Amuro noticed Cerwin Faulkner enter the room with a disturbed look on his face. He walked over to Amuro and put his arm on her shoulder but said nothing at the moment.

"Begging the Senate's pardon," interrupted Amuro. "The record should reflect that the pattern of attack exhibited by tribes was never encountered by any of the officers in this room in prior battles."

"I shall enter your concern Princess Marshal Jenitzen into the record," noted Luminas. "What happened next?"

"We detected the Tribal Army approaching our position," stated Julius. "The remaining soldiers and command staff bunkered ourselves in the ruins to give us a better chance of holding out. We also sent a distress signal. However, we did not anticipate that Marshal Rhone was conducting war games at Fort Capricorn during the armistice. Realizing that relief was close by, we chose to stand our ground rather than surrender."

"Lord Alwein and Lord Cambridge died before the Tribal Army appeared before you?" asked Luminas.

"Yes," replied Julius.

"Your majesty, it is apparent from the inquisition that there is no fault by any member of the command staff presiding over the negotiations," pleaded Luminas as he tore up another card. "Tragically, it seems that both Lord Alwein and Lord Cambridge disobeyed a direct order from a commanding officer, and the resulting disobedience of that order resulted in their deaths from an aggressive and vengeful enemy. Thus all matters against them should be dropped."

"I concur," stated Stephen. "I do have a question myself, Marshal. Did the tribes give you a reason for their attack?"

"They wished to take us hostage," replied Julius.

"Hostage?" asked Stephen.

"They wanted to exchange us for Aramas's granddaughters."

"Why would any tribe outright murder two Acadian knight-errants but seek to hold hostage alliance marshals?" asked a confused Stephen. "The chief let his daughters remain here for their own safety. It's completely out of Aramas's nature to renege on an agreement."

"The tribes attacked because Chieftain Aramas was killed" interjected Cedric. "The way he was killed made it appear as if Central Acadian templars had done it. The tribal leaders feared that we had already taken Hippolyte and Minerva prisoner."

Laughter filled the chamber. However, Stephen saw the seriousness in Cedric's face and knew something was definitely wrong.

"That's just beautiful!" taunted a laughing Jonas. "I think we were set up from the beginning. The barbarians drove us out to some out-of-the-way location so they could accuse us of murdering their chief and then butcher our men! It was nothing more than a simple coup your highness and because Aramas handed his granddaughter's over to us, we are obviously the bad guy."

The senators seemed to agree with Jonas's sentiments. In the gallery, Cassandra noticed Wilhelm von Angelhardt enter. Walking straight to the brass rail, the duke silently placed his hands on it. For a moment he turned to Cassandra and looked her over. He smiled, waved, and soon returned his focus to the proceedings. The princess wondered what that had been about. She stared at the Titan duke for some time and felt a warm feeling inside for a moment. However, Luminas's next question captured her attention.

"Marshal Rhone, if they were so intent on taking our men, how did you defuse the situation?"

"I spoke with Captain Huskal, who served as Chieftain Aramas's Alpha. It is the equivalent of Jonas Marimon's position. Soldier to soldier, we were able to come to an agreement."

"An agreement? What authority did you have to make any agreements?"

"I have authority as a Crown Prince of Titanus and as Marshal Commandant of the Alliance Army based on the laws of my country and the alliance charter."

"I know you do; I just wanted to establish the record. What agreement did you make?"

"If you would indulge me for a few moments, I believe greater details are necessary to understand the situation," began Cedric. "I have a credible source that informed me last evening that the Nephilim conducted an attack on the Wolf Tribe encampment. The army was present at the Armistice so it was an easy target."

Beads of sweat dripping from his forehead, the formerly smug Celius stood to challenge Cedric. Cecilia knew that the Wizards Guild had indeed made a deal with the devil and wondered how her brother would trap him.

"I must interject, your majesty," challenged Celius. "Long has Titanus over-exaggerated the threat of the Nephilim. The self-righteous, scripture-thumpers, believe the old elven fairy tales and myths of demonic houses that once ruled the world."

"Titanus is not the only nation to recognize the risks of these people," shouted Cerwin Faulkner as he stepped forward. "I should know. I was there when the Demonkin attempted to take the life of a young Hayden Marisol and interfere with the formation of the alliance between Hayden and Ulysses."

"The Nephilim that you dismiss have powerful allies," explained Cedric. "Among their Demonkin slaves are the duco-mutatios. These shape-shifters assimilated human form and used Acadian weapons in the attack. All but one that is, the being that actually killed Aramas is named Abaddon. Abaddon is a fallen angel sent to Terminus Mundus for a purpose. The first stage of his plan was to incite a great conflict between the alliance and the tribes. Aramas died, and the tribes took the bait. However, it wasn't going to be enough, so the duco-mutatios disguised themselves as members of the Wolf Tribes and killed our knight-errants as well. The plans of Abaddon are clear—incite a conflagration between our troops and execute whatever his diabolical plan is when chaos reigns. However, we have the opportunity before us to foil such plans."

"I assume this has something to do with your actions concerning Aramas's daughters," suggested Luminas.

"Unlike the other three tribes that elect their leaders, the chieftain of the Wolf Tribe is hereditary. Aramas's son, Aegis, was killed in the Battle of the Terrace River; thus, Hippolyte is now the lawful chief of the Wolf Tribe."

"Some luck at last, my liege!" beamed a proud Jonas. "We've got the chief of the Wolf Tribe; those barbarians will have to do whatever we say now."

"You just don't understand, Jonas!" argued Cedric with an edge in his voice. "King Stephen, I brokered the deal. The tribes have agreed to lay down their arms and come back to the table if we return Hippolyte and Minerva to the Tribal Confederation. If we do this, I guarantee that I can get the tribes to agree to stand with us against Abaddon and his Nephilim."

"The Nephilim did not attack us at the Istle Hill Ruins and kill our men," said Luminas. "That was the actions of your beloved barbarians."

"You still refuse to believe how far the Nephilim have infiltrated us. Julius, I need your help with something. Did you ever relay a message back to Central Acadia that the negotiations were a success?

"We weren't able to send a message back to Central Acadia. Our communications were scrambled from the second we went to the Istle Hills. The only reason we picked up Fort Capricorn because their receiver was close. I thought the effect was based on some natural weather disturbance, but I believe Marshal Rhone has a different conclusion."

"A dampening field was placed over the whole of the area of the Istle Hills. The closer my riders came to the ruins, the harder it became for us to send a signal."

"Yet everyone in the city seemed to know of the attack on our men before we did."

"I have a detailed log from the officer on duty of a transmission from a soldier claiming that there was an attack by the tribes," countered Luminas. "The line went dead after that. The barbarians must have taken the equipment."

"No way. With all due respect, Count Luminas, something is not adding up here," interrupted Cagius. "If you're disobeying a direct order from your superior officers, you're not going to be carrying communication equipment around with you."

"It is a funny thing how the accused hurls his accusations at the investigators," taunted Jonas.

"I accused no one. All I am saying is that it's clear the Nephilim have infiltrated Verian as well," warned Cedric. "The technician was either a duco-mutatio or on the take. It would further light the conflagration between our people if the girls had been killed. Then there would be no hope for peace."

"What proof do you offer?" asked Luminas.

"The Wizards Guild has been meeting with the leader of the Nephilim. He is named Basarabas."

"Is that true, Master Celius?"

"We have had contacts with a Basarabas, but he is only a merchant from the east," feigned Celius still trying to composing himself. "He deals in rare alchemical ingredients; nothing more. This foolish boy is turning us against one another with baseless conspiracy theories."

"No one knows the Nephilim better than Titanus," said Stephen.

"Your majesty, our powers are such that we could clearly recognize an agent of the enemy. The Titans are hysterical fools! I will not stand here and been insulted by a traitor"

"I think we've heard enough," announced Stephen as he took a deep breath. "I'm bringing the inquisition to a close. We know all we need to know about what's going on here. While I must concede Cedric Rhone makes a strong case for someone working behind the scenes against our interests, I fear it is in the best interests of the alliance to have Titanus surrender Hippolyte and Minerva back into the custody of Central Acadia."

Attempting to "split the baby," Stephen hoped the compromise would be enough to calm everyone down. The Titans grew enraged at the order. Seeking strength from his faith, Cedric began to pray the rosary. Cassandra stood in shock on the balcony as well.

"Father, you can't do this! You can't put Cedric in this situation where he'd have to compromise his honor."

Standing from her throne, Civilia went to her son. Stephen could see the searing rage in the eyes of the Matriarch of Destruction as she put her hands to his shoulder. She'd never understand the delicate position he was in. Caught between the tempest of nobles rioting in the streets and a phantom war against a demon enemy, Stephen chose to deal with the evil closest to home.

"Why?" asked Civilia.

"I commend the efforts of your son in trying to avoid further bloodshed. However, there is truth in what Jonas Marimon has said. The chief of the Wolf Tribe in our custody will be powerful leverage. You need not fear; those girls are worth far more alive to us then dead. However, they are our prisoners and per the agreement I had with Aramas, they are our property now."

"The tribes will never hold to that agreement, Prince Marshal Rhone," added Luminas. "You did all you had to do. It is on our heads, not yours. I join the king in commending your efforts once more. I deem under the circumstances that you did, in fact, act quite rationally. However, I must say that it seems quite presumptuous of you to think that a few 'boogeymen' could have coordinated such a precise attack. We are going to have to ask you to hand them over without delay. The last thing Verian needs is another surprise. Our soldiers will escort them back to the castle where they will be held in house arrest."

"I will not comply with such an order."

Gasps filled the halls of the Senate. Even Julius and Amuro stared at Cedric wondering if he had lost his mind. Cedric turned to his mother, who smiled at him with tears forming in her eyes. Nodding in approval, the queen returned to her seat. Stephen was taken aback by Cedric's defiance. He figured that he had to reason with him further.

"I know how important honor is to the Titans. Prince Rhone, this is my decision. Let no man or woman claim . . ."

"I seek absolution only from God. I warned you before this inquisition began that I did not recognize its authority to proceed as ordered. I only came to present you with the facts surrounding the true crisis and enemy we face. I plan to return Hippolyte and Minerva safely to the Tribal Confederation as soon as possible."

"You would dare to defy the steward?"

"Absolutely. King Stephen, you are a man of reason and justice. I stand before you offering peace for a simple act of good faith. Yet you dismiss this offer. I demand to know whether a war has been declared without consultation with the marshals."

"Is it true?" insisted Julius. "Are we at war with the tribes?"

"There was an emergency session this morning of the senate where a vote on a declaration of war was cast," answered Warrington.

"I was aware of no such meeting!" screamed an angry Polonius. "How could you have achieved a quorum without us?"

"I fear that in the haste to convene the matter, some senators were not able to attend," explained Warrington. "Count Luminas offered an interpretation that allowed us to vote without a quorum."

"Now that a quorum can be achieved, I ask for the specific nature of the vote."

"The vote was to declare war on the tribes for a direct violation of the armistice agreement they signed."

"The agreement wasn't even ratified yet! The senate had to approve the final details first as we were promised. Mister president, I demand the floor."

"Need I remind you this is not an ordered session of the senate but rather an inquisition."

"Senator Polonius, When tribes signed armistice, they were bound to it," argued Luminas. "They chose to fight us first! Even if what Prince Rhone says is true, the tribes clearly showed their propensity for vendetta and misplaced anger. They can no longer be trusted to hold their lands and must be brought under our protection."

"The menace will be dealt with once and for all," urged on Jonas.

"I have already consulted with Lords Jenitzen and Fenidor of Evengard and Caesar Constantine," described Stephen. "They all have their reservations about going to war again. Prince Marshal Julius Imperia, you have been selected to serve as the sole alliance commander, the position once held by Lord Marshal Hector Reed. Your father has vowed to honor whatever decision you make. Will you lead our army?"

"Yes, my liege," answered Julius, stepping forward.

Cedric shot a cold stare at Julius. The vast majority of the people in the room stood from their seats and gave him a standing ovation. Covering his face, Cagius turned his back on his brother.

"Why?" asked Cedric.

"I agree with Luminas. You're chasing the villains of fairy tales. This is real, Cedric. We've been at a defacto war with these tribes for far too long. Perhaps nearly getting killed has given me a new perspective on things. This is not a perfect solution, but I'm tired of ridicule from defending you."

"Princess Amuro Jenitzen, your father left you orders to command the elf forces in the campaign if Prince Julius Imperia agreed to take command," described Stephen.

Amuro started to cry. Sucking her tears back, she felt Malcolm's warm hand on her shoulder. She turned to Cerwin with hope that what the king said wasn't true. However, he simply shook his head.

"Then I have no choice. I obey King Stephen."

"Cedric, let's drop the formalities between us," insisted Stephen. "You have been called the greatest knight ever to wear armor on Terminus Mundus. Your long record of victories and triumphs do nothing but make that the understatement of all times. You are a man of faith, honor, discipline, and principle. You are to marry my daughter, and I have always been fond of you. That's why I am pleading with you now."

Wilhelm stared from the gallery with a smile on his face. Nervously tiptoeing to where he stood, Cassandra could hear the duke talking to himself.

"Cedric. . . it is time. . ." acknowledged Wilhelm.

"Time for what?" asked Cassandra.

"It's time to see, my dear, whether you know the man you love," answered Wilhelm as he embraced her. "You are about to find out whether or not he will protect you."

"What does that mean?" demanded Cassandra as tears began to fall.

"I ask you, Cedric, to lead the armies of Titanus against the tribes," pleaded Stephen. "If you do this, I don't care about anything you did this morning. What do you owe the tribes? We are the ones that failed them, not you. Is every accolade and position you achieved in this alliance worth nothing to you? What does my daughter mean to you? Please, end this meaningless protest and do your duties according to your rank."

Cedric lifted his eyes when Stephen mentioned Cassandra's name. Wilhelm took a deep breath as well and folded his hands in prayer. Finished with his prayer, Cedric put the rosary away. He clicked his heels together and saluted Stephen. Stephen went to mouth a "thank you," but Cedric interrupted him.

"Since you and I no longer share the same goal, I can no longer in good conscience hold the position of marshal in the Alliance Army. My final order before I tender my resignation is to ask that all men and women of good conscience stand down against this insanity. It has been an honor to serve you King Stephen."

Cedric dropped the salute and tore the marshal insignia from his military coat. The room was left in a state of disbelief. Crying harder, Malcolm took Amuro's head to his shoulder. On the balcony, Cassandra smiled and cried tears of joy. She hugged Felicia tightly.

"I knew it! Cedric is the Permaneo Eques Ordinares."

Bowing his head, Stephen graciously accepted his resignation.

"I respect your decision, but you've left me no choice. The inquisition is over. Cedric Rhone, Crown Prince of Titanus, you are found guilty of trespass, assault on Acadian knights and soldiers, and high treason.

"Arrest him!" shouted Jonas.

The Templars in the room, along with the guards, readied their weapons. However, the armed delegations of Titanus, Napolitan, and Evengard drew their weapons in Cedric's defense. Neither side wished to move forward at the risk of antagonizing the other.

"Since you stand convicted of high treason, I will not allow you to marry my daughter," commanded Stephen.

"Allow!" yelled Civilia. "You have no authority to do so according to the contract!"

"Since you see fit to do as you please, I will do as I please in my own kingdom, Queen Civilia! Though your son has chosen to defy me, Titanus is still a military member of the alliance. Princess Vice-Marshal Cecilia Rhone, under my royal authority, I promote. . ."

"If you think I'm going to lead my people into this petty war of yours, you are sadly mistaken. I follow the final orders of my brother and stand down from the Alliance Army."

"I agree with the sentiment of the prince and princess. I, Freigraf Horace Irvine, stand down from the Alliance Army."

"Colonel Christian DeVries of Titanus, I stand down from the Alliance Army."

"Prince Cagius Imperia of Napolitan, I stand down from the Alliance Army."

"Lord Antonio Valentine of Napolitan, standing down."

"Lord Captain Sirius of Evengard, I stand down."

Echoing the shouts of the initial six, more and more members from Titanus, Napolitan, and Evengard followed the commands of Cedric Rhone. Julius stared at Cagius, wondering what he had just done, but Cagius just stood there and shook his head. There was no way he was going to have any part in this madness. Perceiving all he had worked for over twenty-five revolutions falling to pieces, Stephen slumped down in his throne in disbelief. However, he had not yet receive the greatest undercut of all.

"I, Lord Captain Jonathan Walker, formally stand down from the Alliance Army."

Clutching his heart, Stephen knew that Walker was held in high regard by many soldiers in the Acadian regular army. Stephen had gambled by casting his lot with the Acadian nobles and lost. His true base of power, the alliance nations and their armies had left him in favor of the defiant Titan prince. Standing from her throne, Civilia cleared her throat.

"Stephen, the only thing that prevents me from formally withdrawing Titanus from the alliance is the fear you will do anything to put those girls in chains. I never should have let you talk me into placing Titan soldiers under an alliance banner again. It is a mistake that I can correct by withdrawing our army in accordance with the alliance charter. All these revolutions, all I the trust I had in you was but a pillar of salt on the shore. My son proudly echoes the sentiments of our nation."

"You are within your rights Civilia. Jonas, I ask you to have your men stand down. I doubt you'd even have the power to take Cedric Rhone into custody if stood alone. However, Prince Rhone is banished from Verian for the rest of his life. If you set foot in this city again, you will be arrested and summarily executed. I'm sorry it ended like this."

"We all make our own choices. It is the blessing and burden of free will. I pray you don't live to regret this."

Cedric walked past Julius and Amuro to the safety of the delegation. Cagius flashed a "thumbs up" and gave the appearance of "right on, man" while Walker stood with eyes closed and fists clenched in rage.

"Cedric. . . please. . . we need you. . ." pleaded Amuro.

"Not for them. . . never again for them," defended Cedric.

"Let him go, Amuro!" said Julius. "I never thought you would be a loser, Cedric."

"If the choice is to lose or become the hero of a massacre, I chose to be a loser. Julius, I'm sure you'll enjoy your triumphant parade while the bodies of the slaughtered paint a red trail from the back of your horse."

Furious at the comment but too ashamed to retaliate, Julius let it go in passing. The Titans surrounded Cedric in case anyone chose to start anything. Standing at the edge of the rail above, Cassandra didn't care if anyone saw her anymore. Her makeup was completely ruined by running tears at this point.

"CEDRIC, I LOVE YOU AND I BEG YOU TO LET ME KEEP LOVING YOU BECAUSE OF WHAT YOU DO! BE GRATEFUL AND REJOICE THIS HOUR, CENTRAL ACADIA, FOR THE LAST KNIGHT WAS IN YOUR PRESENCE!"

Cedric turned to her as Cassandra dropped a favor from her hand into his. Holding the favor to his heart for a moment, the sword master placed it in the spot where his marshal insignia was torn. Relieved for a brief moment, he blew the princess a kiss. Cassandra even earned Cecilia's respect as she nodded in approval with a smile on his face.

"I have been and will always be yours, My Lady!" exclaimed Cedric. "Cassie, no matter what may come, I won't let them have you!"

Joining the Titan delegation were all of the soldiers and senators that vowed to stand down. As he passed by his older brother, Julius grabbed Cagius's arm.

"Don't do this to me, Cagius! I will not allow my own brother to embarrass me here."

"This is wrong! We were there, bro! We know this is wrong because nothing adds up! He begged us to help him and you're going to turn your back on him."

"Cagius, this isn't the time to be a purist! Something has to be done."

"A purist? Julius, please tell me why the doves want war while our hawks are suing for peace."

"Father agreed with Stephen!"

"No, he didn't! Father said 'he would honor whatever decision you made.' There's no way he believed the information given to him by the Acadians over your word. He was counting on you to determine the validity of the matter and make the final decision. That's why the Acadians didn't want him here, you'd never be able to look father in the eye and tell him you did the right thing."

"They tried to kill us!"

"You know that's not true! If they wanted to kill us, why were they so careful? Their actions with us don't match what happened to Alwein and Cambridge? You are searching for reasons and that is not like you. Are you looking to gain your precious political capital with the Acadians? You're so obsessed with Felicia that you're willing to sell your own soul."

"Maybe I am . . . so what?"

"You're going to give up everything for love . . . or is it pride, Julius? Cedric burned you three times today. Your head is so far stuck up your ass right now you couldn't see this for what it was. Julius, I love you, but I don't know how you could stand to stare your son in eyes after what you just did."

Julius grabbed Cagius and shoved him against the wall.

"I knew it!" said Cagius. "One more thing, brother—when I stand down, the legions will stand down with me. I did them a favor by not allowing them to become hired butchers for the Acadians. You'd better ask yourself whether you want to be one as well."

"SHUT UP AND GET OUT OF MY SIGHT!" shouted Julius.

As he watched the senators leave the chamber, Walker slipped up the staircase toward the gallery. Moving to restore order, Luminas banged his gavel many times.

"This inquisition is adjourned."

There were already clamors from senators about getting new riches and war trophies. There were comments in support of Stephen for standing up to Titanus and others. The glories that were Central Acadia were finally being restored in their minds. Julius Imperia was receiving praise too, and many were warming to the idea of him being joined to Marie Acadia. Finally they had a poster boy to counter the power of the allied nations. Felicia held Cassandra tightly as she cried. Approaching from the rear staircase, Walker rushed to the two women.

"My lady, I think it would be best if we got you out of here."

"Thank you, Walker," said Cassandra as she lifted her head and nodded.

"Come with me quickly. I owe an old friend a favor."

Infuriated by the proceedings, the allied nations crossed the bridge of the Senate. Wilhelm stood ready to greet Civilia but his presence was unwelcome.

"Fine time you showing up now!" shouted Cecilia. "Where were you when we needed you?"

"I would have been no help in there, princess. When men close their minds and hearts, they lose the capacity to reason. However, I may be able to help you now, but only if we work quickly."

"Stephen is set on his war; there's nothing we can do," said Civilia. "I'm afraid we failed Wilhelm."

"There may be someone who knows how to stop this," countered the duke.

"Who?" asked Martha.

"Garrett Greensage."

"The blind kobold?" questioned Horace.

"Garrett has served Titanus faithfully for four generations of kings. If anyone could give us insight into defeating our foes, it would be him. Cedric, Christian—Garrett specifically asked to speak with both of you. I need you to come with me right away."

"Since I'm banished from Verian anyway, it shouldn't be too much of a problem."

"Well, I would suggest we slip into some ranger uniforms to cover our identities in the wild," insisted Christian.

"What about the rest of us?" interrupted Cagius. "Are we going to form an army?"

"How many troops do you have?" asked Cecilia.

"The Gold Dragon Legion arrived in Verian just before the senate session began. I could have two more legions on the Gold Highway by tomorrow if necessary."

"Laying siege to Verian won't do us any good," retorted Civilia. "I am prepared to give Stephen some time to come to his senses. Until then, we'd better be very careful."

"Oh, sister dear," teased Cedric.

"Yes, brother dearest," teased Cecilia right back.

"Would you do me a big favor?"

"How can I help?"

"I want you to take command of the embassy. We'll give you twenty-thousand extra riders to hold the embassy in case any 'situations' arrive. Colin will be here as well; use his services wisely. I fear it's going to be difficult to smuggle Hippolyte and Minerva out of the city right now. However, once I finish with Garrett, we'll coordinate with the tribes straightaway."

"I just hope they try something and bring enough body bags with them."

"I'm going to return to Fort Hawkeye with Martha and Horace," announced Civilia. "Stephen is quite set in his ways right now, and I fear my presence will only antagonize him further. I'll call up the remainder of the armada and have them stationed at Hawkeye just in case."

"At this point, I think dividing our forces is a good idea," recommended Wilhelm. "Many issues are drawing our attention all over the west. Everyone be very careful—we've used up all of our mistakes already."

Embracing her son tightly, Civilia kissed him good-bye.

"Cedric, do what you must! Remember I am still you mother, so keep yourself safe."

"I will, Mom."

"Watch over him, Christian. We need heroes, not martyrs."

"Absolutely, your highness. He will be well protected."

"Cagius, Sirius keep in constant communication with our people," ordered Cecilia. "Seal your embassies and station archers on the walls and rooftops. Don't take anything for granted, and if there's trouble, use the underground to get to the Titan Embassy; we have the strongest fortifications."

The two nodded and went to take care of their details. Just about ready to duck into a safe house and get changed, Cedric and Christian stopped when Walker came running up to them.

"Marshal Rhone, wait up!"

"You don't have to call me marshal anymore, Walker. I'm not your commander anymore."

"Warriors of true honor forever hold titles beyond what men can strip them of. Marshal, I just want you to know, anytime . . . anywhere . . . if you need me, I am at your service."

"I appreciate that," said Cedric as he took an ear bud from Walker.

"I am exposed now in front of my countrymen, but I couldn't let you stand alone in there. It's just . . . what you did in there was the bravest thing I ever saw. This is an emergency frequency that only I and the princess communicate on. I'm going under deep cover now, but no matter what transmissions jam, this one will get through."

Walker stepped back and saluted him. Cedric answered the salute.

"I've got one last present for your marshal," stated Walker as he signaled Cassandra to come forward with Felicia.

Heartbroken, Cedric saw the tears streaming down Cassandra's face. Without a word, she grabbed him tightly. Kissing him on the cheek twice, the princess finally relented and gave him a last kiss on the mouth.

"Cedric, you take care of yourself," sobbed Cassandra. "If you dare die in the wilderness because of me . . . I'll never forgive you."

"I've got to go get Cassandra out of here now," remarked Walker. "Good luck, Marshal, and keep in touch.

Walker hurried away with Cassandra and Felicia in tow. Moving his eyes to heaven, Cedric smiled and prayed.

"Reed, if you're watching down from heaven, I'm telling you, you raised a fine son."

"You're doing pretty good. If the Acadians try to kill you, you've got a lot of people willing to take that arrow for you," joked Christian.

"Let's just pray I don't have to ask you to."

"I didn't say me, buddy. Come on, I know an abandoned house where we can slip out discreetly."

In the Wizards Guild, the scene was much different. Celius stormed in the room and began to pace back and forth. Abaddon sat reading *The Titan Battle Manual* with Basarabas standing behind him.

"What is the problem?" asked Basarabas.

"Prince Rhone—he resigned his commission rather than surrender the two girls," responded Celius.

"Yes, that has become apparent to me," instructed Abaddon as he slammed the book shut. "I've just been in the mind of a genius."

"My lord, I doubt that reading will help us in this hour," said Celius.

"Basarabas, I'm disappointed at how little you told me about this this boy's abilities," said Abaddon ignoring Celius completely. "This is about more than just driving you back into the wilderness. He is good and he knows it."

"But my lord, he cannot possibly oppose you."

"His faith is a rock. Do you why I set this plan in motion? I was testing Prince Rhone. At first, I really thought he would make a simple sacrifice of two girls to save the alliance. Every page I read in this book proved to me how foolish that thought was. The test is over; I will never safely take Cassandra while Cedric Rhone is alive."

"My lord, what are we going to do?" inquired Celius. "We don't have the girls."

"We will proceed to the secondary objective," ordered Abaddon. "You are aware of what you must do?"

"The Titans know!" added Celius.

"It is irrelevant whether they know or not. I watched the events, I know that the alliance goes to war. They've turned their backs on the Titans; the city will be empty! We have what we wanted."

"You cannot underestimate them. Civilia Rhone has a relationship with Stephen that no one has. If she..."

"I will deal with the Titans when the time comes. They are strong and cunning, but even with their prowess they cannot defeat me in battle. We are very close to achieving our goals. This is not the time to back away."

"I had no intention of doing so."

"That's good because if you did, I would have killed you and found another wizard to take your place. Begin preparations to transport my associate Virgus Tattenberg into the Guild Hall. After that, finish transporting our Nephilim and Demonkin allies. We will strike on my orders."

"Yes, my lord," murmured Celius as he swallowed hard at Abaddon's words.

"Why all this attention for one divikin?" asked Basarabas.

"It's just... he reminds me of someone. Someone who believed I should have been something more than I was. You know what you have to do. I want Cassandra to disappear in the early chaos."

TITAN EMBASSY

"Even as a princess, I had to climb every rung of the ladder in the Titan armada. The job I hated the most was breaking the news to a distraught parent or spouse that their brave son or daughter had been killed in action. No two-rank promotion is worth that."

—Cecilia Rhone

In the Titan embassy, Cecilia was left to hold down the fort. Trying to come to grips with everything that had happened, the vanadis gathered her thoughts. She couldn't get the image of Cassandra screaming at Cedric out of her mind.

"Is it possible?" wondered Cecilia out loud. "Could Cedric be the *Permaneo Eques Ordinares*? It sounds like a bad bar joke but I can't shake the feeling it's true."

Cecilia's attention turned to the lobby bar. She saw many of her comrades fooling around and having a good time. Knights and valkyries were drinking, horsing around, and swapping good war stories. Drawn to the bar, Cecilia desired a late afternoon whiskey more than anything else after the crazy events of the rotation. Interrupting her, Keiko fluttered to give a report to the princess. Cecilia's face fell and she was completely annoyed at the sylph's presence before a word was uttered.

"Lady Cecilia, where is Lord Cedric?"

"Cedric left with Wilhelm and Christian on urgent business."

"I guess it can't be helped. I'm afraid I'm going to have to ask you to fill in for him for the time being."

"You are not following me around like a lovesick puppy. I have a reputation to maintain."

"I was talking about Hippolyte and Minerva."

"What happened? Don't tell me that wolf took a limb off someone!"

"They need to be told that their grandfather was murdered."

The harsh reality hit Cecilia hard. When they had arrived in the embassy, they barely had the time to get changed and go to the inquisition. While the banners had been lowered to half-mast, she doubted that either had seen it. Resigning herself to the fact someone had to tell them, Cecilia shook her head.

"I don't envy your position, Keiko."

"Mistress Cecilia, they need to know from someone with authority who was there."

"Let me just go get a drink first; I'll go over and tell them afterward," pleaded Cecilia after she took a deep breath.

Trying to make a quick exit, only the condescending tone of Keiko stopped the vanadis in her tracks.

"My lady!"

"Fine, you go tell them and I'll be standing there with you to fill in the details."

"No, *you* need to tell them, your highness!"

"You're right, Keiko. Thank you for reminding me of my duty. I'll go right away."

"Thank you, your highness."

Cecilia walked into the hotel. Clicking her boots against the marble staircase, she reached the second level. Intentionally taking her time, the princess thought about what she was going to say as she strolled down a nicely furnished hallway to one of the larger rooms at the end. Two maids in the hallway stopped what they were doing and curtsied. The large suite at the end of the hallway was now hosting the "political refugees." Colin had been on duty for hours and kept fighting the lure of sleep off. Staring intently at the assassin, Hippolyte was doing everything she could to keep Minerva from finding ways of antagonizing him.

"You don't look and dress like the other Titans," commented Hippolyte.

"I'm not really a Titan; I'm of Acadian descent."

"I didn't think the Acadians grew them so big," teased Minerva.

"If you're Acadian, how did you come to serve Titanus?" asked Hippolyte.

"My mother was a house slave of a wealthy Acadian landowner. She was one of his favored toys and she conceived three children. When he died, his sons divided his property among them. My mother, my two sisters, and I were taken by one of the sons. The caravan we traveled in was attacked by the Wildmen. They killed everyone and raped my mother and sisters to death in front of me. It gave them some sick, twisted pleasure to have me watch them do this before they killed me. My life was not to end that rotation; a Titan patrol lead by master Cedric attacked the wild men. He took the revenge for me because I wasn't strong enough. At that hour, I became his apprentice and vowed I would never be weak again. My abilities led me down the path of the duelist, and I end the lives of those that bring about evil and misery."

Hippolyte and Minerva welled up.

"I'm sorry," said Hippolyte.

"I don't have trouble talking about my past. The key is that you grow stronger from the tragedies that you suffer in life. I would have never been the person I am today if that convoy had made it in one piece. I made a decision that rotation to keep living and fighting. But enough about me... if there's nothing else I can do for you ladies, I really need to catch a few winks."

"We would like to know what's going on," requested Hippolyte.

Everyone heard a rapping on the door. Looking through the peephole, Colin was relieved to see Cecilia stand there.

"Don't worry; it's only the princess."

Colin opened the door and Cecilia entered. Not used to seeing the titan princess without her armor on, Hippolyte and Minerva were very impressed at her assets. The younger sister looked down at her own chest disappointedly before staring at Cecilia's chest again.

I'm so jealous! thought Minerva.

"Colin, I didn't know you were still here. I'll come back later," stated Cecilia, once again trying to escape.

"It's all right, your highness, I was just leaving. Samuel wants to debrief me."

Cecilia looked disappointed when she saw Colin leave her alone. Putting her bravest face on, the vanadis closed the door behind her.

"I think we need some privacy. I don't believe we've had the pleasure. I am Princess Cecilia Rhone of Titanus. I'm Cedric's twin sister."

"Then you are the legendary *Vanadis*!" exclaimed Hippolyte as she stared in awe.

"You could say that," boasted a smiling Cecilia.

"You might say that we're on opposite sides of the Amazon poles," explained Hippolyte. "The tribes are aligned to the powers of Fenrir, while the Titans got your powers from Freya."

"Well, I guess I learned something new."

"Are those goons still out there?" asked Minerva.

"Yes, and I'm afraid they're going to be there for a while. The alliance overwhelmingly favors taking you hostage. My brother chose to relinquish his command rather than give you up."

"Why?" asked Hippolyte. "He owes us nothing."

"Titans don't believe you necessarily do things just because you owe someone something. You instead try to do good works throughout your rotations and hopefully that gets you into heaven."

"So I guess we can't go home yet," cried Minerva.

"It's too risky to do anything right now. We're doing the best we can to get you out of here safely," offered Cecilia before dramatically changing her tone. "Besides, there's another matter that you girls need to be made aware of. I've never come up with a good way of handling this so, I'll just tell you. Your grandfather Aramas was murdered."

Sitting in disbelief for a few moments, the news hit Hippolyte and Minerva hard. Hippolyte just broke down and started to cry, but Minerva remained in denial. Standing up, she took two swings at Cecilia. The vanadis prudently stepped away from the attacks.

"Murdered! By whom? How?"

Taking the young girl in her arms, Cecilia tried to calm Minerva down.

"The deed was done by a being named Abaddon. He was in allegiance with our enemies, the Nephilim. They wanted to start a war between the alliance and the Tribal Confederation, so they made it look like Acadian knights killed Aramas. Huskal led an attack against our forces, but my brother intervened before the war could start. Now the Acadians have taken the bait and walked right into the trap. That's why they wanted you so badly."

Filled with sorrow and rage, Hippolyte tried to form words but was too choked up. The wolf princess collapsed into Cecilia's arms, dripping with tears. Civilia had been impressed over the revolutions at the maternal instincts that her daughter displayed. The vanadis was glad to see she could put it to good use.

"It's all right, child," comforted Cecilia. "Don't ever feel embarrassed when you cry, its part of a woman's courage."

"Grandpa was so strong!" stated Minerva.

"This Abaddon is a fallen angel, a divine being from the beginning of time. The members of our alliance dismiss this as myth and fairy tale, but our kingdom has seen the power of the Nephilim. My brother rides now to try and stop this war."

"I'm the lawful chief of the Wolf Tribe," pronounced Hippolyte. "You have to get me back to my people. If the Acadians declared war on us, we must have a leader."

"That was what we planned on doing," countered Cecilia. "Huskal promised that he would stand down if you two were released. Titanus has every intention of keeping Cedric's vow. I swear we will get you home."

"But the war... if the alliance... will you... ?" asked Hippolyte.

"It's difficult to say what we're going to do right now. You can rest assured we're not going to be part of an alliance army that will attack you. Nothing good has ever come from us walking down that road. We are focused solely on defeating the Nephilim. Are you going to be all right Hippolyte?"

"Now it's only me and my sister; we're the only ones left."

"I am truly sorry, Hippolyte. My brother and I had every intention of trying to protect your people. We guessed the wrong target and Aramas died. We'll try to make the two of you as comfortable as possible. If you wish, you may attend services tomorrow morning. Your grandfather is being remembered. If you require anything, don't hesitate to ask."

"Will you speak with us again?"

"If you summon me or just need to talk, I'll do whatever I can for you."

"Thank you. I can't believe how wrong we were about Titans all these revolutions."

Cecilia let go of the girls and walked out of the room. Dealing with her depression, the princess hit her fist into the wall a few times.

"I think I earned that drink now."

Hippolyte and Minerva turned to each other. Grabbing each other tightly, the girls spent the evening crying their eyes out. Stryker's howls joined them in their sorrow.

Forest of the Eternal Spring, Evengard, the Next Rotation

"When I was born, I was both blessed and cursed by God. It took many revolutions for me to realize that my curse was actually a blessing and my blessing was actually a curse."

—Ramblings of Garrett

Calvary flew above the old forest that stretched about one hundred kilometers north of the border between Evengard and Central Acadia. It was a vast maze of lush, healthy, and bountiful forest where trunks of trees gave the appearance of being around for tens of thousands of rotations. Despite the abundance of limbs, branches, streams, and rock, a natural trail was carved away for travelers in the soil. Trotting along the trail, Wilhelm, Christian, and Cedric rode their horses among deciduous trees that towered high into the sky. Fae folk darted back and forth. Every once in a while they would startle the horses, but it didn't cause too much of a problem. Wilhelm stopped after they walked another one hundred meters. Spotting a waterfall cutting through a lush fjord about two thousand meters from where they were, the duke determined the safety of a wooden bridge. The echoing effect of the waterfall reverberated through the whole of the forest.

"The Forest of the Eternal Spring—I never get tired of the wonders of this place," observed Christian. "We should have brought your sister along, Cedric. Maybe we would have gotten a chance to see a unicorn."

"So the elves say!" teased Wilhelm.

"Why did he want to see me?" asked Christian.

"That kobold never tells me anything," responded Wilhelm. "All I know is that when Garrett calls, I answer. I think he's trying to keep me on my toes."

"I'd be more worried about what he's going to say," remarked Cedric.

"It's never good, but he might be the only one who can help us."

The three took their time as they crossed a bridge over the crashing water of the waterfall. After the bridge, they came to a rolling hill covered in green grass. On top of the hill was a hovel. A large, circular porch surrounded the house. On that deck sat Garrett Greensage, who was rocking away on his rocking chair. Moving in and out of his lips, Garrett smoked a long white pipe. His white hair was brushed back in a close crop away from his completely white eyes save for the small outline of an iris. Shaking, his pointed ears heard the approach of three horses. Picking up his cane, Garrett rocked himself forward and removed the pipe from his mouth. Calvary flew in and landed on Cedric's shoulder. The knight took a piece of raw meat from his belt pouch and fed him.

A kobold on Terminus Mundus, was not quite human and not quite dwarf. Clean-shaven, Garrett stood a little less than five feet tall. Small of stature, frail of body, Garrett Greensage was the most powerful mystic on the planet. In addition to receiving visions of the future, the kobold also proved to be a master strategist. His advice had led many Titan kings to victory over the revolutions. When Garrett heard the three horses come to a stop, he started to speak.

"I didn't think it would take you long to get here. I am well aware of the events that have come to pass. However, you should know that these tragedies are just the beginning. A gathering of this importance hasn't happened in some time. Master Krystos of the Powers choir, Prince Cedric Rhone of Titanus, Prince Dulles Marisol of Evengard, I bid you welcome to my humble hovel."

"Garrett, please!" shouted an angry Christian.

"So you still deny your true place?"

"I serve the country that accepted me not the one who would have me killed."

"It pains me to hear you say those things. I loved your mother very much, and I don't think you should be embarrassed of who you are. However, it is not my duty to judge your path. Perhaps God placed you on this road so you could help your friend now. Come inside; we have much to talk about."

The three entered the hovel where a table was set up with chairs. Despite his blindness, Garrett walked perfectly. Sidestepping the objects, the kobold hurried to his table. The interior of the hovel was built like a home of stone and mahogany wood. The rooms were clearly divided, though the party had to mind the low white ceilings from time to time. Surrounding the table, the room was littered with papers. Everyone took a seat. Pouring from a jar in the center of the table, Garrett passed out glasses to each of his guests.

"Enjoy my drink and company. Let no man, elf, dwarf, or divine say that Garrett does not honor the sacred laws of hospitality."

"I prefer something less sweet then your mead," commented Cedric.

"Your friends seem to enjoy it."

Cedric turned to see Christian and Garrett drinking heartily.

"I've never had much of a sweet tooth," said Cedric, who took the drink anyway and drank it.

"Since you know everything else that's going on, perhaps you can provide us with some help," queried Wilhelm.

"Yes," replied Garrett as he reached for a book on a stand near the table. "I assume that since you trained him, Prince Rhone is familiar with the Ragnarok."

"I gave him the legendary weapon that bears same name for that purpose," added Wilhelm.

"Interestingly enough, Ragnarok has many different meanings among many cultures. However, to Divikin it is the war that this Abaddon took part in before recorded time. His force was the commando unit that was supposed to lead the Siege of the Great Gates while Lucifer's army drew out Archangel Michael's forces. However, the Powers choir remained behind and held the flank."

"I know, Garrett. Lest you forget, I was there."

"I'm sure you have many dramatic tales to tell."

"I've heard them all," interrupted Cedric.

"Not all of them. Cedric I need you to read this book."

"I think I'm familiar with the history of the Ragnarok," refused Cedric politely.

"This book speaks beyond what happened in the battle. It also provides the detailed plans of the forces of darkness as they strive to achieve the victory they were denied that day. Terminus Mundus is central to this plan because it stands on the borders between creation and the celestial realm. The prior attempts to subvert us have all been abysmal failures, but this time there is a weapon that will give them the real chance. Abaddon is like a fox; he knows every trick. He had been waiting in his castle for revolutions for the right opportunity to ingratiate himself to the Prince once more. The event we dreaded has finally come."

"Cassandra!" exclaimed Cedric.

"You are wise, young Rhone. Never would have I believed that when your mother came to me with two nestlings on each arm and a desire to maintain the throne she received from her father, that you would become the man you are today."

"Well I guess your visions aren't right about everything. So how do we stop Abaddon?"

"We cannot. For all you victories and training, no mere divikin can kill this dark angel. Only one warrior has the power to kill Abaddon and bind his soul in hell. Krystos, we need Lord Camael."

"Lord Camael is beyond our reach," remarked Wilhelm as his eyes fell. "He gave himself willingly to God after the battle and I haven't heard from him since. I fear my friend is lost to us."

"No, the Lord Father has revealed to me in a dream that the Sefiroth himself has been incarnated on Terminus Mundus."

"IMPOSSIBLE!" exclaimed Wilhelm. "A Sefiroth cannot be incarnated into creation the same way an angel can. It was terrible enough for angels like myself and Lord Teman to surrender most of our divinity just to cross the barrier. If a Sefiroth were to cross the barrier, Garrett, he would lose all of his divinity."

"Camael is not a true Sefiroth anymore Krystos. Remember Teman had to purge him of the evil that whittled away at his soul. All is revealed to me by the will of God alone. Yes, Camael could never come into creation without sacrificing tremendous power. However, there is no restriction for the powers choir lord to restore his full powers as a result of living in creation. Camael is driven to end the disgrace he endured in heaven. Your task now is to go to the Kablisha Tribe. They will assist you in finding Lord Camael."

"It must be desperate times if I am forced to prostrate myself before those isolationists and beg for their assistance. Garrett, they have separated themselves from our world, I doubt their haughtiness will allow them to help us now. I am still a member of the Powers choir, can I stop Abaddon?"

"You are powerless against Abaddon in your state. He will be able to control the poisons in your body and leave you no more than a hulking shell. You alone have the power to penetrate the ancient Kablisha barrier without additional magic. Bishop Wulf will have further instructions for you. God has made him aware of your coming."

"What am I supposed to do?" asked Cedric.

"I don't know. If the enemy gains a hold on Cassandra, it could mean oblivion for everything."

"Why did you summon me to tell me something I already know!" demanded Cedric as he prepared to leave. "By drawing me away from Verian, I can't protect her."

"You don't understand, I'm trying to save your life! I know you've never lost a battle in war and you've never been defeated in combat. God knows if you've even ever been wounded. Despite all this, you can't protect her, Cedric."

The sword master was ready to draw Ragnarok and strike down the kobold where he stood. Garrett felt the storm forming around him, yet he would speak his peace.

"My visions were quite clear that if you fight Abaddon, you will die. This is not a matter of you not being prepared or strong enough. You are far too important to this world and our people to die in a meaningless battle. My interpretation of what I saw is that no amount of faith you have in God or yourself will grant you victory. You'll die and Cassandra will be his."

"There's no such thing as an invincible opponent!"

"I know that's not what you wanted to hear. Don't be foolish; take care of Cassandra when the time comes. Now there is one last detail to attend to."

"The coup against King Stephen?" asked Christian.

"Yes, Dulles, that was why I called you here. It has not been revealed to me who is involved and when the exact hour is. I can tell you that it will happen soon. You'll have to find out the rest."

"Well, I guess I should thank you for the heads up."

"We don't have any time to lose then," ordered Cedric. "Well, Garrett, I don't like cutting our business short."

"Prince Rhone, I do not consider it a slight; there is much to do."

Cedric and Christian stood. When he felt the presence of the Titan prince over him, Garrett was unsure if he was about to die. Kneeling down, the sword master embraced to the kobold, to his delight.

"Please, I know you haven't in the past, but heed the prophecy. If you fight Abaddon, you will die!"

"I believe you, Garrett, but that doesn't mean I'm going to do as you ask."

"Then fulfill an old kobold's last request and read the book!"

Unfazed despite being informed of imminent death, Cedric turned his focus to everyone in the room and started to give out orders.

"Good luck, Wilhelm. I know the Kablisha don't necessarily hold you in the highest regard."

"Bishop Wulf is wise and may be about the only member of the Kablisha who will listen to reason. I'm sure he has a lead. I'm also pretty sure that he won't sic that sword-wielding captain on me when I show up with ill news."

"Before you go, send a last transmission to the embassy on code two. Start with the code word *seti*; tell them that we're going to sneak back into Verian and that we'll be camping at the northern ridge," added Christian.

"The Acadians have broken code two," remarked Wilhelm.

"Exactly," schemed Christian as he put on his gloves. "If my theory is correct and the communications center is infiltrated, they'll bring it back to their masters."

"You've got it."

"Clever like a fox, this one. Old Hayden would have loved to play chess against you," complimented Garrett. "He certainly would have wished for a descendant like you."

Christian smiled and followed Cedric out the door. The two leapt onto their horses. Calvary flew off Cedric's shoulder and led them back along the path.

"You're putting a heavy burden on one person," commented Wilhelm. "His love for Cassandra is stronger than you can imagine, and no angel in heaven or devil in hell is going to take her from him."

"He's strong enough to handle it," acknowledged Garrett.

"You know, though, that if it comes to down to Abaddon or Cassandra, he's going to disobey your orders."

"I have foreseen it. Well Wilhelm, could you ask for a better man to protect your daughter? God, please bless Cedric Rhone."

CASTLE ACADIA, THAT EVENING

"My daughter is a free spirit. She received the best and worst of both worlds being a half-breed. However, I have never been able to bear her anger with me for a prolonged period of time, and somehow she knows how to make me cave."

—*Journal of King Stephen Acadia*

Seated at her vanity, Cassandra tied up her robe over her nightgown. Her arms were crossed under her chest and her legs were crossed. Choosing to say nothing, Felicia continued to brush her hair in preparation for bed. Despite the princess's mannerisms, she showed no anger toward Felicia.

"Mistress, you haven't eaten in two rotations," commented Felicia. "Do you wish me to send for something from the kitchen?"

Her continued silence caused her handmaiden to sigh. The gently rapping on the outer apartment door distracted Felicia from her silent companion. Walking into the outer room to answer to door, the handmaiden opened it to see the king standing outside. Felicia curtsied without haste.

"Your majesty."

"Hello, Felicia. Would you be able to convince my daughter to see me?"

"I'll try, my liege," said Felicia as she walked back toward Cassandra. "Mistress, your father wishes to speak with you."

Cassandra said nothing but rather continued to twitch her bare foot back and forth. Aggravated at the prospect of returning messages back and forth between the two scorned royals, Felicia decided to assert herself.

"Please, I beg your pardon mistress, but I do believe you should hear what he has to say."

Cassandra stopped twitching her foot. Standing, she silently walked out of the bedroom and into her parlor. Stephen was somewhat relieved to see her come into her parlor. Closing the door to respect their privacy, Felicia moved to the back of the bedroom. Stephen expected some sort of greeting from his daughter, but Cassandra simply walked over to her parlor couch and sat down. Crossing her hands under her chest again, the princess stared her father in the eyes. Stephen sat down in a chair, sighed, and focused on his beloved daughter.

"Well, at least you still came out to see me," remarked Stephen as he stared for any sign of a response from his daughter. "You haven't eaten or left your room since the inquisition. I know it caused you great pain, but I'm worried about what you're doing to yourself."

Watching his daughter say nothing, Stephen continued to search for something to break her down with. He shook his head.

"Sweetheart, please don't act this way. You know I can't stand it when you're mad at me. Please say something!"

"You are wrong!" replied an angry Cassandra. "And you know you are wrong!"

Stephen was a bit taken back by the angry statements. Burning like fire as they passed princess's lips, Cassandra twitched her foot back and forth again. Stephen was forced to hang his head in acknowledgment of Cassandra's truth. Standing, he paced back and forth in the parlor.

"I've dwelt on it these past two rotations. My behavior at the inquisition was not consistent with my true beliefs. I am supposed to be the king of justice and yet I let the nobles goad me into a fight. It was my duty to stand above them like I've done in the past, not cave into their senseless demands for violence and blood. Yet the Titan prince stood in the middle of that room with everyone waiting to rain arrows down on him. Cedric carried my honor and he was right to do so. The warriors in that room, they couldn't wait to stand up and prove him right. *La Morte Angelus* understands war better than I ever could. He knew what it would take for Huskal and the Wolf Tribe to stand down, and he knew we were going to fight a war we didn't need. We all heard the evidence before the inquisition. The tribes are not to blame for the deaths of Alwein and Cambridge; we brought this doom upon ourselves."

Apparently warming to her father's reconciliation, Cassandra stopped twitching her foot and dropped her arms to her lap. The princess continued to listen to her father's every word.

"Maybe it was my stubborn pride that made my ears deaf to his words. I think back now to what I said, I would have the blood of two innocent girls on my hands. Aramas had two granddaughters just like I had two daughters. What if our positions were reversed? Aramas would have never imprisoned and executed you and Marie. Cedric Rhone was trying to warn me about what was coming. Every nation and tribe has always had more honor than us. Maybe this is my version of a necessary confession, but I just can't stand the thought of you hating me. I couldn't live with it, sweetheart."

Cassandra started to cry. Jumping from her seat, she found herself in the warm embrace of her father's arms. Reconciled now, Stephen smiled and held his daughter tightly just as he had done every time something had gone wrong in her life. Twenty revolutions later, the king could never shake the feeling of something terrible happening to Cassie.

"Oh, Daddy," cried Cassandra.

"Still quick to cry, that's one part of you that hasn't changed since you were a little girl. Cassie, I want only the best for you and I want you to be happy."

"Daddy, you know there's only one way I'm really going to forgive you."

"I know," surmised Stephen. "This foolish campaign is going to end tomorrow before it begins. I've made arrangements with Count Luminas. The armies are yet to march, so it will be easy. You and I will travel to Castle Titan in Rhinegard."

Cassandra looked at her father with bright eyes,

"Then?"

"I will pay my penance to Civilia and she will revel in every minute of it. I hope my arthritis doesn't kick in when she makes me kneel."

"Thank you, Daddy."

"It's not my place to deny your happiness. A father can only protect his daughter for so long, the only man I trust with that responsibility is the greatest knight who ever wore armor on Terminus Mundus. Now I've heard your uncle speaking very highly of your training."

"I'm out to do my best."

"Maybe I'll stop by and see you sometime. I'm sure you'll be much better than when you almost inadvertently burnt the castle down."

"No one ever lets me live this one down," laughed Cassandra through her tears.

There was a knock on the door, and a halberdier entered the room.

"My liege, your presence is needed in the throne room immediately."

"I'm busy with my daughter," announced an angry Stephen.

"Please, my lord, it requires your immediate attention."

"I'm sorry," said Stephen as he kissed his daughter of the forehead.

"It's all right, Daddy. You've given me the only words I needed."

"We do have much left to discuss on the journey tomorrow. Good night, sweetheart."

Turning back to Cassandra before he left, Stephen had a puzzled expression on his face.

"Oh, and do you know where Captain Walker is?" asked Stephen. "We last saw him escorting you back to the castle."

"I haven't seen him since. He told me he had something to do."

Stephen nodded and left the room with the halberdier. As soon as he was gone, Cassandra clapped her hands together and started jumping around the parlor. Opening the door again, Felicia sighed at the sight of the childishness of her mistress.

In the courtyard below, a young teenage boy was still working on the anvil of the castle blacksmith. The boy used his large muscles to hammer a sword he was working on. Shaking the sweat out of his mop of brown hair, the young man's green eyes provided the bright spot on a face covered with soot. Towering over the other Central Acadians despite his young age, the boy watched a man covered in rags approaching the forge. Nervously staring at his covered face, the young man appeared concerned that a leper approached him.

"That's far enough, mister," commanded the boy. "I don't know if you're clean or not."

"I'm no leper, if that's what you mean," remarked the man. "However, these severe burns are not a sight for man to behold. I just came to purchase the fruits of your labors."

"I've got some freshly made weapons in the back. My name's Joshua; holler if you need me."

The man nodded and walked back. Examining the weapons with great care, the ragged man nodded in approval. Interrupting his time at the anvil again, Joshua could hear the sound of armor clanking in the courtyard. Staring ahead, he saw templar knights on horseback racing through the city. A group of eight halberdiers came running toward the forge. Prepared to defend himself, Joshua grabbed a blacksmith hammer in his right hand and kept a pot of scalding water just under his left hand out of sight. Watching the halberdiers cutting down servants and squires in the courtyard, the young blacksmith knew something was wrong. The halberdiers turned to Joshua and came charging at him with their pikes down. Not panicking, Joshua threw the water into the face of one of them and melted the skin from his face. A second halberdier was crushed over the head with his blacksmith hammer. Six more halberdiers still in pursuit, Joshua made a mad scramble to the other side of the forge to get his weapons. Dropping his rags to the ground by the weapons, Walker drew Sigmund and the Oath Shield. Joshua stared dumbfounded as the Lord Knight repelled the attacks of his traitorous countrymen. In a matter of ten slashes he managed to get rid of three of them, causing the others to turn tail and run. Returning his blade to his sheath, Walker grabbed Joshua on the shoulder.

"You're... Captain Walker. What's going on?"

"A revolution is breaking out in the capital. I don't know all the details. The Templar Army, the Verian City Guard, and their demon allies are marching on the embassy. Fortunately Cecilia and Cagius have a little surprise waiting for them. Now I need your help to get Princess Cassandra and your mother out of the city."

"I don't know what you're talking about."

"You're a brave lad, but don't play coy with me! I know exactly who you are and who your father is. Now if you want to stay alive, grab a sword and do exactly as I say."

Joshua obeyed the veteran warrior. He took a leather bag and loaded it up with weapons and whetstones. The two ran over to an alcove in the castle wall and entered through a sewer grating.

Northern Ridge, Twenty Kilometers Northeast of Verian

"The first step to beating a trap is to know one exists."

—*Old Elf Proverb*

Jericho and Christian's horse were tied up to a tree at the edge of the forest right at the entrance to the Acadian plains. Bulging sleeping bags lay next to a large and blazing fire. Twenty Demonkin orks crawled silently through the grassy plains. Commanding the demonkin was a Nephilim warrior dressed in black plate mail. They crawled right within ten meters of the sleeping bags.

"Just where they said they would be," ordered the Nephilim warrior, signaling to his underlings to advance. "Make it quick!"

The orks slowly moved toward the sleeping bags. Striking fiercely at bag with their cleavers, the demonkin watched down feathers instead of blood emerge from the bag. Abruptly stopping their hacks, the orks turned to the Nephilim for orders.

"This isn't right!" screamed the Nephilim.

The attackers felt a breeze near the tree where the horses were tied. Removing his invisibility cloak, a smiling Christian moved his hands in a summoning pattern like he had done in the castle. This time, however, fire appeared around him and he yelled, "Fire Jujitsu!" Erupting around the orks was a fire that not only scolded their bodies but drew the strength from them. Collapsing to the ground, none of the demonkin could move.

The Nephilim turned to run when he saw Cedric standing behind him. Cedric yelled, "Lunar" and his saber magic enchanted his blade once more. Ragnarok shined with a pale blue light. Thrusting the blade into the Nephilim's shoulder, the sword master watched as his spell did its work. Despite it only being a minor wound, the commander fell right to the ground, writhing in agony.

"I... can't... move..." screamed the Nephilim.

"The power of the lunar saber, it literally saps the strength from your body and gives it to me," explained Cedric.

Cedric stabbed the Nephilim in the thigh for good measure so he couldn't take off or run. Attempting desperately to escape, the commander spread his black wings. However he could not garner enough power for take off. Rolling on the ground in agony, the Nephilim watched as Cedric and Christian killed ten orks each. Christian slit their throats while Cedric would thrust the blade into their black hearts. When they had finished the deed, Christian walked over to the Nephilim and knelt down.

"You... set us up..." yelled the Nephilim.

"There is an old elf proverb that says 'The first step to beating a trap is to know that one exists,'" teased Christian. "You and your friends were quite careless. Did you really think we would allow ourselves to be murdered so easily? Now I need some information . . ."

"You think I would be stupid enough to give up, my lord?" laughed the Nephilim. "There's no torture or craft you have that could be worse than the place reserved for me in hell if I speak."

"You seem sure about. Well I guess that's too bad because I really was trying to save you."

Grabbing the back of his neck, Christian forced the Nephilim to stare at the Titan prince. Cedric had pressed his hands together and chanted in a language similar to the one Posha had used to invoke Huskal's spirit beast. Bathed in an eerie glow, even Christian feared what his friend was doing at this point. The Nephilim had lost his haughty attitude and his copper face fell white with terror. He turned to Christian who shook his head.

"Sorry buddy, you should have dealt with me."

"Are you aware of the rare spell branch domination magic?" asked Cedric.

"You're bluffing!" taunted the desperate Nephilim.

"The base level spells revolve around simple hypnosis and other parlor tricks. However, the more advanced spells are very effective in interrogation. Unlike torture, it gets the results you seek one-hundred percent of the time. You see, men in love do very desperate things. Your master messed with the wrong guy."

Cedric grabbed the Nephilim on either side of his temple. Convulsing and writhing, he tried to break Cedric's grip but it was too strong. Yellow light flowed from Cedric's hands into the Nephilim's head. A few moments of this torture was all Christian could take. The sadistic face of his enraged friend made the spy master wonder what demon Abaddon had unleashed within him. As the Nephilim's eyes rolled all the way back into his head, the sword master released his grip. Nothing more than a twitching vegetable now, Cedric had drained every memory and piece of information out of the Nephilim's brain.

"I never understood until now why you refused to use that spell," remarked a fearful Christian. "God, I hope you didn't do that to him for nothing. What did you find out?"

"It's worse than we thought. They've got the whole damned city under their control, and that's only the beginning. Virgus Tattenberg's created some kind of tachyon field that's going to ward off all of Central Acadia and prevent anyone from getting in or out. The coup against Stephen is a feint attack to draw our armies into the barrier and pick us off."

"What the hell are we going to do?" asked Christian.

"Get on the line with the embassy, call my sister, and order a full retreat. Let her coordinate with Napolitan, Evengard, and let her send out a general alarm to get all Acadians out of the city who want to go. We've got to warn the Kingdoms not to send any troops to Verian."

"We're running away?"

"We can't stop it, and if we get caught in that field, we're dead. When you're done, get your armor on; we're going to Fort Orion."

"Aren't we needed in Verian?"

"Julius and the others are in danger; they need our help."

"Fine, but what are you going to do?"

"I'm calling the one ally we have left in Central Acadia. With luck, Walker may be able to get Cassandra to the security of the embassy and my sister can get her out before Abaddon succeeds."

"Let me see if I can try and raise Orion. Orion emergency code alpha-theta-epsilon... warning extreme danger... trust no one and get out."

In the command center, Julius and Amuro were looking at a map in the main tactical room. There were no technicians left in the room, and only four guards. Amuro's mind wandered while Julius was focused on a detailed strategy. Malcolm was sitting in the corner of the room with his head down. Every once in a while his head would twitch up as if he sensed something, but as he listened closely he came up with nothing.

"Huskal has had sufficient time to retreat with his army into the mountain stronghold," explained Julius. "That's going to be very dangerous. Since Lurac and the dwarves are vassals of Titanus, they probably won't let us go through the tunnels. That's going to be a long trek, and we'll be exposed on all sides."

Angrily looking at his elf comrade, Julius demanded Amuro offer him some response. Not paying attention, Amuro bit her lower lip and occasionally sucked her tears back.

"Amuro, are you even listening to me?"

"I'm sorry, Julius, did you say something?"

"I am discussing our battle plans here."

"It will be a glorious and wonderful victory. We'll have won it without either of our armies."

"What's wrong? I expect this from your flighty sister but not you."

"I'm not comfortable with this war."

"First Cedric, then my brother, now you . . . isn't there anyone that sees the importance of this?"

"Even if they did attack us at the ruins, this all seems a little too much. The Acadians are talking as if this is going to be genocide. We're not leading our national armies into battle; we're leading Acadians! They duped us into the last war and now we're following the same path again. I don't want to lose everything for them."

"We won't let that happen. I agree with you that this isn't perfect but defacto war isn't the answer either. The tribes are leaderless; it is the opportune time to strike. A quick victory and then we won't have to worry about this problem anymore. Come on, Amuro, you know me! I would never allow the soldiers under my command to commit war crimes."

"Can you say the same for Jonas Marimon?"

"He won't fight."

"Then it's General Rene Palias! Do you know why they call him the peacock? It's because he proudly displays every medal that the Acadians will award him."

"I can handle Palias. It is not wise to antagonize the man you'll be serving soon."

"It never stopped them before! You saw what happened with Cedric and Cassandra. Marie is a much more volatile situation. Besides, what if Cedric's right?"

"Don't tell me you believe in the boogeyman too?"

"You know Cedric as well as I do. Would he have risked everything just to save those two girls unless there was a reason? My people have dealt with the Nephilim; they are a threat."

"I hate to be so cynical, but it could have simply been a ploy on his part to bring the tribes closer to a vassalage agreement. You know the Titans covet that alliance."

"You could be right," cried Amuro, who slammed her hand into the table. "I just don't know if I can take that chance."

Malcolm stood up from the window and went to comfort her. Holding her around the waist, the ranger kissed her cheek.

"What do you think, Malcolm?" asked Amuro.

"I think Cedric is right," responded Malcolm emphatically. "If not for my love of you, I would have joined the chorus of the others in the room and stood down. Do you ever take time to truly listen to nature Julius?"

"No, Malcolm, I'm not a freak like you."

"Point well taken, but the trees give off a foreboding sound. Something is not right with the world right now. I think the Titans have figured it out and sooner we get on the same page the better."

A transmission began to come in scratchy in the room. Amuro ran over to the computer and started to type.

"I'm picking up something. It sounds like its coming in over the emergency channel, but I can't make it out."

A second transmission began to come in. Julius went over to this one and tried to read it.

"A second emergency transmission from Verian," read Julius. "I can't make it out either."

Channels and frequencies began to sound all over the room. The officers watched as troop movements appeared all over the map.

"This board is lighting up like the night sky," observed Malcolm as he stared at the main screen. "Can you make anything out?"

"It's as if the same dampening field that . . . was at the ruins is being used against us now" interjected a panicked Amuro.

"Everybody out now!" screamed Julius.

It was too late. The door opened, and armed Acadian knights entered the room. Without armor and holding no weapons, the three marshals were in no position to fight. The commanding Acadian knight delivered the terms.

"We have no interest in killing the three of you. You're unarmed and we have your people captured in the fort already. If you resist, even if you kill us they will all die. Our intent is to use you to secure pacts of non-aggression with Napolitan and Evengard. Events have been set in motion that you can do nothing about. Verian will be secured shortly, and this will all be over. Our orders are to make sure no harm comes to you or your people. You'll remain locked in here for now and we'll send food down to you."

The knights left and three looked at each other.

"They knew how to hit us," reasoned Amuro. "I guess we're going to have to trust in Cecilia and Cagius to defend Verian now."

"If they can," said Julius. "Valentine is due for a report in an hour. If I don't report, he'll know something is wrong.

"Then I guess we'll just have to wait it out then."

CASTLE ACADIA

"Concerning Central Acadia, the Acadian Royal Family has long placed its trust in a Demonkin to handle affairs of state. I refer, of course, to Count Maximilian Luminas. They refuse to see the danger that such an infiltration poses to their court and country. The count may appear trustworthy, but in the end all Demonkin must return to their masters."

—Duke Wilhelm von Angelhardt Third Report

King Stephen Acadia sat on his throne with his hand on his chin. Surrounded by his saints and royal guard, they did not protect him but rather held the king at sword point. Entering the room, Count Luminas bowed before his king.

"My liege, I trust you have been made aware of the events around you."

Haunted by the screams of dying servants and loyalists in every room of his Castle, Stephen seethed in anger at the vampire he trusted.

"What was your price?"

The clicking of high heels against the marble floor drew Stephen's attention to a dressed up Sharon. Sashaying by him, she kissed Luminas on the lips. Stricken by the irony of the situation, Stephen couldn't help but laugh.

"So the power whore finally seduced the highest rung on the ladder!"

"Count Luminas can satisfy my needs in ways you never could," retorted Sharon.

"Sharon is quite convincing," explained Luminas. "Though I have to admit, it didn't take much. Jonas turned on you for nothing, the others for paltry sums. You made a lot of enemies during your twenty-five-revolution reign. Perhaps no Central Acadian King should ever reign that long, especially at the expense of his own country for the sake of some fruitless alliance. In the end, the royal court, the Wizards Guild, the temple, and the nobles all turned against you. Your performance at the inquisition was brilliant, my liege. You managed to alienate the only people keeping you alive."

"So Cedric had it all figured out, didn't he?" asked Stephen, shaking his head.

"Of course he did. It took a lot to maintain my composure at the inquisition. I don't know how he did it, but he knew. It doesn't matter now. You see, we laid a little trap for him. *La Morte Angelus* is now long dead. Fort Orion is in our hands. The last remaining opposition in this city is under siege. No one is going to save you, Stephen."

"Where are Cassandra and Marie?"

"Don't worry; they won't be harmed. Lord Abaddon has important designs for them," informed Sharon.

"Just relax and enjoy the show while you still can," comforted Luminas. "It will be over soon. Even if your alliance friends rally to save you, they will be walking right into a trap."

"Only an arrogant fool would believe that Cedric Rhone is dead without seeing the stabbed and arrow-ridden body for themselves. There isn't a soul in Terminus Mundus that can stop him from coming here. He'll rescue Cassandra; you can count on it."

"You misplaced your faith," argued Sharon. "It would have been wise to side with us over them. It may have saved your life, but indulge me one last time."

Sharon walked over to him and kissed him.

"Jezebel!"

"Such language, my love."

In another room, Cassandra was tied to a chair with silk ropes around her wrists. Quite embarrassed not at her predicament, but rather that she was dressed only in a negligee with a torn robe. Listening to the door open,

Cassie swallowed hard when she watched Abaddon enter and close the door behind them.

"I must apologize to you, your highness," pleaded Abaddon. "I have personally dealt with the men who roughed you up."

"I see you don't have the decency to see a lady properly dressed," retorted Cassandra.

"Trust me, my dear, we'll be getting to know each other quite intimately soon enough."

"Who are you?"

Pulling up a chair, Abaddon sat almost nose to nose with Cassandra. He started to trace his finger along her cheek, but she pulled away. Captivated by her beauty for a few moments, Abaddon shook his head to compose himself.

"I am Lord Abaddon, the Locust King, ruler of the sixth plane of hell, my princess, and I have been searching for you for a very long time."

"Why?"

"You're unique, unlike any other that has ever graced creation. You were born a half-breed, yes, but with all of the strengths and none of the failings of the elf and human race. Then you were given a second gift, and though you are not aware of it yet, you have the power to finally give me and my comrades the opportunity to achieve our goal."

"I guess you'll just have to kill me then, because I'm not helping you."

"I respect courage, your highness, but do you even know what you're truly dealing with?"

"You must be one of those Nephilim!"

"No, my dear, I am much more powerful than those fallen half-breeds," pronounced Abaddon as he unleashed his wings to Cassandra's shock. "I am what you call a fallen angel. I seek to avenge my Prince's defeat on the Asphodel Fields so many eons ago. Your powers will give us the edge we need. I won't lie to you. Everything you know and love is about to come to an end. If you would join with us, you will take your rightful place at the left hand of the Prince. Power, majesty, and riches would all be yours. We mean you no harm because you are sacred to us."

Abaddon traced his fingers along Cassandra's face again.

"So beautiful, you remind me so much of Nadia. That's impossible because Eva and Nadia didn't share anything in common. Why must I be tormented by what I can't have? I would treated Nadia like a Queen and yet so chose that traitor!

No longer able to resist her beauty, Abaddon tried to kiss Cassie. The princess moved the chair back but Abaddon grabbed the back of her head to force her forward. In a last ditch effort to break away, Cassandra actually butted her head into Abaddon's nose. This caused the fallen angel to pull back and laugh.

"No one kisses me without my permission!" cried Cassandra.

"I love a brave spirit. I wish I had the time to properly seduce you but I not sure if you're grandfather would approve."

The confusion in Cassandra's eyes by Abaddon's words gave the dark angel an opening. He put his hands on Cassandra's forehead.

"What are you doing?" demanded Cassandra.

"Since you won't give of yourself to the Prince willingly, I will give you a taste of the power you will soon wield. You may have some divine blood in you, but you're still susceptible to my magic."

Three glowing red marks appeared on Cassandra's forehead. Feeling a change coursing in her body, the princess's green eyes were covered in golden tint. Like a demoness, a slit formed in the center of the iris.

"WHAT ARE YOU DOING TO ME?"

"I hate to kill your spirit like this, but your willpower is simply getting in the way. When the powers of the Prince finally infiltrate and corrupt your soul, you'll come to me and beg me to finish the transformation. Don't bother trying to chant a counterspell; you cannot deny your true nature. So sit back and relax, there's no point trying to fight it. Your defeat is inevitable."

Just then Basarabas opened the door, interrupting Abaddon's boasting. Angrily, the fallen angel faced his nervous subordinate.

"Lord Abaddon!"

"I left orders not to disturb me!"

"We have a situation. A Nephilim commander and his unit were dispatched without your orders to kill Cedric Rhone. They were found slaughtered."

"Fools . . . how could they be so arrogant?"

"There's something more troubling—we found the Nephilim nothing more than a twitching vegetable. Virgus operated on his head; his brain was stripped of every single wrinkle."

"Memory? That could only be done . . ."

Now longer gloating over the captured princess, Abaddon stood in a panic. Cassandra started to chuckle.

"You might be better off releasing me now. When my boyfriend comes back, you are going to be in a world of trouble."

"I grow weary of this knight interfering in my plans. I'm going to order Virgus to begin his final sequences immediately! If Prince Rhone did what I think he did, he knows everything. Post two guards on this room; no one gets in! I want the princess brought to me as soon as I ask."

"Of course, my lord."

Abaddon left and closed the door behind him. Struggling against the ropes and the evil magic taking hold her body, Cassandra cried heavily. With every ounce her strength, she tried to prevent it from taking hold of her. After a few moments, her sobs turned into a light laughter as a malevolent smile started to grow across her face.

Walker kicked open the door to Cassandra's room, a trail of dead guards behind him. Disappointed to find the room completely deserted, the lord captain took out his frustration with fists to the wall. Jumping at the sound of someone entering the room, Walker was shocked to see Felicia standing in front of him. She was no longer dressed in her maid's outfit but rather was dressed in a green ranger's suit, the same kind that Malcolm wore. The hood of her cloak pulled above her head, the handmaiden wore sixteen daggers on her belt with two dirks in the front. Noticing six dead bodies in the room adjacent, Walker admired her handiwork.

"Walker?" asked Felicia. "Joshua!"

She ran to her son and held him tightly, kissing him several times.

"Where's the princess?" questioned Walker.

"They came in and took her. I was in my chambers at the time, but I knew there was nothing I could do to rescue her then and there. Cassandra fought like a wildcat, but she was taken quickly. From what I gathered, they brought her to the eastern tower on the fourteenth floor. I'll show you the fastest way."

"I believe the time for pretense and secrets between us is over, Felicia," said Walker. "Just who the hell are you?"

"I am Felicia of House Yannis, a ranger of Evengard. When Cassandra turned five, Cerwin had me smuggled into Castle Acadia and personally charged me with being her bodyguard. We elves protect our own, and I felt that serving as her doting handmaiden would allow me to keep close without arousing suspicions. However, my love for Julius put everything in jeopardy. Now tell me what's going on?"

"There's been a coup. I've been deep undercover for two rotations trying to find out what I can. Count Luminas has King Stephen as his prisoner in the throne room. Apparently one of the people involved in the plot has designs for the princess. It's not safe; many of the servants and loyalists have been killed. That's why I went for your son first."

"Thank you, Walker. Now let's go get Cassandra."

Outside, the city of Verian was engulfed in flames. Demonkin were igniting kerosene with fire and throwing them into the Titan embassy. Leading a coalition of forces into battle against the rebels and demonkin cretins, Cecilia bravely held the embassy courtyard. Colin, Samuel, Cagius, Valentine, Sirius, Cerwin, Hippolyte, Minerva, and Stryker joined her in battle. Refugees from the embassies and civilians from the city of Verian poured in through the open back postern gates seeking the protection of the coalition forces. After driving back a third rebel charge, Cecilia picked up a spear staked in the ground. She reared back and launched it so it landed right in the chest of a Templar knight. Riding across her line, the vanadis did all she could to keep the morale of her soldiers high.

"Is that all you've got? Is that all you've got? How dare you insult the vanadis? You'd better bring well over a thousand body bags for me alone if you dare to kill me."

Inspired by Cecilia's performance, Hippolyte readied her spear for the next wave. She had known the legends of the vanadis's twin brother but had never seen a woman command forces like this.

"What's wrong, sis?" asked Minerva.

"I honestly thought no woman could ever match me, but Cecilia... she truly is a man among women."

"I don't know if that's really a compliment, sis. In truth, I'm pretty sure someone with her assets wouldn't appreciate it. Well, if we live through this we'll have a great story to tell by the fire."

Flying out of the embassy, Keiko fluttered past the chaos of battles and falling debris from the buildings in search of Cecilia. Annoyed by the disturbance in the middle of battle waves, Cecilia grabbed the sylph quickly.

"Anything?"

"We can't stay in the embassy any longer," responded Keiko. "Fires have broken out everywhere. We can't control them!"

"Get the civilians to the rear of the defense guard with the stone wall behind them. Destroy all the files and crash the hard drives. I don't want to leave these traitors a damn thing."

"Yes, my lady."

Wavering back into embassy, she watched technicians desperately trying to work amid the coming fire. They tried everything they could to reach the other nations and inform them of the situation. As the fires spread, technicians grabbed extinguishers and did the best to contain what they could.

"Destroy everything!" ordered Keiko. "We can't hold them anymore. It is the orders of the princess."

Loading up the computers with viruses, the technicians typed a series of codes to initiate a full crash of the hard drive. As they all ran out of the room with Keiko, the last technician hit a switch near the door that began a series of explosions in the room. The exterior walls of the embassy became compromised and crushed the causeways below them. Staring in disbelief at their persistence, Cecilia watched the Acadians attempt another charge. Cagius ordered his men to get their spears down and blocked them off with the shield wall. Cecilia picked up a transmission and hit her ear bud.

"God, Walker, I thought you'd never call! Our defenses are breached and we can't hold them. I'm littered with civilians who've never even seen a sword, let alone used one. My brother has ordered us out!"

"Cecilia, I'm not going to make it to our rendezvous point," replied Walker over the communicator.

"How close are you? We'll break through and get you."

"They moved Cassandra. It's going to take too long to get her to you. You've got to leave me behind, Cecilia. I'll just have to find another way out."

"I wish you were born one of us, Walker." cried Cecilia wiping the tears from her eyes. "I'd be proud to have a soldier like you in my army."

"Good luck, Cecilia, and wish me the same."

"Good luck, Walker."

Hanging her head in disgrace, Cecilia signaled for Cagius to join her.

"I think it's time we made our escape," ordered Cecilia.

"I thought we were waiting for Walker," retorted Cagius.

"There's no rescue for Walker, but we've got to get these civilians to safety. Divide your legions into two groups. They'll protect the immediate flanks. We'll put the archers on point while my horses bring up the rear. Civilians will be in the middle, covered on all sides. We'll move toward the city gate and engage only when necessary."

"Okay, let's get started," exclaimed Cagius as he divided his men. "One group with Legate Polonius on the left; the other with me on the right!"

"Just like the old days!" recollected Polonius in his old legion armor.

The legions beat their shields in encouragement while the other confused troops tried to figure out what was going on.

"Colin, what are we doing?" asked Hippolyte.

"We're making a break for it."

"We're running away?" questioned Minerva.

"Our orders are to get the civilians to safety, and there are almost ten thousand of them. If we don't leave now, we're not getting them out."

"Hey, old man, you think you can clear us a path?" yelled Valentine to Cerwin.

"Have a little respect for your elders, Valentine!" retorted Cerwin as he finished his elvish chant. "Blaze wall!"

The fire spell caused the attacking forces to run for cover. Twirling her spear, Cecilia moved to the front of the column. A huge shield wall emerged and cut off the enemy forces when Cecilia yelled, "Defense." The spell was taxing, as Acadians slashed at the wall with their swords. Screaming in agony, every blow against the shield caused Cecilia to endure severe pain.

"Break out! Get the civilians to safety!"

The army and civilians began running for the gate. Protecting the outside, the legions warded off flanking attackers while the archers on point filled straggling guards with arrows. Holding the shield as long as she could, Cecilia was forced to drop it when the demonkin magical weapons penetrated it. The vanadis joined Samuel and the other Titan riders at the rear of the column. As the coalition forces drew closer to the city gates, the rebels broke off their pursuit. Content with the army's escape from Verian, suffering heavy casualties, and tired of fighting, the rebels returned to the safety of Castle Acadia. The large exodus of civilians cleared the gates and the city of Verian. Alliance soldiers from all four nations allowed the long train to rest once they got a kilometer from the city. The civilians collapsed to the ground in exhaustion and many soldiers were glad for the short respite.

"They're not coming!" observed Cecilia.

"I'm not surprised," added Samuel. "We killed too many of them to stomach any more losses."

"You have your orders."

"Your highness, I am not one to question orders, but..."

"You're a good soldier, son. Have faith and get our people home!"

"Of course, your highness."

Turning to face the exiled, Samuel's heart was filled with pity. Families who had lived in Verian for revolutions had just lost everything. Bewildered children sought comfort from parents who had no answers. He screamed as far as his voice could carry him so there would no misunderstanding of the orders.

"EVERYONE LISTEN TO ME! FOLLOW THE SOLDIERS FROM YOUR NATIONS TO YOUR HOMELANDS. THOSE OF YOU FROM VERIAN ARE WELCOME IN ANY OF THE COUNTRIES. IT IS IMPORTANT THAT YOU CLEAR THE CITY LIMITS VERY QUICKLY. DO NOT STOP AND REST UNTIL YOU REACH THE BORDER. TRUST ME, THE REASONS WILL BECOME CLEAR TO YOU SOON! TITANS WITH ME!"

The nations divided themselves up. Cagius noticed Cecilia and Colin had planted themselves in a location away from the rest of the Titans. He walked over to the vanadis.

"I'd like to know where you're going, Cecilia," inquired Cagius rhetorically.

"I'm waiting here for my brother. We've got to make sure that we get the princesses out of that city."

"I'm surprised at you, Cecilia. Here you have the foremost cavalier in the whole of Terminus Mundus and you didn't even ask me to help rescue a damsel-in-distress. Count me in."

Polonius and Valentine walked up to Cagius.

"I sure hope you know what you're doing," said Polonius.

"Felicia is still in that city and I know my brother. Someone has to stay here and make sure he gets home safely."

"Don't sell yourself short, soldier. We can't lose good men like you."

"I know what I have to do."

Polonius left with the Napolitan group. A large number of the Acadian refugees tagged along with the legions. Cagius dismissed Valentine so he could go with them, but the assassin wouldn't move. Laughing, the dragoon didn't need a worded response from the assassin to read his mind. The elves marched back to the north while the Titans rode south. Many of the riders offered their horses to the elderly, women, and children. Remaining behind, Cecilia, Keiko, Cagius, Valentine, Cerwin, and Colin prepared for their next assault. While it certainly wasn't the best organized commando team in the history of the world, it certainly featured a great degree of skill. Talon flew down to the vanadis's shoulder; Cecilia dismounted and walked over to Hippolyte, Minerva, and Stryker.

"I guess this is where we say good-bye."

"Good-bye?" wondered Hippolyte.

"Bad things are going to happen here, and you've got a duty to the tribes now, Hippolyte. The roads will be safe back to your home. The enemy's pulled everything into Verian."

"What are you going to do?" asked Minerva.

"When my brother gets here, he's going to launch a rescue mission for Princess Cassandra and Princess Marie."

"We're staying, Cecilia," demanded Hippolyte.

"You don't understand. If you don't leave right now, we cannot get you home. It's impossible with what's going to happen."

"It doesn't matter. Our people always reward kindness with kindness. Princess Cassandra treated me as a person, and I can't let her stay trapped in that castle awaiting a diabolical fate. Your brother risked his life and career to rescue us. I won't owe him such a debt."

"Yeah, sis," exclaimed Minerva. "We'll show those steel-bellies!"

"God help us," teased Cecilia as she closed her eyes. "All right, as long as you understand the consequences; there's nothing we can do. Rest up; when my brother finally gets here, all hell is going to break loose."

Starting a fire, Cagius and Valentine put on a pot of coffee. Checking their rations, the soldiers made sure each of their packs was loaded with jerky, supplies, and canteens filled with water. Everyone sat down and started to eat and drink. Balling her eyes out, Keiko stared at the magnificent city of Verian engulfed in flames.

"What's wrong, little one?" asked Cerwin.

"I never thought I would ever see a city burn that was built on water."

"Built on pillars of salt and sand... it's not buildings that concern me. They will be rebuilt, but life can never be replaced. Cassandra, be strong!"

FORT ORION

"Finally, draw your strength from the Lord and from his mighty
power. Put on the armor of God so that you may be able to
stand firm against the tactics of the devil. For our struggle
is not with flesh and blood but with principalities, with the
power, with the world rulers of this present darkness, with the
evil spirits in the heavens. Therefore, put on the armor of God
that you may be able to resist on the evil day and having done
everything to hold your ground. So stand fast with your loins
girded in truth, clothed with righteousness as a breastplate,
and your feet shod in readiness for the gospel of peace. In all
circumstances hold faith as a shield to quench all flaming
arrows of the evil one. And take the helmet of salvation and
sword of the spirit, which is the word of God."

—The Letter to the Titans 6:10–17

Cedric and Christian, now in full armor, stood outside of Fort Orion
ready for battle. The shining fort still looked impressive from the
outside at night. Kneeling on the ground with his sword in front of him,
Cedric silently prayed for strength in this dark hour. Christian examined
the front of the fort through his glasses and started to laugh.

"Could you believe these amateurs?" mocked Christian. "They left the
gate portcullis open. You got a plan, boss?"

"I'm going right through the front gate," replied Cedric as he blessed
himself and stood.

"You worry me when you say things like that."

"You told me you scanned only thirty of them. It's fifteen each; shouldn't be a problem for the two of us."

"It's not that."

"What's wrong?"

"I'm worried about what Garrett told you."

"An enemy that can't be killed! I'm sorry, Christian, that's impossible. If he's in creation, an angel is still flesh and blood."

"No, I'm worried about you. I've known you for thirty revolutions now from when we were playing crusaders at age five to our graduation from the academy. I study people, and I know that you have a martyr complex. If push comes to shove, you'll fight Abaddon no matter what Garrett told you."

"Christian, is your fiancé, Rosa Landon worth living for?"

"Don't play these games with me now Cedric."

Looking down at the ring on his finger, Christian knew he had to make a choice. He would either follow his friend into hell or leave his side. When he opened his eyes again, the spy master made his decision.

"Yes Cedric. She's worth's living for."

"Then when this business is all over with, you, Rosa, Cassie, and I should have dinner. I think the girls would get along famously."

"All right, then. Well, I guess there's no point hanging around here anymore. Not when there's work to be done."

Christian and Cedric gave each other a high-five as they started walking up the path toward the fort entrance. Cedric removed his flask from his cloak and took a drink before replacing it. As they got closer, one of the Acadian guards realized what was coming their way.

"It can't be!" exclaimed the guard. "They said they killed him!"

"Greetings. I was wondering if you wouldn't terribly mind releasing the marshals," asked Christian half-heartedly.

"All to arms! Enemy in the fort!" screamed the guard.

Christian and Cedric heard the rustling of armor. Christian rolled his eyes as he drew his dagger and killed the first guard by sticking his dagger into his throat. The guards funneled their way into the courtyard to be met by Cedric with Ragnarok. Cedric quickly dispatched three of the amateurs with five sword slashes. Inside the fort was a run on the armory by the other soldiers. They pulled out swords, spears, bows, and arrows.

"Are we under attack?" asked a guard. "That's the alarm!"

"By what?" asked another. "A division?"

"Worse! By *La Morte Angelus*!"

Cedric moved into one of the fort hallways. He chanted, "Fire" and ignited flames on his sword through his saber magic. Sensing an ambush, he reared back and swung down a corridor in the fort. The backswing ignited a flame wall in a small corridor that roasted five more guards alive. In the main conference room, Julius was lying down on the table with his hands folded over his stomach. Still stewing in his own juices, he was annoyed by Amuro constantly tapping the wall looking for a weak spot.

"Impossible," commented Malcolm. "Even if you found a weak spot, the magical wards built into the walls prevent you from using your magic in here."

"We'll never know unless we try," countered Amuro.

"Do you hear something?"

Amuro stopped and listened.

"It sounds like screaming. Did the Acadians betray us?"

Just then one of the guards went flying through the door, causing Julius to stand up. The body seemed burned not with fire but with thunder bolts.

"It's about time you got here!" taunted Julius.

Entering the room, Cedric and Christian carried a large chest. As they put it down, Julius, Amuro, and Malcolm got their armor and weapons out.

"Is Maiden all right?" asked Amuro.

"She's fine; just startled," reassured Christian.

"We were all startled," replied Amuro

"So it's a coup?" asked Julius as he put on his breastplate.

"Yes," answered Cedric.

"We're calculating that if we don't get the princesses out in the next two hours, we're not going to get them out," said Christian.

"The Imperial Legions are at Dragonstone. They can't get here that fast," reasoned Julius.

"No troops," commanded Cedric.

"How are we going to siege the castle without troops?" questioned Malcolm.

"A small elite force will be able to penetrate the castle and get the princesses out," explained Christian. "We already dismissed the rest of your men and women. They're returning to their countries as we speak."

"I guess that means us. However, I noticed you didn't mention anything about King Stephen," inquired Amuro.

"It's too late to save Stephen," regretted Cedric. "He's under heavy guard in the middle of the castle. I fear we can only target him as a secondary objective. Besides, we have a second concern. Our enemy has a weapon that is going to seal off Central Acadia from the rest of the West. There is a very good chance that any force that goes into Verian is going to get caught behind us. I can't give you an order to come with me. I'm asking you to do this."

"Let's make this clear," stated Julius. "I'll go, but I'm not doing this for you. If you're going to get Cassandra out, I want Felicia and Joshua out as well. I'm going with you for their sakes. However, I will admit that I was wrong about you in the senate, and I'm sorry."

Putting both of their hands out in respect, Cedric and Julius gripped each other at the forearm. Smiling widely and laughing, Amuro threw her arms up in the air.

"Well, it looks like the three marshals are back together. Once again, we may be all that stands in the way of Terminus Mundus and total annihilation. Now let's go get our friends to safety."

The five broke out on horseback north from Fort Orion to Verian.

Eagle's Gate,
the Griffin Mountain Pass

"It is ironic that Castle Titan has been called the 'fortress that cannot be sieged,' since no army has been able to test that 'jinx' since the construction of Eagle's gate."

—*King Frederick Rhone at the Imperial Invasion*

Two giant stone eagles were carved in Griffin Mountains, shadowing over a paved mountain pass going south. In between these stone eagles was a steel gate reinforced with stone facing outward. The pride of the reign of Queen Marion Rhone, the gate has held throughout numerous invasions attempts by both the tribes and the War of the First Alliance during the reign of King Frederick Rhone. Extending half a kilometer into the mountain pass from where it began, catapults and scorpions lined the parapets with plenty of holes for mercenary archers to fire from. A half-kilometer deeper in the mountain pass, Fort Hawkeye was built on the mountain hills. Reinforced by steel walls, the two forts were connected by a single bridge. Thus one twin of Fort Hawkeye could be resupplied by the other twin during a siege. The Titan Armada was positioned just outside of Eagle's gate, with Queen Civilia in the lead and Horace puffing a cigar next to her. Making way to let the scientist pass, Martha floated on a hover platform with a computer attached at the front of it.

"My queen, it's as I feared. Virgus completed his research."

In the distance, a flash of light from Castle Acadia emerged bright enough to be seen over the whole of the west.

"What is that?" asked Civilia.

"It's a tachyon wave, your highness!"

Spreading out in a series of beams, the light would envelop the borders of Central Acadia on all sides. In Napolitan, Evengard, and among the Tribal Confederation, inhabitants could do nothing but stare in awe at these beams rising out of the center of their lands. The beams spread and connected from one point to another. They destroyed absolutely nothing, but rather just set up a giant protective shield. Looking on with trepidation, the Titans pondered how they could confront such a weapon. A light-armor knight rode back to queen's position from the valley.

"Your highness, Captain Samuel's company returns from Verian!"

The riders let up a cheer behind the column as the riders and civilians approached the gate. In Napolitan and Evengard the sight of the approaching civilians and forces were a welcome sight after the terrifying beams of light they had just seen. Breaking formation to greet the coming riders and civilians, hugs and kisses were exchanged by families and friends. Horace rode out to debrief his son. Samuel saluted him.

"Report, Captain," demanded Horace.

"Sir, all civilians in the Titan embassy have been evacuated. We suffered only twelve minor injuries in the skirmish."

"Excellent work, son!"

"Dad, I feel horrible about leaving them behind."

"You had your mission to accomplish, and you succeeded. It's up to the prince and princess to accomplish their mission."

Surprising his son with an outward display of affection, Horace removed his cigar and kissed him on the cheek. Salutations were exchanged by the Titan officers as they returned to the queen.

"Captain Samuel Irvine, you shall receive a commendation for your bravery and thoroughness in completing this mission," announced Civilia.

"Thank you, your highness."

"Freigraf Marshal, order the armada to stand down. There's nothing more we can do until we get Cedric's signal."

"Yes, your highness. I'm sure those two will be able to pull this off."

"I don't doubt it," acknowledged a smiling Civilia.

"Well, I have my own work to do," interrupted Martha. "I'd better obtain a deeper understanding of Virgus's tachyon theories. I'll leave the soldiery to those who do it best."

Civilia blessed herself and bowed her head.

"Holy Mother, please watch over them and may their guardian angels protect them."

ONE KILOMETER SOUTH OF VERIAN

"I do not confront evil; I destroy it!"

—*Prince Cedric Rhone*

Cedric, Julius, Amuro, Malcolm, and Christian walked their horses over to a blazing fire where Civilia and the others that had decided to stay and fight were resting. Percolating on top of the fire was hot coffee and everyone partook of a cup. Minerva found the taste a bit strong but didn't want to appear like a child in front of the others. Cecilia embraced Cedric before pointing out Hippolyte and Minerva. She had an expression that seemed to say, "I'm sorry."

"You were supposed to get out of here!" demanded Cedric.

"Blood brother of the Wolf Tribe, you placed your life on the line for us," said Hippolyte. "We pay our debts and honor an alliance with you. Besides, Cassie is my friend too."

"Very well, but it's not going to be easy. In about ten minutes, you're going to wish you had left."

"What was with the light show?" asked Cagius.

"Acadia is protecting itself with a giant tachyon shield," explained Cedric, as he drank a second cup of coffee. "They originally intended to draw the three allied armies into this shield as a trap. However, once Christian and I got wind of their plans, they changed it to a method of defense. We are locked in this barrier for now. There is no way to return to our own kingdoms."

"What are we up against?" asked Valentine.

"The entire royal court turned against Stephen," responded Christian. "The wizards, the temple, the nobles, and even Queen Sharon are all following Count Luminas. We can expect a resistance of the Templar Army, the Verian City Guard, and the armies of the Demonkin."

"It figures. So the one point that eludes me is, if we're trapped, how are we going to get the princesses out?"

"We follow the ancient tunnels secretly carved into the Acadian Royal Crypt. Cedric cut a deal with Margrave Dennis of Deniva. If we deliver the princesses safely to the trade city, he will give us sanctuary."

"The crypt is filled with the undead," interjected Cerwin. "It will be a perilous journey."

"There's no other way. We go to the crypt or we stay behind."

"We all knew what we were getting into when this operation began," announced Cedric. "I'm proud my closest friends are standing together of their own free will. It is incredibly important that we have an heir to Central Acadia in order to rally our forces for the rotation we have our revenge."

"You know, after this is over I don't want to hear any peasant ever complain about how the aristocracy does nothing for the alliance again," commented Cagius.

"We're defending their right to say that," added Julius. "Any other need to know information for before we head in?"

"One last thing, the main enemy we fight is a fallen angel named Abaddon," described Cedric. "Under no circumstances should you engage him in combat; he's much too powerful for us right now."

"Well, I don't have a death wish," joked Julius. "As long as I get Felicia and my son out of there, I'll be satisfied."

"Well, no point hanging around here any longer; let's go," ordered Amuro.

Overly excited about the adventure, the wolf tribe princesses yelled "Right". Surprising their new allies, they put their hands on top of one another. The girls looked at the royals expecting them to join in.

"We do this in the tribes before we go out on a hunt," explained Hippolyte. "It gets everyone riled up."

Confused and not wanting to embarrass themselves, the others waited for Colin to step in and put his hand down first. Defeated, the others shrugged their shoulders and followed suit. Adapting to the tradition, they put the other hand on the shoulder of the warrior next them. The warriors shared a brief smile before they screamed and saddled up. Cedric, Julius, and Amuro went to the front of the column with the others following behind them. Calvary and Talon took point from the skies above. Accepting a free ride on Myst, Keiko conserved her energy for the coming battle. Stryker choose to remain running at Hippolyte's side. Twenty minutes later, the assault force reached the destroyed city gate of Verian. Guards on the walls stared at the group approaching.

"Are those the marshals?"

"What are they, suicidal?"

Minerva and Malcolm readied their bows. From horseback they fired and struck the two guards on the wall. Malcolm winked at Minerva in appreciation of the fine shot. Running to the gate, halberdiers put down their pikes to stop the charge. Cecilia and Hippolyte readied their spears and took the center two out. Ranks broken, the rebels fled as the marshals trampled them under their horses. Panic spread through the castle like wildfire, soldiers, demonkin, and Nephilim scrambled to prepare for the imminent assault. The group in the throne room was running from one corner of the room to the next in terror as Stephen sat on his throne with a smile. Jonas conferred with his subordinates, trying to figure out what was happening.

"What is going on?" asked Luminas.

"Our sentries are reporting that warriors have entered Verian," reported Jonas.

"Warriors?" queried Sharon. "Could it be the marshals? We've already lost contact with Fort Orion!"

"Cedric wouldn't risk that much for Cassandra?" asked a confused Celius. "Would he?"

"You seem to underestimate the love the Titan prince has for my daughter," boasted Stephen.

"Shut up!" cried a panicked Sharon. "What would that warmonger know of love?"

"They couldn't be coming for the king?" reasoned a nervous Luminas. "No, that's not like Cedric, Julius, and Amuro; they're here for the princesses."

"Great. While our gracious mercenary is out trying to get this damn shield up, we've got the marshals to deal with," moaned Jonas.

"Take the saints and kill them!" ordered Luminas.

"Where are the princesses being held?" asked Jonas.

"We put them in the eastern tower on separate floors," replied Celius.

Jonas went to his earpiece and started to try to communicate with soldiers he had there.

"I'm not getting any response. No one has seen Walker in two rotations, but we had a commotion at the castle blacksmith some time ago. I bet he's making his way to the tower. I'll deal with him."

"No, you won't!" interjected Basarabas, dressed in his armor. "Abaddon has left me in charge. I will deliver the princesses to him. My Nephilim will be more than a match. Do not allow the king to leave your sight!"

Basarabas signaled to some Nephilim standing in the room. Following him out the eastern door, the conspirators were left alone to ponder what to do with Stephen.

In the eastern tower, two guards remained on steadfast alert at the door where Cassandra was behind held. Whirling out of a dark hallway, a dagger caught one of the guards in the throat. The other panicked, but Walker grabbed him from behind and stabbed him in the back. Felicia retrieved her dagger while Joshua kept an eye on the hallway around them. Kicking the door open, Walker spotted Cassandra tied to her chair and head slumped over.

"Mistress Cassandra!" shouted Felicia.

Running to her charge, Felicia cut the silk binds along her wrists. She touched her neck for a pulse first and then went to her heart.

"Something's wrong. Her heart rate seems much higher than usual."

"Was she drugged?" asked Walker.

"I don't know."

Felicia continued to work on Cassandra when she noticed her eyes begin to flutter. Kneeling down in front of the princess, Walker tried to rouse her.

"Your highness, are you all right?"

Cassandra opened her eyes to Walker's horror. The whites of her eyes had gone to blood red and her green eyes were now slit like a demoness. Ejecting waves of green magic from her body, Walker and Felicia were both caught in its power. Walker was saved when his oath shield absorbed the harmful magic but Felicia's eyes became covered in a green mist. With a smile, she grabbed one of Walker's arms when Cassandra lunged for the other. Despite his strength, an otherworldly force pushed the lord captain to floor. Unable to wound either woman, Walker watched helplessly as a terrifying smile formed across Cassandra's blood-red lips.

"I should thank you, noble Walker! Not only did you free me from my binds but you've also provided me a snack. Now I can reach my true potential for lord Abaddon."

"Hey, Felicia, will you snap out of it?"

"Relax, lord captain, and accept the will of the mistress as I have."

"Now, my loyal protector, I need but a kiss and your soul will be mine. Fear not. I will use your energy in further service to the darkness I pledge myself to!"

"Don't do it, Cassandra!" pleaded Walker. "This isn't you!"

She was about to press her lips against his, but Cassandra hit the floor with a loud thud, unconscious. Staring at Joshua with his hand raised in a martial arts stance—a knifehand chop in the forward position—Walker breathed a sigh of relief. Felicia quickly shook her head, now freed from the spell. After bowing deeply to apologize to Walker, she examined Cassandra's body closely. The handmaiden noticed the mark that Abaddon had made on her forehead and how it was glowing blood-red.

"Good thinking, kid," complimented Walker.

"I hope she's all right," worried Joshua.

"What in the name of hell happened to her?" asked Walker.

"It might be a curse. No whatever spell this was, it involved awakening something within her. It's almost as if she had become a succubus or something."

"We have to bring her to Cedric. The Titans have methods of healing that are beyond my powers of white magic. Hey Dad, thanks again for the Oath Shield."

"Yes," agreed Felicia.

"Joshua, please carefully carry the princess," commanded Walker.

"Why me?" asked Joshua.

"Do as he says, son!" ordered Felicia.

"Yes, Mom."

Gently picking up the Princess, Joshua placed her arms over his shoulders. He hunched himself over to keep her in balance.

"She'd better not wake up and tear my soul out. I'm still getting used to it."

"Just be very careful when you're carrying her!" warned Walker.

"I got it! I got it!"

"It's a warning because if anything happens to her, Cedric is going to blame you. Then you'll know why we call him *La Morte Angelus*."

In the main hallway, the marshals and company dismounted. The ornate halls were now littered with blood and collapsing rubble. Anticipating an assault, the warriors drew their weapons and formed a circle. Demonkin orks, imps, and goblins took up position on the stairs, and adjoining hallways. Frothing rabidly at the mouth, they held their axes and swords in battle position. Determined to encircle and flank the warriors, Julius and Cedric smiled at another.

"Well, it looks like we've got them surrounded," observed Julius.

Laughing at the quip, Cerwin turned to Amuro with a wild look in his eye. Amuro picked up on it and held her sword in front of her.

"Amuro, why don't you have some fun?" teased Cerwin.

"Thanks, Grandpa!"

Chanting, the elf maiden brought her red sword in front of her chest and a second yellow light began to reflect off of it. Shouting, "earthquake," Amuro hit her sword into the ground. The strike formed a wide fissure, cracking the stone under the twin staircases. The resulting shaking caused both staircases to collapse. Crushing the demonkin soldiers standing on the stairs and below them, the spell buried other soldiers with plaster from the ceiling above. The warriors started to laugh and invited the attacks of their enemies with their eyes and hands. The remaining orks charged at the warriors. Fast and fierce attacks, forced the rescuers to move quickly with their melee weapons. Slice, dice, and move to the next opponent was the most effective method. Lacking the skill and protective armor necessary for combat, demonkin bodies piled up quickly in the main hall. Reinforcements came charging down the western hall to relieve their comrades.

Keiko gathered magic in her hand, started to chant, and finally shouted, "Missile!" Unleashing a powerful holy energy blast, the sylph vaporized all of the orks coming down the corridor. Spent after the single attack, Keiko retreated to the protection of the inner circle. Leaping into the air, Cagius crashed into the ground trident first. The crater sent the orks in the area flying. Julius and Cedric invoked holy saber due to its effectiveness against enemies of the light. Backswings from Ragnarok and Excalibur wiped out ten to twelve enemies at a time. Malcolm stuck his arrow in one of the goblin's necks. Pulling the arrow out, he drew his bow with such force, it went through two enemies. Cecilia used her power attack from her spear and took out ten more. Hippolyte and Minerva fought in tandem, Hippolyte in front with her spear and Minerva shooting arrows for cover. Speeding through the enemies rapidly with their short swords and daggers, Christian and Valentine ripped up their sector of enemies. Preferring his opponents come to him, Colin unleashed large arcing attacks with his sword to keep them off him. Twenty minutes of heavy fighting wiped out the demonkin columns. Exhausted, Minerva and Malcolm watched for more enemies as the warriors took a swallow of water and a bite of jerky.

"A good start," commented Cedric, tapping his earpiece. "Walker, are you there?"

In another part of the castle, Walker fended off three Nephilim and tried to protect his bounty. Unlike the mindless footsoldiers the marshals dealt with, Walker was having trouble with these skilled warriors. Using his sword and shield in defense, he baited his enemies by creating an opening. Finally, one of them made a careless lunge; the captain slashed his throat with his shield before finishing him with Sigmund. From that first attack, he threw the other away with his shield and thrust through the third one. Suffering a concussion from the shield bash, the Nephilim ran away in hopes of getting reinforcements. Felicia aimed her dagger and struck him in the back of the neck before he could get away. Kicking open the door, Walker was surprised to have Marie give him a hug.

"Your highness, are you all right?" asked Walker.

Cautious over what happened to him the last time, the captain gave a girl a thorough check; Felicia began to examine her as well. Marie smiled, but there was nothing out of the ordinary about her. However, the young princess grew nervous at the extensive search by the two. Satisfied nothing was out of place, the two cleared her.

"Lord Captain, I didn't expect... " started Marie.

"Come on, we're rescuing you!" ordered Walker.

"Of course."

Spotting Cassandra draped over Joshua's tiring shoulders, Marie began to cry. Brushing her raven hair back, the younger princess noticed Abaddon's marks burning brightly on her forehead.

"What's wrong with my sister?"

"She's been the victim of some terrible magic," explained Felicia. "She needs help quickly and, trust me, it's best that she's kept unconscious for now. The marshals are coordinating a rescue."

"Hang on, Cassie, you'll be fine."

Distractions aside, Walker finally got a chance to hit his earpiece and answer the frantic calls of his commanding marshal. The captain breathed a sigh of relief.

"I didn't think you'd ever make it."

"Where are you?" asked Cedric over the communicator.

"They stuck Cassandra at the top of the eastern tower. We're working our way down. On the ninth we secured Marie. We have both packages accounted for, and they are very fragile. Cedric, I have to warn you, Abaddon's done something to Cassandra. It's beyond my power to aid her."

"You'll never make it under those conditions; we'll come up and meet you."

"Right. I left my beacon on so you can track it."

"We've got more company!" screamed Felicia as she took out her daggers.

An arrow came flying in and hit Walker in the chest before he could get his shield up. He glanced down and saw that it hadn't fully penetrated his plate.

"Captain!" screamed Marie.

"Get behind me!" ordered Walker. "It's only a scratch!"

Despite the wound, Walker pulled the girls and Joshua behind his large shield. Under a shower of arrows, Walker used the corridors to deflect the attacks from their targets. In the main foyer, Cedric ordered his warriors.

"All right, we're going to have to meet Walker. Julius... "

Not noticing the other marshal had slipped away, Cedric hung his head in disgust.

"He must have gone after Felicia!" determined Amuro.

"Don't worry; he can take care of himself!" reassured Valentine.

"All right, we've got bigger fish to fry right now," ordered Cedric. "Christian, Cecilia, Cagius, and Cerwin, you'll come with me. We'll go get Walker. Amuro take everybody else and the animals with you. I need you to clear a path for us to get to the crypt. We're going to be coming in hot. Use the disability ramps in the castle to get our horses down there; we're going to need them."

"No problem, Cedric," affirmed Amuro. "May I say I told you so when you insisted those ramps were a waste of vassalage taxes. My team with me!"

Rushing down the east hall, Amuro watched Cedric and his command disappear as her assembled went west. When Amuro reached a corridor underneath a balcony, she heard her sister Saria scream, "Amuro!"

"Adonai, please no!" prayed Amuro with her eyes closed.

Staring at the balcony, she watched her younger sister waving happily on the balcony. Flawlessly leaping from the balcony, the young princess did a somersault, twisted in the air, and landed gracefully on her feet. Though impressed by her gymnastics display, Amuro was frantic and in a panic.

"What are you doing here?"

"King Stephen had asked me to perform for him. However, when the violence broke out, some servants rushed me into a secret passage so I'd be safe," cried Saria. "It was horrible, sis. They didn't say a word; they just started killing."

"I'm sorry, Saria. I would have hoped to spare you from this."

"I know. I'll be all right now since my big sister is her to save me! Let's go back to Evengard."

"We can't!" We're trapped, Saria. You're going to have to come with me."

"You mean there's no way out?"

Slumping her head, the group couldn't help but acknowledge how adorable Saria looked. Quivers of arrow brought them back to reality. Malcolm and Minerva took to their arrows and shot at the archers on the balcony.

"Come on, sis!" commanded Amuro.

Grabbing her sister's forearm, the group sprinted to the ramps Cedric has discussed. Using her magic to make a hole in the wall, Amuro directed her command to take the horses from the courtyard and bring them down the ramps.

"Upstairs, Walker was showing the scars of battle. Engaged with a Nephilim warrior, he was struck in the back with another arrow. Distracted by the pain, a second warrior stabbed him under the arm. The stab cut through the chain mail between his plate and skin. Blood squirting out of his body, Walker managed to finish off his opponent. Falling to his knees, the captain watched as a halberdier charged him pike down. Prepared to prevent his untimely demise, Joshua intercepted the halberdier with a broadsword. Knocking him back, the young blacksmith drove the sword into the side of the attacker. Hearing the snap of a bow, Walker put up the Oath Shield and deflected an arrow meant for Joshua's head. Marie and Felicia stared at the approaching Basarabas at the head of his command.

"There you are, ladies!" taunted Basarabas. "For your insolence, Lord Captain, you shall die first!"

Staggering from the effects of three arrow wounds, Walker raised his sword and shield in anticipation of the coming attack. Reading his spear, Basarabas charged down the hall. As he reached Walker's position, Julius rammed the Nephilim leader into the wall shield first.

"Julius!" screamed Marie. "I knew you'd come!"

Outnumbered, but not outclassed, Julius fought off the company like a man possessed. Loading Excalibur with the power of saint saber, his enhanced attacks dealt extra damage to each of the combatants. Whenever his sword got lodged, he would use his Sacred Shield to stab them through the neck. Basarabas grunted and attacked Julius with his broad sword. Matching sword patterns, the Nephilim displayed his skill at a an equal level of his paladin opponent.

"The Dragon Paladin of Napolitan," screamed Basarabas.

"I guess I should have believed to all of Cedric's rantings about demons."

"We consider ourselves a higher order."

"Well, as a Paladin, it's my duty to cast you back into the darkness."

Walker fell to his knees and again chanted, "heal light." Slapping his right hand to his wounds, the knight tried desperately to alleviate the bleeding and pain temporarily. Julius shoved Basarabas back and slashed him across the chest. The Nephilim pushed himself with his feet away from the conflict as demonkin swarmed the paladin. Julius flipped the first one, spun, and knelt with a strike. He caught the cleaver of another with a shield and stabbed him. Not to be outdone, Walker barreled into an enemy and went back-to-back with Julius so they could spell each other. Working in tandem, the warriors managed to hold them off. Picking off targets with her daggers, Felicia chose her targets carefully as Joshua shielded her from further melee attacks. As the demons got closer, Marie picked up a dagger and stabbed the enemies trying to take her sister. Vision fading, Basarabas was relieved to see Abaddon join the assault.

"My lord, we cannot defeat these foes," pleaded Basarabas.

"It's time to stop playing games."

Abaddon opened his hands and created a huge ball of dark energy. Targeting Julius, the dark angel fired catching the paladin blind to his attack. Before it struck, Felicia shoved Julius out of way. Tearing a hole through her heart, Julius stared in agony as Felicia fell dead before she hit the ground.

Dropping his shield, Julius tore the war crown from his forehead. Lost in a mess of tears and dripping saliva, the marshal put a second hand on the sword. He knifed through the remaining enemies around him as if they were warm butter. Joshua, with tears in his eyes, tried to shake his mother, but she was already gone. Feeling the burnt hole above her heart, the boy put his head to her chest and wept. Dispatching the demonkin, Julius exerted his full attention to Abaddon. Watching the paladin charge their position, Basarabas grabbed his spear and threw it at him. The spear hit Julius in the shoulder but bounced right off his plate mail. Leaping into the air, Julius turned Excalibur into a strike position and drove it deep into the nephilim's leader brain. Not satisfied he had suffered enough, the marshal continued slash and hack away at Basarabas's body before kicking him off a catwalk. Patiently, Abaddon observed the fire in his opponent's eyes. Readying his blades, the dark angel anticipated his attack

"You took my light from me!" screamed Julius.

"What a waste to die for you!" taunted Abaddon.

Launching into an attack, Excalibur was calmly met by Abaddon's two swords at every swing. Devoid of control, Julius rage accelerated with every failed attack. Baiting the trap, Abaddon continued to taunt the paladin.

"Why do you invite death?"

"The elves were wrong! I know now that I have the power to destroy evil! I am the Last Knight, not Cedric!"

"No, my friend... everything you believe is a lie!"

Catching Julius' attack with his left sword, Abaddon spun and disarmed the terrified paladin with his right sword. The inevitable accepted Julius stood helplessly as Abaddon thrust both swords into his chest. The plate mail stopped the attacks at first, but black energy covered the swords, shattering the paladin's armor. Organs shredded to pieces and bleeding profusely, the Napolitan prince fell backwards. Choking up blood, Julius desperately tried to crawl to Felicia's body. His attentions unknown,

Marie ran to Julius. Pressing her dress into his wounds, she desperately tried to stop the bleeding, but to no avail. Distraught with the paladin's defeat, Walker was jumped by two Nephilim warriors. They pinned him to the ground by a spear in his shoulder and thigh. Uninhibited, Abaddon claimed his spoils.

With Basarabas killed, Valadrim, one of his chief lieutenants, bowed before Abaddon, awaiting orders. The new commander sweated profusely from his bald head due to the battles. More muscular and stronger than Basarabas, banded tattoos covered his exposed skin and arms.

"I am at your service, lord Abaddon."

"I want you to take Princess Marie and lock her in the wizard's tower. I have more important things to take care of and I'm not risking another attempted rescue."

Valadrim bowed in compliance. Grabbing Marie by the wrist, the young princess fought him tooth and nail to stay with Julius. Furious at her resistance, the new commander summoned green magic to his eyes. Forced to look into the green swirls, Marie was instantly hypnotized and fell docilely into Valadrim's arms. Dragging her away, Abaddon opened his hands. Opening her demoness eyes, Cassandra bowed before Abaddon submissively.

"That's it, child! It's time for you to come back home."

"Cassie, don't!" screamed Walker.

"I have to go home. My grandfather awaits me!" mindlessly chanted Cassandra as she floated past her protector.

"Finally you understand," crowed a smiling Abaddon.

Driven by the memories of the princess he swore to protect, Walker tore himself loose from the spears. He punched one of his tormentors off of the catwalk before breaking the neck of the other.

"I swore my life and my sacred honor to the protection of Princess Cassandra."

Raising his Oath Shield, Walker bull rushed the distracted dark angel. Abaddon lost his balance and hooked his heel on the edge of the catwalk to keep from falling. Primed to tear the resilient knight protector to pieces, he was struck by a marble column surrounded by blue light. The resulting impact sent Abaddon into the tower wall, driving him down into the main castle area. Spreading his wings to break the fall, the fallen angel sprained the joint coming from his tricep. On the ground once more, Abaddon tried to fly to the eastern tower but couldn't get any lift with the sprain. Yelling in agony, Cerwin taunted him from the catwalk above.

"When you can't kill something, throw something larger at it."

Approaching the catwalk, Cedric replaced his sword and removed his helmet. Pondering what to do with the transformed princess, the new demoness stared at the sword master with repulsion.

"*Permaneo Eques Ordinares*, you are an abomination. Why waste your time defending this vain world and vain people from the inevitable corruption of my grandfather."

Bowing his head, Cedric fears were confirmed from the words from her lips. Cecilia brought her spear up behind her twin brother. Tears streaming down her face, the vanadis readied an attack.

"Cedric, I'm sorry. This is too much for you to handle. I'll take care of her as mercifully as possible."

Cedric calmly put his hand on the Göttin-speer and forced it down. Knowing what he resolved to do, his twin sister grabbed his arm to stop the sword master. The look in his brown eyes forced her to pull the hand away.

"It can only end one way Cecilia. Abaddon needs me to kill her. Cassandra's soul will be damned if she dies like this, and that will deliver her right into the Prince's hand. I'm afraid I'm going to have to try something a little more drastic."

His brother's body convulsing on the ground, Cagius knelt down beside him. The dragoon held the paladin on his chest and right hand to stop him from shaking. Julius smiled at the sight and warmth of his brother.

"Cagius, is it you?"

"Easy, bro, I'm here."

"I couldn't stop him... Abaddon... he took Marie and has total control over Cassandra... I didn't have the power to stop him. What kind of a paladin am I?"

"Don't sell yourself short. Have you seen the bodies piled up around here? You did more than anyone could have asked you. Julius, you honored your vow. You defended the weak and remained the star shining in a sea of darkness."

"All my life... it wasn't me... it was you... "

"I don't understand."

"You're the one that needs to lead Napolitan... you are the leader of men... the legions love and respect you... I was merely a trophy for our father... "

"I never thought of you that way. You were my older brother and I looked up to you."

"When the time comes... you will sit on the dragon throne... Napolitan will be better for it... a true consul just like the times of old; not another moody tyrannical caesar. Take care of Joshua in my place... "

"You know you didn't need to ask me."

Choking on the blood in his mouth, Julius garnered the strength to unlatch his gauntlets.

"Give these to Cedric... he will need them... make sure Cedric wears them... this enemy requires a true paladin and these gauntlets is the only thing can help that self-righteous sword master."

"I will."

"Tell my friend... that I'm glad we never became enemies... "

Julius closed his eyes. Kissing his dead brother on the forehead, tears fell from the closed eyes of the dragoon. Furious that there was no way to bring his body, Cagius gathered as many of the paladin's treasures and possessions he could carry.

Setting herself in a predatory stance, Cassandra levitated to Cedric's position. The sword master let her grab him around his neck. Smiling widely, she pushed her head forward, but the titan prince held her back.

"We can't stay here, Cedric!" demanded Christian. "I don't know how we can bring her with us like this!"

"Cedric, she's under a powerful spell!" described Cerwin. "No craft we have can cure her. You have to let her go!"

"No, I have faith I can do this. This is the path I must walk because I hold the light and the darkness in my heart."

"Cedric, a Divikin is poisoned by the darkness she is emitting," cried Cecilia. "It'll tear you apart from within. I won't let you die!"

Closing his eyes, the sword master surrounded his body with swirling circles of white and black magic. The princess lunged forward and kissed him. At first, green energy flowed from his body to her lips. The demoness was filled with pleasure at the delicious taste of his soul energy. When his eyes opened again, Cedric took his hands and grabbed Cassandra on either side of her head. The demoness in her tried to pull away as the green light changed to gold. The mark on her forehead was infected with the same power and started to peel away. Drawing the poison from her soul, the sword master could feel evil attempting to taint him. Try as it may, the darkness could not corrupt him.

Cecilia bit her lips as she watched her brother's body began to convulse. Grabbing him from behind, she tried to steady him, but was forced away by the red light now surrounding him. When Cassandra finally opened her eyes again, they had returned to their normal green color. Staring at what her fiancé was doing, she used all of her strength to push him away. Not being able to stand seeing him torn apart, his comrades screamed "let go." The sword master would not release his grip until all of the taint was destroyed. Falling to his knees, Cedric's hands fell from Cassandra's face. Convulsing and screaming in agony, Cassandra returned his kiss.

The ensuing white magic emitted from both princess and sword master resulted in a burst of gold power around them. Pulling her forearm down from shielding her eyes, Cecilia shoved a leather strap into Cedric's mouth. Cassandra cast every healing spell she could remember on his body. Riddled with agonizing pain, Cedric willed himself to stand.

"We've got to go!" ordered Christian. "Everybody get ready to move!"

Cagius went over to Joshua, who was still broken over the loss of his mother. Dragging his brother's body behind him, Cagius set him down next to Felicia. Angered by the moping boy, Cagius smacked him in the back of the head.

"You're alive, and if you don't live, then she did die for nothing."

"What can I do... "

"If you don't get your act together, so help me, I'm going to bring the roof of this castle down upon you. I'm your Uncle Cagius and right now I'm your family!"

"Right."

Cagius and Joshua interlaced the hands of Julius and Felicia. The two wiped tears away for a moment with the knowledge that the two could finally be happy together in death. Hurrying to Walker, the two put the lord captain on their backs and shoulders, while Cerwin tried to stabilize his wounds. Bleeding heavily from seemingly innumerable wounds, sheer will was the only thing keeping the knight alive.

"Just leave me," stammered Walker. "I'll slow you down. Keep the princess safe."

"Shut up!" ordered Cagius. "We're rescuing you!"

"Why thank you, Marshal Cagius... "

Cecilia steadied her brother as best she could before he nodded it was okay. Noticing the blush on Cassandra's cheeks from the lack of a proper outfit, Cedric unlatched his cloak and handed it to her. Of course, he rescued his flask first, and tucked it into his belt. Frantically, Cassandra searched the room.

"Felicia!"

Horrified to see her handmaiden lay dead, Cassie went to her. Christian kept signaling Cedric to get her moving, but the sword master gave her a moment.

"How could I let this happen to you? I'm so sorry, I shouldn't have let Abaddon control me like that. You were always there for me."

Running out of time, Cedric cut the memorial short. Bowing to the princess, Cedric scooped her up in his arms to carry her down the remaining stairs. Satisfied by his actions, Cecilia accepted the fact that her brother was fine for now. When they reached a lower level, Christian turned around and moved his hands. Boulders began to fall from the ceiling and block the corridors behind them.

Quietly making their ways down the ramps, Colin and Valentine were using horse whispering techniques to calm the horses. Malcolm spotted fifty Acadian halberdiers guarding the entrance to the crypt.

"How many more of these Acadians do we have to kill?"

"I'll go in full force first; the rest of you start picking them off when they swarm me," volunteered Valentine.

Not ready to accept the plan, Amuro got a devious smile on her face. Staring at her sister, the elf marshal knew what to do.

"Saria... take the left flank," ordered Amuro.

"Amuro, are you sure?" asked a bewildered Malcolm.

"Right, sis," acknowledged a smiling Saria.

The two elf sisters moved from their cover to the clear view of the enemy. The halberdiers stared in shock as Saria ran to the left wall. Looking left and back to the center at Amuro, the guards kept their heads on a swivel.

"Don't let those elves out of your sight."

"You boys are in for a treat," announced Amuro.

"Explain yourself, Marshal!"

"She's mysterious! She's sexy! And just for you she's getting naked!"

Pointing her left finger at her sister, the guards couldn't believe their luck. Common sense was that Saria was a prude, but they harbored the deep desire she was truly an exhibitionist. The guards couldn't pull their eyes away from her as Saria reached for the strap on her gown. Seductively pulling it down, she acted with a "come hither" look on her face.

"Come and get it, boys!"

The few seconds was all the time Amuro needed to chant. Sword glowing bright red, she shouted her favorite spell, "Explosion!" Lacking any restrictions, the circle of fire engulfed the distracted. As terror gripped their final thoughts, the massive magic explosion wiped them away. Disgusted at their behavior, Saria replaced the strap on her dress.

"Serves you right, you nasty perverts."

"How did you ever think of that?" asked Valentine.

"I always wanted to try that," replied Amuro.

"Your antics are going to get us all killed," commented Malcolm.

"Not now, sweetie pie!"

The group walked toward a large stone door marked with elf runes all over it. Glowing in bright blue, Amuro read the runes. The smile on her face disappeared.

"We can't open this door unless we have someone with royal blood."

In the main throne room, Stephen witnessed the conversation between the conspirators growing with intensity. Unnoticed, the king switched on the castle loudspeaker from the panel on his throne. Everyone left in the castle could now hear what was being discussed in the throne room.

"I say we get rid of Stephen now, Luminas!" demanded Celius.

"The last thing we need is the marshals coming here," reasoned Jonas.

"That wasn't the plan," countered Luminas.

"It wasn't the plan to have the marshals performing special operation rescues here, either," argued Celius. "Basarabas hasn't come back yet, and I do not want to risk Cassandra asking Cedric Rhone to save her father."

"Please, darling" said Sharon seductively.

"I want no part of it," bellowed Luminas as he shook his head. "Let it be on your hands."

Striding away in anger, Stephen accepted the inevitable as his last defender had deserted him. Nodding in agreement, Celius and Sharon made the final decision.

"Jonas, kill him," ordered Sharon.

"The wizard was the one that first came up with the idea," argued Jonas. "I say we give him the honor of the kill."

"No, a king must die by the sword," demanded Celius.

"So you're putting it on me!"

"We all knew what we were getting into. He will be executed in the old way."

"Fine, if none of you cowards have the courage."

Drawing his sword, Jonas climbed the steps to Stephen. Smiling at his executioner, the king sat up on his throne. He dusted off his robes and fixed his hair.

"So, you've become a common headsman!"

Cedric was still carrying Cassandra through the hallways. Hearing her father's predicament, the princess tried to kick herself loose. The sword master wouldn't release his grip even as she attempted to jump out of his arms. Tears streaming from her face, her eyes pleaded with her fiancé. Maintaining his course, Cedric held her tighter at the waist.

"Cedric, please, we have to save my father!"

The Titan prince continued to run. Realizing he would not go back, Cassandra buried her crying eyes into his shoulder. In the castle foyer, Abaddon rushed to the throne room. Raising his sword in the air, Jonas measured the king.

"I trusted you with my life, Jonas."

"So will the next king of Central Acadia!"

Reaching into his pocket, Stephen pulled out a gold coin. Flipping it on his thumb, the coin rolled to Jonas' foot. Disgusted by the insult, Jonas gritted his teeth.

"You should be thankful, Jonas; I have the courtesy to tip the headsman before the execution. Cassie, if you hear me, fight on! I abdicate in favor of you, my dearest daughter. Never stop fighting until you restore our family to this throne! I love you, Cassie! Cedric, she's yours now. You protect her with the same fervor as you protected those tribal girls. I've had my last words, Jonas, finish it!"

Writhing in agony, it broke the heart of the other warriors to see Cassandra as she was. Cedric murmured something under his lips. Shouting knowing he couldn't hear her, Cassandra made peace with her father.

"Daddy, I'm sorry... I love you... "

Smiling arrogantly, Jonas brought his sword back.

"Long live the king!"

He took one swing and sliced off the head of the king. Gracious enough to use a saber, the cut was quick and clean. Sharon looked on, a little disgusted at the sight of the head and body of the deceased Stephen slumping off the throne. Luminas shook his head in the corner. Walking up to the intercom, Sharon offered her terms.

"There's no one left to save! Surrender yourselves at once!"

The throne room doors kicked open. The conspirators expected to see the marshals, but instead it was Abaddon and his men. Filled with rage, the dark angel intimidated everyone in the room.

"What have you done?" asked Abaddon.

"We did what was necessary," explained Jonas. "The marshals won't bother to come here anymore."

"Fools, we needed him! The marshals have Cassandra! He just abdicated in her favor. Legally, she is the rightful Queen! All of Acadia that is disloyal to us will rally to her!"

The conspirators were dumbfounded. However, Luminas realized the truth in Abaddon's words. He cursed himself for not acting sooner.

"What about Basarabas?"

"He's dead, Luminas. I've lost Cassandra's trail. Where the hell could they be going? They're trapped in this shield."

"That's not like them. Cedric would have never come in here without an exit strategy."

Jonas tapped his earpiece.

"Checkpoints, sound off!"

Voices began to sound off over Jonas's earpiece. Jonas switched it over so everyone in the room could hear what was going on. One, two, three, and five checked in immediately, but there was no response from four.

"Four, do you copy?" demanded Jonas. "Answer immediately!"

"Where was that guard stationed?" asked Abaddon.

"The dungeon, near the entrance to the Acadian crypt."

"That's where they are."

"The crypt is filled with undead horrors," warned Celius.

"Yes, but those tunnels run deep underground," explained Luminas. "What if they've come up with some way to compromise the barrier?"

"At the very least, it's how they think they're going to escape," noted Abaddon. "I'm going to cut them off. The rest of you set up a choke point coming out of the dungeon. No one gets out of here alive! Understand?"

"Of course."

"And Celius?"

"Yes, Lord Abaddon."

"I will never leave you in charge again."

Pacing back and forth in front of the door, Amuro heard the foot steps of Cedric's team approaching. She got a big smile on her face but it disappeared when she noticed who was missing.

"Where's Julius?"

"He's dead, Amuro," replied Cagius.

"How?"

"Abaddon killed him."

"And Marie?"

"She was taken as well," said Cerwin. "She's with Abaddon now, and we can't risk going after her."

"What about the door?" asked Cedric.

"The elves must have made it so only one of Acadian royal blood can disintegrate the runes. If Cassandra doesn't get it open, we've got no chance of getting out of here."

Putting down the princess, Cedric stared at her face. Staring blankly at him, Cassandra cried for the loss of her friend and her father.

"Cassie, we will have a time to mourn for their sacrifice. Right now, I need you to help me save the rest of us. If you don't remove the runes on that door, we're all going to die."

"I don't know. Are you certain you want to go in there?"

"It's the only way out. We can't die here; we'll take our chances in the crypt."

Inspired by the faith the Titan prince had in her, Cassandra began to trace her fingers along the runes. With each trace she completed, a blue light would melt the rune away. However, the process was slow and tedious because there were many runes, and any misstep forced Cassandra to restart the process. Plenty of jobs kept the others busy while Cassandra worked. Cagius and Joshua brought Walker's body over to Amuro. Gasping at the severity of his wounds, Amuro went to work on his body. As she lay her healing hands against his body, Walker could feel his strength return. His first sight was Amuro's gentle face with a few tears in her eyes.

"Rest easy, soldier. You've completed your mission."

"I never figured I'd see you as an angel of mercy. You just patch me up and get me ready to fight; we're not out of this yet!"

Saria tapped Cagius on the shoulder. Filled with empathy for his brother's death, Saria buried herself in his chest.

"Cagius... I'm so sorry for you... "

Shocked at Saria's presence, he instinctively held the elf maiden tightly. Willing to do anything to help the dragoon, she kissed his cheeks.

"What are you doing here Saria?"

"That's what I was trying to figure out. Apparently it was a matter of being at the wrong place at the wrong time."

"Don't worry, my lady. I'll show you how good a protector a cavalier really is."

"Thank you, my brave cavalier."

Turning his head to see Cedric guarding the area, Cagius remembered his promise. The sword master's vision blurred and he had difficulty holding Ragnarok steady. Not missing a trick, Cecilia, Colin, and Christian stood guard with him.

"You get the feeling we're being hunted?" asked Christian rhetorically. "How are you holding up, Cedric?"

"Not good. My muscles are starting to give up, and I think I used up all of my mana reserves."

"Jesus Christ, Cedric!" shouted Cecilia. "Did you really have to degrade yourself to this point? Surely there was another way."

"With any luck, we'll be long gone before it becomes a problem!" commented Christian.

"Cedric," interrupted Cagius. "I have to speak with you."

"What?

"Julius said that I need to give these to you."

Handing his brother's gauntlets to Cedric, the sword master wondered what the master plan of his fallen friend was. Staking Ragnarok into the ground, the Titan prince removed his own gauntlets. Carefully strapping the new armor to his hands and wrists, Cedric approved of his friend's final gift. Lifting his flask in the air, Cedric offered a toast.

"Lead the way for our soldiers of the future Julius. Don't worry; I know what you're trying to tell me."

Hippolyte and Minerva stared at the door intently as Cassandra continued to disintegrate the runes around it.

"What is this crypt we're going into anyway?" asked Hippolyte.

"The resting place of the Acadian royal family, until it was defiled by King Jacob Acadia and his perversions of necromancy," lectured Cerwin. "Jacob declared war on the empire, and when it turned badly, he sealed himself and his royal guard in the crypt with the aid of necromancers. He cursed all who entered to be attacked by the legions of dead if they dared defile his resting place."

"And we're going in there?" exclaimed Minerva. "That's crazy!"

"They'd be crazy to follow us. Hurry up on that door, Cassandra!"

Cassandra had reached the top of the door and now worked her way down the other side. Furrowing her brow at the comments from the peanut gallery, she concentrated on getting the job done.

"Patience is supposed to be a virtue, uncle!"

"Not when you have a fallen angel on your tail."

Breathing heavier from the toll of the exhaustion and anxiety, the warriors helplessly watched as Cassandra finished tracing the final runes. Smiling proudly, the princess was ready to go.

"Now let's get out of here!"

Sounds of shifting stone reverberated throughout the room as the doors slowly opened on their own. Loud screeches beckoned the warriors from the pitch black they stared into. Covering their noses from the horrendous smell, it was time to saddle up. Saria and Cassandra's were both set up as side-saddle to the amazement of the tribal princesses. As they started to ride, the floor on top of them collapsed. Descending from above, Abaddon landed on his knees with one fist pressed against the floor. His eyes focused intently on Cassandra, who was riding next to Cecilia.

"Clever exit strategy! However, I am going to make this crypt your tomb."

Dismounting Jericho, the Titan prince took out a white talisman with a horse head on it. Recalling the summoned horse, Jericho's essence returned to the talisman.

"I'll stay; you go!" offered Cerwin.

"No offense, Grandpa, but you won't last five seconds against a being that smells of this much blood. I'll hold him off while you seal the crypt. I've got a feeling you still have a larger part to play in this escape. Cagius, Amuro, lead them on!"

The old wizard knew there was no arguing with Cedric. Cecilia tried to ride back but Christian blocked her path.

"This is his fight."

"You told me that Garrett said that if he fights him he dies! Besides, you saw what that curse did to him, he doesn't stand a chance!"

"What are you going to put your faith in Cecilia? The rambling dreams of some mystic or the divikin who would surrender everything to protect he loves!"

Cecilia calmed her emotions and thought of the prophecy in her mind. *In Our Hour of Darkness; When Evil Infests Our World; When Courage is No Longer a Shield; When the Hearts of the Bravest Lie Broken; The Last Knight Shall Take up his Sword and the Prayers of the World; And Inherit the Power to Destroy Evil.*

"You're right," said Cecilia as she flashed her thumb up at her brother. "You send this fiend packing straight to hell."

Abaddon rose from the ground and Cedric knew he was running out of time. Hearing the wailing and tears of Cassandra, the sword master threw his rosary beads to her.

"You just pray as hard as you can because where I'm going, I'm going to need them!" said Cedric.

"Cedric!" shouted Cagius. "You show this bastard who his daddy is! You get me!"

Armor now glowing in a pale blue light, Cedric brought Ragnarok to the center of his chest. This stunned the dark angel for a moment because no opponent had exuded such confidence against him since Camael at the gates of heaven. Drawing his own swords, Abaddon resolved he had no chance of taking Cassandra until he dealt with the final obstacle blocking him. Cassandra gripped Cedric's rosary tightly as her tears flowed freely. Cecilia took the reins of her horse and tied them to Myst. They trotted into the crypt first, with the other following behind them. Watching them depart, Abaddon tried to run around Cedric. The sword master simply slid to his position and met his blades with Ragnarok. Pressing their weapons, the opponents tested each other's strength.

"You'll never touch her again!"

"Prince Cedric Rhone, La Morte Angelus, I presume."

"Abaddon, Locust King of the sixth plane!"

"We know each other well. Drop your attack, boy. I don't want to kill you and I understand you're probably upset with the liberties I took with Cassandra. Let me be candid, I can use a Divikin like you. Wouldn't it be better to live with Cassandra in peace rather than die meaninglessly in this dungeon? If you swear fealty to the Prince and help me deliver him his granddaughter, he will make you a noble of hell with your own plane. You don't even have to offer your soul. What say you?"

"I assume you read my book."

"Of course I did."

"Then don't ask a question when you know the answer!"

"I thought it was against your religion to commit suicide."

"There is no greater love than to lay down one's life for the sake of his friends."

"How noble of you! You quote the scriptures and cling to your faith until the end. Facts trump faith! No one in heaven can help you. Daddy has rules and we don't. You're all alone, and soon you'll be dead. She's belongs to us Cedric not you! Wouldn't it be better to be at the side of the Prince than in his way? Now what's it going to be?"

Screaming, Cedric threw Abaddon back with his sword. Not believing any divikin possessed that strength, Abaddon broke the skin on his lower lip with his teeth. Cedric took one hand off of his sword and motioned for Abaddon to come get him.

"Fine, Cedric, I'll test you!"

Abaddon screamed and charged him. His attacks were incredibly fast; however, Cedric managed to either deflect or avoid every one of them. The sword master returned two slashes and a thrust. On the thrust, Abaddon pushed his two swords down onto Ragnarok. The combatants gritted their teeth as they pressed against one another. Managing to close the stone door, the escaping warriors lost sight of Abaddon and Cedric.

"Amuro! Saria! Help me!" screamed Cerwin.

"What are you doing?" asked Cassandra.

"We have to seal this door or else Abaddon will follow us."

"He's not dead! If you seal the door, Cedric will be trapped!"

"He was fully aware of that when he ordered us in here, your highness," said Christian.

Crying hysterically, Cassandra ran to the stone door. Pounding away at it, she shouted at the top of her lungs.

"Don't do this for me, Cedric! Don't throw away your life to protect me!"

Cecilia grabbed her from behind. The vanadis dragged her away from the door.

"Cecilia, let me go... Please... "

"It's killing all of us Cassandra... mark my words, that dark angel doesn't know what he's asking for."

Embracing Cecilia, Cassandra cried on the Titan princess's shoulder. Amuro, Saria, and Cerwin each took a section of the door. Dark blue runes burned into the stone surrounding the door as the elves traced away. However, it took a long time just to make one mark, and there was a lot of door to go. In the dungeon, Abaddon and Cedric held their position.

"Are you so arrogant that you expect to defeat a divine being?"

"It is unwise to underestimate an opponent!"

Raising Ragnarok, Cedric forced Abaddon to stagger back. Off balance, the dark angel was hit with a crescent kick by his sword master opponent. The dark angel rubbed the new welt on his face.

"You've been trained well divikin. It's as if you know all of our ancient combat techniques."

Charging his swords with black energy, Abaddon whipped his swords forward to create a backswing. A direct hit on the sword master sent him skidding into the wall. As the dark angel charged in for a finishing blow, the Titan Prince rolled underneath his blades. Cedric chanted and charged his sword with ice saber this time. Freezing Ragnarok to increase its power, Abaddon could feel a chill in the air around him. When the opponents struck the blades together again, the dark angel could no longer create friction against the sword master's blade.

"You're full of surprises."

"Well, I figured it would be only fitting to give an angel my best."

Pressing their blades into one another, Abaddon's breath was becoming visible from the immense cold generated by the saber magic. A thrust of angel's wings broke Cedric's attack. Despite the pain it caused him, Abaddon darted for a second killing blow. Once again, the sword master rolled backward to avoid it. Growing impatient at his ability to kill this divikin, Abaddon spit blood at him.

"Did anyone ever mention how annoying you are?"

"Not so easy when you're fighting someone who knows what they're fighting for. It would be disappointing if you simply expected me to lie down and die."

Capitalizing on its success last time, Abaddon used his backswing attack. Baiting a trap, Cedric allowed the attack to hit him. Cedric called the power of thunder saber to Ragnarok as Abaddon closed the gap. Quickly slashing the now giant electrical conductor, the sword master blinded the dark angel temporarily. Flailing maniacally, Abaddon struggled to maintain his feet.

Cedric took the opportunity. He belted Abaddon with a backhand across the angel's face. Chambering a side kick, the sword master struck his opponent. Arms spread and defenseless, the titan prince went for the kill. Cedric screamed and spun one-eighty. He struck Abaddon in the chest with all his might as the fallen angel stared on in horror. That was brief, however, as Cedric observed only a few pieces of armor had broken off and there wasn't even a scratch below that.

"*I just hit him with everything I had, and I didn't even make him bleed,*" Cedric wondered to himself. "*Oh, God!*"

Cedric reflected back on what his sister had said to him during his rescue of Cassandra. Accepting his death was now inevitable, the sword master was determined to make it an end worthy of song. Cedric lowered his eyes and murmured a curse in the ancient tongue under his breath. In the end, he had said it to the dark angel, it was time to give up his life for the love of his friends.

"Is that all the 'greatest knight on Terminus Mundus' can do?" taunted Abaddon mockingly.

Invigorated by his opponent's weakness, Abaddon chanted a spell. Cedric felt a shift in the balance of the room as if Abaddon was reaching into the void itself to summon a far darker power. When Abaddon shouted, "Fury of hell" at the end of his chants, Cedric's worst fears were confirmed. Generated from the hands of the angel was a dark hellish attack. Flowing freely into his swords, he made it so the backswing was directed at the sword master. Cedric held his ground, throwing up his sword to deflect the power, but it went right through Ragnarok and even Cedric's magic shield. Thrown back by the power of the spell, the titan prince felt the magic tearing at his already weakened insides. His screams defined the intense pain he was in as the magic trembled through his body.

"You're mine boy!"

Abaddon came again. Three swipes of his swords were blocked by Ragnarok despite the agony of each block. On the fourth swipe, Abaddon brought Cedric to his knees. The fallen angel stabbed with all his might. As it was before with Julius, the dark magic broke through Cedric's right pauldron and severely injured his shoulder. Screaming in agony, the sword master endured the mocking taunts of his foe.

"Good-bye, boy!"

Abaddon reared back his sword for the final blow when Cedric rose up his right gauntlet and caught the sword. Abaddon was shocked at the true power of paladin gauntlets and how the Titan had mastered them so quickly. The master plan of Julius fulfilled, Cedric Rhone now possessed all of the powers of both a sword master and a paladin without the aid of a physical shield. Shoving the sword back, the Titan swept Abaddon's legs out from under him. Cedric twirled Ragnarok above his head and struck at Abaddon from a kneeling position. Dodging the attack at the last possible second, Ragnarok harmlessly hit the ground. The dark angel was breathing heavily and cursed himself for the arrogance that had nearly gotten him killed. Returning to their original positions, the foes prepared to spar again. Cedric's shoulder was bleeding badly, but his flowing adrenaline allowed him to ignore it. Abaddon wondered what was keeping his opponent on his feet as the sword master brought Ragnarok into a fighting position.

"You couldn't beat me with two healthy arms. What chance do you think you have with one?"

"That sounds like a wager to me."

The slight smile haunted Abaddon as they two pressed their swords once more. Though he wouldn't show it, the wound had an effect on Cedric. Unable to push with the same force, Abaddon overpowered him. Shoving him into a column, Abaddon slashed twice at his head. Cedric jumped behind the column and swung. The cracking marble pillar collapsed on the dark angel. Knowing he only had seconds, Cedric cast healing light on his shoulder. However, the bleeding was too intense for that level of magic to be effective. Mana pool failing to regenerate, the magic promptly sputtered away. With a scream, Abaddon emerged from the rubble with his wings spread wide. He fired another magic attack at Cedric. Easily entering his wounds, the poison caused the sword master's muscles to fail him.

"This magic will tear you apart, but I don't have time for games."

Abaddon charged him again. Cedric blocked two attacks and tried a thrust. However, he missed badly, and Abaddon slit Cedric across his midsection. The plate cracked and shattered around his stomach. Gasping for air, Cedric choked on his own blood. The wound was too deep and it was over. Collapsed in agony, Cedric's fingers trembled for Ragnarok. Turning to the door, Abaddon knew nothing stood in his way. The three elves were working desperately to try and complete the seal.

"We're running out of time!" shouted Cagius.

"We can't work any faster," replied Cerwin.

"Come on!" cried Christian. "Cedric's dying out there for us! You have to get it done."

Magic blasts rocked the stone door and threatened the integrity of the ceiling above the escaping warriors.

"We're too late," said Cecilia.

Abaddon was putting his full force of magic into the door. Slipping one of his swords through the slit of the stone door, he started to wedge it open. The warriors all threw their shoulders into the door to stop him from being able to open it. The elves worked frantically now to complete the spell.

"Cecilia!" ordered Cagius. "Get Cassandra out of here! We'll hold him off as long as we can."

"If my brother couldn't stop him, what chance do any of us have?" countered Cecilia.

The warriors seemed resigned to their defeat but drew their weapons anyway. Laughing, Abaddon taunted his new foes.

"Just give me what is mine and you can live... "

Abaddon screamed the last word. From behind, he felt the crack of his back plate and blood dripping from a new wound. Cedric had bulled into the angel from behind and Ragnarok made its mark. The part of the sword that Abaddon had wedged in the door broke. Sealed once more, the elves continued their work unimpeded. Snorting, Abaddon faced a bloody but not broken Cedric Rhone.

"A wounded animal is a very dangerous opponent," mocked Cedric.

The group in the crypt had the confidence they needed.

"The sonuvabitch is still alive!" shouted Christian.

"Finish the seal!" ordered Cagius.

The three elves finished carving their final runes. Glowing in blue light, the group was now behind the dark angel's reach.

"Let's ride!" commanded Cecilia.

Everyone mounted their horses and took off. Cecilia ran to the door and pressed her forehead against it.

"Cedric, take my prayers and destroy this evil!"

Cecilia leapt on Myst and rode with the others. Boiling with rage, Abaddon cursed himself for allowing the princess to escape him. Spitting blood away from his smiling face, Cedric beckoned Abaddon to him once more. Torn from his prize, Abaddon promised to oblige this insolent fool with his one remaining sword.

"Die, you bastard!"

Abaddon charged Cedric, and the two began a fury of swordplay. One sword each put them on even terms, and the two struck each other's sword on ten different occasions.

"Why? Why can't I kill you? You're a mere Divikin!"

"It's faith, Abaddon. I'm not fighting to die; I'm fighting to live for Cassandra!"

Three more deflections and the two foes pressed their swords a last time. Abaddon hit Cedric with a third "fury of hell" attack. Nothing left in his arsenal to stop it; the magic broke pieces off his armor and tore at skin. The strap on the Rising Moon Helmet broke and the helmet bounced on the ground. Abaddon reared back and struck Cedric through the center of his chest.

"I will bleed you like a stuck pig!"

Gasping for air and in cardiac arrest, Cedric mustered his strength to pull himself off the sword. Failing to do so, his vision faded away. Abaddon was finally starting to savor his victory, though it had been much harder than he anticipated.

"No more snide remarks or quips? Let's face facts, Cedric Rhone, you gambled and you lost. You may have delayed them from being in my hands temporarily, but I will hunt them down. There's nowhere on this planet that Cassandra can go where she will avoid me. Die knowing that you didn't have the strength to defend the woman you gave everything for. What do you have to say to that?"

Spitting blood into the eyes of the dark angel, Cedric appeared to murmur something. Laughing at his weakness, Abaddon taunted him again.

"What was that? Speak up!"

"Join me... in hell!"

Awed by the statement, Abaddon's mind failed to register the taunt of his bloodied opponent. It was over; he was dying!

"I hold the light and the darkness in my heart!" chanted Cedric.

Infused with the powers of dark and holy saber magics, Ragnarok erupted with golden power. Lifting his head, Abaddon stared into Cedric's brown eyes burning with holy fire. As the dark angel backed away, the divikin grabbed him at his throat. Squeezing the life from him, Abaddon struggled for air.

"You may have studied the divikin, but never the beauty of how we die. As we approach death we become less human and more like our divine selves. This is my duel blade, the master technique of my race and class."

"You baited me?"

"After I drew your poison from Cassandra, I could never beat you on normal terms, but I gave up everything to save her!"

Striking upward with Ragnarok, Cedric broke Abaddon's blade. The piece lodged in the sword's master body fell to the ground.

"God, give me the strength!"

Shoving Abaddon to the ground with the strength of an angel, Cedric twirled Ragnarok in his hands once and fell to one knee. He drove the sword into Abaddon's chest where he had previously made the hole in his armor. The sword went all the way through and pinned the dark angel's body to the ground. Penetrated with the holy and dark magic infused in Ragnarok, Abaddon felt his body burning from within. Convulsing on the ground, Abaddon's countenance took on a fearful inevitability. Finally the attack subsided, and Cedric's blood dripped down on the dark angel's face.

"Looks like I lost again, Dad," admitted Abaddon as he stared at Cedric. "*Permaneo Eques Ordinares*. Hell, you've earned the knight's title: *La Morte Angelus*. I salute you."

A white light shot out from the center of Abaddon's body. Decomposing to ash before Cedric's eyes, all evidence of the dark angel faded from the history of Terminus Mundus. Exhausted and mortally wounded, Cedric vomited blood. He crawled to a pillar, and used it and his sword to work back to his feet. It was to no avail as he collapsed on the pillar.

"Father in heaven, my body is broken, but my soul is still strong!"

Cedric tried everything to move, but found his body wouldn't respond. Accepting his fate, the sword master sat himself up against the pillar and reached for his flask. He drank the last of the brandy and smiled.

"The sweetest taste in the world—one last swallow of brandy for one last victory. In nomine Patris et Filii et Spiritus Sancti... "

Summoning his will, Cedric blessed himself after three attempts at failing.

"God... I never prayed for selfishness in my life... I knew I could win because You are always with me. With your will and power, anything is possible. Father, I am not embarrassed to submit myself to you. I can't die until I see her again... into your hands, I commend my spirit... thy will be done!"

Cedric closed his eyes and stopped breathing. He lay against the pillar as a calming smile of peace came across his face. His hand, holding the brandy flask, fell to the ground.

Secret Tunnels, the Royal Crypt

"I curse your wretched empire. Shall anyone defile the sanctity
of my resting place, my Jacobin Legions and I will tear
them to pieces."

—*King Jacob the Mad, before being buried alive*

Striding on horseback down the ancient secret passages, the warriors
followed the light of Cerwin's staff through the crypt. The tunnels
were built with a low arched ceiling, but it was still comfortable for the
warriors to ride through in columns of three. Three burial stacks were
carved into each wall, and the warriors could see stone outcroppings of
the people buried ages ago. Even though they rode through what appeared
to be a main tunnel, a maze of tunnels greeted them at every turn.

"Are you sure this is the right way?" asked Cagius.

"No!" shouted Cerwin. "I've never been here!"

"We're done for."

Cerwin made a gesture with his hand for silence as his horse came to
a stop. Creaking of hinges made it sound like hundreds of coffins were
opening at once.

"The Jacobin Legions; it's not a legend!" exclaimed Walker.

"I would suggest an immediate exit!" interjected Cagius.

"This way!" commanded Cerwin.

Cerwin led the group down the tunnel. Groans closed from behind them in the darkness, as if something was on top of them. Risking more light, Cerwin turned his staff behind the warriors. An army of mummified knights was in full pursuit carrying large swords and axes.

"We're not going make it with them on our tails," screeched Cerwin.

"Then we stand and fight," directed Cecilia as she twirled her spear.

The group stopped their horses and dismounted. Cassandra found her courage and put her hands in the air. Chanting, she was able to create balls of fire in her hands without the aid of a staff. Throwing them at the passage, she lit an area for the warriors to fight. The mummified warriors ran right at the warriors with swords held high. Colin cut the head off of one.

"I thought the Jacobin Legions were only supposed to fight the empire."

"In theory... yes... " stammered Christian as he killed another.

"Well, can't they see we aren't wearing turbans?"

"Knowing King Jacob, I don't think it would matter," observed Walker as he cut the head off of one with the point of his shield.

King Jacob didn't invest heavily in necromancy, because mummified warriors could not compare in strength or agility with their opponents. A few swords slashes later, and they were sluggishly moving in the opposite direction.

"Let's make a break for it," ordered Cerwin as he started to chant the "blaze wall" spell.

Cerwin fired the spell from his staff. Burning from the bandages, the mummies ran in a flaming panic. As they bumped into one another, the other undead creatures burst into flames. The levity of the undead's predicament, was quickly silenced by a terrifying shout. Striking at their hearts, all of the warriors began to shiver.

"That sounded like it was coming from one creature," observed Hippolyte, holding out her spear.

"That's not a mummy... that's the call of a revenant," described Cerwin.

"A *revenant*?" asked Minerva.

"It is a terror created by the art of necromancy, a skeletal manifestation that not only is incredibly skilled with a blade but saps the life from you with every strike. It does not matter if it hits you or not. We cannot fight this creature in his domain; we have to run!"

The group went to their horses and jumped on. They tore through the next corridor of the tunnel. Dirt fell on the warriors as they made an escape. Looking above them, mummified warriors crawled on the ceilings and walls around them.

They're on the walls!" screamed Malcolm.

Malcolm and Minerva went for their bows. Amuro grabbed Malcolm's horse and Hippolyte grabbed her sister's horse by the reins to keep them steady as both archers turned in the saddle. Picking off the mummies one at a time, the undead crashed into the ground. Minerva struck a match on one of her arrows. She fired and hit one of them, causing a conflagration among a group of five. One, however, escaped the flames and headed for Cerwin. Recognizing the attack pattern, Cassandra chanted. A small fireball formed in her two hands. Cassandra made a perfect shot that killed the mummified warrior before it got to Cerwin. The sound of rushing water rattled the ears of the elves. Three stone openings led the path from the crypt into an underground stone tunnel. Three stone bridges crossed an underground stream between the crypt and the path.

"Supposedly this is the fifty kilometer marker and the end of the crypt," shouted Christian. "This is supposed to be a passage to an ancient dwarf tunnel. We're two-thirds of the way to our location. Let's not get careless now. I'll take point."

Testing the first bridge, the center of it gave way to the ground below. Disappointed with its integrity, Christian and Cagius went to the other two bridges. Unnerved by the journey and collapsing bridges, the horses would have to be blindfolded and walked across. Christian carefully went first. Once across, he took a few moments to make sure the other side was safe. Satisfied, he signaled for Cagius to come across the second bridge. Cerwin pulled Cassandra aside.

"I should be thanking you, Cassandra. You never know what a young mage is going to do when they act in the field for the first time."

"Thank you, uncle."

"I guess when we get to Deniva, we need to see about getting your staff."

"Really?"

"It's your time now, Cassie. Your father knew you were destined for great things. Do not carry the burden of the dead with you. It wasn't your fault."

"I know you're right... but Felicia, my father, and Cedric, I just don't understand why all this is happening because of me."

"Cassie... you can't... "

There was the sound of a slice in the darkness. Cassandra looked up to see Cerwin with a large sword sticking through his chest. Choking up blood on Cassandra, the other watched as the light from Cerwin's staff revealed a horrible skeletal face engulfed in flames behind him.

"Uncle!"

With his other hand, the revenant swung a second sword that killed Cassandra's horse. As she fell out the saddle, Cecilia caught her hand. Pulling her up on Myst, the brave gray mare raced across the bridge without aid of a blindfold. Minerva and Malcolm fired arrows at the revenant but they went through the undead monster. Walker cut at the bones of the creature's hand, but as his shield deflected a sword thrust, the creature instantly regenerated. Walker gripped his forearm as acid melted through his armor.

"It regenerates any damage we do!"

Amuro sat back on Maiden and pulled out Enhancer, ready to chant.

"Save it... Amuro... there's enough magic left in these old bones for one more spell," screamed Cerwin.

"That spell is forbidden for a wizard Cerwin! If you use that spell, you'll die... "

"It's fine my sweet elf maiden... I now know why the Father has let me live all these revolutions. I die peacefully with the knowledge that not only will Evengard be safe in yours and Malcolm's hands, but I trained the greatest magic user of us all. Remember the old ways, Amuro, and follow the example of Hayden and the prophets."

Cerwin wedged his staff in the door to prevent the revenant from moving on the others. Racing across the bridges to safety, Cassandra stared at her uncle with tears streaming down her face. Her uncle smiled at her.

"Cassie... you have power inside of you that would rival any magic user in this world or the realms around us. . . you will destroy the false guild of wizards... I love you... leave the old to die and bath this world in the light of rebirth... do not waste my final gift!"

Raising his staff in the air, the revenant behind him sensed the power building up in the old wizard.

"You gave up everything... for this Jacob... no evil is going to take those brave souls... time to pay the piper!"

The revenant tried to pull out his sword as Cerwin chanted. The entire catacombs began to shake as if there had been an earthquake. Recognizing what was coming, Amuro screamed out orders.

"Ride! We need to get clear of this area. Everything around us is going to be leveled!"

"There's a legend about this spell. Fragments of the heavens themselves will fall when chanted!" exclaimed Malcolm.

"Star Fall!" screamed Cerwin.

At the call of the final chant, a vacuum opened around Cerwin and revenant. Star fragments emerged from the vacuum. Dropping his weapon and Cerwin's bloody body, the revenant sought the security of the inner crypt. Collapsing tunnels crushed the skeletal body, as fragments bombarded the tomb. Riding away on Myst, Cassandra watched helplessly as a large meteorite fell on her uncle's body and what was left of the revenant. The impact of the spell began a cave-in along the tunnel. Wondering what other terrors could happen, Cecilia released Talon and Colin released Calvary. The raptors flew through the narrow passages as they honed their senses on breathable air. Dust kicked up around the riders, causing them to cover their mouth's with cloaks. Lighting her wings up, Keiko provided a beacon in the darkness. It was another five kilometers before the raptors finally slowed their pace and went to a steady glide. Ceiling no longer collapsing, the warriors dismounted and walked their tired mounts for a while.

"Rest assured, between the runes on the door and that, no one can follow us," observed Christian. "It may work to our advantage in the long run. Perhaps they'll believe we died in the cave-in."

Continuing on foot the last fifteen kilometers, the group covered the ground as fast as they could. No words were spoken, as if everyone was trying to settle personal grief. Cassandra staggered on all of her steps despite support from Walker. Her once bright green eyes and charming countenance were blank and the princess simply stared straight ahead. The rays of Primus's dawn crept slowly into the tunnel. The fresh smell of oxygen penetrated the olfactories of the warriors. In the distance, Christian and Cagius could see an opening where light emanated. All of the warriors had to squint and cover their eyes at first when the light came down.

"Hold up, everybody. I'm going to go take a look," offered Cagius.

Leaving his mount below, Cagius carefully crept to the surface. Closing his eyes, the legate prayed hard.

"Oh please, let's be outside the barrier."

Facing west, Cagius opened his eyes. The barrier's edge was a good two kilometers west of his position. Breathing a sigh of relief, he turned east. In the distance, the golden spire of Castle Deniva reflected the rays of Primus. The most beautiful sight his eyes could behold was the walled, independent, fiefdom situated in the plains just north of the Arudin Forest.

"The golden spire of Castle Deniva! We made it!" screamed Cagius in the tunnel. "It's okay; you can come on up."

The warriors rode out of the tunnel and into the dawn. Cecilia pointed her spear west to the barrier and Central Acadia. Launching into a tirade of obscenities from the ancient Titan tongue, the Vanadis dealt with reality as best she could. Christian tried to come over and console her but she'd have none of it. The spy master grabbed her, begging her to stop.

Pulling Cedric's cloak tightly across her body, Cassandra silently fell to ground in a crumpled heap. Her tears watered the ground around her and even Cecilia stopped her tantrum at the agony the princess was suffering. Keiko collapsed to the ground next to Cassandra joining her in sorrow and screaming her fallen master's name. Even Hippolyte and Minerva were holding onto each other's shoulders and crying hard for the divikin they were raised to hate.

"Do not think that I do not appreciate or understand sorrows," pleaded Valentine. "We can't stay in this position. The barrier might keep us out, but we don't know if our enemies can pass through it. The princess is exposed."

Walker believed Valentine's words. Moving to Cassandra's position, he put his right hand on her back.

"Your highness."

"They're gone, Walker! They're all gone!"

Tears streaming from her blue elf eyes, Amuro knelt in front of Cassandra. Embracing the princess tightly, a golden light flowed from her body to Cassie's. Malcolm stared at the transfer of elf empathy from one kin to the next. It was the power to comfort those dealing with the savagery of the world. Forcing Cassandra to looked her in the eyes, Amuro pleaded with her to release the pain.

"He killed my whole family, Amuro! Everyone I love is back there!"

"I'm so sorry, Cassie. We never thought it would be like this... we all thought it would be okay. The three marshals could never lose a battle, but we got our butts kicked. It was our own foolish arrogance to believe we'd get out of this without losses."

Saria started to sing a lamentation in the elf tongue. Despite the sad words of the song, the warriors would smile at the memory of those who had fallen. Cassandra lifted her head to the east and saw a wild rose bush.

"Walker, please let me have your dagger."

"Of course, princess."

Walker handed Cassandra a knife from his boot. However, her shield didn't miss a trick and watched what she did carefully out of fear she'd try to take her own life. Cutting five red roses off of the bush, the princess carelessly pricked her fingers on the thorns. Numb to the pain, she placed the five roses at the entrance of the tunnel. Closing her eyes, Cassandra muttered a prayer.

"For Felicia, Julius, my father, Uncle Cerwin, and..."

Cassandra couldn't get Cedric's name out without finally breaking down. It was actually a relief to the others because it returned her to a sense of normalcy. Blood dripping down her face from the cuts on fingers, Cassandra was grabbed by Amuro once more. The elf maiden kissed Cassandra on the forehead, causing the princess to close her eyes and faint into Amuro's waiting arms.

"The grief is too much for you right now. Rest now, dear, we're going to need your strength before this is over."

"What do we do now?" questioned Colin.

"Two marshals dead, our new queen is a wreck," observed Malcolm. "Would it have been better to do nothing at all?"

Moping in self-pity didn't serve Cecilia. She ripped the war crown from her head.

"I'll tell you what we're going to do! We're going to show the same faith my brother did when he stayed behind so we could live. It's a new rotation and as long as we're alive we can keep on fighting. Valentine made an astute observation before, we can't linger here! Saddle up and ride for Deniva! I'll be along in a second."

Dropping to her knees, Cecilia blessed herself and began to silently pray.

"Are you sure you're okay, Cecilia?" questioned Amuro.

"We don't know if my brother is dead yet! We didn't see him die! If he truly was the *Permaneo Eques Ordinares*, then he has the power to defy fate!"

The others let what Cecilia spoke to them sink in. Amuro glanced quickly toward Christian, fearing for the sanity of her spear-wielding companion. Christian's face betrayed the elf marshal had nothing to worry about. Valentine shot a glance toward Cagius, who decided to take a direct leadership approach at this point.

"We need to get to Deniva as quickly as possible. We're just asking for trouble if we stay out in the open like this."

"Come on, Colin, we'll go scout ahead," volunteered Christian after a nod.

"Right behind you, Colonel DeVries!"

Christian and Colin jumped on their horses. Calvary led the way for the two as they went ahead.

"You don't think what Cecilia said is true?" asked Colin.

"All the evidence points to the fact that he is dead," said Christian, taking an official tone.

"Yeah, that's what I thought, but... "

"But there's always room for a miracle, and no one has stronger faith than Cedric."

The two turned to each other, unable to hold back their smiles. Laughing, they carefully observed patterns and trails on the road ahead. The remaining warriors decided it was time to move on and saddled the horses. Minerva was having trouble, so Walker assisted her. Blushing, she stared longingly in his eyes.

"Thanks, Walker."

"You're a crack shot, Minerva."

"You think?"

"A few more revolutions and we'll make a soldier out of you yet."

"A soldier? I'm already a soldier."

"You'll understand what I mean when the time comes," teased Walker as he winked at the girl.

Maiden bent down to accept Amuro and Cassandra on her back. Nuzzling Cassandra slightly as she was placed on her, even the winged unicorn felt sorry for the girl. Settled in the saddle, Cagius offered Amuro her first salute.

"How do you want to proceed?"

"I don't understand."

"This is still a military operation. You're the senior officer now. We're waiting for our orders, Marshal."

Choked up with tears, Amuro finally accepted the reality of command. No longer a trinity of marshals, it was her sole responsibility to order the finest warriors in the world.

"I never wanted it like this. This is no time for me to feel sorry about myself. Let's review what we've got. Christian and Colin are blazing a trail. Let's follow fifty meters behind them, and we'll make Deniva about lunch time. That is, if they're willing to give us lunch."

"Of course, Marshal!" acknowledged Cagius as he saluted her.

Proudly answering the salute, Amuro signaled to the others it was time to go. Bidding final farewells to the fallen, everyone positioned their horse toward Deniva.

The reign of Stephen Acadia, the king of justice, has ended after twenty-five revolutions. Those around him in Central Acadia refused to believe in his vision and chose the path of darkness. The Acadian Insurrection was successful, and now the greater war to restore Cassandra to her rightful place as true queen of Central Acadia began for the Alliance. The path shall not be easy for our heroes. Cut off from one another, the kingdoms of the former alliance must find a way to defeat an enemy impervious to an armed attack. The remnants of the warriors who gave everything to save Princess Cassandra rode for the trade city of Deniva; they must find rest and new allies in order to win back their homes. Prince Julius Imperia and Prince Cedric Rhone died to accomplish their final mission, but their deaths were not in vain. The challenges confronting all would no longer require faith alone, but hope as well. As it had been prophesized, Cedric Rhone fulfilled The Legend of the Last Knight; the Terminus Mundus Saga had just begun.

Epilogue

"Legends Never Die"

—*Old Sentinel Proverb*

Finishing her prayer, Cecilia called Myst to her side. The vanadis mounted her horse and strapped her war crown on her head. Just as she was about to ride away, a feeling in her gut forced Cecilia make a final turn to the barrier. Closing her eyes once more, she bowed her head. Keiko noted her behavior and watched a devious smile creep across Cecilia's face.

"Mistress Cecilia..."

Ignoring the sylph, Cecilia lifted her head. Her eyes burning with the same fire and passion as her twin brother, the vanadis lifted her spear high into sky.

"MY BROTHER IS ALIVE!"

To be continued . . .

www.ingramcontent.com/pod-product-compliance
Lightning Source LLC
Chambersburg PA
CBHW072258020726
47501CB00002B/306